Praise for

SUSAN KRINARD

and her books

"Animal lovers as well as romance readers and
those who enjoy stories about mystical creatures and
what happens when their world collides with ours
will all find Krinard's book impossible to put down."
—*Booklist* on *Lord of the Beasts*

"A poignant tale of redemption."
—*Booklist* on *To Tame a Wolf*

"A master of atmosphere and description."
—*Library Journal*

"Susan Krinard was born to write romance."
—*New York Times* bestselling author Amanda Quick

"Compelling characters and the universal nature
of their underlying conflicts should guarantee an
across-the-board appeal."
—*Library Journal* on *The Forest Lord*

"A different and magical read."
—*Affaire de Coeur* on *The Forest Lord*

"An extraordinary story of love, strength,
courage and compassion."
—*Romantic Times BOOKreviews* on *Secret of the Wolf*

Also available from

SUSAN KRINARD

and HQN Books

Dark of the Moon
Chasing Midnight
Lord of the Beasts
To Tame a Wolf

**Available from Susan Krinard
and LUNA Books**

Shield of the Sky
Hammer of the Earth

**Watch for the latest paranormal romance from
Susan Krinard and HQN Books**

Lord of Legends

Coming in spring 2009

SUSAN KRINARD

Come the Night

H

HQN™

ISBN-13: 978-0-373-77315-2
ISBN-10:   0-373-77315-3

COME THE NIGHT

This edition published by arrangement with Harlequin Books S.A.

www.HQNBooks.com

Printed in U.S.A.

Dear Reader,

One of my favorite types of heroes is the hard-boiled detective…oh, not *too* hard-boiled, but the kind of rough-and-tumble guy who can dish it out *and* take it, who's world-weary and cynical but just ready to fall for the right woman.

Ross Kavanagh is just that sort of guy. First introduced in *Chasing Midnight,* he's an ex-cop who was thrown off the force for a crime he didn't commit. Being a cop was his whole life, and now he's rudderless, waiting for a chance to prove his innocence…when he is reunited with his former love, proper Englishwoman (and werewolf) Gillian Maitland.

For Gillian, seeing Ross again is painful but necessary— her son, Toby, has run away to America to find his father… none other than Ross himself. Ross didn't know that his brief affair with Gillian had produced a child, and now he's determined to claim his fatherly rights. The problem is that he's only a quarter werewolf, unable to Change, and thus—by the laws of Gillian's traditionalist werewolf clan— an unfit mate.

Now Ross has two things to prove: that he's worthy of Gillian, and that he's innocent of the crime that changed his life forever. But first he has to acknowledge his love for the woman who left him so many years ago, and she must defy her father and risk abandoning the life she's known—by recognizing that her love for Ross outweighs even the dangers of defying her clan and provoking its jealous enemies.

I hope you'll enjoy reading *Come the Night* as much as I enjoyed writing it.

Susan Krinard

This above all: to thine own self be true,
And it must follow, as the night the day,
Thou canst not then be false to any man.
—William Shakespeare

PROLOGUE

Cumbria, England, 1910

"CHANGE, DAMN YOU!"

Her father's voice was little more than a hoarse whisper, but to Gillian it sounded like a shout. She curled into a tighter ball and concentrated as hard as she could.

Change. Oh, please Change.

It seemed as if her body was doing everything possible to resist, everything possible to make Papa angrier with her. He'd already chastised her numerous times for lagging so far behind most *loup-garou* children.

"You aren't trying hard enough," he'd accused. "You wish to shirk your responsibilities. Well, I won't have it. You'll do as I tell you, even if I have to beat it into you."

Gillian had believed him. He'd resorted to the belt more times than she could remember, and for far less terrible infractions than this. But oh, if she could only please him. The sun would come out in his eyes then, and the beatings would be forgotten.

She wanted so badly to please him.

Change.

She squeezed her eyes shut with such force that little white lights danced behind her eyelids. Her muscles twitched and protested. She imagined what it would be like when she became a wolf...how different the world would seem, how beautiful, how perfect.

You'll be like the others. You'll belong.

Without understanding why she did so, she let her mind go
blank and her body relax. Her arms and legs went limp. She
could still hear Papa's voice, but it seemed very far away. A
softness flowed through her like liquid sunlight.

And then something shifted, as if invisible gears had
clicked into place. She had expected it to hurt—surely something so difficult would have to hurt—but it didn't. There was
nothing strange about it at all. One moment she was a
fourteen-year-old girl—neither particularly pretty nor unusu-
ally bright, as her father so often reminded her. The next she
was crouched on four large paws, and the universe was exploding with sounds and smells she had never known in all her life
as a human.

She straightened and shook out her golden fur. There was
nothing awkward about her now, nothing to make Papa
ashamed. She looked up at him, daring to allow herself a
shining moment of hope.

Papa was smiling. The warmth of his approval spilled over
Gillian, bathing her in relief and joy. She jumped up high, twisted
in midair, landed again as lightly as a feather. Every muscle and
tendon obeyed her to perfection. She turned toward the wood
behind the house, longing to escape into the fells, to feel the
power of her new shape in all its glory.

But it was not to be. "Enough," Papa said. "I have business
to attend to."

He had already turned away by the time she Changed back.
The crisp morning air brought goose pimples to Gillian's naked
skin. She pulled on the dress she had left lying over a bench,
skinny and plain and awkward once more, and berated herself
for her foolish expectations. Why should there be a celebration
just because she could finally do what any werewolf was
supposed to do? Why should this day be any different?

She slipped her shoes and trudged through the kitchen garden to the servants' entrance, praying that no one would see her. Not even Cook's sympathy would make her feel better now. Cook was only human and couldn't possibly understand.

No one stopped her as she climbed the stairs to the nursery. She was briefly cheered by the thought that Papa would no longer force her to remain in the room she'd occupied since infancy; she'd proven herself a woman today.

A woman whose future was already decided.

Gillian slumped onto her narrow bed and covered her face with her hands. She barely felt it when someone touched her drawn-up knee.

"Gilly? Are you all right?"

She opened her eyes. Hugh was standing beside the bed, his normally cheerful face overcast with worry.

Gillian straightened and found a smile. "Of course I'm all right," she said. "I Changed today."

Hugh's mouth formed an O of surprise. "Cor blimey!"

"You ought not to curse, Hugh."

"Did you really Change, Gilly? What was it like?"

"Wonderful," she lied, remembering how Papa had destroyed her brief pleasure with his casual dismissal.

Hugh shuffled his feet. "Now that you're grown up, you won't play with me anymore."

"Nonsense." She slid off the bed and wrapped her arms around Hugh's thin shoulders. "I'll still be close by. Nothing will really be different."

Hugh allowed her to hold him for a few seconds and then stiffened to indicate that he'd had enough coddling. *He's growing up, too*, Gillian thought. But it would be easier for him when it was his time. He'd always been Papa's favorite. That was a fact Gillian had accepted long ago.

Just as she had accepted that he must never know how badly their father made her feel.

She pushed Hugh's brown hair away from his forehead. "It's

almost time for lessons," she said. "Would you like to go outside and throw the ball for a little while?"

Hugh's grin was answer enough. He ran to fetch the ball and raced ahead of her down the stairs, his small feet thudding loudly in the stillness. Papa might take him to task for his noise—if Papa were paying any attention. If Sir Averil Maitland was involved in his "business," nothing else would matter.

Gillian descended the stairs and joined Hugh on the lawn, catching the ball and throwing it back with just enough force to satisfy a rapidly growing boy. She'd almost forgotten that she was to meet Ethan by the beck this evening after supper, when Papa was in the library with his books. Ethan was human; there were a lot of things he couldn't understand. But she'd told him about *loups-garous* years ago, and he wasn't afraid. He would listen patiently, the way he always did, and in the end she would feel just a little bit better.

Mrs. Beattie rang the nursery bell, and Hugh heaved a great sigh. It was time for lessons, and there would be no more play for the rest of the day. Nothing had really changed. Except that now Papa would begin thinking about a suitable mate for Gillian, a man of pure werewolf blood who would be the father of her pure werewolf children.

Gillian looked one last time toward the woods and reminded herself all over again that there was no such thing as freedom.

CHAPTER ONE

New York City, July, 1927

ROSS KAVANAGH contemplated the half-empty bottle of whiskey and wondered how much more it would take to get him stinking drunk.

It wasn't the first time, and it wouldn't be the last. He'd never been a drinker before they threw him off the force. There hadn't seemed to be much point; even a man only one-quarter werewolf had a hard time becoming inebriated. And he'd been content with the world.

Content. Until everything had been taken away from him, he hadn't really thought about what the word meant. He'd given up on anything beyond that a long time ago. It was enough to have the work, the company of the guys in the homicide squad, the knowledge that he'd kept a few criminals off the streets for one more day.

Now that was gone. And it wasn't coming back.

He lifted the bottle and took another swig. The whiskey was bitter on his tongue. He finished the rest of the bottle without taking a breath and set it with exaggerated care down on the scarred coffee table.

Maybe he should put on a clean shirt and find himself another couple of bottles. Ed Bower kept every kind of liquor hidden behind his counter, available for anyone who knew what to ask for. Sure, Ed Bower was breaking the law. But what did the law matter now?

What did anything matter?

Ross scraped his hand across his unshaven face and got up from the sofa. He walked all too steadily into the bathroom and stared into the spotted mirror. His face looked ten years older than it had two weeks ago. Deep hollows crouched beneath his eyes, and his hair had gone gray at the temples. He wondered if Ma and Pa would even recognize him if he went home to Arizona.

But he wasn't going home. That would mean he was licked, and he wasn't that far gone.

Maybe tomorrow. Maybe tomorrow he would sober up and start looking for the guy who'd made a mockery of his life. The bum who had gotten away with murder.

Ross sagged over the sink, studying the brown stains in the cracked bowl. Clean up. Get dressed. Think about living again, even though no cop in the city would give him the time of day and the mobsters he'd fought for twelve years would laugh in his face.

Someone knocked on the door, pulling Ross out of his dark thoughts. *Who the hell can that be?* he thought. It wasn't like he had a lot of civilian friends. As far as he knew, Griffin and Allie were still in Europe. They were the only ones he could imagine showing up at his apartment in the middle of the day.

Maybe it's the chief coming to give me my job back. Maybe they found the guy.

He laughed at his own delusions. The person at the door knocked again. Kavanagh swallowed a stubborn surge of hope, threw on his shirt and went to the door.

The man on the landing was a stranger, his precisely cut suit perfectly pressed and his shoes polished to a high sheen. His face was chiseled and handsome; his hands were manicured and free of calluses. Ross sized him up in a second.

Money, Ross thought. *Education.* Maybe one of Griffin's friends, though there was something about the guy's face that set off alarm bells in Ross's mind.

"Mr. Kavanagh?" the man said in a very proper upper-class English accent.

Ross met the man's cool gaze. "That's me," he said.

"My name is Ethan Warbrick." He didn't offer his hand but looked over Ross's shoulder as if he expected to be invited in. "I have a matter of some importance to discuss with you, Mr. Kavanagh."

"What is it?"

"Something I would prefer not to discuss in the doorway."

Ross stepped back, letting Warbrick into the apartment. The Englishman glanced around, his upper lip twitching. Ross didn't offer him a seat.

"Okay," Ross said, leaning casually against the nearest wall as if he didn't give a damn. "What's this about?"

Warbrick gave the room another once-over and seemed to decide he would rather continue standing. "I will come right to the point, Mr. Kavanagh. I've come to see you on behalf of a certain party in England with whom you were briefly acquainted during the War. She has asked me to locate you and warn you about a visit you may presently be receiving."

The Englishman's statement took a moment to penetrate, but when it did, Ross couldn't believe it meant what he thought it did.

She. England. The War. Put those words together and they meant only one thing: Gillian Maitland. The girl he'd believed himself in love with twelve years ago. The one who'd left him standing on a London kerb feeling as if somebody had shot him through the heart.

"Sorry," Ross said, returning to the door. "Not interested."

"Perhaps you ought to hear what I have to say, Mr. Kavanagh."

"Make it fast."

"To put it simply, Mrs. Delvaux, whom you once knew as Gillian Maitland, expects her son to be arriving in New York at any moment."

Ross turned his back on the Englishman. He'd been right. *Gillian*.

"What does her son have to do with me?" he asked.

"He believes you to be his father."

The floor dropped out from under Ross's feet. "What did you say?"

"Young Tobias is under the mistaken impression that you are his father. He stowed away on a ship bound for America, and every indication suggests that he is on his way to you."

It took a good minute, but the world finally stopped spinning. Ross made his way to the sofa and sat down, resenting the empty bottle on the table before him. "How old is he?" he asked hoarsely.

"Eleven years. Mrs. Delvaux has asked me to intercept him and send him home."

Ross jumped up again, unable to banish the pain in his chest. "*Is* he my son?"

Warbrick hesitated just an instant too long. "Mrs. Delvaux married a Belgian gentleman shortly after her return from her volunteer work in London. Tobias was born nine months later."

Gillian, married. To "a Belgian gentleman"—*gentleman* being the key word. And Ross was willing to bet he was a full-blooded werewolf. Just like Gillian.

Warbrick wasn't a werewolf. Not that Ross could always be sure the way some shifters could, but he had a pretty good knack for figuring out what made people tick.

Even so, if Gillian knew the guy well enough to send him after her son, odds were that *he* knew about the existence of *loups-garous* and knew that Gillian was one of them. He wouldn't be the first human to be privy to that information. Not by a long shot.

And if he knew about werewolves, he ought to know how dangerous it was to tangle with one. Even a part-blood like Ross.

"How do you know Jill?" he said, deliberately using the nickname he'd given her in London.

"Not that it is any of your business, Mr. Kavanagh, but Mrs. Delvaux and I are neighbors and old friends."

"Where is *Mr.* Delvaux?" Ross asked abruptly.

"He died in the War, shortly after their marriage."

Ross released his breath. Gillian was a widow. She'd never remarried. He didn't know what that meant. He shouldn't care. He *didn't.*

But there was one thing he *did* care about. He spun on his foot and strode toward Warbrick, stopping only when he had a fistful of the Englishman's lapel in his grip.

"He *is* my son, isn't he?"

To his credit, Warbrick didn't flinch. His face remained deceptively calm, but Ross wasn't fooled. This guy was no fighter.

"I'll find out one way or another," Ross said. "So you might as well tell me now and save us both a lot of trouble."

Ross could see Warbrick weighing the chances of his getting out of the apartment with his pretty face intact. He made the right decision.

"Yes," he said. "Kindly release me."

Ross let him go. Warbrick smoothed his jacket.

"The fact that Tobias is your son is of no consequence," he said. "He doesn't know you. He wasn't even aware of your existence until a fortnight ago."

"How did he find out?"

"It was entirely an accident, I assure you."

"And he decided to come to New York all by himself?"

"He is a precocious child, but he is still a child. You can have no possible interest in a boy you have never seen."

Ross stepped back, cursing the booze for muddling his thoughts. Warbrick was right, wasn't he? Maybe the kid was bright, but he was Ross's son in name only.

Gillian had made sure of that. She could have written, sent a telegram. She hadn't bothered. Instead, she'd married this Delvaux guy and passed the boy off as his.

Ross knew how easy it would be to let his anger get out of control. "Let me get this straight," he said. "Mrs. Delvaux asked you to run me down and make sure I hand over the kid as soon as he turns up."

"That is correct."

"How is he supposed to find me?"

"The same way I located you. He knows that you worked for the New York City police."

Worked. Past tense. "He learned all this by accident?"

"It hardly matters, Mr. Kavanagh. You will be doing Mrs. Delvaux a great service, and she is sensible of that. We are prepared to offer you a substantial sum of money for your cooperation."

Sure. Buy the dumb American off. Neat, convenient, painless.

"Why didn't she come herself?" he asked. "If she's so worried about the kid…"

"Since she knows that I have been resident in New York for nearly a year," Warbrick said, "it was hardly necessary for her to come in person." He withdrew a piece of paper from his jacket pocket. "I have been authorized to present you with this check for one thousand dollars as soon as the child is safely in my custody. Even if I am able to locate him first, you will receive it as consideration for your—"

"Get out."

"I beg your pardon?"

"You heard me." He grabbed the Englishman's shoulder and propelled him toward the door. "You can tell Mrs. Delvaux that I don't need her money."

The heels of Warbrick's shoes scraped on the landing. "You are making a serious mistake," he said, anger rising in his voice. "If necessary, I will enlist the police to—"

"You do that." Ross pushed Warbrick toward the stairs. "Don't trip on your way down."

He listened until he heard the door in the lobby snap shut. His hands had begun to shake. He went back into his apartment, closed the door and leaned against it, waiting for the fury to pass.

For eleven years he'd had a son he didn't know about. For eleven years Gillian hadn't bothered to contact him—until she needed something from the American chump who'd been stupid enough to fall for a lady of wealth and privilege and pure werewolf blood.

He was still a chump, letting her get to him this way. He had to start thinking rationally again. Think about what he would do if the boy did show up. It wasn't as if he had anything to say to the kid.

Maybe Warbrick would find him before he got this far. That would solve everybody's problems.

Then you can go back to drinking again. Forget about the kid, forget about Mrs. Delvaux, forget about the job.

There were just too damned many things to forget.

He went into the bathroom, turned on the faucet in the bathtub and stuck his head under the stream of cold water. When his mind was clear, he shed his clothes and scrubbed himself from head to foot. He got out his razor and shaved the stubble from his chin. He was just taking his last clean shirt and trousers from the closet when the telephone rang. He let it ring a dozen times before he picked up the receiver.

"Kavanagh?"

Ross knew the voice well. Art Bowen had been one of the last of his fellow cops to stand by him when everyone else had left him hanging in the wind. But finally even Bowen had decided that it wasn't worth jeopardizing his career to associate with a suspected murderer.

"Hello, Art," Ross said. "How are you?"

There was a beat of uncomfortable silence. "Listen, Ross. You need to get down to the station right away."

Ross's fingers went numb. *They found the real killer. They know I'm innocent. It's over.*

"There's someone here looking for you," Art continued. "He claims he's from England."

The floor began to heave again. "Who?" he croaked.

"His name is Tobias Delvaux. He says he's your son."

ETHAN HAILED A TAXI and gave terse instructions to the cabbie, promising a generous tip for a quick ride back to his hotel.

As unbelievable as it seemed, Kavanagh had gotten the better of him. Considering the ex-policeman's circumstances, Ethan hadn't been prepared for his hostility, let alone his refusal of the check. The man had lost everything, including his means of support, and he was clearly not in a position to refuse financial assistance.

But he had—and far worse, he'd presumed to treat Ethan as if he were a commoner.

Of course, he had made a mistake in allowing Kavanagh to know that Toby was his son. He had been too eager to observe the American's expression when he realized that Gillian had concealed the boy's presence all these years, that she hadn't had the slightest desire to renew their relationship.

He had received some satisfaction in that, at least. Kavanagh's pretense at indifference had been spoiled by the anger he had unsuccessfully attempted to conceal.

But was the anger merely at Gillian's deception? Or was there something more behind it? Something that would make Kavanagh far more of a problem than Ethan had anticipated?

He had no intention of taking a chance. When the cab pulled up in front of his hotel, he already knew what he must do.

Bianchi's secretary was polite and apologetic when she informed Ethan that the boss was on holiday. When Ethan pressed, she provided him with the mobster's location, though she carefully reminded him that the boss didn't like to be disturbed when he was fishing in the Catskills.

Ethan dismissed her warnings. He'd become quite wealthy as a result of skilled investments in American industry and less "legitimate" pursuits, and he'd contributed generously to Bianchi's defense the last time the boss had been under investigation.

Bianchi owed him, and what he wanted wasn't much of an inconvenience for a man of the boss's power and influence. Ethan knew that there was some risk in leaving town at this juncture, but he had a number of hired men watching for Toby, including several in the police department.

And if something *were* to happen to the boy…why, even that tragedy could be turned to his advantage.

Ethan rang the concierge to arrange for a car and began to pack.

WALKING INTO THE precinct was like walking into the kind of nightmare where everything starts out perfectly normal before going all to hell. Ross stepped through the doors the way he had thousands of times before. He passed a couple of uniforms loitering near the entrance. They started when they saw him; then their faces went hard and blank.

It was the same with every cop he met on the way to the reception desk. Guys who'd been closer to him than brothers turned their backs as he went by. He heard more than one curse crackling in the air behind him. The young officer at the desk gave him a cold stare and suddenly became absorbed in his paperwork.

"I'm here to see Art Bowen," Ross said.

The officer pretended not to hear him. Ross leaned over the desk, forcing the uniform to lean back.

"He's expecting me," Ross said. "Why don't you be a good kid and let him know I'm here?"

The young cop obviously wanted to go on ignoring Ross. Nevertheless, he picked up the telephone and did as Ross asked, resentment in every line of his body.

Art came into the room five minutes later. He didn't offer his hand.

"Hello, Ross," he said.

"Art." Ross looked past his shoulder. "You said you have my—"

Art made a cautionary gesture and glanced at the uniform behind the desk. "Let's go someplace where we can talk."

Ross nodded and dropped into step behind Art. He'd endured another half-dozen cold shoulders by the time they reached one of the interrogations rooms. Art waved Ross in ahead of him and locked the door.

Sitting behind the table was a smallish kid who could have been anywhere between nine and twelve years old. He jumped up as soon as he saw Ross, and they stared at each other in mutual fascination.

The first thing Ross noticed was that Tobias looked exactly like his mother. Oh, not feminine in any way, but fine-boned and intelligent, a little wary, with even and unremarkable features, light brown hair and Gillian's hazel eyes. His smell was distinctly his own, but it held traces of something half-familiar. Something that reminded Ross as much of himself as Gillian.

"Is this your son, Ross?" Art asked behind him.

Ross looked for any sign of himself in the kid. Maybe there was something in the chin, the line of the mouth, the straight and serious brows. Or maybe that was just an illusion.

The boy stepped forward. "How do you do, sir," he said. His voice, like Warbrick's, was that of a cultured resident of England, high with eleven-year-old nervousness, but clear and strong. The kid wasn't afraid. Of that much Ross was certain.

"Hello, Tobias," he said, his own voice less than steady.

"Toby, sir. If you don't mind."

Art cleared his throat. "I guess you aren't surprised to see him," he said. "I didn't know you had any children."

Ross couldn't think of a single good way to answer that question. "How much has he told you?"

"Just that he's come all the way from England to see you. Looks like he came alone."

"I did," Toby said, lifting his chin. He eyed Art warily. "Am I under arrest?"

Laughter caught in Ross's throat. "What have you been telling him, Art?"

"Nothing." He gave Ross a direct look that suggested he had more to say on that subject. "I made a few calls. No record of a kid by his name on any ship's manifest."

Warbrick had said he'd stowed away. Suddenly feeling far older than his thirty-one years, Ross crouched to the boy's level.

My son.

He took himself firmly in hand. The only way he was going to be able to deal with this mess was by treating it like any other case. Leave everything personal out of it.

"Tobias—" he began.

"Toby," the boy said, meeting his gaze.

"Toby. I'm going to ask you some questions, and I expect you to answer them honestly."

"Of course, Father."

Funny how much of a punch such a common word could pack.

"Did you really travel on a ship from England by yourself?" he asked.

"I wasn't any trouble. No one knew I was there."

"But you didn't tell anyone you'd left home."

Toby gazed down at his badly scuffed shoes. "No," he said quietly.

"How long have you been in New York?"

Toby brushed at his soiled short pants, which Ross guessed he'd been wearing for several days, if not longer. "Just a few days," he said. He mover closer to Ross and lowered his voice. "I think someone was after me," he said, "so I hid until they went away."

"Who was after you?"

"I thought they might be gangsters, but I don't really have anything worth stealing."

Ross glanced at the battered suitcase standing beside the table. It might have held a couple of changes of clothing and a few other necessities, but not much else. "I don't think it was gangsters, Toby. But if you thought you were in danger, you should have come straight to the police."

"Maybe it *was* the police," Toby whispered, rolling his eyes in Art's direction. "I had to come here because it was the only way I knew how to find you." Unexpectedly, he grinned, the expression transforming his features the same way Gillian's smiles had always done. "I knew you'd come for me."

Ross straightened, reminding himself not to swear in front of a kid. "Okay," he said. "I need to talk to Art for a few minutes. Can you wait here a little longer?"

"Of course, Father."

With a wince, Ross turned for the door. Art went with him.

"You didn't know about him, did you?" Art said as soon as they were in the corridor.

There wasn't any way to avoid answering, and Ross didn't see the point in lying. "Not until this morning," he admitted.

Art nodded sympathetically. "The War?"

"Something like that."

Mercifully, Art didn't pursue that line of questioning. "Did Warbrick come to see you?" he asked.

"You talked to him?"

"Yeah. He came in first thing this morning, asking to speak to the Chief. I got stuck with him." Art's lip curled in contempt. "He demanded that we inform him if a certain kid turned up. Said the boy had run away and might come to the station."

"Did he tell you why?"

"It came out after he asked where you lived. Except he claimed the kid mistakenly thought you were his father, and made noises about going higher up if we didn't do exactly as he said." Art snorted. "Damned Limey, thinks he can lord it over us."

"He showed up at my place with the same story," Ross said. "I threw him out."

Speculation brimmed in Art's eyes. He controlled it. "I wasn't much in the mood to kowtow to Warbrick, so when the kid turned up, I called you instead of him."

"Thanks, Art. I owe you one."

Art shrugged. "I can always play dumb if the higher-ups come after me," he said. "Only a couple of uniforms know he's here, so you can…" He hesitated. "You *are* going to take him, aren't you?"

Ross saw the chasm opening up before him. He knew he could walk away, find out where Ethan Warbrick was staying and send Tobias to him, just as *Mrs. Delvaux* wanted.

But it wasn't that easy. Ross couldn't look away from the cold hard evidence of the boy's parentage. *Gillian's son.*

His son.

"Yeah," he said. "I'll take him."

Art's relief was obvious. "Right. It might be a good idea to go out the back door."

Ross nodded, and then an unpleasant thought occurred to him. "He doesn't know…you didn't tell him…"

"No. As far as he knows, you still work here."

"That's another one I owe you."

Art shifted his weight. "Do you, uh…if you need a little cash, I'd be glad to—"

"Thanks, but I'm fine," Ross said, more sharply than he'd intended. "The kid won't starve before he gets back to England."

Their eyes met, and Ross realized what he'd just said. He'd already assumed he was sending Toby back to his mother.

And what else are you supposed to do with him?

"I gotta get back to work," Art said. "Take care, Ross."

They shook hands. Art strode away, his thoughts probably on whatever case he was working on now. The way Ross's would have been not so long ago.

Hell.

Ross blew out his breath and opened the interrogation room door. Toby sprang back as the door swung in, guilt flashing across his face.

What did you expect? Ross thought. He walked past Toby and picked up the suitcase.

"Come with me," he said.

"Are we going home?" Toby asked, hurrying to join him.

Home? "To my place, yes," he said. Where else was there to go?

He led Toby down the corridor and around several corners until they reached one of the back doors, encountering only a couple of detectives along the way. If Toby noticed their stares, he didn't let on. The door opened up onto an alley, where several patrol cars were parked. Ross continued on to West Fifty-fourth Street and kept walking, one eye on Toby, until they'd left the station some distance behind. Only then did he stop, pull Toby out of the crowd of busy pedestrians and ask the rest of his questions.

"How did you find out I'm your father?" he asked.

Toby's body began to vibrate, as if he could barely contain his emotions. "Mother wrote it all down. She didn't think I'd ever find out, but I…" The spate of words trickled to a stop. "You *are* my father."

It was as much question as statement, the one crack of uncertainty in the boy's otherwise confident facade.

"I know you didn't expect me," Toby said, slipping into a surprisingly engaging diffidence. "Mother never told you about me. She was never going to tell *me,* either. That was wrong, wasn't it?"

If it hadn't been for the boy's age, Ross might have suspected he was being played. But Toby was as sincere as any eleven-year-old kid could be.

"You said she wrote it all down," Ross said. "Did she say… *why* she didn't want to tell us?"

"Yes." Tobias frowned, a swift debate going on behind his eyes. "But it doesn't matter to *me,* Father. I don't care if you're only part werewolf and can't Change."

Ross was careful not to let his face reveal his emotions. He'd known, of course. Lovesick fool that he'd been, even at nineteen he'd been able to guess the reason why she'd left him.

"You aren't angry, are you?" Toby said into the silence. "You won't send me back? I promise I won't be any trouble."

Ross stifled a laugh. *Trouble?* Hell, none of this was the kid's fault. Ross knew who to blame. And she didn't even have the courage to face the situation she'd created.

With a little bit of help from you, Ross, me boyo...

Toby continued to gaze up at him, committed to the belief that had carried him across the Atlantic. If there was the slightest trace of doubt in his eyes, it was buried by stubborn determination. And blind, foolish, unshakable faith. Just like the kind Ross had had, once upon a time.

A small, firm hand worked its way into his.

"Are you all right?" Toby asked, his eyes as worried as they had been resolute a moment before.

The feel of that trusting hand was unlike anything Ross could remember. He felt strangely humbled and deeply inadequate. Nothing and no one had made him feel that way in a very long time.

"I'm all right, kid," he said. "It's just that I'm not exactly used to this sort of thing."

"Neither am I."

Ross bit back another laugh. Toby only reached halfway up to his chest, but he was every bit as precocious as Warbrick had said. Maybe that would make it easier.

Easier to do what? To convince him he has to go back to his mother? That whatever he thinks he's looking for, I'm not it?

"I gotta warn you, Toby," he said, "The way you're used to living...well, I'm pretty sure it's a lot different from my place."

Toby gave a little bounce of excitement, as if something tightly wound inside him was beginning to give way. "Don't worry," he said. "I've read Dashiell Hammett. I know all about American detectives."

Ross rolled his eyes. How did a kid his age get hold of Hammett's books, especially in England? That was rough stuff for an eleven-year-old boy. And it had probably given him ideas no real cop or detective could live up to. Especially not Ross Kavanagh.

To think that just a few hours ago he'd thought his problems couldn't get any worse.

Start simple, he told himself. "You hungry?" he asked.

Toby turned on that high-voltage grin. "Oh, yes! May we have frankfurters, please?"

"You've never had a hot dog?"

"I've only read about them. They must be the cat's pajamas."

The American slang sounded funny coming out of this kid's mouth. "Yeah. The height of gourmet dining." Ross spotted a vendor down the street, a guy he'd known almost as long as he'd been on the job.

"Mr. Kavanagh!" Petrocelli said cheerfully. "It's been a while, hasn't it?"

You had to give it to Petrocelli. He'd never indicated that he knew anything about Ross's disgrace, even though it had been in all the papers. "Two dogs, Luigi. Easy on the sauerkraut."

"You bet." The man began slathering two buns with mustard, ketchup and sauerkraut. Toby stood on his toes and watched, politely restrained, but clearly ravenous. He thanked the vendor very graciously, glanced at Ross for permission, then bit into his hot dog with every indication of pure bliss, just like any red-blooded American boy.

"Relative of yours?" Petrocelli asked. "There's something familiar about him."

The vendor's casual words hit Ross like a line drive. He grabbed Toby and pulled him away before he was tempted to make up some pathetic story about a long-lost nephew.

At least the long-lost part is accurate.

Oblivious to Ross's turmoil, Toby drifted along the sidewalk, hot dog in hand, turning in slow circles as he took in the towering buildings on every side. Ross plucked him from the edge of the kerb when he would have walked right into the street.

"Listen, kid," he said, planting Toby in front of him. "This is New York. Haven't you ever been in a big city before?"

Toby gazed at him with the slightly blank expression of a rube just off the train from Podunk. "Grandfather, Mother and I went to London once, when I was very small. I don't really remember."

Ross was momentarily distracted by thoughts of Gillian and grimly forced his attention back to the matter at hand. "London ain't New York," he said. "You can get yourself hurt a hundred different ways here if you're not careful."

"Oh! You don't have to worry. I can take care of myself."

Ross tried to imagine what it must have been like for a little boy to cross the ocean alone and make his way from the docks to Midtown without adult assistance. The kid had guts, no doubt of that. "Do you have any money?" he asked.

Toby plunged his hand into his trousers and removed a wad of badly crinkled bills. "I have pound notes and a few American dollars," he said. "Do you need them, Father?"

Damn. "You hold on to them for now." He frowned at Toby's gray tweed suit with its perfectly cut jacket and short trousers, now disheveled and stained. "That the only outfit you've got?"

"Oh, no. I have another suit in my bag. I'm sorry I didn't have time to change."

His expression was suddenly anxious, as if he expected Ross to blame him for the state of his clothes. Ross reached out and put his hand on the boy's shoulder.

"Listen," he said. "I'm down to my last clean shirt myself. Guys in my line of work—" *my former line of work* "—don't always have time to look pretty."

Toby relaxed for about ten seconds before his facile mind latched on to a new subject. "Have you arrested lots of criminals, Father?"

Ross wondered why he was so bent on making the kid think well of him. "I've taken a few bad guys off the streets in my day."

"Capital!" Toby's eyes swept the streets as if he expected a mobster to appear right in front of them. "Do you think we'l meet any bootleggers?" he asked eagerly.

"We aren't going to see any bootleggers, mobsters or criminals of any kind."

Toby's face fell. "You said New York was dangerous."

"It's not like there's a gunfight every few minutes. You jus have to be careful." He resisted the urge to take out his handkerchief and wipe a bit of mustard from Toby's upper lip. "You wouldn't have made it this far if you weren't pretty good at that."

Another lightning-quick change of mood and Toby wa grinning again. "Will you show me all around New York? Wil we see the Woolworth Building and Coney Island?"

Ross cleared his throat. He still wasn't prepared to lie to the kid, but he didn't have to tell the whole truth, either. "I'll see what I can do," he said. "You need a wash-up, first. And a nap."

"Oh, I don't take naps anymore."

"You will today."

Toby groaned. "You sound just like Mother."

Ross grabbed Toby's hand and flagged down a taxi. "How is she?" he asked.

The question was out before he could stop it. *Don't kid yourself. You'd have asked it sooner or later.*

"Oh, she's all right."

Ross said nothing until a cab pulled up, and he and Toby were in the backseat. "Does she live alone?" he asked. "I mean…" *Idiot.* He shut up before he dug the hole any deeper.

But Toby was too bright to have missed his intent. "I haven't got another father," he said. "I always knew my real father wasn't dead."

"Mr. Delvaux…"

"Mother never talked about him. I'm not even sure he's real."

"You mean your mother wasn't really married?"

Now you've done it, he thought. But Toby didn't seem to be offended.

"I don't know," the boy said. "Some of the pages in her diary were missing, but there was enough in it to help me find you."

Gillian had kept a diary. About him. And she'd somehow known that he'd gone into the force when he returned to America. He hadn't even thought about it himself until he was standing on the East River docks, trying to think of the best way to forget Gillian Maitland.

Why hadn't she forgotten him?

"Didn't you think how upset your mother would be when you ran away?" he asked, resolutely focusing on the present.

Toby hunched his shoulders. "She has enough things to worry about."

Ross swallowed the questions that immediately popped into his head. "Your mother has done a lot more than just worry."

A speculative look came into Toby's hazel eyes. "How do you know that, Father?"

"She sent someone to look for you. A man called Ethan Warbrick."

"Uncle Ethan?" Toby's forehead creased with concern. "Don't tell him I'm here." He tugged at Ross's sleeve. "Please, Father."

"Don't you like him?"

"He's all right, but…" He lowered his voice. "I think he wants to marry my mother."

"War— Uncle Ethan isn't a werewolf, is he?"

Toby looked up at him curiously. "No," he said. "Did you think he was?"

"He knows all about werewolves."

"Mother and Uncle Ethan were secret friends when they were children."

"Does *she* want to marry Uncle Ethan?" he asked, cursing himself for his weakness.

"I don't know," Toby said slowly, as if he'd given the matter some thought. "You wouldn't let him, would you?"

Ross didn't get a chance to come up with an answer, because the cab had arrived at his building and someone was standing by the door. Someone Ross recognized the moment she turned her head and looked straight into his eyes.

Gillian Maitland.

CHAPTER TWO

SHE'D CHANGED.

Oh, not so much in outward appearance; she'd always thought of herself as plain, but to Ross, she'd been beautiful from the first moment he'd laid eyes on her in the hospital. She still was. Her features were a little stronger now, a little more fully formed with experience and maturity; the faintest of lines radiated out from the outer corners of her eyes; and her golden hair had grown long, gathered in an old-fashioned chignon at the base of her slender neck.

No, it wasn't so much her appearance that had altered, or the cut of her clothing. Her suit was conservative, the skirt reaching below her knees, the long jacket and high-necked blouse sober and without embellishments of any kind. Ross remembered when he'd first seen her out of uniform; she'd been very proper even then, as far from being a "modern girl" as he could have imagined. Nor had her scent changed, that intriguing combination of natural femininity and lavender soap.

But her eyes…oh, that was where Ross saw the difference. They were cool and distant, even as her expression registered the natural shock of seeing him again after so many years. The hazel depths he'd always admired were barred like a prison, holding the world at bay. Behind those bars crouched emotions Ross couldn't read, experiences he hadn't been permitted to share. And a heart as frigid as an ice storm in January.

She looked from his face to Toby's, and her straight, slender

body unbent with relief. He'd been wrong. Her heart wasn'
cold. Not where her son was concerned.

"Toby," she said. "Thank God."

Toby stood very still, his face ashen. He began to walk towar
his mother, not unlike a prisoner going to his well-earned pun
ishment. Gillian knelt on the rough pavement and smiled, he
eyes coming to life.

"Mother," Toby said, his voice catching, and walked into he
arms.

Gillian closed her eyes, kissed Toby's flushed cheek and hel
him tight for a dozen heartbeats. Then she let him go and stoo
up, keeping her hand on her son's shoulder.

"Thank you," she said to Ross, sincere and utterly formal
"Thank you for finding him."

Ross opened his mouth to answer and found his tongue a
thick and unwieldy as a block of concrete. "I didn't find him,"
he managed to say at last. "He found me."

"At the police station," Toby offered, his brief moment of re
pentance already vanished. He looked from Ross to his mother
wide-eyed innocence concealing something uncomfortably lik
calculation. "You needn't have worried, Mother. I was never i
any danger."

Gillian tightened her fingers on his shoulder, her gaze steady
on Ross's. "I'm sorry that you were put to so much trouble,"
she said. "I didn't know he had left England until the ship ha
already departed."

"Yeah." Ross locked his hands behind his back. "Your frien
Ethan Warbrick told me the story. He implied that you weren'
coming."

The barest hint of color touched Gillian's smooth cheeks
"Perhaps Lord Warbrick misunderstood." She glanced away
"Again, I apologize, Mr. Kavanagh. If you've incurred any
expenses…"

"I bought him a hot dog," Ross said, a wave of heat rising

under his collar. "It didn't exactly break the bank." He smiled the kind of smile he reserved for suspects in the interrogation room. "As I told Warbrick, I don't need any 'consideration,' either."

"I don't understand."

That little hint of vulnerability was a nice touch, Ross thought. "Tell Warbrick he can tear up the check."

"The—" Her eyes widened. "Oh, no. You mustn't think such a thing, Ross. You—" She caught herself, donning the mantle of aristocratic dignity again. "We shan't trouble you any longer, Mr. Kavanagh."

She turned to go, taking Toby with her. He dug in his heels and wouldn't budge. Ross pushed past the burning wall of his anger and crossed the space between them until he was blocking her path of escape.

"Is that it?" he asked softly. "Nothing else to say…Mrs. Delvaux?"

Most people would have shrunk away from the finely tuned menace in Ross's voice. Gillian wasn't most people.

"I had not thought," she said, "that you would wish to prolong the conversation."

"I didn't know we were having one," he said. "Not the kind you'd expect between old friends."

Gillian understood him. She understood him very well, but she wasn't about to crack. "This is neither the time nor the place," she said, holding on to Toby as if she expected him to bolt.

Ross showed his teeth. "As it so happens," he said, "my schedule is pretty open at the moment. You pick the time and place. I'll be there."

She looked down at Toby. He was listening intently to every word, his head slightly cocked.

"We will not be staying in America long," she said. "The ship—"

"Mother!" Toby cried. "We've only just arrived." He turned pleading eyes on Ross. "Father promised he'd take me to Coney Island."

Ross had promised nothing of the kind, but under the circumstances, he wasn't prepared to dispute Toby's claim. He was certain he'd seen Gillian flinch when Toby said "Father." Did she really believe he would have accepted Warbrick's lie about the kid being some other guy's son?

"I'm surprised that Mr. Kavanagh has had time to make such promises," she said, her voice chilly.

"Toby knows what he wants," Ross said. "I like that in a man."

"He's hardly a—" She clamped her mouth shut. "If you have no objection, I'll take Toby back to our hotel. My brother is also stopping there. He can watch Toby while you and I—"

"Uncle Hugh came, too?" Toby interrupted.

"Yes. And you will remain with him while I make arrangements for our return to England."

"But Mother—"

"Do as your mother says," Ross said. "I'll come along with you."

"And we'll go to Coney Island before I leave?"

"Maybe." He stared at Gillian until she met his gaze. "You don't mind if I accompany you to your hotel?"

She stiffened. "That is hardly necessary, Mr. Kavanagh."

"New York is a complicated city, Mrs. Delvaux. I'll feel better knowing you aren't traveling alone."

Gillian had never been anything but bright. She knew she was licked, at least for the moment. She inclined her head with all the condescension of a queen.

"As you wish," she said. She gave the address of her hotel—one of the fancy kind an ordinary homicide detective seldom had occasion to set foot in—and Ross escorted her and Toby back to Tenth Avenue, where he flagged down a taxi.

The ride to Midtown was about as pleasant as a Manhattan heat wave. Toby sat between Ross and Gillian, darting glances from one to the other, but remaining uncharacteristically silent. If Gillian felt any shame about the situation, her forbidding demeanor concealed it perfectly. Ross's temper continued to simmer, held in check by the thought that he would soon have Gillian alone.

And when he did…by God, when he *did*…

"Roosevelt Hotel," the cabbie announced as he pulled his vehicle up to the kerb. Ross stepped out first, circled the cab and opened the door for Gillian, extending his hand to help her up.

She hesitated for just a moment, then put her gloved hand in his.

Ross knew he shouldn't have felt anything. Not a damned thing. He couldn't even feel her skin through the kid gloves, and she let go as soon as her feet were firmly planted on the sidewalk.

But there was something he couldn't deny, a spark of awareness, a memory of flesh on flesh in a far more intimate setting. Unwillingly, he glanced at Gillian to see if she'd felt it, too, but her attention was fixed on her pocketbook as she counted out the fare. Ross was just a few seconds too late to stop her. She took Toby's hand as he bounced up beside her and marched across the sidewalk without a word to Ross; the doorman hurried to open the door and tipped his hat as she swept into the lobby.

"Nice family you got there, mister," the cabbie said as Ross stared after her.

There was genuine admiration in the guy's voice. Ross pressed another buck into the guy's hand and started after Gillian, walking in a way that advised anyone in his path to step aside.

His skin began to prickle as soon as he entered the lobby. He'd spent his childhood up to his knees in manure and mud or coated with dust and sweat, working his parents' ranch alongside the hired hands. There hadn't been much extra money in those days, though the Kavanaghs always managed to keep their heads above water. Ross had received most of his education in a one-room schoolhouse, and the folks with whom his family associated had all been simple, hardworking ranchers, not much different from Chantal and Sim Kavanagh except in their unadulterated humanity.

The Roosevelt Hotel had never been intended for the common man. It was only a few years old, its carpets and fancy uphol-stery pristine, every metal surface sparkling, porters and spot-lessly uniformed bellhops poised to fulfill every guest's slightest wish. One of the bellhops rushed forward to take Toby's suitcase; Ross gave the kid a hard look and lifted the bag out of Gillian's hand.

Gillian continued to the elevators without stopping; though no one would take her for a glamour girl, her inborn werewolf grace naturally attracted attention. Ross bristled at the expen-sively suited swells who watched her progress across the lobby with appreciative stares; Gillian simply ignored them. Rich or not, they were only human.

The boy in the elevator seemed very aware of Ross's mood. He stood quietly in his corner until the elevator settled to a stop and Gillian got out.

The corridor smelled of perfume and fresh flowers from the vases set on marble stands between the widely spaced doors. Gillian paused before one of the doors, produced a key and entered.

The door led to a luxurious suite, complete with an obviously well-stocked and illegal bar. A handsome young man sprawled on the brocade sofa, drink in hand, his wayward hair several shades darker than Gillian's gold. The young man sprang to his feet when he saw Gillian and Toby.

"Gilly!" he exclaimed. "You found him!"

Toby hung back, waiting for Ross to enter the suite. The young man's gaze fixed on Ross in surprise.

Gillian's posture was as rigid as it could be without losing any of its grace. "Hugh," she said, "may I present Mr. Ross Kavanagh. Mr. Kavanagh, my brother, Hugh Maitland."

IF A BOMBSHELL had gone off in the room, the shock couldn't have been more palpable. Hugh's nostrils flared, taking in Ross's scent as Gillian's words began to penetrate.

"Ross Kavanagh?" he said. "*The* Ross Kavanagh?"

Gillian had no intention of belaboring the point. The day had already proven to be an unmitigated disaster, and Hugh's involvement was only likely to make matters worse. Her hopes of keeping the truth from Ross had been naive from the start.

So had her conviction that seeing him again would have no effect on her heart.

If it hadn't been for Toby, she might not have been able to maintain her composure, but he kept her focused. She would deal with Ross—and her own unacceptable weakness—once her son was safely out of danger.

She took Toby's hand firmly in hers. "You'll excuse me," she said, "but Toby must have a bath and then a nap. Hugh, I'm sure you will provide Mr. Kavanagh with appropriate refreshments."

Hugh gazed at her with lingering astonishment. "Yes. Yes, of course."

"I'm not at all tired, Mother," Toby said, his jaw setting in that stubborn expression that so perfectly mirrored Ross Kavanagh's. "Mayn't I—"

Gillian stared into Toby's eyes. She seldom felt the need to bring the full weight of her authority to bear, but she was desperate…to get him away from Ross's influence. Toby shrank ever so slightly under her gaze, acknowledging the wolf he had yet to become. He was very subdued as he accompanied her into the ornate water closet.

There were no further arguments from him as she ran a bath and left him to soak in the hot water. She retreated to her bedroom and went to the window, staring out at this cold, modern city of steel canyons and seething humanity.

She'd thought herself prepared. She'd thought that she could face Ross in the same way she'd dealt with New York itself: by keeping a firm grip on who she was, where she had come from and why she was here. By reminding herself that what she and Ross had shared had been no more than a few weeks' passion, that they'd never had anything in common save for their youth and reckless disregard for propriety.

All her careful preparations had disappeared when Ross had arrived at the apartment building with Toby beside him. The image she'd held had been that of a boy only slightly older than she'd been twelve years ago: a handsome young man with striking light brown eyes and hair a few shades darker, unpolished yet undeniably compelling. A young man who'd claimed to love her…just before he admitted that he was only one-quarter werewolf and unable to Change.

That boy was gone. The man who'd stared at her with such accusation might have been another person entirely. He was no longer young; the lines in his forehead and around his eyes testified to a life of conflict, a career spent enforcing the law for the humans whose blood he shared. He was still handsome, but it was a grim sort of attractiveness, touched with bitterness that Gillian dared not examine too closely.

But it was what lay beneath the surface that had startled her most. At the hospital in London he had seemed so completely human that she'd never questioned her initial assumption; even after he'd told her the truth, she'd hardly been able to recognize the wolf within him.

No longer. The life he'd lived since the War had chiseled away at his humanity, revealing the core of his werewolf nature. It gleamed yellow under the brown of his eyes, sculpted the bone and muscle of his face, stalked in his every movement.

Those changes alone would have been enough to shake her equilibrium. But it was something within herself that had stripped her of her defenses, something she couldn't possibly have anticipated that struck at her with all the force of a hurricane.

Gillian pressed her forehead to the cool window glass. Years had passed—years of dedication to duty, to her father, to her son. It should not even be possible for her to still desire a man she had known for only a handful of weeks amid the chaos of war, a man who could never become her mate. She had almost forgotten what it was to feel that kind of excitement, that kind of pleasure. Such things had no place in the life of a sequestered widow, and she had accepted that they would have no part in her forthcoming marriage.

Why, then, had this happened now? Was it her punishment for refusing to recognize Toby's incipient rebellion, for neglecting to meet needs she hadn't understood? Or was it a gift in disguise, a reminder that she must never let down her guard, never for a moment surrender to her own natural weakness?

She had felt weak in Ross's presence. Weak and vulnerable. But he would never know it. She would make certain of that. She would take Toby home as quickly as possible. And then…

"Gilly?"

Hugh's voice held a note of concern that reminded her how long she'd been gone. She answered her brother's tap on the bedroom door with a calm that was almost sincere.

"I'm sorry, Hugh," she said. "Give me a few more moments to put Toby to bed, then I'll join you."

"You'd better," Hugh said. "Kavanagh isn't much for small talk, and I don't want to be the one giving all the explanations."

Explanations. Was that what Ross wanted of her? The strength of his anger had been almost overwhelming, all the more effective for its quietness; she could well envision criminals quailing before him, begging to confess rather than face that simmering stare.

She returned to the bathroom to find Toby dozing in the cooling water. She woke him, left him to towel himself dry and then steered him into his room.

"Is Father still here?" he asked sleepily, hovering near the door.

"Mr. Kavanagh is with Hugh at the moment. But you are to

sleep now, young man. You've had quite enough adventure fo
one day. We shall have a good long talk about this later."

Ordinarily Toby might have been concerned about his in
evitable punishment, but his mind was on other subjects. "I'll se
Father tomorrow, won't I?"

Toby had been this way since he could talk: direct, fearles
and frightfully stubborn. Gillian had simply failed to realize—
had not let herself realize—how much he would be like the ma
who had sired him.

She had only lied to him once, and the unfortunate results o
that deception were plain to see.

"I don't know," she said. "Mr. Kavanagh and I have no
spoken in many years."

"Because you didn't tell him about me."

"I shall make my decisions based upon your welfare and
nothing else."

Toby glared at her, jaw set. That expression had been all to
common of late; he was poised on that terrible brink betwee
boy and man, cub and wolf. Gillian could feel him beginning t
slip out of her grasp, and she wasn't ready to let him go.

*There is no need to rush. He will Change when the time i
right. He* will *Change….*

She shook off her pointless worries and herded him towar
the bed. "Go to sleep, Toby," she said. "I will inform you of m
decision in the morning."

"But if you—"

"*Sleep.*"

He crawled into bed, defying her with every movement of hi
rapidly growing body. She waited until he'd tucked himself i
and then switched off the bedroom light.

There was no delaying the inevitable. She smoothed her skirt
made sure that her chignon was still in place and walked bacl
to the sitting room.

Hugh was standing by the mantelpiece, a drink in his hand and his shoulders hunched. Ross hovered a few feet away, arms held loosely at his sides, as if he might spring into action at any moment. His head swung toward Gillian as she entered the room; the impact of his stare almost broke the measured rhythm of her stride.

She didn't stop until she had reached the sofa. "Won't you be seated, Mr. Kavanagh?" she asked.

"I prefer to stand, Mrs. Delvaux."

"As you wish." She glanced at Hugh. He looked deeply uncomfortable, and she had no desire to inflict the coming unpleasantness on someone who'd had no part in creating it.

"The evening is very mild, Hugh," she said. "We've had little opportunity to see the city. Perhaps you'd enjoy a walk."

Hugh shifted from foot to foot and looked from her to Ross. "I'd rather stay, if you don't mind," he said.

Gillian's heart turned over. She'd always understood that Hugh needed protecting, even though he was Father's favorite. He was good-natured to a fault, but foolish and feckless; the more formidable wolf characteristics Sir Averil had done so much to encourage were almost never in evidence behind that ready grin. But now he was prepared to give up his own comfort in defense of his sister, and Gillian loved him the more for it.

"You'd better beat it, kid," Ross growled. "This is between me and the lady."

The way he said "lady" was clearly not meant as a compliment. Hugh's head sank a little lower between his shoulders.

"Since the subject under discussion involves my nephew," he said, "it also concerns me."

Ross gave Hugh a long, appraising look. He made a rumbling sound deep in his throat; his lips stretched to show the tips of his upper teeth. Quarter werewolf or not, he dominated Hugh as easily as a collie does a sheep.

"I'm sure your sister will fill you in," he said. "Make yourself scarce, and we won't have any arguments."

Hugh's face revealed the progress of his thoughts. He passed quickly from anger and indignation to uncertainty and, finally, resignation.

"All right," he said, making an attempt at severity, "but if you need me, Gilly, I won't be far."

He gave a little jerk to his tie, spun around and walked through the door, trailing a wake of wounded dignity behind him.

"Hugh doesn't deserve your scorn," Gillian said once Hugh had closed the door. "He was a child when you and I knew each other."

Ross shrugged. "I have nothing against him." He glanced toward the hall. "Is the boy asleep?"

"He will be presently."

"Then we can speak freely."

She held his gaze, struggling to disregard the half-familiar scent of his body beneath the inexpensive suit. Surely that warm, masculine fragrance hadn't been quite so potent in London. Surely his shoulders hadn't been so broad, his movements so steeped with barely leashed power. Surely she hadn't forgotten so much….

"I always knew you came from money," Ross said, leaving his post by the door to wander around the sitting room. "I just didn't realize how much until now."

It wasn't the way Gillian had expected the conversation to begin. Accusation had seethed in his voice when they'd spoken outside his apartment building, and Gillian could still feel a suggestion of violence beneath his deceptive calm. But he was attempting to approach their differences in a relatively civilized manner, and for that she should be grateful.

"I guess that's why Warbrick offered to buy me off," Ross said, picking up a fragile vase of intricately engraved crystal. "You'd hardly notice losing a thousand bucks."

Gillian turned to face him, the solidity of the sofa at her back. "I must apologize," she said, "for any insult Mr. Warbrick may have unintentionally given you. He and I had not discussed—"

"Unintentionally?" Ross laughed. "Where *is* your friend, by the way? He seemed pretty anxious to spare you any inconvenience."

"I don't know where he is at the moment," Gillian said. That was the truth; she'd tried calling Ethan's hotel when she and Hugh had arrived, but he hadn't been in. "I assure you that he meant no harm. He—"

"Tried to make me believe that Toby wasn't my son." Ross set down the vase. "Was that your idea or his?"

Gillian revised her hopes for a civilized discussion. "I didn't authorize him to deceive you," she said.

"Even though that's what you've been doing for the past twelve years?"

There was no sense in denying obvious fact, no point in stammering excuses that would only ring hollow. "I'm sorry that it has come to this, Ross," she said, pushing past the barrier of his name. "It was never my intention to cause you pain."

She expected another harsh retort, but Ross surprised her. His face emptied of all emotion. "I don't remember saying anything about pain," he said.

That was when Gillian realized he wasn't going to speak of what he'd felt on the day she'd left him. She had assumed that a large part of his anger was directed at her—not because of Toby, but because she'd cut off all contact with him the day after he'd made his declaration. She couldn't blame him; she had endured months of confusion, unhappiness and self-reproach before she'd come to terms with her decision and recognized its inevitability.

She had gradually erased all speculation about Ross's feelings. Even if part of her had wished he would search her out and sweep her away, she had known such an act would be a terrible mistake. And when he hadn't come for her, she'd assumed that his love had been like hers, built on a transient passion that would never have endured.

Apparently Ross had come to the same conclusion. If he was

bitter, it wasn't because he still loved her. If he was angry, it was because his pride had been damaged, not his heart.

Strange how little relief she felt.

Gillian released her breath. "I assume," she said slowly, "that you have questions about Toby."

Ross walked to the window and pushed back the silk drapes. "When did you marry Delvaux?"

Again he'd caught her off guard. She briefly considered telling him the real story, which Toby would have discovered for himself if her diary had been intact.

No. She would tell Ross exactly what she'd told Toby when he was old enough to understand.

"Jacques Delvaux," she said, "was the man I was engaged to marry before I went to London."

Ross stiffened, every muscle frozen, and then gradually relaxed.

"You were engaged?" he asked.

"Yes. My work as a nurse only postponed our wedding."

"Let me guess. He was pure *loup-garou.*"

There. He had reached the obvious conclusion, as she'd known he would. The unpalatable truth lay between them, stinking of shattered dreams.

"Yes," she said.

He could have berated her then, could have brought it all out in the open, painting her as the unredeemed villainess. But Ross said nothing about her lack of honesty. He laid no blame, offered no reproach. He simply waited, calm and remote, as if he were a priest awaiting a supplicant's confession.

"Jacques and I were married a month after I returned to Snowfell," she said. "Only a few days before he left to join his regiment on the front lines. He died within the week."

Ross gazed at the wall behind her. "You knew Toby wasn't his," he said.

Of course she'd known. How could she not have recognized the changes in her own body? A werewolf female knew instinctively when she was with child. It ran in the blood as surely as the Change.

"I knew," she admitted.

"Did you tell him?"

Gillian took a deep breath. What *would* she have done, if events had occurred just as she'd claimed? What if Sir Averil had been able to keep her pregnancy a secret and her arranged marriage—the *real* marriage—had happened exactly as Sir Averil had so carefully planned?

Let Ross think the very worst of her. It didn't matter now.

"No," she said. "There was no time."

"But no one questioned that Toby was Delvaux's," Ross said. "You were together long enough to give your son a legitimate, acceptable father."

The bitterness was gone. She'd done nothing to soothe his pride; she'd only given him more reason to despise her. But Ross's words were rational, almost detached. It was as if he had become a different person than the one she'd been speaking to only an hour ago.

An hour. Had it really been such a short time? Could they have passed so easily through the turmoil of their reunion and emerged relatively unscathed?

"The world hasn't changed so very much," she said. "Toby would have been subject to harsh judgment if anyone knew that he was illegitimate."

"But you weren't really worried about what regular people might think. All those other *loups-garous* with their plans for the werewolf race wouldn't have been too happy with you, either."

Oh, yes. He clearly remembered her attempts to explain what had seemed so important for him to understand in those days, even before she'd known he was a little more than human.

"I was concerned with Toby's future, yes," she said.

"What about your family? You never talked about them. How were they involved in all this?"

Now he was striking much too close to the truth. "They approved of my marriage to Jacques, of course. Our families had been connected in the past."

"So you couldn't tell *them* about me, either."

"They would not have understood. They trusted me...my honor. I could not have disappointed them."

He cocked his head, as if he sensed how much she was omitting, but couldn't frame the right questions.

"You did what you had to do to protect Toby," he said evenly. "Where did you go after Delvaux died?"

"To Snowfell, the estate where I grew up. My family welcomed me."

"Are your parents still living?"

She wondered why he would ask. Or care. "My mother died long ago. My father...has become rather eccentric in his old age, and seldom leaves Snowfell. I do what I can for him."

"So you've never left."

"Toby and I have everything we need there."

"And Toby was doing all right without knowing about his real dad. The only mistake you made was to write the truth down so that he could find it."

He was right. It had been a terrible mistake. She'd remembered having destroyed the diary a year after Toby's birth, after she'd learned that Ross had found employment with the New York City police force. But her memory had played tricks on her...she'd only torn out certain pages, leaving a patchwork of notations that had revealed the very things she'd never wanted Toby to know.

"Why did you keep track of me?" Ross asked.

She couldn't invent a convincing reason. "I don't know," she said.

He seemed to accept her answer. "What did Toby do when he found out that Delvaux wasn't his father?"

"He was...intrigued," Gillian said carefully. "A boy of his age is incessantly curious about everything, especially himself. It was only natural that he should wish to know more about you."

"What did you tell him?"

"I had little chance to discuss the matter with him before he ran away."

"And you didn't notice he was gone until he'd gotten all the way to the ship?"

Gillian felt a prickle of heat rushing over her skin. "He's run away before, but never went farther than the neighboring estate."

"Sounds like he didn't have everything he needed at Snowfell after all."

"Boys of his age are naturally restless."

He offered no contradiction. "You never considered letting him meet his real father, even in secret?"

Another question filled with pitfalls. "It would hardly have been fair to him—or to you," she said. "My…writings did not continue beyond the first few years. I knew nothing of your present life. You might have had a wife, children of your own. I could not anticipate that you would wish…to be…burdened with the knowledge."

The corner of his mouth twitched. "Mighty considerate of you," he said, lapsing into that peculiar Western dialect she remembered from London. "But you were wrong on all counts, Mrs. Delvaux. No wife. No kids. Never had much use for the idea."

"Then I see no real difficulty in our…in the situation. Toby has met you. His curiosity has been satisfied."

"Has it?"

She remembered what Toby had said to her in the bedroom. "Toby is a boy of intelligence and ability beyond his years," she said. "He is affectionate with those who have earned his trust. But he can also be rash and stubborn. He has done a very dangerous thing by traveling alone to America. Such behavior must not be rewarded."

"So he should be punished for wanting to know the truth?"

Her stomach began to knot. "I have answered your questions," she said. "What more do you want of us?"

Ross looked at her and then down at the carpet between his feet, and she recognized something she hadn't expected to see: uncertainty. She might almost have called it vulnerability. But the moment passed quickly, and when he spoke again, it was without any trace of hesitation.

"I want to see more of my son," he said.

CHAPTER THREE

PANIC SWELLED in Gillian's throat, but she fought it down. She needed to use reason now, not emotion. Unless Ross had lost the basic decency that had been such a fundamental part of the boy she had known, he would listen to a sensible argument.

"Please be seated," she asked.

He regarded her as warily as if she'd asked him to jump out the window, but he acceded to her request. He selected one of the deep armchairs, and she took a seat on the sofa, holding herself still and erect.

"I understand," she began, "that you are curious about Toby. That's only to be expected. I can see that you are also concerned about his welfare." She paused, trying to collect her thoughts. "Since you lack experience with children, you may not realize... how impressionable a young boy can be."

"Impressionable." Ross got up abruptly, went to the illegally stocked sideboard where Hugh had left his bottle of brandy and poured himself a glass. "You mean he might be susceptible to bad influences."

How easily he twisted her words. "He may be entering the transition at any time. Additional distractions will only serve to confuse him and make him unhappy at such a crucial juncture in his life."

Ross emptied the glass. "You think I'll confuse him?" he asked. "You think he'll lose his ability to Change just by being around me?"

Gillian flinched. "I implied no such thing," she said stiffly.

"But you're worried about it, aren't you? He's my son, and that means…" He paused to pour himself another glass and inspected it critically. "What else are you worried about, Mrs. Delvaux? Afraid I'll give Toby a yen to be a cop like his old dad?"

Gillian pushed her anger back into the little hollow deep inside her chest. "You can only hurt him if you give him reason to believe…if you allow him to form an attachment to you which cannot last."

"Hurt him?" Ross quickly swallowed the second drink and set it down so hard that Gillian expected the glass to shatter. "Is that what you think I'm trying to do?"

"No, of course not. But Toby's future is in England, and you surely would not wish him to be torn—"

"Between you and me?" He pushed the half-empty brandy bottle aside with a sweep of his hand. "Do you think I could take him away from you?"

Ice water rolled through Gillian's veins. "Is that what you intend to do?"

Ross dragged his palm over his face and returned to the chair. "No." He met her gaze with an earnestness that battered at her defenses more surely than a barrage of curses. "I don't steal kids from their mothers. But he's blood of my blood. You can't make that fact disappear, no matter how much you want to."

"I have no wish to deny it."

He gave her cynical smile. "Yeah. I guess it's a little too late for that." He sobered. "All I'm asking is a few days. Just a few days, Jill."

Gillian swallowed and looked away. "Jill" had been Ross's pet name for her; she still remembered when he'd told her, with a teasing sort of tenderness in his eyes, that "Gillian" was too "highfalutin" for everyday use. She'd thought that it was his way of bridging the gap of wealth and class that lay between them, differences she had been just as ready to set aside.

Until he'd tried to make their affair more than it could ever be.

She rested her hands in her lap, deliberately relaxing her fingers and letting all emotion drain away. "I know you have no reason to trust me," she said, "but I must ask you to believe that I know what is best for our…for Toby. He has romantic notions that may perhaps have led him to believe that he will find something—something mysterious and wonderful—here with you that he hasn't found at home. He has an idealized image of the father he never knew."

Ross dropped his hands between his knees. "I never claimed to be anyone's ideal. I won't lie to the kid." His voice grew husky. "Am I asking so much, Jill? A few days out of a lifetime?"

His question hung between them, so saturated with unspoken feeling that Gillian felt worse than if he'd shouted and raged. The gentleness of his voice didn't change the circumstances in the least, but her mouth simply refused to speak the words that necessity should have made so simple.

He was asking her to trust him. Trust him with the most important thing in her life, when he had every reason to resent her. She had known from childhood that emotions could change in an instant, that one could never rely on anyone else's behavior, only one's own. His motives were still a mystery to her; it wasn't as if he knew more than a trifle about Toby or could even begin to understand him.

But what other purpose could he have? If he were planning some sort of retaliation for the assaults on his pride, surely he wouldn't be here in her hotel room bargaining with her.

The brash young doughboy she'd known in London would never have sought revenge. Such dark emotions had been alien to him, even after he'd faced death on the battlefield. That was only one reason she'd found it so easy to believe, however briefly, that she loved him.

"I shall consider everything you've suggested," she said. "Will it be acceptable if I telephone you tomorrow?"

He pushed his hands into his trouser pockets, a gesture she remembered all too well. "I guess it'll have to be." He glanced toward the door to the bedrooms. "Do you mind if I look in on him before I go?"

The wolf in Gillian wanted nothing more than to rush across the room and block the door with her body. The woman was nearly paralyzed and hated herself for it.

"Of course," she said. "But please don't wake him."

"He won't even know I'm there." Ross picked up his hat and headed unerringly for the room where Toby was sleeping. He made no sound at all when he stepped into the bedroom. Gillian paused in the doorway as he went to the bed and looked down at the boy sprawled beneath the covers.

There should have been nothing remarkable in the sight of a father watching his son while he slept. It happened all over the world every day. But Gillian could hardly breathe as Ross knelt beside the bed, reached out with one big hand and touched Toby's hair with such gentleness that Toby didn't so much as stir the tip of one little finger.

The moment lasted for a dozen heartbeats, and then Ross withdrew. He met Gillian's gaze, and the gentle wonder that lingered in his face warmed her like a fire in winter.

"Thanks," he said simply, and slipped out of the room. Her skin hummed beneath the sleeve of the blouse he had brushed in passing. She compelled her feet to follow him to the outer door, astonished at how difficult it was to regain control of her own body.

Ross opened the door to the hall and turned to face her, his expression unreadable once again. "I'll be expecting your call," he said.

"Ross—"

"Good night, Gillian." He placed his hat on his head, nodded briefly and walked away.

Gillian leaned heavily against the doorjamb, watching him

until he reached the elevator and stepped inside. She felt nervous, a little sick to her stomach and oddly exhilarated.

The first two symptoms she understood well enough. But the third…that one made no sense at all. Physical yearning was a thing of the body alone, easily governed by the mind. It was only a ghost, a dream, a memory with no validity in the present.

She backed away from the door, closed it firmly and returned to Toby's bedroom. He was sitting up, his chin resting on his bent knees.

"He's gone, isn't he?" he asked.

"Yes." Gillian sat in the chair nearest the bed and folded her hands in her lap. "Did we wake you?"

He shook his head. "I had a dream that Father was teaching me how to fish."

"How to fish?"

"Mmm-hmm. Except I was very small. And Father was living with us at Snowfell."

Gillian's nails pressed tiny crescents into her palms. "Toby… it would be wise…it would be better if you didn't call Mr. Kavanagh 'Father.'"

His bright, direct gaze focused on her. "Why not? He *is* my father."

"In a literal sense, yes. But once we return to England, it's likely that you'll never see him again. You will find it easier to adjust if you—"

"If I pretend I never met him?" Toby leaned back against the pillows and folded his arms across his chest. "*I* can't forget, even if you can."

It was surprising, Gillian thought, how much a child's thoughtless words could sting. "Tell me," she said, "why you're so fond of Mr. Kavanagh when you've spent scarcely any time with him."

Toby considered her question with a lightning shift to that precocious maturity that still had the power to surprise her. "Isn't one *supposed* to like one's father?" he asked.

If she hadn't known better, she might have thought he was testing her. But she'd been careful, so very careful, to keep him away from Sir Averil and his volatile moods.

"That isn't an answer, Toby."

"I just like him. He doesn't treat me like a child."

"But you *are* a child. There are many things you don't understand."

"I understand that you wrote that you didn't think Ross was good enough to be my father because he wasn't like you and Hugh and Grandfather."

Gillian felt light-headed. He'd read just enough to confuse him, and now she had to set it right.

"Do you remember when we talked about how rare were-wolves are in the world?" she asked.

He tangled his fingers in the sheets, his expression turning sullen. "Yes," he muttered.

"Wise men realized that the only way to save our kind was to marry those of *loup-garou* blood to each other, to preserve our abilities and our way of life. That is the purpose of the Convocation. That is why we must sometimes set aside the things we…might think we want in order to help all our people."

"And Mr. Delvaux was the right kind of werewolf."

Oh, how she had tried to keep this from him. How she had danced around the subject, knowing that one day Toby might discover his mixed heritage and what it could mean.

How much had he read in those damning notations?

"Mr. Delvaux," she said, "was from a family that could trace its bloodlines back to the fourteenth century and beyond. No one questioned that he had all the qualities necessary to strengthen our people."

"You didn't even love him."

"You can hardly make such judgments, Toby, when he died before you were born."

He gave her a hard, direct look. "I know you didn't love him,

ut you still thought he was better than my real father." His jaw
et in a way that reminded Gillian far too much of Ross. "There
sn't anything wrong with Father, whatever you say."

Dangerous, dangerous waters. "You're right, Toby," Gillian
aid gently. "There's nothing wrong with Mr. Kavanagh. I've no
oubt that he is very competent in everything he does. I'm certain
e has a full life here, with his work as a police officer."

Toby wasn't to be distracted. "He wasn't a police officer
vhen you met," Toby said. "He was a soldier, wasn't he?"

"Yes, but—"

"Did you know, then, that he was only part werewolf?"

Dear God. "I…it isn't always possible to tell."

"But you liked him anyway, didn't you?"

"Yes. I liked him, Toby."

"I know the facts of life, Mother." His cheeks colored, raising
a spattering of freckles. "You decided to have a baby with him,
didn't you?"

The facts of life. Toby had only the weakest grasp on the nature
of relationships between men and women, but he knew enough.

"Sometimes," she said, "we don't always expect what's going
o happen."

"You didn't want me to be born?"

"Oh, Toby." She moved quickly toward the bed and sat down,
er arms trembling with the need to embrace him. "You were a
miracle. A wonderful gift."

"But I'm part human."

He knew, and there was no going back. "Yes. But your were-
volf blood is of the very strongest. You don't have anything to—"

Be afraid of. But he wasn't afraid. Not…yet. She had almost
lipped, almost revealed too much.

"Even if Father isn't like Mr. Delvaux, he's still a werewolf,"
Toby said, speaking into her sudden silence. "I'll bet he could
hrash anyone coming to the Convocation." He bit his lower lip.
"Maybe you don't *have* to Change to be a real *loup-garou.*"

Gillian began to shake. He was talking as much about himself as Ross. Either he'd seen through her private fears or he'd drawn the natural conclusions from what he'd read.

She couldn't lie. But she wouldn't tell the whole truth.

"You're very real," she said, cupping his face between her hands. "And there are many admirable things about humans. Think of Uncle Ethan. Haven't we been good friends?"

"Would you marry him if he asked you?"

For a few seconds she was too stunned to answer. "Ethan? Where did you get such an idea, Toby?"

"It wouldn't matter whom you married if you weren't going to have any more babies, would it? You could even marry Father."

If he really believed that, she had succeeded in one thing, at least: she had kept him busy enough at Snowfell—and isolated enough, when the occasion required it—that he hadn't grasped how little her life was her own, or how hard she'd striven not to let him feel the weight of burdens he was too young to bear.

But he would have to be told about what awaited them both at the Convocation. And soon.

"No," she said gently. "That is quite out of the question. Our lives have become too different. We are too different."

He frowned at the counterpane. "What if Father wants me to stay in America?"

"He knows that is impossible, Toby. A boy belongs with his mother."

"What if he asks you to stay, too?"

That icy river sluiced anew through Gillian's veins. "He will not. You must put any notion of our remaining in America out of your mind."

She could see right away how little impact that command had on Toby. She should have found a better way to control him, to raise him with enough discipline to have prevented him from considering such a mad course as running away from England. But each time she'd considered treating him more strictly, she'd thought of Sir Averil, and all such resolutions had deserted her.

There was only one way of getting through to him now. And it would mean sacrifice…and faith that her bargain would be enough.

"You would like to see your father again," she said.

Toby sat up. "Oh, yes!"

"Then I propose a compromise."

"He'll come to visit England with us!"

Oh, Lord. He had no idea. None whatever.

"No," she said. "You know the Convocation is soon to begin, and there won't be room for more visitors. I propose that we remain in New York for a few days, and you may see Mr. Kavanagh, if he is agreeable. But at the end of that time, you must promise to return with me to the ship without protest."

Toby cocked his head. "Two weeks."

"A few days, no more."

His chest rose and fell in a great sigh. "Agreed," he said. "May I ring him now?"

"Tomorrow morning is soon enough." She rose, letting him see nothing of her apprehension. "Back to sleep, young man."

He plunged back under the sheets with the energy of any ordinary eleven-year-old boy. Gillian was almost out the door when his voice brought her to a halt.

"Thank you, Mother," he said.

Unable to trust her own voice, Gillian left the room. She almost went straight to the sideboard and the half-empty bottle of brandy, but she didn't. Alcohol was a refuge of which she had no need.

Ross had. But he wasn't the one who'd lost the skirmish between them. An hour or two was all the time it had taken him to win Toby over. He had never held a wailing infant in his arms, changed a nappy or soothed a little boy's hurt, but Toby was already halfway his.

Was that how it happened to me?

The front door clicked. Hugh stuck his head into the room and glanced about warily.

"Is it safe?" he asked.

"Mr. Kavanagh is gone." Gillian pulled the pins out of her hair and let it tumble down around her shoulders. "Did you enjoy your walk?"

Hugh snorted. "Enjoy it? I was worried sick about you."

"There was no need." She sat on the sofa. "Mr. Kavanagh was quite civil."

Hugh eyed the brandy as he sat in one of the armchairs. "What now? Do I buy a gun or start packing my bags?"

The idea of Hugh wielding a gun was as ludicrous as the notion of Ross among the delegates at the Convocation.

"I have decided that Toby will visit with Mr. Kavanagh over the course of the next few days," she said.

Hugh hummed through his teeth. "That *is* civilized," he said. "I have to say, I'm a little surprised you trust him so much."

"I trust him because I will be with him and Toby every moment they are together."

"Won't that be a trifle…awkward?"

"I assure you that I will survive his company."

"No doubt. It's Kavanagh I'm worried about."

Gillian began to be irritated. "What do you mean?"

But Hugh had fallen into a rare contemplative mood, and he rose and wandered aimlessly around the room until he reached the window. "I should be able to find something to do for a few days," he murmured. "Yes, it ought to be rather interesting."

Gillian didn't ask him what he meant. She got up, went into the WC and drew herself a bath, grateful that there were no servants to deceive with a smile and a few hollow words. She sank into the hot water with a sigh. The liquid ran exploratory fingers over her thighs and arms and breasts, soothing her into a state of nearly complete relaxation….

Ross pushed her hair away from her face, letting her short urls run through his fingers.

"Are you sure?" he asked. "Is this what you want, Jill?"

She pressed her hands into his back, feeling the flex of muscle nd the strong beat of his heart. "Yes," she whispered. "I'm sure, Ross."

"I haven't…" He flushed beneath his tan. "I haven't got any protection with me. If you want, I can find something to…"

"No." She lifted her head to kiss the ridge of his collarbone. "I don't want to wait. Nothing will happen."

A slight frown crossed his face, but it lasted no longer than it took for her to pull him down. His hands were eager and a little rough as he touched her hips and breasts. She briefly wondered if he'd ever had a woman before. In a way, she wished he hadn't. Then they would be the same, if only for this short while.

All thoughts fled as he began to caress that very private place between her legs. She hadn't known there could be such a feeling in the world.

Ross was no longer awkward. He took one of her nipples into his mouth and began to suckle, while his fingers continued to work their magic below. Gillian began to get very hot and very wet, and her breath grew short.

"Now, Jill?" Ross whispered, his lips brushing her ear.

She squeezed her eyes shut. "Yes. Now, Ross. Now…"

Gillian sat bolt upright in the bathtub, splashing lukewarm water over its porcelain sides. She pressed her palms to her flushed cheeks, fighting her way out of the dream.

She was alone. No one had touched her; no one had brought her to the brink only to abandon her, gasping and unfulfilled. Her memory had turned traitor, reaching up out of the past with cruel, grasping fingers.

Gillian got out of the bathtub and found a thick towel, wrapping herself tightly in the soft white cloth. At least she was alone; no one had witnessed her lapse.

And tomorrow? Would Ross look at her and surmise what had been going through her mind?

She went to the mirror and relaxed all the muscles of her face until there was no further sign of agitation. Not even full-blooded werewolves could read thoughts. And unless she were an utter fool, she wouldn't betray by a single word or action that she ever remembered their lovemaking.

The face in the mirror gazed serenely back at her. The lines about her eyes and mouth could scarcely be detected; no one would guess that she was thirty years old. Ross would have no reason to believe that she'd enjoyed anything less than a life of perfect contentment.

And hadn't she? Hadn't she found her place and purpose? Hadn't she been given the most wonderful son in the world?

And who gave you that son?

Gillian spun away from the mirror and rushed to her bedroom, where she slipped into the luxurious silk-and-velvet dressing gown provided by the hotel. It felt decadent against her skin, and she almost took it off again.

Sir Averil's wealth had paid for this expensive suite. There had never been any fine silk dressing gowns at Snowfell, but Sir Averil was a proud man. His daughter must have the best accommodations on those rare occasions when she appeared in public, even though he had heartily disapproved of her coming to America.

Gillian rubbed her cheek against the velvet collar. There was no harm in the dressing gown. Just as there would be no harm in seeing Ross again. Both would soon be far out of reach.

She sat down at the dressing table and began to brush out her hair with long, rhythmic strokes. Tonight her sleep would be empty of dreams.

CHAPTER FOUR

CONEY ISLAND, Ross mused, was a place most werewolves would go out of their way to avoid, especially on a Sunday in May. And that suited him just fine.

He'd been sitting on his sofa, wide-awake after a sleepless night, when Gillian had telephoned. Her voice had startled him, even though he'd been expecting her call; he still wasn't used to the richness of her tone, or the way it played along his nerves like the bow of a costly violin.

"Coney Island," he'd suggested, after they'd dispensed with the exchange of meaningless courtesies and she'd made her proposal. "Toby seems to have his heart set on it."

The sound of Gillian's breathing had filled the silence over the line as she considered his recommendation. "Is it a suitable place for a boy of his age?"

Strange that she actually valued his opinion now that she'd decided to let Toby see him again; he'd begun to wonder if he'd judged her a little too harshly. But when she'd made it clear that she would be coming along, Ross had almost nixed the idea. He didn't want her there. It wasn't part of his plan.

Then he'd pictured Gillian surrounded by the hoi polloi of humanity in all its brash, loud and malodorous glory, and he'd changed his mind.

This was *his* world. She had stepped into it whether she'd intended to or not. All that mattered was that he had a couple of days to find a chance to talk to Toby alone. It wouldn't take many questions to find out how Toby felt about being part-human...or if Gillian had done anything to make him feel bad about it, deliberately or otherwise.

Ross shoved his hands into his pockets and scanned the street. Automobiles and streetcars puttered up and down Surf Avenue, narrowly avoiding the hordes of pedestrians that crossed boldly in front of them. Gillian had said that she and Toby would arrive in a limousine. There weren't too many of those on Coney Island these days; ever since the new subway extension had been put in and the beaches had opened to the public, Manhattan's most humble citizens had become the majority of the island's visitors.

That wouldn't bother Toby, Ross was certain. There wasn't a prejudiced bone in his body; he was a democrat at heart. And when he got a look at the Thunderbolt...

Ross caught himself. He'd never suspected how easy it would be to slip into that dangerous kind of thinking. There was no logical basis for it; he'd spent less than an hour with Toby yesterday, and yet he already thought he understood the kid just because he'd had something to do with bringing the boy into the world.

All he really knew was that Toby had any normal child's appreciation for hot dogs and amusement parks. That he didn't share all his mother's views. And that he was brave, smart and determined to get what he thought he wanted.

Ross had believed the same things of Gillian when they'd met. Brave and smart and willing to throw caution to the winds once she'd decided that she wanted a doughboy boneheaded enough to wear his heart on his sleeve.

A young man and his girl brushed by Ross, hand in hand. Ross watched them walk through Luna Park's garish entrance. Gillian's qualities and his former relationship with her, good or bad, had little to do with his purpose now. The whole point of this meeting, and any others he could finagle, was to determine if Toby was safe and happy.

The first step had been convincing Gillian that there wouldn't
e any harm in letting him see his son. He'd played her the same
ay he played suspects, harsh at first and then gradually relent-
g, so that she started to think he was harmless. Reasonable.
Villing to compromise.

Ross loosened his tie as the sun emerged from behind a cloud,
eflecting heat up from the sidewalk under his feet. Obviously
oby hadn't realized that he was part human until he'd found the
iary. But had he sensed something amiss, something he could
ever quite define?

He's eleven years old, for God's sake. He didn't act like a kid
who'd had a difficult upbringing. But Ross couldn't ignore the
ossibility that Toby was hiding his own private fears—fears he
vouldn't share with his mother. If there was any chance that
oby was going to suffer just for being Ross's son, Ross wanted
o know about it. If the kid was going to grow up feeling that
omething was wrong with him, Ross intended to do whatever
vas necessary to make sure that didn't happen.

A few days was all Ross had to get at the truth. Gillian hadn't
iven in because she had any regard for him; she'd just realized
hat he wasn't going to walk away quietly, and that compromise
vas better than an outright battle.

Still, Ross knew she would never have let Toby anywhere near
im if she'd heard about the scandal. The longer she stayed in
Jew York, the more likely she was to run across that informa-
ion. She'd said that Toby had an idealized image of the father
e'd never known. And ideals…they had a way of crumbling
nder your feet when you least expected it.

The blare of a horn interrupted Ross's thoughts. A black lim-
usine pulled up at the kerb, and a uniformed chauffeur got out.
Ross beat him to the back door and opened it.

Gillian looked up at him from beneath the brim of her rolled
ilk hat, and he caught his breath. Nothing in her appearance had
hanged since yesterday. That was the problem. She could still

make him feel as addled as a schoolboy catching his first glimps
of a girl's knees.

He held out his hand, and she accepted it, rising from the au
tomobile like a swan unfurling its wings. Her georgette frock
plain enough to be almost severe, was a shade of green tha
brought out the same color in her eyes. She wore no rouge o
lipstick. She needed none.

Damn her.

"Good afternoon, Mr. Kavanagh," she said. She lifted he
head, and her nostrils flared to take in the cacophony of smell
that even the least sensitive werewolf would find overwhelming
A large, laughing family bearing baskets stuffed with bread an
sausages careened by, trailing the scents of garlic, perspiratio
and smoke. Gillian watched them recede into the crowd, her fac
expressionless.

"Hallo, Father!" Toby popped up beside them, nearly burstin
out of his blue serge suit. His face was scrubbed pink, his hai
was neatly groomed and his shoes had been shined to a mirro
finish; he looked as if he ought to have been in church instea
of on the boardwalk.

"Hello, Toby," Ross said, taken aback by the sudden tightnes
in his throat. "Glad you could make it."

"So am I." Toby's gaze swept over the street, the vividl
painted buildings and the people hurrying from one attraction t
the next. "It's even better than I imagined."

Ross tried to remember when he'd last felt as excited as Tob
was now. "Are those the clothes you usually wear when you g
to an amusement park?" he asked.

Toby looked down at himself in surprise. "I've never been t
one before. Mother always insists that I dress like a gentlema
when we are away from Snowfell." He grinned. "But I don't se
any gentlemen around here."

Ross glanced at Gillian, who didn't seem to be listening

"Does that bother you, Toby?" he asked. "Would you rather go someplace where your clothes won't get dirty?"

Toby raised his fair brows in exaggerated disbelief. "You must be joking. I'd much rather wear dungarees like a cowboy, or a jumper and plus-fours like Uncle Hugh."

"Maybe that can be arranged, once we're back in the city."

"Capital!" Toby tapped the leather bag dangling from a strap over his shoulder. "Mother *did* let me bring my bathing costume," he said, lifting the bag for Ross's inspection.

Ross hid his astonishment. Obviously Gillian had no conception of what the beaches would be like, swarming with uncouth human bathers competing for their small patches of sand. His treacherous thoughts shifted, constructing a detailed picture of Gillian in one of those revealing one-piece jersey swimming suits, her curves no longer hidden by a shapeless, low-waisted frock.

"Did your mother bring hers?" he blurted.

This time Gillian was paying attention. Her fair skin went pink. "I do not own a bathing costume," she said. "We purchased Toby's at a shop near the hotel." She looked from side to side as if she were seeking escape. "If you will excuse me, I need to speak to the chauffeur."

"You don't have to keep him here," Ross said. "I'll make sure you get home safe and sound."

She hesitated, probably wondering just how far she should trust him. "Yes," she said. "Of course." She turned to address the driver, who touched the brim of his cap and returned to the car.

Toby had spent the brief interlude bouncing in place, ready to bolt for the park entrance as soon the adults finished their boring conversation. Gillian moved to take his hand. He shook himself free as unconsciously as a dog shakes water from its back.

Gillian dropped her hands to her sides. "Where do we begin?" she asked.

Her voice was brisk, but there was uncertainty in it. She was as out of place here as Ross had been in the Roosevelt Hotel. Her wealth and perfect breeding bought her nothing in this egalitar ian human world. She was lost, and that was exactly how Ross wanted her to feel.

But she hadn't been that way in London. She'd worked among soldiers of all classes and had treated them equally, as had the other upper-class women who'd joined in the war effort. She'd never shown any outward sign of discomfort in her role as a common nurse. Even when she'd been faced with devastating injuries and suffering, she'd never faltered. And she'd given herself to a guy she'd assumed was human, a man not even from her own country.

Ross cursed under his breath. What the hell was he thinking? *This* was the real Gillian Maitland, the one who'd returned to her old life without a backward glance. That other Gillian had been a mask she'd temporarily worn, the way a little girl tries on her mother's clothes and oversized shoes. And this Gillian—Mrs. Delvaux—had thrown away whatever spirit of rebellion and adventure had led her to volunteer in the first place.

Just like she'd thrown away his love.

Toby tugged at Ross's arm. "May we go now, Father?"

"Toby!" Gillian said, inserting herself between him and Ross. "I doubt Mr. Kavanagh wishes his arm to be pulled from its socket."

"Don't trouble yourself on my account, Mrs. Delvaux," Ross said. "I think I can handle my own son."

She blanched and stepped back as if he'd struck her. Ross pretended he didn't care. He ruffled Toby's hair.

"What first?" he asked. "The Aerial Swing or the Dragon Gorge?"

"Which one is least frightening?" Toby asked in a low voice.

"Being scared is part of the fun, isn't it?"

"Oh, I'm not worried about myself. But Mother is with us."

"Do you think she'd be afraid?"

"I don't know. She's never been to a place like this before either. I think she's a little nervous."

So even Toby saw it, though he wouldn't realize that Gillian's ꜱease had nothing to do with the amusements themselves. He ꜣas capable of a child's unthinking callousness, but he also ꜣanted to protect his mother. Would he feel that way if he resented ꜣr, if he hadn't already forgiven her those years of deception?

Ross cleared his throat. "Let's start her off easy with the ꜣragon's Gorge," he suggested. "Mrs. Delvaux?"

"Yes, Mr. Kavanagh?"

"We're off to see the Dragon's Gorge," Toby said. "You ꜣedn't worry, Mother. You have two men to protect you."

Gillian met Ross's gaze. He could have sworn there was ꜣdness in her eyes.

Because Toby wasn't her little boy anymore. He was growing ꜣ. She was bound to lose him eventually, just like any mother. ꜣut for her, it was a hundred times worse. She might lose him ꜣ his humanity.

A sense of chivalry Ross had given up years ago compelled him ꜣ offer Gillian his arm. She ignored him and started toward the ꜣrk entrance. Toby lingered to make sure Ross was following, and ꜣen he darted ahead. They waited in line to purchase their tickets ꜣd joined the stream of people sweeping into the concourse.

The Dragon's Gorge was one of Luna Park's primary attrac-ꜣns, and the crowd was considerable. Miniature railroad cars ꜣoved one by one along a winding track into the open maw of ꜣvast cave, guarded on either side by snarling winged dragons. ꜣoby walked at a rapid clip to the end of the line, trying to peer ꜣer the heads of the people ahead of him.

Gillian joined Toby, and Ross fell in behind them. The top of ꜣillian's head was just level with Ross's mouth; the smell of her ꜣin and her hair, unsullied by the heavy perfumes so many ꜣomen used, was far more intoxicating than the whiskey to which ꜣ'd become so attached since the hearing and its aftermath.

Both the whiskey and the woman were a kind of poison. Both ꜣnfused his brain and his senses, made it all too easy to deny the hard facts of life. Ross backed away, bumping into the man behind him. He muttered an apology and deliberately closed off his senses until he, Gillian and Toby had reached the head of the line.

He wasn't sure quite how it happened, but suddenly Toby was sprawled across the last seat of the waiting railroad car, leaving Ross and Gillian to take the first seat in the car behind it. The attendant gestured impatiently; Ross stepped into the car and helped Gillian in after him.

She sat just as stiffly as she had in her hotel room, her gloved hands tucked in her lap and her gaze fixed on the car ahead. Toby twisted in his seat and waved happily as the car lurched into motion.

"Is it quite safe for him to ride alone?" Gillian asked, speaking as if the words had been pried out of her by red-hot pokers.

"He isn't a baby," Ross said. "You can't keep him in high chairs and diapers for the rest of his life."

She glared at him, her eyes glowing as the shadows of the cave closed in around them. "You think me overprotective," she said. "You think that Toby is as…worldly as any boy his age. He is not. He has lived all his life—"

"Around people just like him, where he's safe from anything that could challenge what he's been taught."

"You know nothing of how he's been raised."

"I can guess." He leaned back on the hard wooden seat, careful to keep from touching her. "The lessons don't seem to have taken, though. He's not a stuck-up little prig."

Her breath came fast. "No," she said, "he is not. But you, Mr. Kavanagh, are certainly not lacking in arrogance."

"Because I'm honest?"

"Are you?" She searched his eyes. "Are you really?"

Ross started to answer and found he couldn't speak. He was convinced in that moment that she could see right through him, right down to the core of the miserable failure he'd become.

He was saved as the railcar, which had been chugging its way to the top of a steep incline, suddenly plunged from darkness into a brilliant white scene of the North Pole. Ross hardly noticed. The car rolled on to the next exhibit, but he was no longer paying attention. He thought of all the places he'd read about and longed to see when he was a kid at his parents' ranch in Cold Creek Valley, places with exotic names that seemed a million miles away: Timbuktu, Istanbul, Singapore. When he'd turned seventeen and the Great War was already raging in Europe, he'd seen joining up as a chance to escape Arizona and explore a little of the world. Ma had been against it at first, but Pa had understood Ross's need to be part of something bigger than himself. They'd added to his own store of carefully saved money to send him on a boat to France.

There hadn't been many American volunteers at the time; the United States was still years away from officially joining the War. But Ross had found exciting and often dangerous work as a driver for the American Volunteer Motor Ambulance Corps. He'd served for about three months when his vehicle hit a mine; somehow he'd gotten mixed in with a bunch of British wounded and been shipped off to recover in a London hospital.

That had been where he'd met Gillian. Of course he hadn't known her name in the beginning; his injuries had been pretty severe, though not disfiguring, and at first he'd hardly been able to tell the difference between the succession of doctors, nurses and volunteers who passed by his bed.

But then he started to heal—fast, with the help of his werewolf blood—and he'd seen her visiting the men in the ward. He'd become increasingly intrigued by her poise, her grace, her untouchability. If anyone in the place represented his idea of a European aristocrat, loaded to the gills with "good breeding," she was it.

It soon became obvious that she was very skilled at what she did; ice queen or not, she had a gentle touch and soothing voice for soldiers who needed comfort, and she was more competent than many of the professional nurses. Plenty of guys seemed to find her attractive. But she seldom smiled and never laughed, and no one seemed to be able to breach her air of cool superiority.

Ross had almost dismissed her as a just another arrogant, privileged blue blood. But then his condition had begun to improve, and he'd had set himself a challenge: to find out what made Gillian Maitland tick.

His first few attempts had failed. Maybe she was put off by his American drawl, or his easy manner and informal ways; he treated her as if she were his equal, and that didn't sit well with her in the beginning. But eventually she began dropping by his bed more often, and he would regale her with the stories of the "Wild West" he'd learned at his father's knee. She started to smile a little more. Warmth crept into her hazel eyes. He learned that her father was a baronet, and she came from a grand estate in the north of England. He figured that she'd never known a day of want in her life, which made her work at the hospital all the more admirable.

Little by little their relationship had evolved from a cautious friendship to a deeper bond. One night, after Ross was finally allowed to walk again, she'd let him kiss her.

A new Gillian had emerged after that brief incident, a girl of passion and hidden fire. Ross had felt like the peasant boy who'd won the heart of the king's daughter. He and Gillian had kept their relationship carefully hidden from the hospital staff and patients. They had walked on the grounds after midnight, hand in hand, speaking little and feeling much.

One late night, on his way to meet her, Ross had seen Gillian Change from wolf to human form on the hospital lawn behind a clump of trees. He'd quickly overcome his shock, realizing that he'd already felt the difference in her without knowing it. He'd told her then, with perfect honesty, that he knew about the existence of werewolves, at least in America. She didn't ask how or why he knew about *loups-garous,* and he didn't reveal his own mixed heritage, unsure how she would feel about it.

After that, Gillian had told him all about the werewolves in Europe. They were trying to save the werewolf race from extinction, she'd explained. The number of *loups-garous* in the world was rapidly shrinking; they had to live secretly among humans, constantly fearing exposure. Ancient European families had been working tirelessly to preserve the pure werewolf bloodlines and unique gifts.

Ross had listened, strangely uncomfortable with the driven, almost mechanical way Gillian spoke of the Europeans' efforts. She'd recited the information almost like a schoolgirl who'd learned her lessons by rote; the passionate, animated woman Ross had discovered beneath her aristocratic veneer seeming to vanish.

But then she'd self-consciously asked him to make love to her, and he'd forgotten the things that had troubled him. Their joining had been like a miracle, a gift Ross knew he didn't deserve. He'd finally admitted that he was of werewolf blood. She'd laughed, her eyes filled with happiness and relief. Ross had believed that his dreams were about to come true.

Until she'd asked him to run as a wolf beside her, and he'd had to tell her that he couldn't do it, that his mother was human and his father only half-werewolf. He hadn't noticed then how quiet she'd become. He'd been certain, in spite of what she'd said about the European devotion to werewolf purity, that it couldn't possibly matter. They loved each other. And he wanted her to marry him.

There had been no explanations, no warning. Gillian simply never showed up at their next planned rendezvous. She'd left her work at the hospital and disappeared without a word. And in his shock, Ross had remembered what he hadn't wanted to acknowledge: the look in her eyes when he'd told her he couldn't Change.

The look of a princess who'd just been told that her knight in shining armor was nothing but a crippled beggar after all.

A sharp movement jostled Ross out of the past. The car had made another turn and was descending into a new tableau, this one depicting the Grand Canyon. He looked at Gillian; she was gazing at the diorama with her lips slightly parted and an almost childlike expression of wonder on her face, as if she'd completely forgotten that Ross was there.

"Why didn't you remarry?" he asked.

She started and clutched at the car's railing as if she expected to be pitched out onto the ground. "I…beg your pardon?"

"Delvaux died before Toby was born. Why didn't you find Toby another father?"

It was a stupid thing to ask. Ross knew he wasn't thinking clearly, hadn't been since Gillian had stepped out of the limousine.

He dug the hole a little deeper. "There must have been other acceptable candidates, even after the War," he said. "Or did you run out of all the pure-blooded types in your part of the world?"

She turned toward him, her hair bleached white by the harsh overhead lights. "I had no desire to marry again."

"Delvaux was that great, huh? You just couldn't let go of his memory?"

Damn and double-damn. Now he'd given her reason to think he could be jealous, when he felt nothing of the kind. But Gillian didn't offer the cutting reply he'd expected. She sighed and leaned back in her seat, the wonders of the Dragon's Gorge forgotten.

"My time with Jacques was short," she said. "He would not have wished me to grieve unduly."

Ross's heart lurched and slowly resumed its regular rhythm. *She didn't love him. Not any more than she loved me.*

"But you still didn't think Toby needed a man in his life," he said.

"What makes you think he didn't have one?"

Touché. Just because Gillian hadn't married again didn't mean she couldn't have had a whole string of lovers. Her coolness hadn't kept plenty of wounded soldiers from falling in love with her, though she'd given none of them a second glance.

They'd all been human, of course. But she'd thought Ross was human up until the time they'd made love, and that hadn't stopped her.

"Is it Warbrick?" he asked in a bored tone.

"What?"

"Toby said Warbrick wanted to marry you. Or was it something more casual?"

Gillian might have been an excellent actress, but her discomposure seemed genuine. "There is nothing between… Children, as you know, have vivid imaginations. Ethan has been a good friend to Toby."

"That must be why he begged me not to let Warbrick find him."

"Toby knew that what he'd done was wrong and was hoping to avoid the consequences."

"Was Warbrick likely to punish him? Isn't that your job?"

Gillian didn't seem to hear the second part of his question. "He is a good man," she said quietly.

"Sure. But he's got one serious flaw. He can't Change."

CHAPTER FIVE

ROSS KNEW HE'D gone too far, said out loud things he hadn't meant to bring up in Gillian's presence. But now it was done, and she had nothing to say. They rode on in silence until the car reentered the vast, openmouthed cave where the ride had begun and descended to the platform, where Toby was waiting for them.

"That was capital!" Toby exclaimed, his gaze darting from Gillian to Ross and back again. "You weren't afraid, Mother?"

She managed a smile for him, excluding Ross. "Not in the least. I found it quite delightful."

Toby gave Ross a pointed look, as if he were trying to convey some secret message. Ross found himself at a loss, and Toby turned away.

"May we try the Aerial Swing?" he asked.

They made their way to the Aerial Swing, which consisted of four large gondolas suspended from the ends of crossbeams projecting from a tall, narrow tower. The crossbeams rotated around the tower as they moved up and down, swinging the gondolas in a wide circle far above the earth.

This time Gillian maneuvered herself so that she and Toby shared the same seat and Ross was relegated to the one behind them, wedged in next to a portly gentleman with a very red face. The man giggled during the entire ride. Ross was deeply grateful when it was over.

Gillian was a little gray when she stepped out of the gondola, but she didn't complain.

"I suggest we head for Steeplechase Park," Ross said. "They opened the Thunderbolt roller coaster there two years ago. It's the tallest one on Coney Island, famous all over the world."

He half expected Gillian to balk, but she allowed him to usher her and Toby across the esplanade and through a knot of park-goers clustered around the carousel. "We can grab one of the streetcars on Surf Avenue," he said.

Gillian maintained her silence, absorbed in her own thoughts, as if she were pretending she was somewhere else. It wasn't possible for Ross to talk to Toby privately once they were packed into the streetcar, but he kept the kid entertained by pointing out the various attractions along Surf Avenue as the vehicle carried them toward Steeplechase Park.

"You've been here lots of times," Toby commented, a wistful note in his voice.

"Not when I was a kid. I lived too far away, and my family didn't do much traveling."

"Where did you live?"

Obviously that was something Gillian hadn't written down in her diary. And why should she? "We had a ranch in southern Arizona, near the Castillo Mountains."

"I know where Arizona is," Toby said with a touch of pride. "Did you rope cattle and fight outlaws?"

"Lots of roping, but most of the outlaws and cattle rustlers were gone by the time I was born."

"At least you had plenty of bad guys to fight in New York." He kicked his heels against the bottom of the seat. "What made you decide to become a policeman?"

"It seemed like it might be something I'd be good at," he said.

"Yes," Toby said. "You could do all sorts of useful things, like smelling the criminals before they could see you coming, or just being a lot better at fighting." He paused as if a thought had just popped into his head. "Are there lots of werewolves in New York, Father?"

It wasn't an unexpected question, but Ross knew he had to tread carefully. "Maybe a hundred," he said.

"Truly? We haven't nearly so many in England. Are any of them policemen like you?"

"Not that I know of."

"All the European werewolves Mother told me about live in big houses in the countryside, where they don't have much to do with regular people. Is it the same in America?"

Ross realized that Toby had given him an opening to learn more about how Gillian lived. "I don't know how it is other places in the States," he said, "but in Manhattan, most werewolves belong to one pack."

"A hundred in one pack?" Toby frowned. "It isn't like that with us at all. We have families instead."

"Are there other werewolf families living near you?"

"There are some in Northumberland, Lancashire and Yorkshire, but we don't see them very often."

"But there must be other houses nearby, even if they aren't occupied by werewolves."

"Oh, yes. Uncle Ethan lives at Highwick, which is right next door to Snowfell. And there are farmers all around the fells, and people in the village."

"Then you have other kids to play with."

Toby glanced at his mother, who was gazing at the passing scene. "I'm much too old to play children's games."

"You must have friends."

"Of course. I—" He squirmed, scuffing his feet on the floor, and then seemed to reach a decision. "I talk to the servants all the time."

The servants. Fuming, Ross reminded himself that he was talking to a boy, not a man. "If you don't play with anyone," he said, "what do you do to have fun?"

"There are lots of things to do at Snowfell. Mother and I read a great deal. She orders books from London. We play chess nearly every day. And we've even found some old Roman ruins,

where soldiers used to guard the border against the barbarians."
He beamed. "I've begun a collection of ancient coins."

"That sounds…very interesting. Do you ever take trips away
from Snowfell?"

"I've been to Kendal, of course, and Carlisle and Penrith, and
once to London."

"What do you do there?"

"Sometimes we go to museums or visit the park. But we
don't go very often."

"And your mother? Does she go out alone sometimes?"

"Mother? Oh, no. Only when she takes me."

"Does anyone come to see her?"

Toby's speculative glance was keen enough for a kid half again
his age. "No one comes to Snowfell. Not even Uncle Ethan. But
sometimes Mother meets him where Snowfell borders Highwick."

Warbrick again. Ross hid his scowl, but he needn't have
bothered, because Toby's interest had been caught by the structure towering over the streetcar as it began to slow. "Is that the
Thunderbolt?"

The boy craned his neck, peering up at the steel struts and
towers, the sweeping curves of the massive roller coaster that pro-
jected above the fence running alongside Surf Avenue. He might
have jumped off the still-moving vehicle if Ross hadn't grabbed
his arm.

"Stay right here," he warned Toby, and turned back to help
Gillian, who had already stepped down to the street. The day was
growing warmer by the minute, but somehow Ross knew that the
perspiration gathering on Gillian's forehead had nothing to do
with the temperature. She gazed at the vast structure before
them.

"Toby," she said quietly.

The boy obviously heard a world of warning in those two syl-
lables. "It's not as dangerous as it looks," he assured her. "I'll
ride with Father. You stay here."

Gillian continued to stare at the roller coaster. Ross sensed that it wasn't so much the potential danger of the ride that worried her as much as Coney Island itself, this vast and very human place. She dropped her gaze to the unruly line winding around the base of the coaster, then looked around like a wild animal surrounded by hidden hunters, seeking the source of danger in an ever-changing, faceless crowd.

Toby had said she never went out and that no one came to Snowfell. How long had it been since Gillian was engaged with the world, as she'd been in London? What kind of life had she led before he'd met her? She'd said her family had welcomed her back after Delvaux's death, but what exactly had she gone back to?

Was it possible that he'd never really known her, that he'd been mistaking arrogance for fear all along? Had she been battling demons of her own from the very beginning?

Hell, no. Not Jill. Upset that she'd let herself fall for a guy who was mostly human, sure. And worried about betraying her high-flown principles, concerned about Toby and his attachment to Ross, less than enamored with crowds of noisy, malodorous humans. That was the sum total of it. The rest was sheer fantasy.

He emerged from his thoughts to find her staring at him, the uncertainty in her eyes vanishing behind a wall of determination.

"We must go," she said. She grabbed Toby's hand. "Please show us to the exit, Mr. Kavanagh."

"But we've hardly done anything, Mother!" Toby protested. He looked at Ross for support. "It isn't fair." Before Ross could respond, Toby tried another tack. "Mother, why don't you go back to the hotel and rest? Father and I will go on alone."

"Certainly not," she said. "We have done quite enough for one day. I am certain that Mr. Kavanagh will understand."

"Mr. Kavanagh doesn't," Ross said. "We had a deal. I'll take you back to the hotel, and then Toby and I—"

But Gillian was already walking away, dragging Toby behind

her, body tensed as if she were about to break into an all-out run. Ross caught up with her.

"For God's sake, Gillian."

She spun. Her lips curled back from her teeth, wolflike. "Where?" she demanded. "Where is the way out?"

Ross was on the verge of another argument when he noticed that Gillian had suddenly gone still. He turned to follow her stare. Behind him, a crowd had gathered at the base of the platform where the coaster's cars came to rest after each circuit.

Gillian pushed Toby toward Ross and set off for the platform at a run. By the time Ross and Toby caught up with her, she had shoved her way through the circle of gaping observers and crouched beside the boy who lay on the ground, flopping like a fish thrown onto dry land. A cut on his forehead was bleeding profusely, and Ross guessed that he had somehow fallen from the platform.

"What's wrong?" someone asked. "What's wrong with him?"

Gillian didn't answer. She had rolled the boy onto his side and placed a wadded piece of cloth under his head, watching him intently as the muscles of his body contracted violently and then released. When a man from the crowd tried to help by restraining the child, she warned him off. He persisted. Ross told Toby to stay put, told the guy to back off and crouched beside Gillian.

"It's a Grand Mal seizure," she said, in a tone meant only for werewolf ears. "Either he's an epileptic, or he's dangerously ill."

As she spoke, the boy's convulsions grew weaker and gradually ceased. Gillian produced another strip of fabric—torn, he presumed, from some part of her clothing—and pressed it to the child's wound. Ross glanced at Gillian's profile. She hardly seemed to realize that she was the center of attention; the boy was all that mattered.

"Someone ring for an ambulance," she said. "I'm only a nurse. Someone needs to find a doctor, if one is available."

After a brief hesitation, several men huddled together and ran off in different directions. A shriek silenced the murmurs of the observers, and a woman stumbled into the center of the circle.

"Bobby!" she cried, dropping to her knees. "Bobby!"

"It will be all right," Gillian said, nothing but compassion and understanding in her voice. "Ross, please watch Bobby and hold this cloth in place. He should regain consciousness presently. I must speak to his mother."

Ross moved so that he was level with Bobby's head, listening to Gillian as he waited for the boy to wake up. Gillian began to ask the sobbing mother a series of questions, each spoken so calmly that their rhythm slowly eased the woman's hysteria. She squeezed the woman's trembling arm gently and turned back to Ross.

"This has never happened to him before," she said. "It's possible for children to develop epilepsy at any time, but Bobby must have a full medical examination to rule out an infection. It's fortunate that he wasn't more badly injured in the fall." She passed the back of her hand across her forehead. "We must move him to a cool, quiet place."

Ross knew that she didn't have to explain anything to him, but the fact that she was doing so, and asking for his help, meant a lot more to him than he was willing to admit even to himself. He lifted the boy in his arms while Gillian assisted the mother to stand and gave her an arm to lean on. Ross made sure that Toby was following and aimed for a vendor whose booth was fitted out with a wide awning.

Not long after they'd made Bobby comfortable on a blanket provided by the vendor, he began to regain consciousness. Gillian smiled at him and asked him how he was feeling. The boy, obviously confused, tried to answer, but his mother's weeping distracted him, and Gillian left them alone.

One of the observers returned a few minutes later with a harried, bespectacled man whose day's amusements had obviously been interrupted. He introduced himself as a doctor and

spoke briefly with Gillian, examined the boy and assured himself
that someone had summoned an ambulance. As soon as he'd
taken charge, Gillian faded into the background.

But she was not to be allowed to resume her anonymity.
Several of the men and women who'd followed them to the
vendor's booth gathered around her, exclaiming and congratulating her. She answered rigidly, all the ease she'd shown with
the boy instantly gone. Ross wedged himself between her and
the man closest to her.

"Give the lady a little room," he said gruffly. The people retreated, responding to the quiet authority he'd honed to near
perfection during his years on the job. Gillian seemed to breathe
more easily, though she was much too pale for Ross's liking.

"Are you all right?" he asked, taking her elbow.

She stared in the direction of the vendor's stall. "Where is Toby?"

"Here, Mother." Toby joined them, clutching his bag and
grinning up at his mother with obvious pride. "That was smash-
ing, wasn't it, Father?"

"Yes." Ross heard the wail of a distant siren. "The ambulance
is coming. I think it's time for us to leave."

"But there's a man who wants to talk to Mother. He says he's
a reporter for a newspaper."

Ross's neck prickled. "Not today, Toby."

"But he wants to know about the lady who saved the little
boy's life!"

"I did not save him," Gillian said faintly. "I merely made him
comfortable until he emerged from the seizure."

"But he could have hurt himself," Toby said, pugnacious in
defense of his mother's expertise. "Isn't that right, Father?"

That was probably true, and by the end of the day a lot of
people on Coney Island would probably regard the mysterious
English lady as a heroine. But one look at Gillian's face told Ross
that she didn't want anything to do with newspapers or the no-
toriety they could bring.

He gazed over the heads of the people still hovering nearby. A man was striding toward them at a fast pace, his hat jammed down on his forehead and a notepad clutched in one hand.

His name was O'Grady, and he'd been a gadfly biting at Ross's heels all during the hearings and even after Ross had been released for lack of evidence. Once he'd recognized his victim, any chance of keeping Gillian and Toby ignorant of the scandal would be over.

"No reporters," Ross growled. "We're leaving."

Toby's face fell, then brightened again.

"Will we take the subway?" he asked.

The last thing Gillian would want now was to be sandwiched into a subway car jammed with weekend revelers. "We'll find a taxi," he said.

But before he got Gillian and Toby moving, O'Grady had caught up with them.

"So this is your mother?" the reporter said loudly, striding alongside Toby while he simultaneously noted Ross's presence and tipped his hat in Gillian's direction. "Morning, ma'am. Miles O'Grady, *New York Sentinel*."

"The lady's got nothing to say to you, O'Grady," Ross said, keeping his hand firmly on Toby's shoulder as he hurried Gillian toward a waiting cab. "Get lost."

O'Grady wasn't put off. "What's the lady to you, Kavanagh?" he asked. "Mrs. Delvaux, your boy said."

Toby was smart enough to recognize the edge of hostility in the reporter's tone. "She doesn't want to talk to you," he said belligerently. "And my— Mr. Kavanagh doesn't want to talk to you, either."

Ross cursed under his breath. "Toby," he said without breaking stride, "you tell the cabbie to take you and your mother to the place where we started. Go back exactly the way we came, okay?"

In answer, Toby hurried to Gillian's other side and took her and. Gillian was moving like a sleepwalker, in spite of Toby's urgent tugging. Ross came to a stop and grabbed O'Grady by the arm to keep him from following.

O'Grady grinned. "Same old Kavanagh," he said. "Better let me go, or I'll see you arrested for assault."

Ross snorted with disgust and released the reporter. "You may think you have friends on the force," he said, "but they don't like you any better than they like me."

"Why not? We're all on the same side. Trying to bring a killer to justice." He watched Gillian and Toby as they climbed into the cab. "You know, I didn't think this would be much of a story. Now…"

"You stay away from them," Ross snarled.

"Why? I'd be doing her a favor by sticking around. She's pretty, slender, blond…just like the other one, but with a lot more class. You grazing in richer pastures, Kavanagh?"

Ross could have had the bastard on the ground in two seconds flat, but he knew what would happen if he so much as waved a fist in O'Grady's direction.

"I was cleared," he said. "And when I find the real killer, I'll make you choke on your newspaper."

The reporter laughed, but he wasn't quite as immune to Ross's anger as he wanted to believe. "Cleared?" he repeated. "You were released for lack of evidence. Not quite the same thing, is it? But who knows? Maybe I can find something nice to say about you if you cooperate." He slipped a thoroughly chewed pencil from behind his ear and held it poised over the notepad. "Who is she? She's from England, right? What's your relationship with her and the kid? Does she realize—"

He grunted in surprise as Ross tore the notepad and pencil from his hands and threw them to the ground. "If you get anywhere near her, I may have to do something stupid," Ross said.

O'Grady stared at the notebook, its pages splayed and fluttering in the light breeze. "You already have, Kavanagh."

Ross leaned toward the reporter, his breath stirrin O'Grady's thin reddish hair. "You're right," he said softly. "I have to have been pretty crazy to murder that girl. And if I' crazy, why should I stop with her? Why not try something dif ferent this time?"

As if compelled by forces beyond his control, O'Grady me Ross's gaze. He opened his mouth. No sound came out. He too a step backward. He kept up his retreat until he was well out c Ross's reach.

"I know where you live, Kavanagh!" he said, all bluster agai "I'll get my story."

"Leave us alone."

Gillian had returned. Her voice was clear, sharp and startling ringing with such natural authority that everyone within hearin distance stopped and stared. She ignored her audience, her at tention completely focused on O'Grady.

"No more questions," she said. "I must take my son home."

O'Grady made the mistake of thinking he'd found a nev opening. "Sure, I understand. Just tell me where you can b reached, and I'll …"

He trailed off, his bravado crushed by Gillian's witherin stare. When she moved, he jumped like a rabbit. He stayed pu as she stalked away, a muscle under his eye twitching franticall

"What the hell…?" he breathed.

Ross couldn't have put it better himself. What had he jus seen? One minute Gillian was calm and confident, the nex nervous and uncertain, then aggressive and strong. How man different women lived inside that sleek, graceful body?

He fell into step beside her. "I don't think you should g directly back to the hotel."

She glanced at him without breaking stride, her hand stil clamped around Toby's, conflicting emotions passing behin her eyes.

"Why?" she asked. "Will that man follow us?"

"I know the guy. He's a persistent bas— He won't give up easily. And he knows your name."

"I'm sorry," Toby said, abashed. "I didn't think there would be any harm…."

"It's okay," Ross said. "O'Grady could get a clam to confess. But I think it would be a good idea to throw him off the scent."

"How do you propose to do that?" Gillian asked.

Her tone held the same conflicting emotions as her eyes, anxious and angry at the same time, but Ross had seen how much she detested the kind of attention she'd attracted as a result of her good deed. She would probably do just about anything to avoid answering the reporter's questions, no matter how benign they might seem.

Ross certainly didn't want to tell her that O'Grady held a grudge against him and was likely to be even more obnoxious than usual in trying to uncover the nature of their relationship.

"I've got a friend who lives over on Long Island," he said. "Grif and his wife have been out of the country for months, so the place is vacant. They won't mind if we stay there until O'Grady finds a more interesting story. Shouldn't take more than a few days."

"A few days? That is impossible."

"I think you'll find Oak Hollow comfortable, even if Grif isn't as big on the luxuries you're used to."

Gillian opened her mouth, hesitated, and closed it again, clearly torn. Then she saw or smelled something that worried her, because she moved a little closer to Toby and drew herself into a defensive posture.

"How will you make certain that the reporter doesn't follow us to Long Island?" she asked.

"I'm going to give you instructions on how to take the subway back to Penn Station, where you'll catch the train to Long Island. While you're doing that, I'm going to lure O'Grady in another direction. I'll join you as soon as I can. Once we're at Oak

Hollow, you can call Hugh and arrange to have some of your things sent over."

Gillian nodded with obvious reluctance. He could sense that she wanted to say something else, but was finding it difficult to spit out the words.

"Thank you," she said at last. "Thank you, Ross."

"It's nothing," he said curtly. "Listen carefully. This is what you do...."

He gave her the promised instructions and accompanied her to the Coney Island station, keeping an eye out for O'Grady all the while. When the reporter appeared as expected—obviously having convinced himself that he'd followed them without being detected—Ross managed to distract him while Gillian and Toby boarded their train. By the time the reporter realized he'd been had, his intended victims were long gone and he settled for his secondary target.

After a couple of hours of following Ross around Manhattan, O'Grady finally surrendered to the inevitable and gave up. Even so, Ross waited another hour until he was sure the reporter had called it quits before he caught the train to Long Island.

The Bridgehampton railroad station was well-lit and relatively clean, reflecting the money and taste of the local residents. Nevertheless, Ross had advised Gillian and Toby to wait for him at one of the local hotels, where he found them eating supper in the attached restaurant. He tipped the hotel's concierge to call a taxi, which carried them the three miles to Oak Hollow.

The wrought-iron gates at the entrance to the estate were locked, but Ross knew where Griffin kept a spare key under a rock nearby. He opened the gates and waved the taxi through, following on foot. The cobbled, tree-lined road led up to a carriage circle in front of the columned entrance of a Georgian-style manor house, where the cabbie let Gillian and Toby off.

It was obvious right away that someone had been keeping up the place in Griffin's and Allie's absence. The lawn was cut, the hedges neatly trimmed and the flower beds to either side of the porch filled with new plantings. Gillian stood gazing at the portico. Whatever she thought of the place didn't show on her face, but Toby had his own opinions.

"It's not nearly as big as Snowfell," he pronounced, "but it looks much nicer."

"What's not nice about Snowfell?" Ross asked, unlocking the front door.

"Oh, I don't know. It was built in the sixteenth century, but most of it burnt down, and then they rebuilt it, and then it burnt down again, so my great-grandfather had it rebuilt. Some of the old parts are still standing. It ended up a patchwork, not very pretty." He sniffed. "There must be lots of servants here."

"Only two, as far as I know."

"Two!" Toby whistled, earning a reproving glance from Gillian. Ross ushered them ahead of him into the cool central hall. Immediately Gillian stopped, wrapping her arms around her chest.

She might have sensed it, of course. Even though she hadn't recognized Ross as a werewolf when they'd first met, she might be able to smell a full-blooded one.

"There's something I didn't tell you," Ross said, coming up beside her. "Griffin Durant is a werewolf, and he's married to a vampire."

Gillian stared at him. "I beg your pardon?"

"I never met a vampire in Europe, so I don't know how you feel about them over there. But Allie's all right. She—"

"A real vampire?" Toby interrupted, the final syllable rising into a squeak. "Are we going to meet her?"

"Like I said, they're out of town." He met Gillian's gaze. "All you need to know is that you'd be welcome here."

"I see."

Ross was pretty sure she didn't see at all. She was probably horrified at the idea of a vampire-werewolf marriage, but was too polite to show it. Of course, Ross had been skeptical himself until he'd seen with his own eyes just how well such an improbable union could turn out.

But Gillian wasn't in any state to listen to him explain what she probably didn't want to hear anyway. He started up the stairs. "I'll show you some spare bedrooms you can use," he said. "Once you've rested, we can telephone your brother."

Gillian uncrossed her arms and seemed to relax a little. "Thank you."

Ross was beginning to get sick of those two words. Without replying, he showed Gillian and Toby the guest bedrooms. When he and Gillian were alone in the room Gillian had chosen, he decided to say what he'd been thinking ever since they'd left Coney Island.

"You did good, Mrs. Delvaux," he said, lingering in the doorway. "Helping that kid…it might not have seemed like much to you, but I'm sure his mother appreciated it."

She stood beside the four-poster, as self-conscious as he'd ever seen her. "Anyone could have done it," she said curtly.

He shook his head. "Most people would have made it worse." He ran his fingers along the doorjamb. "I'd almost forgotten how capable you were at the hospital, how well you looked after the patients. You were the best nurse there. Better than the ones who had a lot more training than you did."

"There was nothing exceptional about my work. Others did far more."

"We'll have to agree to disagree on that subject." He laughed briefly. "Among others."

All too aware that he was standing on the edge of a precipice, Ross retreated. He was halfway down the stairs when the front door swept open and Allegra Durant stepped into the hall.

"Ross!" she exclaimed, dropping her suitcase on the paneled wooden floor. "What are you doing here?"

As had happened more than once, Ross was momentarily at a loss for words. Allie had that effect on a lot of men, regardless f ancestry. She wore only a slightly more conservative dress han she had in her bachelor girl days, one that didn't quite reveal her knees, and her aqua eyes sparkled.

But Ross was seeing another woman in her place, a woman with golden hair and grave hazel eyes.

"Okay," Allie said, walking farther into the foyer. "Something's up, I can tell. Don't tell me someone's been murdered on Long Island. It's such a boring—"

She broke off, her gaze flying up the staircase. Ross turned. Gillian was poised on the landing, her features registering astonishment before she brought them under control.

"Well, well," Allie said, grinning. "Now I've seen everything. How many girls have you brought out here, Kavanagh? Or is she the first?"

CHAPTER SIX

GILLIAN FROZE at the other woman's question. She had already taken in the short dress, the bobbed hair and the bright red lipstick that identified Allie as one of the flappers who seemed so common in London. The two women stared at each other, and Gillian felt a stirring of instinctive hostility.

Ross was quick to fill the silence. "I've never brought anyone here before," he said, a little stiffly. "I didn't know you were coming back."

"We didn't, either." Allie's gaze returned to Gillian. "Any friend of yours is welcome here." Abruptly she started for the staircase, nearly running up the steps until she was standing just below Gillian. "Sorry about the quip. I didn't mean to be rude." She thrust out her hand. "Allie Durant."

Gillian's training overcame her aversion. She took the proffered hand. "Gillian Delvaux," she said. The sound of rapid footsteps warned her that Toby had heard the voices and come to join them. "This is my son, Tobias."

Toby careened to a halt at Gillian's side, remembered his manners and gave a little bow. "How do you do, Mrs. Durant?" he said. "Are you the vampire?"

Allie burst into laughter. "I see that Ross has told you all about me," she said when she had caught her breath again. "That makes things easier." She smiled at Toby. "Yes, I'm the vampire. You aren't scared, are you?"

A look of faint scorn crossed Toby's face. "Certainly not." He glanced at Gillian. "Werewolves are just as strong as vampires, aren't they?"

"I don't know," Gillian said, meeting Allie's gaze. "I have no vampires among my acquaintance."

Allie's smile never wavered, but her eyes took on a sharper expression. "You're *loup-garou?*" she asked. "From England, right?"

"Yes," Gillian said. "I apologize for visiting at such an inconvenient time. We shall leave immediately."

"Don't be ridiculous." Allie turned her head slightly as Ross came up behind her. "I have a feeling there's a very interesting story behind all this, but I'm famished. Grif will be here any moment. Would you like something to eat?"

Gillian was at a loss, a feeling she had experienced all too frequently since she'd met Ross again. The day's events—the pressing human crowds, the emergency with the boy, the reporter's intrusions—had shaken her more than she liked to admit. And now she was face-to-face with a vampire for the first time in her life—a remarkably hospitable vampire, for all her forwardness.

"Thank you," she said, "but Toby and I have recently dined."

"Then you won't mind if I make myself a sandwich." Allie addressed Toby. "Did Ross tell you that vampires can eat just like normal people?"

"I didn't get the chance," Ross said. He gave Gillian an encouraging glance. "Mrs. Delvaux only arrived from England a short time ago, and it's been kind of a rough day."

"Mr. Kavanagh exaggerates," Gillian said, wishing she could sink into the landing and disappear.

Allie seemed to notice her discomfiture. "That's not something he usually does. I've been a lousy hostess. Ross, you've shown Mrs. Delvaux the bedrooms?"

"Yes. And she needs to rest."

"I am quite well," Gillian said with as much dignity as she could muster.

"In that case, why don't you come downstairs and make yourself comfortable? I—" She stopped as a man walked through the front door. "Here's Grif now."

The gentleman who entered the hall was roughly Ross's age and height, with dark hair, golden eyes and handsome features…far more classically handsome than Ross's rugged contours. Gillian wasn't certain that she would have recognized him as a werewolf if she hadn't known beforehand; she had sensed something when she'd first entered the house, but aside from Ross, she'd met few strangers who had turned out to be werewolves.

Griffin Durant's face registered surprise as he saw Ross and Gillian; he set down the suitcases he had brought inside and continued on to the staircase.

"Ross!" he said with obvious pleasure. "I didn't expect a welcoming committee."

"Yeah," Ross said. "Like I told Allie, I didn't know you were coming back today."

"Completely understandable." Durant's eyes reflected the same curiosity Allie had shown, but he remained cordially reserved as he looked up at Gillian. "May I be introduced?"

"Mrs. Delvaux," Ross said, "this is my friend Griffin Durant. Grif, this is Mrs. Gillian Delvaux."

Griffin reached the landing. "How do you do, Mrs. Delvaux?"

This time Gillian offered her hand first. "Very well, thank you, Mr. Durant. May I present my son, Tobias?"

"Tobias. Pleased to meet you."

Toby stared at Mr. Durant. "Do you belong to the New York pack?"

Durant glanced at Ross, who buried his hands in his trouser pockets. "As I was telling Allie," Ross said, "Toby and Mrs. Delvaux have only been in the States a short time and aren't familiar with the setup here. *Loups-garous* do things differently in England."

"A fascinating subject, I'm sure," Allie said, "but I'm still starving. Let's go downstairs."

Griffin stood aside to let the women precede him. Gillian hung back.

"If you will excuse me for a few moments…" she said, and ushered Toby into the room she'd chosen for him.

"Toby," she said, "listen carefully. You are not to mention anything to the Durants about your relationship to Mr. Kavanagh, or about what happened at Coney Island. Nor are you to quiz Mrs. Durant about her…particular constitution."

Toby understood her readily enough, but his jaw set in incipient rebellion. "You don't want anyone to know that Ross is my father."

"The matter is private and of no concern to people we have just met, even if they are Mr. Kavanagh's friends."

"Then what do you want me to say?"

"You know how to hold a civil conversation." She placed her hands on his shoulders. "I trust you to use good judgment. You may answer general questions about England and what you have observed in America. Say nothing about the method by which you arrived. I am simply an acquaintance of Mr. Durant's, and we are here on holiday."

"What if Father tells them the truth?"

"I believe—" *dear God, let it be so* "—that he will also prefer to keep our private affairs confidential."

"Your mother is right," Ross said, walking into the room. "We won't say anything to embarrass her, will we?"

Gillian listened for sarcasm in his voice and heard none. When he offered her his arm, she took it, well aware that he could make things very unpleasant if he chose to do so. His tacit promise to hide their secret only strengthened the emotions with which she'd struggled ever since he'd taken such trouble to protect her and Toby from the intrusive interest of the crowd.

It had taken more effort than she would have supposed to meet

Ross's mocking feints with appropriately composed answers, both in the hotel and at the amusement park. She had wavered constantly between despising him and—to her shame—wanting desperately to be near him. Only his sarcastic manner and biting questions had kept her leaning toward the former.

But his behavior had changed completely from the moment she had tried to help the boy. His support had been immediate. He had realized—all too well, as she had just discovered—how much she wanted to avoid the public notice her actions had attracted. He had been very much the gentleman then, as if he felt he owed her his protection.

Of course he didn't, just as he didn't owe her the compliments he'd paid her a few minutes ago.

She continued down the stairs at his side, concentrating on moving with the dignity and grace that were expected of her, letting such simple thoughts create a barrier between her keen physical awareness and the necessities of her position. She must overcome her attraction, for Toby's sake. Dependence upon Ross's assistance while she remained in New York would hardly persuade Toby to leave the father he had just met, and her memories…

Ah, her memories. They were the greatest obstacle of all. Vivid recollections of her affair with Ross, feeding the unwelcome reactions that overwhelmed her when she was in his presence, whenever she touched him.

Thank God Ross hadn't sensed her emotions. He certainly didn't share them. He'd shown no sign that his feelings for her went beyond the same natural gallantry that had been so much a part of his nature when she had met him. Still, the bitterness and wounded pride she had seen in him during their conversation at the hotel seemed to have given way to a far more sympathetic attitude.

Unless his softening was no more than a new tactic to throw her off her guard. The possibility seemed more likely as she considered it, and it was all she could do not to remove her arm from the crook of his elbow.

If he really did intend to use this new method of attack, she must under no circumstances let him think he had succeeded.

Determined not to reveal the grim nature of her thoughts, Gillian joined the Durants in a pleasant room plainly but comfortably furnished in a rustic American mode very much at odds with the Georgian style of the house itself. Allie pulled back the heavy drapes to reveal French doors that opened onto a well-kept garden, now cloaked in darkness.

"Please, sit," she said. "I'll be back in a few minutes. Do you want anything, Grif?"

"Not at the moment, thanks," her husband said. He waited until Gillian and Toby had taken their seats on the sofa and went to the sideboard standing against one wall. "Would you care for a drink, Mrs. Delvaux? Ross?"

Ross shook his head. "Thank you, but no," Gillian said.

"I don't drink myself," Durant said. He took one of the armchairs. "I was unaware that Ross had friends in England, Mrs. Delvaux," he said, his posture relaxed but alert. "I hope your visit to America has been pleasant thus far."

Gillian prepared herself to tell the necessary lies. "I find your country to be very interesting, Mr. Durant," she said.

"We went to Coney Island today," Toby piped in.

"Did you enjoy it?"

"Immensely. We went into the Dragon's Gorge and then on the Aerial Swing." He bit his lip, eyed Gillian and fell silent.

"Mrs. Delvaux volunteered as a nurse at the hospital in London where I recovered after the War," Ross said. "We became friends. I wrote to her a few times after I returned to America. We lost touch, but she looked me up when she came to the States on holiday with her brother."

He didn't look at Gillian, but she understood his ploy. He was protecting her "honor" by revealing as much of the truth as possible.

"Yes," she said lightly. "My brother, Hugh, insisted that Toby and I come along when he decided to visit the United States. I remembered that Mr. Kavanagh had joined the New York police force after his return." She smiled at Ross. "He has been an excellent guide."

"I told her a bit about you and Allie," Ross said. "I thought I'd show her Oak Hollow…the other side of American life."

"That's a lot to do in one day," Allie said from the doorway, balancing a plate adorned by an enormous sandwich. "And you said you just arrived, Mrs. Delvaux?"

"Yesterday," Ross said. "I'm afraid Toby's been running his poor mother ragged."

"Not at all," Gillian said quickly. "There is so much to see and do, I'm quite certain that we shall leave America with a great many interesting sights unvisited."

"Can't have that," Allie said, falling into the chair nearest her husband. "I guess you haven't had time to see Harlem or visit a speakeasy. That's not really Ross's type of place, though…he's been a cop too long."

"I don't think Mrs. Delvaux would be interested in visiting a speakeasy," Ross said.

"Oh, come on. The best jazz is in the speaks. You can't come to America and not hear the jazz." She took a bite of her sandwich and spoke again as soon as she'd swallowed. "I know the best places. I'll be glad to show you around."

Gillian was beginning to feel very much out of her depth. "Your offer is much appreciated, Mrs. Durant," she said. "But as much as we have enjoyed Mr. Kavanagh's company, Hugh—my brother—wishes to escort us during our visit."

"Call me Allie. Mrs. Durant sounds so…stuffy."

Griffin Durant gave his wife a teasing look. "You'll forgive me if I don't agree…Mrs. Durant."

It was obvious to Gillian that the couple were engaging in a kind of banter with which both were comfortable, an indication of their affection for each other. *A vampire and a werewolf,* she thought, still amazed. She tried to imagine what her father would say to such a union and found even the suggestion impossible to comprehend.

Allie was watching her. "I guess things are a lot more formal in England. Grif spent a lot of time there."

Immediately Gillian recognized the new danger. "Indeed?"

"I don't imagine we'd have many acquaintances in common, Mrs. Delvaux," Durant said. "I didn't actually meet any *loups-garous* when I lived there."

Gillian concealed her relief. The chances that Griffin Durant knew anything of her personal history appeared to be remote. Unless, of course, he was lying out of courtesy.

"You asked if I were a member of the New York pack," Mr. Durant said to Toby. "I am not, for various reasons. Not all werewolves in the United States are attached to a pack."

"Neither are we," Toby said, apparently judging that he was on safe ground. "But sometimes lots of werewolves from all over Europe come together in a big meeting called the Convocation, where everyone—" He caught himself in midsentence. "Do you have Convocations?"

"Not that I've heard," Mr. Durant said. "But I confess that I don't monitor the doings of werewolves in other parts of the country."

Gillian turned hastily to his wife. "Have you been married long, Mrs. Durant?"

"*Allie,* remember?" the vampire said. "Almost a year. Most of that time we've been overseas with Ross's sister, Gemma." She glanced at Ross. "Seems quite a bit has happened while we were gone."

Ross stared at the darkened windows. "Yeah," he said hoarsely. "The clan split up into two factions after Raoul died. It got pretty bad for a while. They've only just reunited under a new leader."

For the first time Allie's high spirits seemed to dim. "We should have been here," she muttered. "We might have helped."

"Wouldn't have made any difference," Ross said. "The clan is no happier about your marriage than the pack is. Not likely that they would have listened to either one of you."

Allie noticed Gillian's oblique glance. "The clan is the big vampire organization in New York."

"From which Allegra fortunately escaped," Griffin said.

"With a little help," she said, reaching over to lay her hand on Griffin's sleeve. "Anyway…the subject won't interest Mrs. Delvaux. I'm the first vampire she's met. Isn't that right?"

"Yes," Gillian said, prompted by the other woman's frankness. "I'm certain they must exist in England, but *loups-garous*…have no dealings with them."

"Let alone get married to them," Allie said wryly. "The prejudice probably goes back thousands of years."

Gillian stiffened. "I didn't intend to cause offense."

"None taken." Allie squeezed Griffin's hand. "Someday, maybe everyone will realize it's love that matters, not that other stuff."

Her words slashed at Gillian's already fragile composure. She was painfully aware of Ross, knowing what he must be thinking. She could hardly bear the thoughts careening through her own head.

If Allie had been in her place, she would have stayed with Ross. She would have flung all other considerations and consequences aside.

But I am not Mrs. Durant. I could never be.

Gillian rose. "We have imposed too much upon your hospitality, Mrs. Durant," she said. "We should return to Manhattan."

Ross cleared his throat. "I'm sure that Griffin and Allie would be happy to put you up tonight," he said.

Gillian knew what he was trying to say. It was still possible that O'Grady would find her and Toby. But the prospect of staying here seemed almost as bad. "I would not wish—" she began.

"Ross is right," Allie said. "It's getting dark, and God knows this heap has plenty of empty rooms." She pursed her lips. "You're a little taller than I am, but I'll bet I could fit you out with anything you'd need."

"Mrs. Durant, I—"

"Can't we stay, Mother?" Toby begged. He yawned expansively behind his hand. "I *am* rather tired."

In spite of Toby's blatant manipulation, Gillian knew that a refusal now would be rude. She had begun to like Allie Chase in spite of her initial doubts, and the prospect of being close to Ross on the trip back to Manhattan was more than a little daunting.

"Very well," she said. "If you are certain our remaining will not be an imposition."

"Not at all," Allie said.

"May I use your telephone? I should ring my brother and tell him where we are."

"Of course. Come with me."

"Perhaps I might put Toby to bed first."

"I'll take him up," Ross offered, getting to his feet. "You do whatever you need to."

Gillian had no desire to behave in a way that would suggest to the Durants that she didn't entirely trust her good friend Ross Kavanagh. "Thank you." She turned to Toby. "I shall say goodnight presently."

Toby nodded, his eyes unfocused. Gillian knew that look. It had nothing to do with boredom or weariness; he was concocting some sort of scheme or other. Reluctantly she followed Allie to a somewhat more formally decorated room that was obviously left unused the majority of the time. An ornate telephone table stood by the door.

"Here it is," Allie said brightly. "I'll give you a little privacy."

But she made no move to leave the room. Instead, she wandered about, clucking her tongue as she brushed her fingertip across a tabletop and her skin came away coated with dust.

"Sorry about the mess," she said. "I never was much of a housekeeper."

Gillian searched her mind for something to say. "Did you enjoy your stay in Europe, Mrs. Durant?"

"If you don't start calling me Allie, I'll think you don't like me."

Gillian looked for somewhere to sit. "We have scarcely met," she said.

"True, but if you're Ross's friend…" Allie trailed off and picked up a porcelain figurine from the table. "So you worked as a nurse during the War?"

There seemed no polite way of escaping Allie's questions. "Yes."

"And that was when you met Ross."

"Yes."

"Your husband must be a pretty modern guy."

"I beg your pardon?"

"The old-fashioned kind—you know, the ones who still have a foot in the last century—they probably don't like their wives to go gallivanting around a foreign country with an unattached male friend."

Informality was one thing, but this was another matter entirely. "I am a widow," Gillian said coldly.

As if realizing she'd gone too far, Allie set down the figurine and met Gillian's eyes with an uncharacteristically serious expression. "I'm sorry," she said, the simple words covering Gillian's loss and her own rudeness. "It really is none of my business." She strode to the door, her short skirt swirling about her knees. "Please let me know if there's anything you need."

She left, closing the door gently behind her. Gillian took a moment to catch her breath. Why had Allie found it necessary to probe into her marital status? Why had she assumed that

Gillian's supposed husband would forbid her to see an old wartime friend?

Because that is exactly what would *happen,* Gillian thought. Of course, if she were married, Toby might never have escaped, and neither of them would have come to the United States.

Unwilling to pursue that line of thought, Gillian picked up the telephone receiver. She dialed the operator and asked for the Roosevelt Hotel. Hugh answered on the third ring.

"Gilly!" he exclaimed. "Where are you? I expected you back hours ago."

"You needn't have worried, Hugh. We are still with Mr. Kavanagh."

"Well, you'd better get back here soon. Warbrick has been haunting the hotel since this morning."

"I did attempt to ring him at his hotel."

"He said he's been out of town. He nearly blew his top when he heard you were with Kavanagh."

Perhaps because he hadn't known that Gillian was coming to America herself, let alone that she might contact Ross directly.

"I tried to explain what had happened," Hugh continued, "but he just kept shaking his head and muttering under his breath. Wouldn't tell me why he was so upset, just that he wasn't going to leave until you got back."

Gillian had already begun to think that she'd made a very poor decision in agreeing to stay at Oak Hollow. "Toby and I are stopping with friends of Mr. Kavanagh's on Long Island. We shall not be back until tomorrow morning."

"It sounds as if you've been very busy, Gilly. I can't wait to hear the details."

That was something Gillian did not anticipate with any degree of pleasure. "I shall see you tomorrow morning, then. Give my regards to Ethan, and assure him that Toby and I are quite well."

"Swell." He paused. "Be careful, Gilly. But then, you're always careful. Or at least you used to be."

He hung up, and Gillian was left with his unsettling words ringing in her ears. Hugh was hardly a model of discretion himself. If *he* thought she had been reckless in her dealings with Ross, he must really be concerned.

But he had agreed that she ought to allow Toby some contact with his father. Even if he hadn't, she would have relied on her own judgment, not his.

Judgment she had begun to doubt more and more as the day went on.

As for Ethan… He had always been protective when they were children, angry when her father had been more critical than usual or had made it difficult for her to leave Snowfell to meet him. When they'd met again as adults, after a separation enforced by Sir Averil and facilitated by Ethan's years away in Europe and the East, she'd told him about Toby's real parentage, but she'd made it very clear that she had no desire to rekindle her past with her American lover. She couldn't guess why he would be so upset about her having met with Ross.

After returning the receiver to its cradle, Gillian stepped out of the room. She was relieved to find the hall empty. Moving quickly to the stairs, she paused at the landing. She heard the low hum of Ross's voice and the higher pitch of Toby's light alto coming from Toby's room.

The temptation to listen was great, but she deliberately closed her ears and continued on to her room. She would bide her time until she could speak to Toby herself, and then she would be free to spend the rest of the night alone.

Alone with the cruel little voice that kept asking her if she'd made the worst mistake of her life on that painful day twelve years ago.

GRIFFIN WAS WAITING for Ross at the bottom of the staircase.

As restrained as Grif had been compared to Allie, Ross had a feeling he wasn't going to get away without answering a few ques-ons. He'd noticed the way Griffin had watched first him and then Jillian, silently appraising, his golden eyes narrowing from time o time as he listened to their brief exchanges…or lack of them.

Whatever Grif was thinking, it was better that he knew at least ome of the facts rather than speculate and come up with all the vrong ideas.

"How about that drink?" Ross suggested.

"Has Mrs. Delvaux retired?" Griffin asked.

"I haven't seen her since I went up." Ross passed Griffin and alked into the summer parlor, heading straight for the side-oard. "What she told you was the truth, you know."

Griffin considered Ross from the doorway, one brow cocked. Which part?" he asked.

"About our meeting while I was recuperating in a London ospital."

"I don't doubt it."

Ross poured himself a brandy. "We got pretty close back en. You know how it was. People formed strong bonds during e War, and it didn't really matter who you were or where you ame from."

"I remember."

"Anyway, she got married, and I went on to join the force." Ie paused, wondering if Grif had heard anything about the candal while he and Allie had been away. "I didn't hear from er until she phoned me from England a couple of weeks ago. he thought we should meet again for old times' sake."

"Old times," Griffin repeated. He wandered toward the vindows. "You don't have to play these games with me. I owe ou more than I can repay. I would never presume to judge you."

Ross downed the drink and poured another before he had time o think. "I don't know what you're talking about."

"And I would accept that, Ross, if it weren't so clear that ou're in some kind of trouble."

He *didn't* know. Ross expelled his breath. "And you think

this 'trouble' I'm in has something to do with an old friend from the War?"

"She's more than an old friend, isn't she?"

The second drink disappeared in seconds. Ross set the glass down a little too forcefully.

"We were close," he said. "Very close. But it didn't work out."

Griffin sat on the sofa, stretching his arm across the back. "What about the boy?"

"What about him?"

"He's yours, isn't he?"

Ross could have denied it. If he had, Griffin might have left it alone. Or, white knight that he was, he might have decided to interfere anyway, his usual courtesy be damned.

"How could you tell?" Ross asked.

"A hunch."

"That's all? A hunch?"

"And the fact that you offered to take Toby up to bed. If you'd never met the child until recently…"

"I hadn't." Ross forced himself to walk away from the sideboard. "Look, it's not something I want to talk about."

"Did Mrs. Delvaux bring Toby to the States to see you?"

"No. And please don't mention any of this to her. She and Toby…" He swallowed. "They might not be in New York much longer."

"I see."

"I doubt it." The impulse to tell Griffin everything gnawed at Ross. He wished he could take the risk of getting drunk. "What do you think of the kid?"

"He seems a fine boy," Grif said. "He looks very much like his mother."

"I'd noticed that." Ross paced across the room. Though it wasn't small, it seemed far too confining. "He's only part werewolf," he said suddenly.

"Is that important?"

"It is to Ji— To Mrs. Delvaux."

Griffin considered that in silence. "You're worried about Toby."

"I want to make sure he has a good life in England," Ross said. He rubbed his hand across the unshaven stubble on his chin. "Hell. I've only known him two days, Grif. And seeing Jill again…"

"Allie told me she's a widow."

Ross wondered what sort of conversation she and Gillian had had. "Yeah."

"Do you still love her?"

CHAPTER SEVEN

THE BLUNTNESS of the question left Ross stammering. "She… I…" He gave himself a hard mental shake. "What makes you think I loved her?"

Griffin looked at him as if he'd said something stupid. Ross wished he were back in his own apartment, with a cheap bottle of whiskey and a stained wall to throw it at.

"It wouldn't have worked," he muttered.

"Yet she's here."

Too much had already been said. Ross opened one of the French doors to the garden and walked out, leaving Grif to his speculations.

The garden smelled strongly of roses, both new and fading. The moon was high and very bright. He wandered aimlessly for a while, across the rolling lawn and then down to the boathouse that stood near the dock. The scent of salt water was so strong that he almost didn't realize that Gillian was already there.

Gillian, yes. But she waited for him on four legs instead of two, and the moonlight caressed sleek golden fur and sparkled in slanted lupine eyes.

Ross stopped, transfixed by memory and Gillian's magnificence. She was more glorious in her maturity than she'd been that first time he'd caught her in wolf shape, but he felt that same sense of shock and realization, understanding that certain puzzles had been solved and mysteries explained. No one, not even the most superstitious human, could have looked at her now and doubted that she was beautiful.

And untouchable. Untouchable because she was what she was, and he could never Change and stand at her side as partner and true equal.

He turned to leave. A low whine brought him to a halt. He didn't move again until he heard her return from the boathouse on two human feet.

"Ross."

She wore a dress cut much shorter than she seemed to prefer—one of Allie's, no doubt—and flat pumps a size too large. Her legs were bare, and her hair hung loose below her shoulders. She looked so unlike the Gillian he'd met two days ago that he could do nothing but stare.

She glanced down at herself. "I suppose I look rather a mess," she said.

She spoke like a girl with her first beau, doubting her own ability to attract the interest of any male. Ross thought of the golden wolf and struggled not to laugh at the desperate irony of it.

"No," he said roughly, blurting out the first words that came into his head. "You look beautiful."

His pronouncement had an unexpected effect. Gillian's face flushed red, and she smoothed her skirt as if she could somehow make it extend farther down her legs. "I thought I would be alone," she said.

"I'll leave."

"No." She brushed her hot cheeks with her fingertips. "That isn't necessary. I was about to return to the house."

"Don't." He realized he'd taken complete leave of his senses, and he didn't care. "Stay."

Gillian took an awkward step, stumbled, then caught herself just as Ross reached her. He grasped her arm and felt her muscles tense. The scent of her hair and skin swirled around his head, far sweeter than any rose.

If Gillian had behaved true to form, she would have extracted herself from his grip immediately. Instead, she laughed. The sound was almost girlish, nervous and bright.

"I'm not usually quite so clumsy," she said.

"I know." He glanced around and noticed a bench near the boathouse, set where the lawn gave way to the beach. He eased her down, though it was clear she didn't need his help. She sat with her back straight and her hands folded at her knees, gazing out at the dark, choppy water.

Ross continued to stand, half-afraid he would send her running off again if he tried to share the bench with her. A little afraid of himself, too.

"Toby's asleep?" he asked.

"He soon will be, if he isn't already," she said. "I didn't realize it was possible to exhaust him."

The ease of her speech, like her laugh, set Ross back on his heels. He'd expected her to be warier after meeting Allie and Grif; Allie could come on pretty strong, especially in comparison to someone as reserved as Gillian. Maybe he seemed less threatening in comparison.

"I guess you don't feel very comfortable with the Durants," Ross said. "I'm sorry it turned out this way."

Gillian raised her hand in a brief, dismissive gesture. "Mrs. Durant is an unusual woman, but quite charming," she said. "Mr. Durant is very pleasant company."

"Yeah." Ross figured that it didn't matter if she was lying just be to be polite, as long as it helped her cope. "I guess this place has one advantage. You're a lot safer Changing here than in the city."

"I hadn't thought about it."

"But you've been living in the countryside. You must find Manhattan pretty confining."

She cast him a distracted look. "We…seldom find occasion to Change at Snowfell."

It was such a strange comment that Ross wasn't sure how to

respond. "I thought Changing was the most important thing for your people."

"It is." She answered so quickly that she hardly seemed to realize what she'd said until the words were spoken. "I… Of course there is a great deal more…. It is simply…" Her shoulders went up in a defensive posture, and Ross had a sudden, inexplicable flash of insight.

"You don't really like it, do you?"

She would have bolted from the bench if Ross hadn't stood in her way. Her scent heightened with some strong emotion.

"If I didn't 'like' it," she said tightly, "why would I do it here?"

Ross had nothing but pure conjecture on his side, yet he couldn't let it go. "I don't know," he said. "Maybe being around people who've broken the rules means you have to remind yourself who you are and what you're supposed to believe."

"I know what I am."

"But are you so sure what you believe?" He leaned over her. "What was it like when you went back to Snowfell, Gillian? What made you this way?"

Waves licked at the beach and receded again, whispering derision at Ross's stupidity. She would never confide in him, not while he treated her like an enemy.

"I'm sorry," he said.

Gillian met his gaze, her hazel eyes searching his as if she thought he was mocking her again. "Why, Ross?"

"Why what?"

"Why are you doing this?"

"I don't know what you mean."

She got up, dodged him and walked to the edge of the water. "What do you really want? It isn't money. You're in no position to keep Toby, even if you were to steal him from me."

He flinched. "I told you I wouldn't take him from his mother."

"If you truly thought it was in Toby's best interests…" She turned to face him. "Wouldn't you? Wouldn't you do anything?"

"If you're asking if I care about Toby, I do. That doesn't mean I'm out to cause you pain."

"Then the man I once knew isn't entirely gone."

"Twelve years is a long time. It changes some things, but not everything."

"Yes. Some things never change." She buried the toe of her pump in the damp sand. "Am I such a terrible mother?"

Seeing this side of Gillian—this doubt and fear, this vulnerability—unmanned Ross more than anything else she could have done. "Jill…"

"Do you hate me, Ross?"

He wouldn't in his wildest dreams have expected her to ask such a question. "For God's sake," he said hoarsely. "I don't hate you. I never—"

But that wasn't true. He *had* hated her, no matter how much he'd tried to deny it. He just hadn't realized how much until the hatred was gone.

For it *was* gone, and he didn't know what do with the empty space it had left inside him.

Unable to find the words, he took Gillian's shoulders, pulled her toward him and kissed her.

If she'd struggled, if she'd pulled away and slapped his face, he wouldn't have blamed her. She did neither. She softened in his arms, as pliant and responsive as she'd been as a girl of eighteen. The distinctive scent of arousal filled his senses, threatening to overwhelm him. He retained enough self-control not to demand too much, so Gillian gave freely in return, locking her arms around his shoulders, accepting the thrust of his tongue with a soft groan of pleasure.

That was when Toby found them.

He made hardly a sound, but Ross smelled him instantly. So did Gillian. She lurched backward, uncharacteristically clumsy once again, and pressed her palm to her mouth. Ross felt as if someone had punched him in the gut.

"Mother," Toby said, his mouth quivering as he fought to conceal an expression he didn't want them to see. "Father."

"What are you doing here?" Ross demanded, aware that Gillian was still struggling to regain her composure. "Why aren't you in bed?"

"I couldn't sleep." He hunched a little under Ross's glare. "I heard voices outside."

Sure he had, the little devil. He'd probably been looking for a chance to escape his room ever since he'd heard his mother leave the house.

"You're going back right now," Ross said. "March."

"I'll take him," Gillian said.

Her voice held no trace of the softening she'd shown since Ross had met her on the beach. Her face was strained and pale.

She'd probably like to shoot herself right about now, Ross thought. *How's she going to explain this to Toby?*

And how was Ross going to explain it to himself? When he'd left the house, kissing Gillian had been the furthest thing from his mind.

"Do you still love her?" Griffin had asked. Hell, it had nothing to do with love. Ross still found Gillian attractive— more than that, he'd been forced to admit he still wanted her. And her response had told him that the attraction and the wanting were mutual.

Maybe she'd had other lovers since her husband's death, but he was beginning to doubt it. Having made the mistake already, she wouldn't have chosen another human, and he had a hunch that English werewolves weren't casual in their sexual relationships, even among themselves.

Then there was the *way* she'd kissed him, tentatively at first, then with an intensity that hinted at passion long denied.

Even though she and Ross had made love only once in London, Gillian had been uninhibited, almost wild in her physical expressions of desire. It was the side of her that had convinced him, in his naiveté, that she might abandon her old life and return with him to America.

He wouldn't make the same mistake twice. Most likely Gillian would never come within touching distance of him again; she wouldn't want Toby getting any more ideas. But even if she did, it wouldn't mean anything except that she was still capable of wanting him.

Ross walked away from the boathouse at a fast clip, hoping to get his wayward body back under control. Gillian would know if he went into the house still in a state of arousal. He just couldn't let her have that kind of power over him. And in spite of what he'd told her, he had yet to make up his mind about Toby. How could he, when he'd barely had time to talk to the kid?

Fresh out of answers, he walked for a good two hours, following the road that ran parallel to the ocean. He passed a dozen fancy mansions, some bigger than Griffin's. It was ironic. He remembered when Griffin had been dead set on marrying off his younger sister, Gemma, to some human guy from high society. Grif had wanted to forget the animal side of himself. Events had finally compelled him to accept his werewolf nature. Could Gillian accept her son's human blood?

Hell, he'd been a cop. Still was, whatever anyone else said. In the end, he had to rely on facts. Maybe he'd jumped to the wrong conclusions about Gillian's fears for Toby, seeing and hearing only what he expected instead of what really existed.

She loved Toby too much to make him suffer for being part-human.

She'd never loved Ross that much.

Another couple of days and I'll be sure. Then I'll know I did everything I could.

Everything but forget.

It was near dawn when Ross returned to the house. He heard Allie moving about and took the stairs quietly, wanting to dodge more probing discussions. A couple of hours' shut-eye would wipe the last confusion out of his head.

But it wasn't going to be quite that simple. He could smell Gillian even from several rooms away, hear the faint movements she made as she stirred in her bed. When he finally did manage to sleep, his dreams were full of her, full of the sounds of her cries as he made love to her, the feel of her nails scraping his back and the brush of her hair across his face.

The first thing he did when he woke was to take a long, cold dip in the bathtub. It didn't do a damned bit of good. And short of hiding in his room, he couldn't avoid Gillian any longer once it was over. He went downstairs to the modern kitchen where Gillian, Toby, Allie and Griffin were eating eggs, bacon and toast.

"Boy, I'll be glad when Starke is back," Allie said, polishing off her last bite.

"You don't like my cooking?" Griffin asked, pretending offense.

"You can cook?"

Griffin showed the tips of his teeth, and Allie laughed. Gillian gazed at them with a strangely bereft look on her face.

She's never seen this kind of thing before, Ross thought. He still knew almost nothing about her parents or her life at Snowfell, and she hadn't had enough of a marriage to develop the kind of easy, bantering devotion that Grif and Allie shared.

He was glad of that, and he despised himself for it.

He sat down and buttered a piece of cold toast, returning Allie's cheerful greeting. Gillian was absorbed in studying the intricate floral pattern of the tablecloth. Toby watched Ross out of the corner of his eye and pushed the remnants of his egg around on his plate with his fork.

"I want to thank you again for your hospitality," Gillian said to Allie and Griffin. "Toby and I will be returning to Manhattan this morning."

"No need to rush," Allie said. "You're welcome to stay here as long as you're in New York."

"That is very kind of you, Mrs. Durant, but we will shall be returning to England very soon."

Ross felt Griffin's gaze. *He's wondering if I'm just going to let my son and his mother walk out of my life.*

No one should know better than Griffin how little Ross was cut out to be a father. But Grif still clung to some of his old-fashioned ideals. Maybe he thought Ross should fight to keep them, the way Grif had fought for Allie when she'd tried to run away from his love.

But that's the difference, Grif. That little emotional complication so many people set such store by.

Ross managed to stay away from Griffin while Gillian went upstairs to freshen up. Allie had insisted that Gillian keep the dress she'd borrowed; Gillian accepted with courteous gratitude that didn't quite hide her reluctance. She remained ill at ease when Griffin insisted on driving her, Toby and Ross to the train station, and she kept her legs pressed firmly together after they boarded the train, as if she feared being mistaken for a woman of loose morals.

Ross laughed under his breath, earning a curious glance from Toby, who was sitting beside his mother. *What would you think if you knew the things going through my mind, Jill? Or are the same things going through yours?*

He wrenched his thoughts from the shapely curves of her calves and ankles and the scent of her skin, turning his mind toward deciding what he should do next. He was still chewing over the possibilities when the train arrived at Penn Station. He whistled down a taxi, bracing himself for the discomfort of sharing an enclosed space with Gillian. He knew that she felt the same tension, but she managed not to show it except when she told him it wasn't necessary for him to escort them into the hotel.

Ross ignored her suggestion. The air was so thick in the lift that he wondered how the elevator boy, human though he was, could possibly fail to sense the charged atmosphere. And maybe he did, because the kid looked almost relieved when the doors opened onto the third floor.

Ross let Gillian and Toby precede him into the hall, so at first he didn't notice the guy waiting at the door to their suite.

"Ethan!" Gillian exclaimed, rushing ahead to meet him. "Hugh told me you'd called. It wasn't necessary for you to worry about us." She half turned toward Ross, her movements a little too jerky. "Lord Warbrick, I believe you have met Mr. Ross Kavanagh. Mr. Kavanagh, Viscount Warbrick of Highwick."

"I remember," Ross said coldly. "A lord, huh? I'm impressed."

Warbrick pretended not to hear. "What are you doing?" he demanded, his gaze locked on Gillian's. "Do you know what this man is? What he's done?"

Toby darted away from his mother and stood in front of Ross as if he anticipated trouble. He probably wasn't far wrong. Ross clenched his fists at his sides, knowing what was to come.

"He's a criminal," Warbrick said, his cultured voice taut with anger. "He just barely avoided a trial, but everyone in this city knows that he committed murder."

AT FIRST Gillian didn't seem to understand him. Ethan wasn't surprised; it wasn't something she would want to accept if she'd already come to trust Kavanagh enough to leave the hotel in his company.

But Gillian had never been lacking in intelligence, in spite of her poor judgment regarding Kavanagh. She searched Ethan's eyes, her own growing increasingly bleak.

"Toby," she said, "please go to your room, close the door and wait for me."

Toby didn't move. "Why are you saying such bad things about my father, Uncle Ethan?" he demanded.

Gillian seized Toby's wrist in an iron grip. "You will go to your room and wait," she said.

"Go on," Kavanagh said, his voice gentle as he spoke to the boy. "It'll be okay, kid."

Jaw set, Toby allowed himself to be steered into the room. Gillian followed him, leaving the door open behind her.

Ethan closed it. "I'll give you one opportunity, Kavanagh," he said, staring into the American's hostile brown eyes. "Leave now. Make no further attempt to contact either Mrs. Delvaux or the boy, and I shall not summon the police."

Kavanagh's smile was as unpleasant as his weather-beaten face. "On what grounds?" he asked. "What's the matter, couldn't take what I dished out?"

Ethan returned the smile with interest. "My mistake was in not dealing with you as you deserved from the very beginning. But do not misunderstand. I will do anything to protect Mrs. Delvaux from you, just as she will do anything to protect her son. Whatever you may have done to win her trust, it will not be enough. You will not get what you want from her."

With an easy, deliberately insolent motion, Kavanagh propped his shoulder against the wall. "How do you know what I want, Warbrick?"

"There can be only one reason why a man like you would pursue a woman he hasn't seen in twelve years. Apparently I didn't offer you enough."

"Pursue?" Ross said, biting off the word. "She came to me. So did Toby."

"He is correct, Ethan," Gillian said from the doorway. "I suggest we continue this conversation inside."

"That would be most unwise," Ethan said, taking firm hold of his temper. "I assure you that I was not exaggerating when I named Kavanagh a murderer."

Gillian's gaze moved from Ethan's to Kavanagh's, level and unafraid. "Considering that Toby and I spent all day with Mr.

Kavanagh and emerged unscathed," she said, "I hardly think we are in immediate danger. Will you come in, Mr. Kavanagh?"

Ross stepped away from the wall and strode past without a second glance, all bluster and bravado. Ethan keenly felt Gillian's rebuke. He had made the mistake of framing his first warning as a reprimand, a self-indulgence he would not repeat, just as he would no longer count on anyone else to do the necessary work as he had so foolishly relied on Bianchi.

He went into Gillian's suite. Kavanagh was already at the sideboard, pouring a glass of brandy.

Drink, by all means, Ethan thought. *Poison your mind. Give me yet another advantage.*

Gillian glanced at Kavanagh, her frown revealing her concern. Ethan clenched his teeth. It wasn't possible that she should still find this lowbred mongrel attractive.

"I ask you to speak softly," Gillian said, standing behind the sofa with her hands resting on its low back. She didn't need to explain further; Toby was doubtless trying to hear what was going on among the adults. Ethan realized he'd been rash to accuse Kavanagh in front of the boy. Amazingly enough, the American had already won some measure of Toby's loyalty.

"Perhaps you had best be seated, Gillian," he said.

She stayed where she was. "What is this about, Ethan?" she asked softly.

"I'll tell you what this is about," Kavanagh said, positioning himself so that he stood at an equal distance from both Ethan and Gillian. "Your friend is going to tell you that I murdered a gangster's moll and was kicked off the force."

Shock and horror would have been a natural reaction to such an announcement, but Gillian's expression never altered. Ethan silently cursed Kavanagh for trying to assume control of the conversation.

"He didn't tell you, did he?" Ethan asked.

"I didn't tell her because it isn't true," Kavanagh said. He took a step toward Gillian. "I *was* kicked off the force. But I didn't murder anyone. Someone set things up to make it look like I killed the girl. They never found enough evidence to bring it to trial."

"So he claims," Ethan said. He'd heard the subtle trace of fear in Kavanagh's voice. The American must know that Gillian would be far more likely to believe an old friend than a man with whom she'd once had a passing fling.

And, Ethan realized, Kavanagh cared for Gillian's opinion. As ridiculous as it seemed, he apparently wanted more from her than money.

Ethan breathed very slowly to control his rage. He would gladly have killed Kavanagh on the spot, but he knew the American's jealousy could be turned to his advantage. Though it was extremely unfortunate that Kavanagh had been permitted to spend time alone with Gillian and Toby, there was considerable satisfaction in knowing that the American regarded Ethan as a threat.

"The prosecutor believed him to be guilty," Ethan said, deliberately calm. "Public opinion was against him. Simply because the authorities lacked the necessary proof—"

"It was a setup," Kavanagh repeated. "I made enemies on the job." He spread his hands in an almost pleading gesture. "There are a lot of powerful people in New York, people who don't like cops who can't be bought. The guy I was investigating…he had connections in the mayor's office. The girl was my contact in the boss's organization. If they found out about her, it would have been easy for them to kill her and make it look like I did it."

Ethan laughed, drawing Gillian's gaze. "A guilty man always has excuses," he said. "Someone else is always to blame."

Kavanagh tightened his hands into fists. "In this case," he said, "someone else is. Someday I'm going to prove it."

Ethan ignored Kavanagh and kept his attention focused on Gillian. "Ask him why even his closest colleagues turned against him," he said. "Men who had trusted him with their lives. They were fully convinced of his guilt."

"Not all of them," Ross said. "There was pressure from above to get rid of me." He jerked a thumb in Ethan's direction. "Ask *him* why he wants you to believe I'm guilty. Ask him why he tried to deny that Toby is my son and then tried to buy me off."

Gillian spoke as Ethan gathered his answer. "I never asked you to lie for me, Ethan," she said.

"I have no regrets for attempting to interfere," Ethan said. "If deception had allowed me to find Toby and keep Kavanagh away from—"

"But it didn't work," Kavanagh said. "I tossed him out, and that's what the little pipsqueak doesn't like. Isn't that right, Warbrick? Or is it just that you can't stand the competition?"

Ethan looked him up and down. "There is no competition," he said. "Mrs. Delvaux has no interest in two-penny scoundrels."

With a swift, sharp motion Kavanagh started toward him. Gillian moved just as quickly, blocking Kavanagh's path.

"That's enough," she said, speaking in the same way she had to Toby minutes ago. "I have heard accusations, but no evidence to support them." She stared at Kavanagh. "If you had told me…" She gave her head an almost imperceptible shake. "It would have been better if you had been honest, Mr. Kavanagh."

Kavanagh was the first to look away. "I should have told you," he muttered. "But I didn't do it, Jill. And I didn't want Toby to think—"

"I think you had better leave," Gillian said.

Ethan swallowed his smile. Even if he had planted sufficient doubt in Gillian's mind, he must not assume victory too quickly. Gillian wasn't herself. Her judgment was still questionable.

"So you're just going to believe this guy?" Kavanagh asked, the muscles of his jaw so tight that the words emerged like bullets.

Her eyes turned cold. "Ethan Warbrick has been a friend for many years," she said. "He has never deceived me."

"What are you going to tell Toby?"

"I don't know."

Kavanagh spun on his heel and charged for the door. He stopped with his hand on the knob.

"You're too smart to make your decision based on one guy's claims, even if he is an 'old friend,'" Kavanagh said. "You'll want to get the whole truth, if only for Toby's sake. When you need it, you know where to find me."

He opened the door and strode into the corridor. For long moments after he had gone, Gillian stood facing the door.

"*Is* it true?" she asked finally.

Ethan thought better of approaching her. "He avoided trial only because of a technicality," he said.

"But he *didn't* go to trial. He wasn't found guilty."

"He wouldn't be the first criminal to escape justice."

She turned to look at him, her back pressed against the door. "You hate him. Why? Because he refused your bribe?"

"Don't be ridiculous, Gillian. He's hardly worth hating. But he must not be allowed to deceive you further. Whatever hold he has on you—"

"He has no hold on me."

The reply was too vehement. Ethan took a seat in one of the chairs. Gillian was disturbed, more so than he had seen her in a long while. As of course she must be, nearly losing her son and then being forced to deal with a man she had wisely rejected years ago.

As for what awaited her in England…

I will *protect you. We shall never be parted again.*

"Has he threatened you?" he asked. "Even if he were to attempt to make a legal claim on Toby, he would find no allies in this city."

"He hasn't threatened me." She walked away from the door, started toward the window and came to a stop, her gaze sweeping around the room as if she had lost something of importance. "He only wanted to see Toby. To make certain he was…" She inhaled deeply. "Toby was with him when I went to his apartment. He had already developed an attachment."

"But surely there can't be any question about the necessity of separating him from Kavanagh."

"Of course not." She drifted back to the sofa and sat down, poised, as always, but oddly distracted. "That would have been the case even had you not told me…" Suddenly her eyes focused on his face. "Whatever you believe, I cannot accept that Ross committed murder."

"How can you make such a claim, Gillian? Spending a single day with a man like Kavanagh is no basis for trust." A new, creeping suspicion formed a hard knot in his chest. "What did you do with him? Where did you go?"

"To an amusement park, and then to the home of his friends on Long Island."

"Friends? It is difficult to believe he has any left."

"One of them was a werewolf. I don't think he'd believe anything of what you've told me."

Ethan wanted to shake her. He pressed his hands against the arms of the chair. "Kavanagh clearly possesses a certain cleverness. Perhaps a few others have been taken in."

"Others such as myself?"

He leaned forward, holding her gaze. "It can't be that you still retain some affection for this man?"

She straightened, as if throwing off an intolerable weight. "You need have no fear for me. I am quite safe."

"Then we must make immediate plans to leave for England."

"I—I must think." She rose again and walked to the sideboard. Ethan had never seen her drink, yet she examined the bottles on display as if she considered them a real temptation. "Where is Hugh?"

The change of subject didn't please Ethan, but he sensed that she could not be pushed any further at the moment. "Your brother said that he was going out today when I spoke to him yesterday evening."

"Where?"

"He declined to say. Considering his tastes, he's likely to be making the rounds of the clubs and speakeasies."

"At this hour of the morning?"

"Many are open all day and night."

"Apparently *he* wasn't worried about Mr. Kavanagh."

"You know as well as I how little your brother can be relied upon."

Gillian seemed poised to argue, but it was only her reflexive desire to defend a member of her family. All her life she had tried to deny the Maitland men's fatal flaws: Sir Averil's vicious unpredictability and Hugh's utter fecklessness. She had protected Hugh since girlhood, accepting blame for his heedless pranks, never protesting when Sir Averil doted on his son and treated her as a possession of less value than his best Thoroughbred mare.

Hugh received all the credit for anything she accomplished. And he must on no account be treated as the overgrown child he was.

In time you will recognize the truth, Ethan thought. *You will see Hugh for the wastrel and poseur that he is. Then you will have no need to defend him ever again.*

"I must find him," Gillian said, oblivious. "Can you show me these clubs?"

"That would be impossible. There must be hundreds in this part of Manhattan alone." He stood. "We shall simply have to make arrangements without him."

But Gillian hardly seemed to be listening, her thoughts following their own troubled path. "I must find a way to explain things to Toby. He will not understand."

"Perhaps if I spoke to him…?"

She shook her head. "I must have more information. Ross— Mr. Kavanagh deserves the chance to properly defend himself."

"You can't see him again. You heard his excuses. He has no scruples, none whatsoever."

"Unless he is innocent."

Her stubbornness left Ethan seething. He had used every conceivable argument to convince her not to come to New York, but she had done so even against Sir Averil's wishes. The prospect of Toby in danger had overridden all her usual caution.

This reckless defiance was an aspect of Gillian's character that had remained almost entirely dormant under Sir Averil's rule, and it didn't please Ethan in the least. Of course, when she returned to her ordinary life and faced her father's displeasure, she would once again recognize that Ethan was her one true friend. The only one who could save her.

"If you need additional proof," he said, "I will provide it. There are men highly placed in the government of this city who will gladly speak to you on the subject of Kavanagh's guilt."

"Then we must stay in America a few more days."

"If that is your wish."

His reasonable tone had a salutary effect on Gillian's demeanor. "Yes," she said in a tone of relief. "Only a little while longer." She started toward the hall that led to the bedrooms. "If you will excuse me, I want to look in on Toby."

As soon as she was out of sight, Ethan let the mask slip. His lips pulled away from his teeth. He was no longer so certain that Gillian had not developed some bizarre attraction to Kavanagh. The American was little better than a savage, to be sure, but Gillian had made the mistake of falling for him once before.

Not that she would abandon her duty for romance. On the one occasion when Ethan had suggested that she and Toby leave Snowfell and accompany him to a place far beyond Sir Averil's reach, she had refused in a way that had warned him never to make such an offer again.

Not until she had no other choice but to accept it.

Ethan rose and was about to follow Gillian when the door to

the suite swung open and Hugh stumbled in, followed by a pair of ruffians with ill-fitting suits and the expressionless faces of professional enforcers.

Hugh half fell into the sofa, his breath still stinking of alcohol. One of the enforcers kicked the door closed, while the other circled the room, his nostrils flaring as he sniffed the air.

"Who are you?" Ethan demanded, slipping his hand inside his jacket. "Hugh, what is this about? Who are these men?"

"I can tell you that," Ross Kavanagh said, stepping into the room and facing the enforcers with a gun in his hand. "They're the pack's bullyboys, and Hugh just got on their bad side."

CHAPTER EIGHT

GILLIAN HEARD the commotion and spun toward the door of Toby's room. She caught the acrid smell of alcohol, combined with Hugh's distinctive scent and the unfamiliar odor of strangers. By the time she'd warned Toby to remain quiet and returned to the living room, Ross was crossing the threshold, his gun pointed unwaveringly at the intruders.

"You're disturbing the lady," he said as Ethan hurried toward Gillian. "What do you want, Rutger?"

The larger of the two strangers stepped away from Hugh, who was half-lying over the back of the couch, and faced Ross. "Look who we have here," he said. "The crooked cop." His sharp-featured face twisted in contempt. "I don't know what you're doing here, Kavanagh, but you'd better run while you still got a chance."

Gillian brushed past Ethan and went to Hugh, who was bone-pale and sported a rapidly darkening bruise on his cheek. He gave her a bleary-eyed look, groaned unintelligibly and closed his eyes.

Satisfied that he was relatively unharmed, she turned to the intruders. "In England," she said, "it is not considered polite to enter a private residence without knocking."

The man Ross had called Rutger glanced at his partner and grinned. "La-di-da. They breed 'em fancy overseas, don't they?"

"If you are representative of what they breed in America," Ethan said, moving up beside Gillian, "I fear for the future of your race."

It took perhaps five seconds before Rutger realized that he had been insulted. His eyes narrowed. "Get the kid, Jaime," he said.

Gillian was already halfway to Toby's room before she realized that the smaller stranger had gone after Hugh. Ross intercepted him, jammed the muzzle of his gun into Jaime's side and backed him away from the sofa.

"Gillian," he said, "stay back." He grabbed Hugh by one arm, heaved him up and pushed him in Gillian's direction. Rutger started after him.

"Stay put, Rutger, unless you want me to put a bullet in Jaime's breadbasket." Ross shifted, his legs slightly bent and his weight resting on the balls of his feet. "The lady wants to know what you're doing here."

Rutger worked his fists. "The Limey trespassed into our territory. We don't let outpack werewolves wander around Manhattan, especially when they come to make trouble."

Gillian glanced from Rutger's face to Ross's, aware that the explosive atmosphere was very close to igniting into violence. She set aside her fear and spoke with a calmness she hoped the intruders would accept as genuine.

"We did not come to America to cause trouble," she said, "nor to trespass on your territory. I am certain that my brother did not intend to offend you."

"Your brother should'a thought of that before he started making eyes at the pack leader's daughter," Rutger growled.

"Is that what this is about?" Ross asked with a derisive chuckle. "The kid made a pass at Ariana Sherrod?"

"It wasn't like that at all," Hugh said. "I was…at a club. This girl…she came up to me and asked where I came from. Said she could tell I was *loup-garou* and did I want to go somewhere where we could have a bit of fun." He swallowed, his face going slightly green. "I…went with her to a speakeasy. They were all werewolves there. Ariana and I…started to dance."

"He had his hands on her," Rutger snarled.

"And someone noticed that Hugh was not of the pack," Ross said, his lips curled in a sneer.

"I never…meant any harm," Hugh said, catching himself as he began to lose his balance. "Didn't know…werewolves here would be so uncivil."

"No outpack werewolf comes into Manhattan without the boss's permission," Rutger said. "We asked him who he was. He didn't cooperate until we persuaded him a little."

"I didn't…tell them anything," Hugh said, his expression crumpling like a child's. "I thought they were letting me go. They…followed me back to the hotel."

"Where we find Kavanagh acting like he's better than scum," Rutger said. He glanced at Gillian dismissively. "Looks like he had to go overseas to find a female who'd let him between her legs."

Gillian had heard crude talk before, among the soldiers whose pain and fear got the better of their tongues. But she had never been addressed in such a way by any stranger, human or werewolf. She opened her mouth, prepared to issue a scathing retort, when Ross crossed the room and backhanded Rutger across the face.

"I may be scum," he said as Rutger reeled away, "but no one talks to Mrs. Delvaux that way. No one." He whirled to confront Jaime as the other man drew his gun.

"Go ahead, belly-scraper. You'll have to shoot everybody in this room, and that'll bring everyone in this hotel down on your head. Mrs. Delvaux has connections in England and New York. You think I have it bad, just wait and see what they do to you if you harm a hair on her or her brother's head."

Rutger straightened, clutching his jaw. Gillian saw no sign that he had taken Ross's threat to heart, and Jaime appeared ready to open fire at any moment, in spite of the obvious dangers. Ethan, who had remained silent throughout the conflict, had made his way slowly across the room to the telephone table by the entrance to the hall.

He'll call the police, Gillian thought. But that would be disaster. Police involvement might lead to publicity she didn' want, awkward explanations, the possibility that Sir Averil woul hear of the incident. Any solution was better than that.

Even the one she found most difficult of all.

"No one's gonna care if you're dead, Kavanagh," Rutger said speaking over her thoughts. "As for the others, they're comin with us to see Sherrod. He'll know what to do with foreigner who think they can steal our females."

"You are not taking us anywhere," Gillian said, prepared to bluf as far as was necessary. "Mr. Kavanagh was quite correct. You wil find yourselves in serious trouble if you harm us in any way."

"That's right," Hugh said, his words no longer slurred. "Ou father, Sir Averil Maitland, knows a lot of people on both side of the Atlantic. People you don't want to tangle with."

Rutger laughed. "Sir Averil Maitland? Never heard of him."

"If your leader has a quarrel with us," Gillian said, "he ma present his case in a neutral location. But we shall not go any where with you, now or at any other time."

As she spoke, Ross had edged closer to her, positioned so tha he could shield Gillian and still manage a good shot at either o the American werewolves. "You heard the lady," he said. "I Sherrod wants to talk to her, he can pick up the phone. As fo me, I haven't got much to lose. Either of you try to use your gun one of you is going to be dead."

The next few seconds unfolded as if in a distorted movin; picture. Toby appeared at the entrance to the hall, crouched lov as if he hoped to remain unnoticed. Ethan picked up the tele phone receiver and began to speak in a rapid whisper. Jaime sav him and charged. Ross swung his gun toward Jaime and then back to Rutger as the bigger werewolf lunged toward Hugh.

For Gillian there was no question of which way to move. Sh spun and ran toward the bedrooms, catching Toby up in her arm as she went. There was a cry of pain from the sitting room, an the thump of a body hitting the floor. Gillian knew there was little chance now that the situation could be defused.

She set Toby down just inside his bedroom door, her heart thumping erratically in her chest.

"Who are those men?" he asked, trying to look over her shoulder. "They have guns!"

"Yes. And that is why, if you do not remain here, I shall not allow you to visit the ruins again for a month after the Convocation ends."

Much to her relief, Toby took the threat seriously. "Yes, Mother," he whispered. "What are you going to do?"

"Close your eyes, Toby."

He did as she commanded, his body pulled tight with real fear. Gillian closed her eyes, as well, preparing her body for the Change.

Ross had been correct when he'd confronted her at Oak Hollow. He'd guessed that she really didn't enjoy the Change. He couldn't know that she'd learned to think of the transformation as a test she had barely passed all those years ago when Sir Averil had stood over her, commanding her to become a wolf and prove her worthiness as a Maitland.

And Ross had also been right in that she only Changed when it was necessary to remind herself what she was, what she must always be…just like that time in London. But now it was different. Now it was a matter of life and death.

By the time the bitter thoughts had finished racing through her mind, she had made the necessary mental preparations. She kicked off her shoes and tore off her dress and chemise, leaving them and in a heap on the bedroom floor with her undergarments. Naked, she called upon the Change and let the transformation take her. She leaped into the hall on four feet and ran into the sitting room.

Ross was on the floor, struggling with Rutger for possession of a gun. Gillian ploughed into Rutger, seized his wrist in her jaws and ground down with her teeth until he shrieked and dropped the weapon. Ross wasted no time in snatching it up. He paused for a fraction of a second to take in Gillian's altered appearance and then punched Rutger in the face as he tried to rise.

Gillian had already begun to move again, her muscles working like pistons beneath her fur. Ethan lay slumped against the telephone table, apparently unconscious. Jaime was facing Hugh, who had raised his fists in a belated attempt to fight. He glimpsed Gillian over Jaime's shoulder, and his eyes widened in astonishment.

Jaime spun and took aim as Gillian sprang at his chest. The bullet was never fired. Ross slammed into Jaime and carried him hard against the wall. Gillian landed lightly, turned back to Rutger and found him on his knees, struggling to tear off his clothing. She knocked him over and straddled him. Her snarl convinced him to abandon any attempts to Change.

The silence was sudden and complete, broken only by Rutger's harsh breathing. Hugh sank onto the sofa, his body shaking. Ross released his hold on Jaime's shoulders, letting the unconscious man slide down to the floor. He left Jaime where he lay and knelt beside Ethan.

"He's out, but he'll be all right," Ross said. He glanced at Gillian and quickly looked away. "Hugh, you're going to help me with these two bums."

Hugh took hold of himself. "What—what do you want me to do?"

"I'm going to find a car and drive them someplace where they'll stay out of trouble for a couple of days. While I'm gone, you're going to find the next ship leaving for England and make sure all of you are on it."

A peculiar weakness coursed through Gillian's limbs when she heard his words. Rutger stirred. She placed both forepaws on his chest.

Ross quickly collected both the enforcers' weapons. "Do you know how to shoot one of these?" he asked. Hugh nodded, licking his lips. "Okay. I'm leaving one with you. Don't use it unless it's absolutely necessary. It's a miracle no one has come banging on the door already. If anyone shows up, you'd better have a good excuse handy."

"I…can't kill…"

"Aim for the leg, then call the police. They know these men as enforcers, even if most of 'em don't realize what else they are. It isn't good for business when the mobs scare off rich foreign tourists. The cops will take your word over Rutger's. Just stick as close to the truth as possible."

Hugh reluctantly took the gun Ross handed to him. "What about Gilly?" he asked. "You should get her and Toby away from here."

Hugh's burst of courage was genuine, Gillian knew, but she couldn't leave Hugh alone with the American pack members while Ethan was unconscious. She growled and shook her head.

"I'll take Toby to the concierge," Ross said. He entered the bedroom hall and returned a few minutes later with Toby, who had put on a new suit.

"Mother?" Toby said, staring around the room with avid interest.

"You go with Mr. Kavanagh," Hugh said. "Your mother will be fine."

"Come on, kid," Ross said. As he hustled Toby out the door, Gillian could hear her son's voice receding down the outer corridor. "Did Mother really fight?"

Gillian laid her ears flat against her head. She held her position, aware that any slight shift in her body might give Rutger some small encouragement to resist. Hugh got up, the gun in his hand, and faced the wall where Jaime still lay unmoving. Ethan's hand twitched. He groaned and tried to pull himself up. Hugh ignored him.

"Gillian," Ethan croaked.

"She's here," Hugh said. "She can't talk right now."

Ethan pushed himself up against the wall, his gaze traveling from Hugh to Jaime and then to Gillian.

"Is Toby all right?" he asked.

"He went with Kavanagh," Hugh said.

"With Kavanagh?" Ethan clawed his way to his feet, grunting with the effort. "Are you mad? Did it ever occur to you—" He bent over, caught his breath and continued with an effort. "This could all have been a ploy by Kavanagh to take Toby. These men—"

"Oh, stuff it, Warbrick," Hugh said. "It's obvious these hooligans despise Kavanagh."

Ethan flushed, and for a moment he looked at Hugh as if he would have liked to knock him down. Unable to speak to either of them, Gillian growled again. Hugh examined his gun, and Ethan became intent on rubbing a sore spot on his jaw.

The minutes crept by very slowly. A werewolf's thoughts were often not as coherent in wolf shape as they were when she walked as human, but Gillian began to wonder if Ethan could be right. What if these men had been working with Ross? If he'd believed that she had condemned him outright because of Ethan's accusations…

"I'm calling the police," Ethan said. He reached for the receiver. Just then the door opened and Ross walked in. He set the valise he was carrying down on the carpet and crouched beside it, removing what appeared to be metal shackles. Rutger tensed; Gillian lowered her muzzle and bared her teeth in his face.

Neither Hugh nor Ethan spoke as Ross took one set of shackles and walked over to Jaime, flipped him onto his back and closed the thick metal cuffs around the enforcer's wrists. Rutger was less cooperative, but Hugh pointed his gun at the man's chest while Ross locked the cuffs. When Rutger began to mutter threats, Ross pulled a handkerchief from his pocket and jammed it into the enforcer's mouth.

"That'll hold 'em as long as necessary," Ross said, sitting back. "Now we just have to get them out to the street."

Hugh shifted his grip on the gun. "You should take someone with you…wherever you're taking *them*."

Gillian didn't wait for Ross's reply. She trotted into the hall and then returned to her own room to Change. She dressed hastily in her most practical skirt and blouse, and hurried to join the men.

"I'll go with Ross," she said, interrupting Ethan in midargument.

Ross stared at her, a wariness in his eyes that hadn't been there a few hours before. "Do you really want to go anywhere with a guy who might have murdered someone?" he asked.

"Is it not a point of both British and American law that one is innocent until proven guilty?"

He laughed. "Tell that to your friend and half of Manhattan."

"The pack's quarrel is with my family. Resolving it is our responsibility."

"*You* can't resolve it. You should get out of New York as soon as possible."

Gillian ignored him. "Hugh," she said, catching her brother's eye, "while I'm gone you will collect Toby, check out of this hotel and find another place to stay until we can make the arrangements for our return to England."

"Utter folly," Ethan said, glaring at Ross. "Kavanagh's interference has only made the situation worse. Let *him* deal with his own kind."

"It's my fault," Hugh said, his head sunk between his shoulders. "If it would do any good…I could try talking to this Sherrod…."

"It is not your fault, Hugh, if the American pack prefers barbarism to reason," Gillian said impatiently. "If not for Toby, I would…" She stopped, hardly recognizing the furious pattern of images in her mind. "Would you please pack Toby's things and have them taken down? I will see that my trunk is ready before I leave with Mr. Kavanagh. Leave a note with the concierge to let me know where you have gone."

"Gillian—" Ross and Ethan said simultaneously.

"There has been enough discussion. Mr. Kavanagh, you said you had a means of getting these men out of the hotel?"

Ross gave her a long, speculative look, nodded and left the

suite. He reappeared in the doorway with a large food trolley draped with a white tablecloth. He beckoned to Hugh and spoke to him softly. Hugh nodded, and together they lifted the half-conscious Jaime and pushed him onto the hidden lower shelf of the cart, adjusting his body so that he was completely concealed by the cloth.

Rutger presented a more thorny problem, but Ross was unfazed. He hauled the enforcer to his feet, shook out a white jacket folded on top of the cart and draped it over Rutger's overly broad shoulders.

"You're going to push the cart," he told Rutger. "I'll be right behind you."

The other werewolf bared his teeth around the gag. "You've gone too far, Kavanagh," he mumbled. "The pack will hunt you down."

"Maybe. But I wouldn't boast about that if I were you. I could decide to kill you, instead, and dump your body in the river." He shoved the gag deeper into Rutger's mouth and positioned the man behind the cart, draping a white towel over his hands to conceal the cuffs. "Come on."

He opened the door to the outer corridor and forced Rutger to precede him. Gillian followed. At the end of the corridor Ross pushed the elevator button and waited with the muzzle of his gun pressed into Rutger's back. When the lift doors opened, he put his hand on Rutger's shoulder, as if they'd been having a pleasant conversation, and herded the enforcer into the elevator. The boy running it looked hard at Rutger's face and then at Ross, as if he suspected something was amiss.

Gillian tucked her arm through the crook of Ross's elbow. "I hope the management appreciates the quality of their employees and rewards this man accordingly," she said, smiling brightly at Rutger.

"You're right, sweetheart," Ross said, beaming at her like a doting husband. "With us standing right beside him, they're bound to give him what he deserves."

The elevator boy yawned. He paid no attention when they reached the ground floor and the cart trundled out. Ross detached himself from Gillian without a word. Instead of continuing across the lobby, he guided Rutger down a side corridor, which passed several service doors and ended at another that, as evidenced by the heightened smells of hot concrete and petrol fumes, led outside. It opened onto a stifling alley cluttered with crates and refuse.

Ross gestured for Gillian to back away, his weapon still fixed on Rutger. He flipped back the tablecloth and peered at the shelf underneath.

"Jaime's still out of commission," he said. "You stay here, Mrs. Delvaux." He grabbed Rutger by the collar and dragged him toward the harsh daylight of the open street. A few minutes later he returned and took the unresisting Jaime from the bottom of the cart. Gillian followed.

A battered automobile of nondescript design was waiting by the kerb. "I wasn't aware that you owned a motor car," Gillian said.

"I don't. I'm just borrowing this one."

Stealing, he meant, though Gillian wasn't of a mind to object. She smelled no humans nearby, perhaps because the heat had discouraged them from leaving the shelter of the nearby buildings. There were no witnesses as Ross heaved Jaime into the backseat.

"Rutger's in the trunk," he told Gillian. "He'll be uncomfortable for a while, but he'll survive." He opened the passenger door. "If you're still determined to come with me…"

"I am." She suddenly found herself shaking in belated reaction to what had happened in the hotel room. She was certain that Hugh, in spite of his irresponsible behavior, would carry through with locating a new hotel for the brief remainder of their visit. Ethan would help make sure of that. But she was worried about what Toby had seen and heard. He'd never been exposed to violence before, and now he'd seen werewolves behaving like common criminals.

Of course, *she* had known, from witnessing her own father's example, that werewolves could be as cruel as humans. At the same time, she had come to accept—in spite of her own reluctance to Change—her father's belief that werewolves were naturally superior to humans in every way. She had believed that by containing a real beast within themselves they were far more capable of controlling their primitive natures than humans, who so often denied that they possessed any bestial side at all.

And yet…she could not deny that this Change, unlike all the others that had gone before, had been different for her. There had been a certain glory in battling the American mobsters, in feeling the flow of lupine strength in her body and the power to face them on their own terms. It was what she might have felt from the time she had first Changed as a girl. What she had not *permitted* herself to feel.

Savagery had been very close to the surface. Yet she still didn't dare believe that the behavior of the American werewolves—or her own—changed the fact that the majority of *loups-garous* were civilized beings ruled by reason and not merely aggressive instinct.

Even if she did have the smallest uncertainty on that score, this was no time to give Toby doubts about his werewolf blood.

Soon we will be gone. Today's incidents made that a necessity, one that even Ross recognized. Gillian would no longer be compelled to choose between trusting Ross and protecting Toby.

Ross isn't a murderer. If I believed he was, I would not be going with him now.

But by going with him now, she was making certain that he had no opportunity to abduct Toby, a possibility she had ceased considering seriously in the wake of Ross's denials. At least not until Ethan had reawakened the suspicion in her mind.

"Get in," Ross said. "We don't have any time to lose."

She slid into the passenger seat. Ross started the engine and pulled away from the kerb. He was silent as he maneuvered through the morning traffic, driving north until the maze of buildings began to thin and patches of open space appeared amid the building sites where new housing was being constructed for New York's ever-expanding population.

"I'm sorry," he said quietly.

Gillian watched a wine-colored Duesenberg turn the corner ahead of them. "It was not your fault," she said.

"Maybe I didn't bring the pack down on your heads, but I should have remembered that they've turned even more paranoid since Sherrod took over. I should have told you—" He broke off, negotiating a pothole in the road. "I should have told you to leave as soon as you showed up looking for Toby."

Gillian kept her agreement to herself. "Is such violence typical of American packs?"

"They've always been highly territorial, but Sherrod's more openly aggressive than the previous leader. There was a lot of confusion after Garret Sloan fled New York in disgrace, and Sherrod's taken advantage of people's fears and the need for strong leadership to coordinate the pack's bootlegging operation." Ross shifted gears, and the car groaned in protest. "Still, it didn't occur to me that Hugh would find a way to run afoul of them so quickly."

You wouldn't say so if you knew Hugh as well as I do, she thought. But he *didn't* know Hugh. And he never would. "Why aren't the police able to control them?"

"They're only one of several gangs competing for the liquor trade. There are vampires involved, as well. It's true that some cops are aware of the nonhumans in the city, but werewolves can pay bribes just as well as the next gang, and there are plenty of guys willing to take the money. It can easily be fatal taking on lawbreakers who are twice as strong and fast as you are."

"Then the city is virtually lawless."

He laughed, the sound like a saw scraping wood. "Some of us actually tried to keep that from happening."

"You told Toby you are not a member of the pack. How did you remain a free agent?"

"It wasn't because of the murder, if that's what you're thinking," he said. "If I'd been one of them, they would have taken action to make sure that the pack couldn't be tied to the girl's death. But I was persona non grata a long time before that. Even if I wasn't a cop…" His fingers tightened on the steering wheel. "I'm something worse—a cop who has werewolf blood, but not quite enough of it."

Gillian sank into her seat. So even the criminal American werewolves found it necessary to reject one whose mixed blood marked him as an outsider. Ross had been denied the fellowship of other *loups-garous,* no matter how crude they might be, yet because of the accusations leveled against him, he had also been ejected from the human society of which he had been a productive member. He could rely only on the friendship of other outcasts, such as the Durants.

Outcasts who cared nothing for their status as exiles among their own people. Griffin and Allegra Durant were perfectly content with each other. They had remarkable courage. Courage Gillian would never possess.

"They didn't much like me," Ross went on, unaware of the grim thoughts marching through her mind. "But the pack leaders and I had a sort of understanding. There were guys on the force I could count on for backup when it was necessary to deal with the pack, but most of those guys aren't talking to me anymore. That's why you've got to get out of the city."

The landscape had opened up into a vista of farms, fields and woodland, but Gillian hardly saw it. "What about you?" she asked. "What will the pack do once they know of your part in the fight?"

He shrugged. "I'll be all right. I can get out of town anytime, and Sherrod isn't going to have me followed over one fight with his enforcers." He stretched, a casual movement that wouldn't have convinced a child in leading strings. "Maybe I'll go out to California, get a look at those movie stars over in Hollywood."

California. The other side of the world from England. Ross really was prepared to let Toby go with no thought of himself.

"I'm sorry that Toby had to find out about the murder," he said. "I knew it was a risk. I just didn't think…"

Gillian heard his shame in the silence, feeling it as if it were her own. "I'm certain that Toby believes in your innocence."

"And you?" He didn't wait for her answer. "Even if you do, it's not enough. Not for either of us. Once you and Toby are back in England, you'll be away from the rumors and gossip. No one ever has to know he's my son."

Tears filled Gillian's eyes. "Ross…"

"Just promise me that he'll never have to be ashamed of his human blood." He turned to stare at her. "Promise me, Jill."

The tears spilled over. "I will never stop loving him," she said.

Whatever he thought of her answer, Ross said no more. He continued to drive for another hour and then pulled onto a smaller road that led into the countryside. After another few miles and several narrow dirt roads, Ross drove up to a ramshackle farmhouse, obviously long abandoned.

"We'll leave Rutger and Jaime here," he said. "I'll chain them up, but leave water within reach. Once you're gone, I'll let Sherrod know where they are."

"And you will be arranging your own departure from New York once we return to the city," she said.

He dropped his hands from the steering wheel and set the brake. "Do you care so much about what happens to me, Jill?"

"I…I want you to be safe."

"No one's ever completely safe. The War taught us that."

Gillian's reply was interrupted by a loud moan from the backseat and banging from the trunk.

"The natives are restless," Ross said. He got out of the automobile, opened the back door and pulled Jaime out. The enforcer's eyes were half-open, but he was still far from capable of much resistance. Ross half carried him to the farmhouse porch and kicked the door open. While he was inside, Gillian left the car and wandered to the rickety fence that divided the overgrown yard from the field beyond.

No one's ever completely safe. He wasn't talking only about himself. He'd implied before that Toby couldn't be protected forever, and he already had some notion of the challenges the boy had yet to face in England. Yet when it came to Toby's well-being, he was willing to put their son entirely in her hands, subject to her judgment.

Gillian touched her lips. Had it been only last night that he'd kissed her? She'd found it so easy to give in, to let old desires reawaken. But then, after she'd learned of the accusations against him, she'd actually asked herself if Ross's tenderness was simply a trick to make her vulnerable.

She didn't believe that any longer, no more than she believed Ethan's wild surmise about Ross working with the enforcers. No, Ross's kiss had been genuine, just as his concern was genuine. As fantastic as it seemed, he still found her desirable. As she did him.

Desire wasn't enough, though. It hadn't been twelve years ago, and it wasn't now. But it was real. And Gillian knew she would never find it with any other man as long as she lived, no matter how pure his werewolf blood.

Ross came out of the farmhouse, glanced toward Gillian and continued on toward the car. He opened the boot, grabbed a cursing Rutger by the collar and lifted him out. He returned five minutes later.

"It's done," he said. His eyes narrowed. "Are you all right?"

"Yes."

He drew closer. "Of course you're not all right. You had to fight because I couldn't handle a couple of lousy belly-scrapers."

How could she tell him of the forbidden exhilaration she'd felt during the fight?

"I wasn't harmed," she said.

"But it must have been hard for you." He set his hands gently on her shoulders. "You've never had to do anything like that before, have you?"

"No." She tried desperately not to feel the warmth of Ross's hands, to smell his spicy masculine scent. "There have been no such altercations at Snowfell."

As soon as she had spoken, she thought of the War and what Ross had endured. But he understood what she meant. He squeezed her arms gently. "You were good, Jill. If I had a right to be proud of you, I'd..." He smiled sadly and let his hands fall. "Today you more than proved that you can take care of yourself and Toby."

His words had a dreadful ring of finality about them. Ross really was letting them go. She had what she'd thought she wanted. She and Toby would return to England and resume the life that was expected of them. And Ross...

Ross would be alone.

"Please," she whispered. "Let's leave this place."

He searched her eyes for a moment longer, then led the way back to the automobile, holding the passenger door open for her. He retraced the path he had taken to the farmhouse, driving much more slowly than necessary. It was almost as if he wanted to delay the inevitable farewells.

Gillian was incapable of saying anything to fill the silence. She was imagining herself, Toby and Hugh standing at the railing of a ship bound for England, watching as Ross's lean, solitary figure vanished in the distance. Toby would be trying manfully not to cry. She would permit herself to feel nothing, knowing that there had never been any hope of an outcome other than this. And Ethan would turn to her, his expression sympathetic, but his eyes shining with satisfaction.

"Stop," she said.

Ross glanced at her, his face drawn and pale. "What?"

"Stop the car."

He slowed and pulled to the side of the road. "What's wrong?" he asked as he set the brake. "Gillian, what—"

She reached across the seat, seized his hand and pulled him toward her. His mouth was half open to ask another question when she pressed her lips to his.

CHAPTER NINE

ROSS RESPONDED ARDENTLY, taking her in his arms and deepening the kiss. Gillian recognized the desperation in his touch, for she was possessed by the same urgency. She welcomed the thrust of his tongue, the erotic warmth that flowed through her body as his hands stroked her back and slid beneath her blouse.

Then he paused, his breathing as rapid and hoarse as her own. "Gillian," he said, resting his face in the hollow of her shoulder. "Why?"

The last thing she wanted now was words. But she couldn't mislead him, not even if the price was his rejection.

"Just once," she whispered, glorying in the earthy scent of his thick brown hair. "Just once before we go."

He went very still, and she could feel the strength of his emotions in the subtle tension of the muscles flexing beneath his skin. "I haven't got any protection," he said.

It was like the first time all over again. Twelve years ago she'd been hardly more than a girl, pretending a confidence she seldom felt, still ignorant in so many ways. She'd told Ross then that it didn't matter, that nothing would happen. She'd been wrong.

But she was no longer quite so ignorant about the workings of her own body. "I'm not…I'm not fertile right now," she said.

He was so quiet that she was certain she had offended him. And why shouldn't he be offended? She had just told him that she wanted him because there was no possibility of her becoming pregnant. No possibility of this impulsive act begetting anything but an hour of mutual pleasure.

She pulled away. "I'm sorry," she said. "I've made a mistake."

He sighed, his breath curling along the nape of her neck. "No," he said. "There's no mistake."

He released her, turned around in his seat and opened the door. His arms were strong and sure as he lifted her from the car and carried her away from the road.

Gillian closed her eyes and clung to his shoulders. Though she had given no thought to where they were, it seemed that fate had chosen an ideal place for lovemaking. There was neither sound nor smell of any other vehicle in the vicinity. She could hear the burble of a brook and the sigh of a breeze in a thick stand of trees; the fragrance of tall grass and rich, loamy earth eased the last of her reservations.

This was right. This would be a time out of time, a sliver of sweet memory to be preserved when nothing else was left.

Ross carried her to a sheltered area, a small clearing where the trees and shrubbery formed a barrier that would hide them from any possible observers. He let her down gently and knelt beside her, such a strange combination of hunger and bewilderment in his eyes that she was afraid he would ask her if she was quite sure she wanted this.

Blessedly, he didn't. He simply looked at her for a long time, his gaze drifting from her face and slowly down her body, undressing her thoroughly before he so much as touched her clothing. She felt hot and cold by turns, and she became very wet between her thighs, a condition that had become familiar to her during the past hours.

Ross leaned over her and kissed her, featherlight, undemanding. She lifted her arms and locked them around his neck, pulling him down. Still he would not let himself go; despite his initial response in the car, part of him held back, treating her as if she were one of her mother's porcelain figurines, gathering dust in cupboards that had not been opened since Gillian's childhood.

And she *was* just like those figurines. No one had taken her out of her cupboard since she had been with Ross in London, though he didn't know it. And she couldn't tell him.

She pressed her lips harder against his, and after a moment he yielded, slipping his tongue inside. She took it gladly, imagining what was soon to come. He rested his weight on his hands on either side of her shoulders, barely grazing the tips of her breasts with his chest. Even that slight contact brought her nipples to aching peaks. Everything they had done in London exploded into her memory in a burst of light and lust.

His lips left hers, brushing her cheeks and teasing the lobe of her ear. He suckled ever so gently, tugging, awakening a sympathetic response in her nipples.

"Ross," she whispered.

He withdrew. His face was flushed, his eyes more than a little dazed.

"Touch me," she said. "*Touch* me."

He rolled onto his side, watching her face as he rested his palm just above her breasts. Her heart felt as if it would leap right into his hand. He teased loose the uppermost button of her blouse and parted the flimsy fabric. His fingers slid into the gap and traced tiny circles, sending wild shivers along the length of her spine.

He was not so hesitant after that. He undid one button and then another, discovering the simple bandeau brassiere that supported her small breasts. It was not particularly sheer or dripping with lace or other fashionable embellishments, but Ross seemed fascinated. He grazed the silk covering one nipple with his fingertip. She arched and gasped.

"Gillian," he said, one word to encompass everything they both were feeling. Then he lowered his head and closed his mouth over the silk, wetting it, suckling her without touching flesh.

She bore with the preliminaries for all of a minute and then pushed him away so that she could undo the rest of the buttons. Ross lifted her and slipped the blouse back over her shoulders. The bandeau came off just as easily. Gillian shivered as the breeze, warm though it was, played over her skin.

The breeze was not to have its way. Ross eased her back down and began to stroke her breasts, the calluses on his finger-tips only heightening the erotic sensation. She bit her lip and closed her eyes.

"Am I…am I too rough?" he asked.

In answer, she took his wrist and pressed his palm over her right breast. "It isn't enough," she whispered.

He didn't force her to explain. He bent over her and flicked his tongue over the peak of her nipple. Pleasure radiated outward to every point of her body, and a rush of warmth soaked her bloomers. She tilted her head back, breathing deeply as he drew her nipple into his mouth and suckled…again, so gently, so carefully.

But perhaps that was as it should be. She was sure she could take him, even after so long, but it would be better if…

Thought became meaningless as he sucked more vigorously, moving from one breast to the other, until both were thoroughly tender and the slightest touch set her gasping. She was so lost in sensation that she moved more by instinct than thought when he reached lower and unhooked her skirt. He slipped it down over her hips, leaving her bloomers, garters and stockings the only barriers between him and her naked flesh.

Her imagination was vivid enough, but even memory could not anticipate the glide of his fingers as they slid inside her bloomers and found the slick wetness beneath.

The training of a lifetime urged her to close her legs tightly and forbid him entrance. Another instinct, far stronger, moaned approval. He stroked the swollen lips, running his fingers up and down the cleft without probing deeper. It was the sweetest torment, unbearable excitement.

Ross made a soft exclamation that Gillian only half understood. "I'd forgotten how wet you were," he whispered. His fingers ventured deeper, sliding over the swollen nub that could bring so much ecstasy. She whimpered. He pinched the nub and released, stroked and withdrew. She began to shudder.

It was coming too soon. She didn't want it, not this way, not with him still outside her. Even when he found her entrance and slid his finger into it, it wasn't what she wanted.

"Ross," she gasped.

"You're tight," he said. "So tight."

"I…I want to feel…"

His finger circled and circled. "There couldn't have been many others," he said, so deep in his throat that no human would ever had heard.

"There have…been no others."

He stopped, frozen by feelings she could well imagine. Relief that there hadn't been dozens of lovers to comfort her in her widowhood, as if he really had believed she could have been such a shameless creature. As if she could ever have wanted anyone else.

She began to roll away. He reached over and turned her toward him again, kissed her lips and forehead, and began the caresses all over again. Then he was removing her bloomers and his warm breath was where his fingers had been.

It was new, what he did to her then. That time in London had been a miracle, but nothing had been totally strange to her; even she, isolated at Snowfell, had known the basic facts of sexual intercourse.

This, though…this was both frightening and wonderful, shockingly daring and liberating all at the same time. His mouth pressed against her, and then his tongue slid over the same moist, swollen flesh his fingers had stroked. She couldn't stop the moans of pleasure as he flicked his tongue up and down, licking up the wetness with relish, thrusting his tongue inside until she could think only of feeling his hardness filling her to the brim.

She didn't have to find the words. When he paused, it was

only to remove his own clothing and lie naked beside her. She opened her eyes to look at him, wondering how much he had changed. Of course he was older; there were new lines on his body, a faded scar or two that must have marked major wounds he couldn't heal without the benefit of the Change, a thickness of muscle gained over years of vigorous physical activity. He was no Greek god, but he was astonishingly beautiful.

And below…

There had been little to compare him with in London, though she had seen plenty of injured and recovering soldiers stripped of their clothing for treatment. Nevertheless, she knew his "cock," as the common soldiers liked to call it, was impressive. It was very hard, ridged beneath and smooth at the top.

Shyly, carefully, she reached down to touch it. He went rigid and blew out his breath in a sharp gust of surprise.

"Show me," she whispered.

But what he had begun was inexorable and not to be delayed for his pleasure alone. He kissed every part of her, starting with her lips and working down to the place he had already so thoroughly explored. She parted her thighs, the emptiness so vast that she could scarcely bear it another second. Emptiness she had refused to acknowledge year by year, pretending such needs didn't exist.

Ross understood those needs. He raised himself onto his arms and crouched over her, his hips above the cradle of her spread thighs.

"I don't want to hurt you," he said hoarsely.

She took his face between her palms and forced him to meet her gaze. "You could never hurt me. Never."

He believed her. With infinite care he eased down, the head of his cock just grazing her wetness, hot and full. When he entered, it was like a homecoming, a fulfillment of dreams she had never held long enough to discard.

The rhythm was gentle at first, testing her readiness. "So

tight," he murmured, leaning down to kiss the corner of her mouth. "Gillian…"

Then he said no more. He tilted back his head and moved more quickly, gliding in and out more forcefully, but never so hard as to cause her anything but the utmost pleasure. She found herself moving with him, arching into his thrusts, joining a dance whose steps she had practiced only once before. The ecstatic tension continued to build and build as Ross's motions grew more urgent. Gillian knew it was nearly over, and she didn't want it to be. She tried to hold him inside. He paused, breathing hard, and then thrust almost violently, shuddering as he reached his completion.

Gillian wasn't far behind. Her hips lifted, and she cried out, waves of indescribable sensation pulsing outward from her core.

Ross withdrew and rolled onto his side, one arm draped possessively over her waist. He stared up at the rustling leaves overhead.

Little by little, as the incredible pleasure faded, Gillian remembered where they were. Not in London, when she had still held on to foolish dreams by the tips of her fingers. Not Snowfell, forbidden to Ross for all time. Just a small quiet grove by an American roadside, apt to vanish like some fairy realm of ancient legend.

She lay quiet and still, hoping that Ross wouldn't speak and ruin the spell that remained. His arm lay heavy on her skin, and his breathing slowed into the cadence of sleep. She turned her head to look at his face. So peaceful now, the harsh lines of experience and adversity so gentled that she could almost recognize the boy he had been.

But the memory was too painful, and suddenly she felt trapped. She lifted his hand from her waist, trying to forget the joy its skillful touch had brought her, and laid his arm at his side. He didn't hear her as she collected her clothing and put them on, smoothing the rumples and becoming Sir Averil's daughter once more.

LIKE ALL good things, the dream had to end.

Ross opened his eyes. The canopy of summer trees whispered

overhead, and the bees went on about their business in the nearby meadow. Nothing had changed except the angle of the sun and the hour displayed on his battered wristwatch.

Gillian was gone. Oh, not far…he could still smell her warm skin and the lingering traces of their passion. She was just out of sight—and forever beyond his grasp.

He got up and reached for the drawers and trousers he'd tossed over a nearby shrub. Gillian's clothes no longer lay where she had left them. Ross put on his shirt, leaving the buttons undone, and went to find her.

She was standing beside the creek, fully dressed in her conservative serge skirt, blouse and flat-heeled pumps. It was evident to Ross that she had done more than simply put on her clothes; she had also cast off the wild, uninhibited Gillian who had so willingly shared her most intimate secrets with a disgraced ex-cop. A cop who'd been stupid enough to hope for what could never be.

She met his gaze, her expression unreadable even to his experienced eyes. "We should go back," she said.

And that was it. No hesitation, no emotion, just carry on as if nothing had happened. Ross despised himself for wanting more.

"You should have woken me up," he said.

"There was no need. I'm certain that Hugh and Ethan will have relocated by the time we return to Manhattan."

"Yeah." Ross turned away and buttoned his shirt, shaking with unreasoning anger. "I'll get my shoes."

She remained behind as he returned to the glade and pulled on his socks, shoes and jacket. He stuffed his tie in his trouser pocket and sniffed out his hat, which he'd flung several yards away in a fit of abandon. He jammed the hat on his head and returned to the creek. The faint tracks of a woman's shoes led away from the soft bank toward the road.

The car was hot after sitting for over an hour in the summer sun, but Gillian didn't seem to notice. She got in before Ross could move to open the passenger door and waited like a proper English schoolgirl while he started the engine. There was no conversation during the drive back to Manhattan. Ross parked on a side street near the Roosevelt. It was well past noon now, and the city was suffused with the heavy, stifling humidity of a midsummer heat wave.

Gillian made no move to get out of the car. She no longer seemed quite so detached as she had an hour ago. Ross knew she was about to say something difficult.

"I have so much to thank you for," she began, her voice very low. "You could have made our time here very unpleasant if you chose to do so. Instead, you have put Toby's welfare above any quarrel you have with me."

Ross stared through the windshield at the sun-baked street. "Yeah. I've done one helluva job."

She glanced in his direction, her eyes focused on a point beyond his shoulder. "Please, Ross. Don't hold yourself responsible. I would prefer that we…" She paused, her slender fingers tensing in her lap. "I would like to think that we may part as friends."

Friends. That was a good one. If she could look back on what they'd just done and think that was something that happened between *friends*…

"Do you want to shake on that, Mrs. Delvaux?" he asked, unable to keep the bitterness from his voice.

She didn't rise to the bait. "I don't expect you to forget what occurred in London," she said. "Nor do I deny that I was wrong to deceive you about Toby. But I shall assure him that I fully share his belief in your innocence."

"Even if Warbrick keeps insisting I'm a killer?"

She finally looked at him. "If I ask him to cease his accusations, he will."

The thought of that smug, sanctimonious face gave Ross a

solid target for his anger. "I wouldn't rely on that guy too much, if I were you. He kept pretty clear of the fight when Sherrod's men showed up."

"He is no more accustomed to such hostilities than I am."

"And since he's only human, it was convenient for him to decide that you could handle other werewolves better than he could."

"You may have reason to dislike Lord Warbrick, but you will not be compelled to bear his company much longer."

Ross clenched his teeth, feeling as helpless as he had when they'd come to arrest him nearly a year ago. He'd met Warbrick only twice, yet his instincts—wolf and cop both—were humming with the conviction that the Englishman couldn't be trusted. And he had not one shred of evidence to support his certainty.

The guy hates me, but not because he thinks I'm a threat to Gillian. He thinks I'm a threat to his chances with her.

Didn't he know she would never marry a human? Or was he after the favors Ross had twice been granted? But if they were such good friends, the viscount had to know that no amount of devotion on his part would sway her from the life she'd chosen.

Ross realized he still knew next to nothing about Gillian's life at Snowfell, except what little Toby had told him. Nor did he know what plans she had for Toby, other than her determination to see the kid prove he was a real werewolf.

He'd made a start on an interrogation at Coney Island, but events there and in the hotel room afterward had interrupted his plans. Now it was too late.

The click of a door handle brought Ross up out of his thoughts. Gillian had obviously taken his silence to mean that their conversation was over.

Ross cursed, got out of the car and followed her. She stopped at the corner of Madison Avenue.

"Perhaps we had better part here," she said. She offered her hand. "Thank you, Ross. I shall not forget what you've done."

He held on to her hand even after she tried to withdraw it. *Don't go,* a voice inside him begged. *Stay with me.*

But he didn't speak the words. He didn't speak because he knew he had nothing to offer Gillian or Toby, nothing but a ruined reputation, an empty wallet and the contempt of the pack.

Except those weren't the real reasons at all. He wouldn't ask because one roll in the hay didn't make him any more a werewolf than he'd been before.

He let go of Gillian's hand. "I'll wait here while you check at the desk for messages. If Hugh did what he was supposed to do, I'll leave." He fished in his pocket for his wallet and withdrew a dog-eared card, the last he'd preserved from his time on the force. He jotted a number on the back. "Here's my number. Call if anything goes wrong, or if you hear from the pack."

She took the card between her fingertips. "Thank you," she repeated. She stared at the card as if it had been handed to her by a stranger. "Goodbye, Ross."

Then she was walking away, and he was standing on the blazing sidewalk like a boxer who'd just taken a rabbit punch to the head. Gillian didn't look back. Finding his legs again, Ross went as far as the hotel entrance and waited. A few minutes later a bellboy emerged and approached him.

"Mr. Kavanagh?" he said. Without waiting for confirmation, he handed Ross a folded piece of paper. "Compliments of Mrs. Delvaux."

Ross unfolded the paper. *All is well,* the note said in Gillian's crisp, neat handwriting. Ross turned the paper over. Nothing else. There was no more to say.

Ross crumpled the paper in his fist and shoved it in his pocket.

"Is there a return message, sir?" the bellboy asked.

The handful of coins in Ross's pocket felt as light as a wad of cotton next to the weight of Gillian's final words. He fished for a quarter and tossed it to the boy.

"No message," he said.

HUGH SAT on the sofa in the new hotel suite, watching Gillian as she moved restlessly about the room. She'd returned from her drive with Ross deeply agitated and had been so for hours, though she didn't show it in a way that would be obvious to most people.

Hugh wasn't most people. He'd grown up with her. He knew how expert she was at concealing her true emotions, something he'd never been any good at. She thought he hadn't seen how upset she'd been ever since she'd met Ross Kavanagh again. She would never guess that he, the hedonistic little brother, would notice how often she looked at Kavanagh, or what shone in her eyes when she did.

He got up, went to the well-stocked bar—hardly different from the one at the Roosevelt—and poured himself a Glenlivet. He'd been working himself up to saying something useful ever since Gillian had turned up at the Algonquin, where he and Toby had relocated. Maybe if it hadn't been for all the little clues in her behavior and the slight change in her scent, he would have chosen the better part of valor and kept his lip buttoned. But he knew he wasn't wrong. Not this time.

He cleared his throat. Gillian glanced up from her ferocious study of the carpet.

"You're certain Ethan said that the ship leaves tomorrow," she said.

Of course she didn't trust *him* to get the facts straight. Why should she? "Yes," he said. "Warbrick said he would ring after he'd confirmed the arrangements."

Gillian nodded, her eyes revealing neither relief nor disappointment. "You will remain in the hotel until tomorrow morning?"

It wasn't really a question, but she was making her usual effort to pretend that he had some say in the matter. "I've learned my lesson," he said, tightening his grip on his glass. "I'm just not so sure you have, Gilly."

For perhaps ten seconds it seemed that Gillian hadn't heard

him. Then she turned slowly, the first hint of real emotion on her face. "I beg your pardon?"

Hugh's first instinct was to retreat. He defied it. "A long time ago," he said, "you had a chance to be happy. You didn't take it. Now you've got another one."

She stared at him as if he'd gone mad. "What are you talking about?"

"You and Kavanagh. And Toby, too." He set down his glass and deliberately walked away from the sideboard, feeling like a convict on his way to the gibbet. "Just for once, Gilly, couldn't you think of yourself instead of Father's cause?"

Comprehension raised a flush of color in her cheeks. "Whatever peculiar notion you have in your head," she said, "I assure you that it is quite mistaken."

"I don't think so. You've never told me the details, but whatever went on between you and Ross twelve years ago isn't over. Not for either one of you. But instead of facing up to it, you're running away."

The wariness in Gillian's expression turned to astonishment, as if she'd just observed a five-year-old child flawlessly reciting one of Shakespeare's more obscure plays. "Mr. Kavanagh and I have reached an amicable agreement," she said. "He is sensible enough to recognize that his present circumstances and the threat of the pack make it inadvisable for us to have further contact with him. That is all it is necessary for you to know. I suggest you go to your room and rest. A night of reckless carousing and offending dangerous men has clearly affected your mind."

Hugh thought longingly of a comfortable bed and taking the easy escape Gillian offered. He squared his shoulders.

"No," he said. "I realize I've never been much of a brother to you, Gilly. Brothers are supposed to protect their sisters, and obviously I've made a hash of that. But I'm finally going to make up for it."

"I require no help from you. I expect nothing."

"But that's just the problem. You're prepared to return to England and marry whomever Father has chosen for you because you think that's all you have a right to do." He took a step toward her. "I'm telling you, Gilly—"

"Lower your voice." She strode to the closed door that separated the main sitting area of the suite from the adjoining bedrooms. "Toby will hear you."

"Maybe Toby *ought* to hear me."

A dangerous light came into her eyes, one he'd seen on only a few occasions in his life. She walked across the room until she was standing right in front of him, the heat of anger rising from her skin like steam from a kettle on the boil.

"I don't know what has provoked this effusion of advice and concern," she said, "but it is unnecessary. There is nothing of any significance between Mr. Kavanagh and me, whatever your imagination may suggest."

"Do you believe what Warbrick said about him?"

"I do not."

"Haven't you wondered why he's so anxious to turn you against Kavanagh?"

"I am well aware that you don't like Ethan, but—"

"He's jealous, Gilly. Ross figured it out right away. Warbrick wants you for himself."

Hugh could see that his argument was already uncomfortably familiar to her, though they'd never discussed it before. "Ethan has…no such interest in me," she stammered. "And he would have no reason to believe—"

"He's observed the same things I have. Since you met Ross…well, I may be a bit dull-witted at times, but I'm not blind."

"You are quite mistaken. If I have seemed…preoccupied, it is only because I have been concerned that Toby's meeting with Mr. Kavanagh would create confusion in his mind. I no longer have reason to feel that Toby will suffer any lasting harm from the acquaintance. He will come to understand—"

"Bollocks." Hugh stiffened his spine and held Gillian's gaze. "Toby might come to understand if life at Snowfell were to stay the same as it's always been. But that isn't going to happen. Father has chosen some fellow at the Convocation to carry you off like a prize of war, and Toby will be surrounded by strangers. Do you honestly think either one of you can be happy in such circumstances? Especially when you love someone else?"

The color drained from Gillian's face. "I do not love anyone," she whispered.

"Then why did you sleep with him?"

CHAPTER TEN

GILLIAN MOVED BEFORE Hugh could prepare himself. The force of her openhanded blow knocked him backward. He reeled several steps, recovered and braced his arms against the sofa. Gillian covered her mouth with her hands.

"I'm sorry," she gasped. "I didn't mean—"

Hugh touched his lip gingerly. "No blood," he said. "I suppose I shall live."

Gillian continued to breathe harshly through her fingers, her expression frozen with horror.

Hugh went to her and took her in his arms.

"There, there," he said. "Everything will be all right, Gilly. You'll see."

She pulled away and studied his face. His cheek still stung, and he imagined it was imprinted with the mark of Gillian's palm. She appeared perilously close to weeping, which she never did. Just as she'd never before raised her hand in violence.

"Forgive me," she said in a small voice.

"Of course. I *was* a little cheeky, wasn't I?"

She tried to smile and failed. "Hugh, you must not ever allow Toby to know."

"I wouldn't. Ever," he said, stepping back. "But he's not stupid, Gilly. In fact, he's quite a bit brighter than I am."

"When we are gone, it won't matter." She folded her arms across her chest. "What happened...will never be repeated."

There was no doubt in Hugh's mind that the conversation was

over. He was almost ashamed of his relief; he would rather have faced a dozen Rutgers than go another round with Gillian the way she was now. But he hadn't done a damned bit of good. She had been shocked into admitting that she and Kavanagh had been together, but she still wouldn't permit herself to consider just what that meant.

A woman like Gillian wasn't the sort to take casual lovers. It wasn't just that their father would forbid it, or because she'd suffered so much after her first fling with Ross. Even if she'd lived completely independent of Father's beliefs and Father's rules, in many ways she was just a typical old-fashioned Englishwoman, inhibited by the unspoken rules of human society to which most werewolves—at least the non-American variety—found it necessary to conform.

Hugh shook his head. No, there was nothing typical about Gillian, however successfully she had played the dutiful daughter. Since leaving England, she'd begun to reveal a side of herself Hugh had only glimpsed a few times during those years when he'd been so stupidly blind to her unhappiness. She'd never seemed to enjoy Changing on those few occasions Sir Averil demanded it of his children, yet this morning she hadn't hesitated to take wolf shape and fight as if she'd been doing it all her life. She'd given herself wholly over to the wolf during the battle, but afterward she'd acted as if nothing unusual had occurred.

With Kavanagh it was the same. She'd deliberately kept Hugh ignorant of her previous relationship with him until Toby's escape from Snowfell, and when she'd finally admitted the details she'd taken such pains to conceal, she'd been very clear that the affair had been no more than a youthful indiscretion.

It hadn't taken Hugh very long to see that she hadn't been honest, with him or with herself. She'd behaved just as recklessly now as she had twelve years ago, then simply pretended there would be no consequences for her actions.

As if you have the right to talk about consequences, Hugh

thought. But unless the entire American pack descended upon them tonight, *his* imprudence wasn't likely to determine the course of several lives.

"I'm going to retire, Hugh," Gillian said. "I suggest you do the same. I shall be expecting Ethan's call."

"Gillian…"

"Good night."

She went through to the bedroom area and shut the door quietly behind her.

Hugh blew out an explosive breath and returned to the sideboard. Another shot of Glenlivet sounded very good just now. *Ineffectual as always, Hugh, old boy. Utterly useless.*

A little while later, as he was just hovering on the pleasantly oblivious verge of inebriation, he heard the padding of familiar footsteps.

"Toby," he said, struggling to focus on the boy in his sober gray pyjamas. "What are you doing awake?"

Toby crept across the room as furtively as a housebreaker. "Mother is asleep," he whispered. "I want to talk to you, Uncle Hugh."

Hugh took great pains to set his half-full glass on the coffee table without spilling the contents. "Come on over here, old chap. We'll have a—a nice con-ver-shayshun."

Toby's nostrils flared. "I don't like that stuff," he said.

"Neither do I." Hugh was able to stand on the third attempt and carried his glass to the sideboard, hiding it in the cupboard. "There." He wove his way back to the sofa, sat down and patted the cushions. "Tell Uncle Hugh what's on your mind."

Casting Hugh a troubled look, Toby chose one of the chairs opposite the sofa and sat gingerly on the edge of the seat. "I heard you talking to Mother," he said.

Hugh widened his eyes. "You did? You know you're…not supposed to listen to other people's…discussions."

"I know. But you were talking about Father. Mother isn't going to let me see him again, is she?"

The faint recognition of danger penetrated the haze in Hugh's brain. "You'd…you'd like to stay with him here? In America?"

"No. I just want what you said, Uncle Hugh. I want Mother to be happy." He leaned forward. "I was very angry with her, but I'm not anymore."

"Why not?"

Toby plucked at the flannel covering his knees. "You said that Mother is going to marry someone chosen by Grandfather at the Convocation."

Hugh's stomach gave a queasy lurch. *Oh, Gilly, you should have told him. Now there'll be hell to pay.*

"Yes," he said carefully. "I'm afraid that's true."

Toby's eyes revealed a complexity of emotions that should have belonged to a man three times his age. "I don't think Mother thinks I know about Grandfather."

"What do you mean, Toby?"

"How nasty he is to her. She tries to keep me from noticing, but I'm not a child anymore."

That was all too obvious. How long had Toby been "noticing" Sir Averil's arrogance, his brutality toward Gilly and his utter disinterest in his grandson? Could you grow up at Snowfell and not know those things, not take them in with every breath?

You did, Hugh mocked himself. *You managed to hide it from yourself very effectively.*

"Who is he making her marry?" Toby prodded.

"I…don't know. Your mother doesn't know, either." He felt the bile rise in his throat. "Some werewolf…of excellent and undoubtedly ancient bloodline."

"And we're supposed to go live with him?"

There was no way to make the facts any more palatable. "Yes."

Toby's fingers clenched on his knees with such force that he seemed apt to tear the sturdy fabric. "She didn't tell me."

"She…she probably thought…"

"You said she loves Father."

Hugh wished that the sofa cushions would collapse and swallow him. "I…I shoudn't have said that."

"You said she…" Toby's freckled skin reddened. "What does it mean, 'sleep together'?"

Hugh was fairly certain that Toby had already guessed exactly what it meant. "Uh…has your mother told you how babies come into the world?"

"Of course." A gleam of calculation entered his eyes. "You mean that Father and Mother were trying to make another baby?"

Oh, Lord. "It isn't…that is, babies don't always happen when men and women…when they come together."

"I know. Mother didn't expect *me* to be born."

Hugh sat up straight. "You must never believe she… Your mother loves you very much."

But Toby was already pursuing another line of thought. "If Mother doesn't love Father, and doesn't want another baby, why would she…?"

"I don't know, Toby." The alcohol was beginning to wear off, and so was the sense of detachment that might have protected him from worrying about Toby's misconceptions…or his keen insight. "No one can really know what goes on in someone else's mind."

"Does Father love Mother?"

"I don't know that, either."

"What are we going to do, Uncle Hugh?"

Hugh felt on the verge of hysterical laughter. Toby was looking to *him* for advice?

"What do you think we should do?" he asked.

"Make Father come to England with us. He won't let Mother marry some stranger. I know he won't."

Hugh was transfixed by the image of Ross Kavanagh meeting Sir Averil Maitland. "The Convocation—"

"You *do* want Mother to be happy, don't you, Uncle Hugh?"

The clever little blighter. "Of course I do," he said faintly. "But I can't see how Mr. Kavanagh's coming to England will make any difference."

The light went out of Toby's eyes. Without so much as a good-night he got up and returned to his room.

Numb and ashamed, Hugh slumped back into the cushions. His head had begun to pound abominably. He closed his eyes, praying that he would sink into blessed oblivion.

When the telephone rang it jerked him from his half sleep, and he managed to answer by the fifth ring.

"Hallo?"

Warbrick's voice was like an electric drill boring into Hugh's skull. "I must speak to Gillian," he said.

"She's asleep," Hugh said, rubbing his face to work some feeling back into it.

"Is she well? Is Kavanagh...?"

"Kavanagh's gone. And Gillian is fine." It was more difficult than usual to keep the hostility out of his voice. "What did you want to tell her?"

"We must be at the pier by eight o'clock tomorrow morning. I shall arrive at your hotel by seven."

"Your escort isn't necessary."

"I intend to take no chances as long as Kavanagh is free."

Hugh stared at the receiver. "What do you mean by 'free'?"

There was a beat of silence. "You will call me if Kavanagh returns?"

"I don't think you have any reason to worry."

"I quite agree, Maitland. I shall see to that."

The recent and very vivid memory of Toby's reproachful expression and the throbbing pain in Hugh's head had driven him to his limit. "You'll never have her, Warbrick."

"I have no idea what you're talking about."

"I've been a bit slow in figuring it out, but I'm on to you now. Whatever you have planned, it won't do you any good."

"She is not so foolish as to make the same mistake twice. Kavanagh belongs in the gutter, and she knows it."

Warbrick had misinterpreted Hugh's comment, but that suited him very well. "Right," he said. "Gilly's always confided just about everything to you, hasn't she? She's probably told you all the details of the affair since you returned to Highwick. Did she explain why she didn't stay with Ross in London, or contact him when she found out she was with child?"

"Kavanagh—"

"Was too human. Or didn't Gilly explain about the Convocation and our father's scheme to ensure the purity of the species?" Hugh snorted. "At least Ross is part werewolf. What are *you*, Warbrick?"

Telephone connections were incapable of conveying anything but disembodied voices, yet Hugh felt Warbrick bristling in fury. "I am her friend," Warbrick said.

"And that's all you are or can ever be. She may trust you, she may confide in you, but she'll never marry you. If it's really marriage you want."

"I would never dishonor—" Warbrick lowered his voice. "You have always disliked me, Hugh. Why?"

"*My* feelings don't matter. You must know that you will only increase Gillian's distress if you expect something from her that she can't give you."

Derisive laughter crackled over the line. "Ah, Hugh. You have always been a weakling. You see everything through a weakling's eyes."

"That may be true. But I didn't see you fighting those gangsters this morning, Warbrick. You may think you've got rid of Kavanagh, but you won't dare come near Snowfell during the Convocation, and when it's over, it will be too late."

"You are very much mistaken if you think I fear Sir Averil or his allies. Gillian has been misled all her life. She will not be compelled to suffer much longer."

Hugh was about to ask what Warbrick meant when the connection went dead. He returned the receiver to its cradle and glanced toward the bedrooms. Gillian must be very deeply asleep not to have been awakened by the phone. That was something to be grateful for.

But the problems posed by Warbrick remained. Gillian trusted the viscount to an extent Hugh found disturbing. But that was hardly surprising; Gillian had always had a much rougher time of it than he had, even though he'd failed to recognize just how much until recently. He'd been useless as a confidant, and Warbrick had been the only other child of her age within miles of Snowfell. He'd accepted her inhuman nature in a way few humans could or would have done.

And he hadn't given up on her, even after they'd spent years with no contact. When Ethan had returned from Europe and Sir Averil had rebuffed his renewed efforts to see Gillian openly, he'd continued to meet her in secret. And when he'd gone to America for an extended holiday, she'd concealed from Sir Averil the fact that she'd asked for Warbrick's help in looking for Toby. Such shared secrets made for strong bonds indeed.

Secrets.

She won't be compelled to suffer much longer, Warbrick had said. Did he actually intend to confront Sir Averil a second time? If he had any notion that he could deal with the werewolves at the Convocation on an equal footing, he was sorely mistaken. He might occupy the estate nearest Snowfell, but there was a chasm between the two houses that could never be bridged.

As for his motive, that remained the biggest mystery of all. Gillian was a mature woman with a son rapidly approaching adolescence. She was hardly the sort to make a man lose all sense.

Was it possible that Warbrick really loved her?

Hugh shook his head. Warbrick saw only what he wanted to see. There was something peculiar in his confidence. Something not quite sane. He would be returning to England on the ship with them, so perhaps he intended to press his suit then.

In some ways, he might have a better a shot at winning her now than at any other time since he'd known her. She'd been different since they'd left England—bolder, more confident, more outspoken—and Hugh knew it was because she was free of Sir Averil's shadow for the first time in years. Seeing her fight as a wolf had been a revelation.

But it couldn't last. She would wrap herself in her old skin the moment they set foot on the Liverpool docks.

Hugh went to the window, flipped back the drapes and looked out on the sparkling city. It wasn't as if *he* were going to escape the demands of his blood, no matter how much more freedom he appeared to possess. If Gilly had been able to find a way to defy Sir Averil—not just in little things, like her friendship with Warbrick or covering for her scapegrace younger brother, but in something really significant—maybe he could have avoided his own inevitable fate, as well.

And isn't that why you tried to make her admit that she loves Kavanagh? It isn't just because you want her to be happy. You want to save yourself.

Filled with self-disgust, Hugh let the drapes fall. What had he thought would happen if Kavanagh had cared for Gillian enough to overcome both pride and scruples and ask her to stay with him? What if she'd agreed? If Kavanagh and Gilly were to remain together in New York, Sir Averil would cut off Gillian's access to the Maitland fortune, at the very least. And at the worst...

Hugh shuddered. If Gillian were left with no other choice, she would find a way to summon that inner strength she'd spent most of her life denying. She would adapt and survive, just as she'd survived thirty years of their father's contempt. And if it meant ensuring Toby's welfare, Hugh believed she could even set aside the old, ingrained beliefs and make a new life without any of the resources Snowfell and Sir Averil provided.

Could he do the same, even for the woman *he* professed to love?

The thread of a pernicious thought curled through Hugh's brain like a parasitic worm. If Sir Averil were gone, his fortune and title would pass to Hugh. His hold over his children would be broken. Wouldn't that solve every problem?

Hugh reeled away from the window, stumbled halfway to the sideboard and stopped. He *was* a weakling. He was a coward, right down to the core.

But Kavanagh *wasn't*. Now that his eyes had been opened, Hugh found he was not quite so inept as he had once been in guessing at people's real emotions. He'd told Toby that he didn't know if Kavanagh loved Gillian, but in fact he suspected there was as much feeling from the American's direction as there was from Gilly's, no matter how well concealed.

With a child's straightforward practicality, Toby had found the solution to the simple problem he perceived: keep his mother and father together. And in so doing, he might have found the solution to Hugh's problems, as well.

Hugh closed his eyes. Sir Averil had position, wealth and influence, even in the human world he so despised. Kavanagh had nothing—except the raw courage to fight for what he believed in.

The idea was quite simply mad.

Abruptly Hugh turned away from the seductive bottles lined up on the sideboard and walked toward the telephone table. It wasn't necessary to reveal his scheme to Kavanagh; all he need do was convince the American to arrive at the docks before the ship set sail.

You're going to pay for this, Hugh told himself. *It'll just be a question of who comes after you first.*

He picked up the receiver and dialed.

CHAPTER ELEVEN

THE SUN HAD BARELY risen over Queens, but the heavy air along the docks was already threatening another day of drenching heat.

Ross stood at the pier, gazing at the grand ship that loomed over the wharf. Porters and ship's personnel were already hurrying up and down the gangway, loading crates of luggage sent ahead by efficient passengers. A few hardy souls, eager to be on their way, were waiting to board: women in furs far too warm for the weather; men in suits and hats purchased from Manhattan's finest haberdasheries; well-dressed children whose fidgeting brought the occasional soft rebuke from their bored parents.

Gillian stood out from the rest. She wore no fur, not even so much as a scrap around her shoulders, and her dress was plain to the point of homeliness. Toby stood beside her, uncharacteristically quiet, only the occasional glance toward the quay suggesting that his thoughts were on something other than the cruise ahead. Ethan Warbrick was engaged in an argument with one of the porters, his voice rising as he pointed to the several large trunks stacked on the ground beside him, while Hugh waited alone, occasionally scuffing one highly polished two-tone oxford on the wooden planking under his feet.

The reason Hugh had given for calling last night was as patently phony as a two-dollar bill. The kid might be a lightweight, and he obviously recognized that he wasn't much use in a fight, but he couldn't really believe that Ross alone was capable of providing sufficient muscle if pack enforcers improbably showed up again.

Maybe Hugh was trying to make up for his stupidity in provoking the pack by offering Ross a chance to see Toby again. But that was sheer speculation; Ross had no idea what motivated Gillian's younger brother. He should have listened to his instincts and stayed home.

But here he was, hunkering in the long morning shadow of the Customs building while more first-class passengers arrived with their luggage, pampered pets and expectant chatter. The smells of oil and exhaust mingled with perfume and perspiration. At seven-thirty the chain across the gangway was removed and the passengers began to embark. Gillian was among the first to board. She took Toby's hand and strode up the incline. Hugh followed at a slower pace. Warbrick lingered, turning to stare toward the Customs House as if he knew Ross was there.

It was another hour before the last stragglers, the ordinary passengers as well as the poorer folks in steerage, clambered up the gangway. Well-wishers crowded the dock, fluttering handkerchiefs and shouting farewells, while their loved ones jostled for position along the ship's railing.

Ross searched the sea of faces, looking for the only ones that mattered. Gillian wasn't there. She probably had Toby locked in their cabin by now, with Warbrick congratulating them on their narrow escape.

The mere thought of Warbrick alone with Gillian was enough to set a match to Ross's heels. He managed to hold his place as the steamer blew its horn. Time had run out. He had known when he arrived that he wouldn't interfere with Gillian's departure. The decision he'd made yesterday had been the right one.

So why did feel as if his heart had been ripped out of his chest?

He turned and walked away, hardly aware of his feet or where they were carrying him. In a few hours he would telephone pack headquarters and let them know where to find Sherrod's henchmen. He would probably have to face a punishment detail, but at least he could give the pack enforcers a good fight.

A good fight. He was almost looking forward to it. Simple, straightforward, something to remind him that he was still alive.

His thoughts were drifting when a certain familiar scent pulled him back to the present. He found himself in a district of dockside warehouses just north of the pier where the steamer was berthed. Astonishment brought him to a halt.

"Toby?"

The boy stepped out from behind a forklift, his body tense with excitement.

"Father," he said.

Ross crossed the distance between them in a few strides and stopped just short of grabbing the boy by his thin shoulders. "What in hell you doing here?" he demanded. "The ship—"

"I want to stay with you," Toby said, holding Ross's gaze with the stubborn determination Ross had begun to expect of him.

Ross swept off his hat and spiked his fingers through his hair. "We have to get you back."

Toby shuffled away, ready to dash off if Ross made any sudden moves. "I don't want to return to England just so that Mother can marry someone she doesn't love. I don't want any father but you."

"What do you mean? Are you talking about Warbrick?"

"No. It's to be some werewolf my grandfather has chosen for her. They're supposed to meet at the Convocation."

Ross felt himself beginning to slide out of his depth. He steered the boy in the direction of the docks. "You're talking about gathering of families you mentioned at the Durants'."

"Yes. A bunch of werewolves from England and Europe come together to talk about keeping us from going extinct. They stopped having it late last century, but Grandfather started it up again."

Grandfather. The mysterious Sir Averil, a man Ross still knew almost nothing about. Hugh had made some extraordinary statements about him to the pack's enforcers, statements that had completely contradicted Gillian's vague references to an eccentric old man in her care.

"Who is your mother supposed to marry?" he asked thickly.

Toby glared at the pavement as they continued on toward the pier. "I don't know. Mother never even told me she was going to get married. I heard her and Hugh talking, and that's how I found out."

Ross was silent, absorbing what Toby had said. Gillian had never mentioned any of this to *him,* either. She obviously hadn't considered it important for him to know…just as she hadn't objected to enjoying a transient sexual encounter when she was already committed to someone else.

It was London all over again.

"When is this Convocation taking place?" he asked.

"I think it's supposed to begin right after we return to Snowfell." Toby glanced at Ross. "Uncle Hugh said that even Mother doesn't know who Grandfather has chosen, but we'll have to go with him to wherever he lives—maybe even to a place like Russia or Germany."

A stab of anger sliced through Ross's nerves. "Why would your mother agree to this, Toby?"

"I don't know." Toby cast him another sideways glance, reminding Ross incongruously of a suspect who was telling part of the truth, but holding other facts in reserve. "Mother has told me something about the Convocations, and Uncle Hugh said it's all about 'excellent bloodlines.'"

Of course. This prospective husband would be purebred, like the long-lost Mr. Delvaux. She'd said she had no desire to marry again. Had that been a lie, like so much else between them?

The blast of a steamer's horn reminded him that he and Toby were almost at the pier. Much to his surprise, the *Terpsichore*'s gangway was still down and the crowd continued to linger, though it had thinned.

Ross stopped well behind the edge of the crowd, and Toby stopped beside him. "You aren't going to make me go, are you?" he asked quietly.

A garishly dressed woman a few feet away laughed raucously, and a stream of cigarette smoke congealed in Ross's nostrils. He stared up at the deck, where a bevy of young women were leaning over the railing, their faces rosy with excitement under cloche hats and penciled brows.

He hardened his heart, though it was already so brittle he thought it might crack. Gillian had made her decision. She'd determined that Toby's welfare lay with some guy she'd never met—a guy with impeccable werewolf credentials—and Ross knew enough by now to realize she wasn't going to change her mind. Not for Toby, and certainly not for him.

"A kid your age needs to be with his mother," he said. "Someday you'll understand."

Toby refused to look at him. "At least you can take me onto the ship."

Ross didn't have the guts to deny him such a small thing. "Okay," he said. "But then you're staying put."

Toby nodded sharply and strode to the gangway. Ross accompanied him up the ramp. They'd just reached the deck when Hugh appeared, his expression changing from worry to relief in an instant.

"Toby! Thank God." He glanced up at Ross. "You *did* come. I'm glad you found Toby before Gillian realized he was gone."

Ross's muscles twitched with the sense of something not quite right. "Did you expect Toby to sneak off the ship?"

"I didn't think it was beyond the realm of possibility." Hugh gave Toby a stern look that was about as convincing as prison stripes on a cherub. "You're going straight to the cabin, young man."

Heaving a great sigh, Toby offered his hand to Ross. "Goodbye, Father," he said solemnly.

Ross enfolded the small hand in his. "Toby, I—"

But Toby spun around and ran off, leaving Ross with a lump in his throat the size of the Rock of Gibraltar.

"Poor little chap," Hugh said. "Things are going to be a bit rough for him once we're back in England."

Ross tensed. "You Maitlands are just full of secrets, aren't you?"

"More than you know." Hugh leaned closer. "Listen, there's something I must discuss with you. I wasn't sure I'd get the chance, but since you're here…"

"Not anymore." Ross started down the gangway.

Hugh ran after him and grabbed his shoulder.

"It's important, Kavanagh. Please."

Ross shook him off. "Well?"

"We must speak privately. You'll have to come up."

"The ship's about to leave."

"Don't worry, I'll have you off in good time."

"If this is about Gillian and this marriage of hers…"

"It's much more than that. Come on."

He led Ross back onto the deck and into a narrow corridor punctuated with cabin doors. The ship's horn blasted again. Hugh took a number of turns and descended down stairs that Ross suspected were mainly used by crew and service personnel.

If he hadn't been brooding over what Toby had told him, he might never have fallen for the trick. Hugh stepped into a room that appeared to be some sort of storage area. Ross followed him. Hugh moved as if to shut the door, but walked through it instead, slamming it closed. By the time Ross reached it, the door was locked.

He tested the lock, but it was too strong for even a pure-blooded werewolf to break. He pounded for several minutes. For the next half hour he continued to look for a means to break down the door. All too soon he felt the telltale lurch of the ship beginning to move away from its berth. He realized that he'd been trapped for a reason, and no one was going to let him out until the ship was well out to sea.

He paced the small room, rage giving way to puzzlement. Who had planned this? Hugh? What in hell did he want? Was he as anxious to save Gillian from her forthcoming marriage as Toby was? Then why hadn't he brought the issue up before? And what did he think Ross could do about it?

Ross slumped against the wall, ignoring the rumbling in his stomach as the times for breakfast and lunch came and went. He reckoned it was close to suppertime when someone opened the door.

The uniformed steward gaped at Ross. "Sir?" he said. "May I ask—"

"Don't," Ross said. "Is there a way I can get off this ship?"

"I…I'm afraid not, sir." He cleared his throat. "Have you a cabin, sir?"

"Are you asking if I'm a stowaway?" Ross laughed. "No, I haven't got a ticket or a cabin or anything else. This is the last place I want to be."

"Am I to understand that you were detained here involuntarily, sir?"

Ross considered how foolish he must look. "Something like that."

The steward dutifully tried to conceal his natural skepticism. "I see. Well…in that case I think it best if we consult the captain."

"By all means." Ross pushed past the steward, who stepped quickly out of his way. Head down and jaw set, Ross stalked after the man while he thought longingly of strangling Hugh Maitland.

The encounter with the captain proved more interesting and far less unpleasant than Ross had anticipated. It transpired that Ross did, in fact, have both a ticket and a stateroom, generously supplied by an anonymous benefactor. A full wardrobe of clothing and other necessities waited in his cabin. All he needed to do was make himself comfortable.

But Ross wasn't interested in comfort. On his way to his cabin he found a steward who directed him to the stateroom occupied by one Hugh Maitland. The only problem was that it was certainly near Gillian's. Ross decided to bide his time. He ordered supper in his cabin and waited until after-dinner cocktails were being served in the lounge. He dressed in the tuxedo his "benefactor" had left in his closet and hovered outside the lounge until, inevitably, Hugh emerged suitably inebriated.

The young man's face underwent a startling loss of color when he caught sight of Ross. He raised his hands unsteadily.

"Sorry, old chap," he stammered. "It was the only way. You see, I—"

Ross seized his collar. "Spit it out—and quick."

"You must come to England, Kavanagh. It's the only way for you to see what's really going on." He coughed. "Look, I know things have been strained between you and Gilly. But I think you care enough about her and Toby to want to know the whole story."

Ross let him go. "I've already heard just about all I want to."

"But you haven't. You have no idea." Hugh glanced up and down the corridor. "You blame Gillian for what happened in the past. Maybe you wouldn't be so quick to judge if you knew the circumstances."

"Are you trying to say she's in some kind of trouble?" Ross felt his emotions beginning to slip out of his control. "If you don't start explaining…"

"I can't. Not here." Hugh gulped audibly. "Little as I may deserve it, I'm asking you to trust me. If you still want to stay out of it afterward, I'll send you back on the next ship, and all you'll have lost is a few weeks of your time."

A few weeks. What were weeks, or even months, in a life that had lost its purpose?

"Was Toby in on this?" he asked.

"Don't blame him. He's very worried about his mother."

The anger drained out of Ross like stale water from a rusty standpipe. "Yeah," he said. "Well, I can't exactly swim back to New York. But I don't want Gillian to know I'm here."

Hugh blew out his breath. "I quite agree."

Ross yanked at his silk tie. "Okay. But you're going to tell me if Warbrick makes any kind of move on Gillian."

"That is extremely unlikely. She isn't speaking to anyone at the moment."

That was the first piece of good news Ross had heard in quite a while. He turned on his heel and took a circuitous route back to his cabin. It was going to be one hell of a long week. And Ross had an idea that he was going to be having some very disturbing dreams.

THE *TERPSICHORE* arrived in Liverpool on a cool, wet afternoon. Ross had already packed the things he'd decided to take off the ship, including a few plain shirts, trousers and a casual jacket. He had little use for the evening clothes Hugh had provided, so he left them in the cabin and finished shaving while the steamer settled into its berth.

Hugh arrived just as he was putting his razor away. They'd spoken only a few times during the voyage, when Hugh had come to assure him that Gillian was still avoiding any company, including Warbrick's. The conversations had been strained and brief; Hugh had obstinately refused to provide any further explanation, insisting that Ross "see for himself."

There was a marked change in the young man now, a kind of nervous energy suggesting that Ross was finally going to get his answers.

"They've started to disembark," Hugh said without preamble. "I'll be going with Gillian and Toby, of course, but it's important that you're close behind us."

"Warbrick?"

"He…doesn't come to Snowfell. He'll be making his own way back to Cumbria."

Ross let his immediate question pass. "What do you expect me to do?"

"Follow and observe. It's important that you don't let Gilly or Father see or smell you."

"Your father will be there?" Ross frowned. "She told me he's an old man who needs her care and almost never leaves the estate."

"That...wasn't quite true."

"I figured as much. Toby told me about this arranged marriage. Did Sir Averil arrange her first one, too?"

Hugh hesitated. "He tried to. Gilly upset his scheme."

Ross sensed the words unspoken. "You said you didn't want your father to see or smell me. Why? Did Gillian tell him about me?"

"It's complicated. You can't imagine how complicated." Hugh hooked a finger under his tight, immaculate collar. "Please, Kavanagh. There's no time for explanations now. Be patient just a little while longer." He met Ross's gaze. "If you won't do it for Gillian, do it for your son."

Despite his confusion, Ross gave a single short nod. Hugh backed out of the cabin. "Give me ten minutes," he said. "I'll signal you from the bottom of the gangway."

Deliberately wiping all further speculation from his mind, Ross waited the requested ten minutes, then picked up his small suitcase and joined the passengers streaming off the ship. Hugh waved from the bottom of the ramp, and when he set off into the crowd of embracing couples, reunited families and eager tourists, Ross followed.

Hugh slowed his pace as the warehouses and shipping offices of the docks gave way to city streets. A veteran with a missing leg held out his bowl as Ross passed by; Ross paused, felt inside his pocket, remembered that he didn't have any English coins and gave the man two bits instead. The man examined the quarter and peered up into Ross's face.

"Yank, ain't you?" he asked in a thick Liverpudlian accent.

Ross glanced up to make sure that Hugh was still in sight. "That's right."

The man offered his hand. "Thanks, mate."

Ross shook the veteran's hand and quickly moved away. This wasn't London, but his brain was already clogged with memories of a time he had no desire to remember. He walked faster until he found Hugh waiting at a kerb lined with automobiles of every description. Hugh noticed him and lifted his hand in a cautioning gesture.

More than twelve years of serving as a soldier and a cop had made certain skills second nature to Ross. He knew how to keep himself hidden and to stay downwind of his quarry. He made his way close to the kerb, found a newsstand, paid for a newspaper and pretended to read while he observed.

He saw Gillian almost at once. Toby was close beside her, standing very still in a way not at all typical for him. But it was the third figure who demanded instant attention.

The man was an English gentleman in the most complete sense of the word. He was tall and evidently fit, with a large frame supporting substantial muscle. His posture was as erect as a general's, his clothing cut to perfection, his face at once stoic and severe. Not a single lock of his graying hair was out of place, and Ross imagined that the razor edge of his mustache must have been trimmed with the aid of a magnifying glass.

Those qualities would have been notable, but hardly extraordinary. What stood out was the power that radiated from the man, power unquestioned and accepted as a natural feature of his existence. Passersby gave the old man a wide berth; a few glanced at him in puzzlement, as if they couldn't decide why they felt such an urge to avoid him.

It was a natural reaction many humans had when in the presence of a werewolf. But not all *loups-garous* inspired such a marked response, especially among their own kind. When they did—when one werewolf rose above the others by sheer virtue of some elementary, inborn power—he or she inevitably climbed to a position of domination. A single look at Gillian's face and the set of her body told Ross that he was witnessing the very thing Hugh had wanted him to see.

The changes in Gillian's bearing seemed subtle at first. They might not even have been noticeable to someone who didn't know her well. Though she'd shown uncertainty and vulnerability in New York, especially at Coney Island and at the Durants', Ross well remembered her calm competence in London, her firmness when she'd argued with him about Toby and stood up to Warbrick's bullying, her courageous stand against the pack's enforcers…and her passionate lovemaking. Though Ross had been glad to see that her shield of superiority could be penetrated, he'd completely dismissed the idea that Jill was capable of being really afraid.

But a different Gillian stood there on the kerb with her son, a woman who seemed to have shrunk in height, whose shoulders were drawn in, who refused to meet her father's gaze. She looked like a defeated enemy facing some crushing humiliation at the hands of her captor.

And her captor, the shadowy figure Gillian had hardly ever mentioned, looked down on his daughter as if she were a serving girl who'd spilled a few drops of water on his gleaming patent leather shoes.

"You were to have returned immediately," he said in a harsh, deep voice. "What was the cause of your delay?"

Gillian gazed at the upper button of Sir Averil's waistcoat. "We did not find Toby immediately, Father," she said, her words barely above a whisper. "I thought I knew where I might find him, but my judgment was incorrect."

"As I expected," Sir Averil said, making no effort to hide his contempt. "You have always—"

"It was entirely my fault," Hugh interrupted, moving to stand beside Gillian. "I…allowed myself to be distracted by the city's attractions."

"Rubbish." Sir Averil leaned over Gillian as if he would crush her with a sweep of his fist. "You met *him,* didn't you? You met with that filthy human again."

"*I'm* the one who found him," Toby said, his voice high. "That's why I went to America. *I* found my father."

Sir Averil glanced at Toby as if a street cur had stood up on its hind legs and spoken. Gillian immediately shifted position so that she stood between her father and her son.

"No harm was done," she said softly. "We are home. This will never happen again."

"So you said the first time." He curled his lip. "You were a whore then, and you remain one now. If anyone at the Convocation should learn about the human, or the truth about Delvaux…"

The next part of the conversation faded so low that Ross couldn't make it out for several minutes. It was bad enough just to watch.

"What did he demand in exchange for his cooperation?" Sir Averil said, loudly enough for Ross to hear.

"Nothing," Gillian said. "He…recognized that Toby's welfare must come first."

"Most fortunate for you. If your son misbehaves again…"

Gillian shrank like a wounded soldier from the surgeon's knife. "He will not, Father."

Sir Averil didn't answer, but lifted his head, his gaze making a circuit of the area, as if something untoward had caught his attention. Instinctively Ross froze, and Sir Averil's stare moved past him without stopping.

He's never seen me. He wouldn't recognize my scent.…

But Gillian would. The breeze off the river had been working to Ross's advantage, and Gillian had been far too preoccupied to sense his presence. Toby glanced once in Ross's direction, but his expression didn't change. He was keeping the secret.

A secret that wasn't likely to remain one much longer.

Ross clenched his fingers on the newspaper as Sir Averil signaled to the chauffeur standing beside the limousine that had pulled up to the kerb. The driver hastened to the back and opened the door for Gillian, who urged Toby into the car ahead of her. Hugh spoke to his father about a missing trunk and began walking back toward the pier, while Sir Averil climbed into the seat next to Gillian.

Hugh appeared at the newsstand a few moments later. "You heard?" he asked.

Newsprint crumpled in Ross's fists. "Yeah," he said. "Your father is a first-class son of a bitch, and you should have told me—"

"What? That Gillian's spent most of her life trying to appease…" His voice trailed off, and he stared at the pavement under his feet. "I thought if you could see for yourself what it's been like for her—"

"I'd punch the bastard's lights out? Maybe you should have thought of that yourself."

"Oh, I have. But I'm a coward, you see. Father doesn't know it, of course. I've always been the fortunate son."

Ross reminded himself that it would do no good to make Hugh suffer the same treatment he would like to give Sir Averil. "The bastard is forcing Gillian into this marriage by threatening Toby, isn't he?" he asked.

"It isn't just Toby. It's years of being told she was a disgrace. Years of having it drummed into her head that her only reason for existing was to do her part in ensuring the purity of the race."

The eggs and toast Ross had eaten for breakfast threatened a violent escape. "All those things she said in London—"

"Might have come directly out of our father's mouth," Hugh finished.

Ross's fingers punched through the thin newsprint, and the paper fluttered to the ground. "What about Toby?"

"The boy represents Gilly's betrayal of everything Sir Averil believes in. He knows the one thing she could never bear is being separated from him."

So that was the hold he had over her. "Then why did she come back to England, after…" He swallowed. "Why in hell did she tell him Toby was my son, when he could have been Delvaux's?"

"I don't think she ever mentioned your name, but you know that females of our kind…she must have realized she was expecting as soon as she left London. Delvaux…" He seemed to think better of what he'd been about to say. "She must have thought if she confessed to the affair instead of trying to hide it, the old man might forgive her. But even if she kept the details from him, he would have made it his business to find out who and what you were."

More than half-human. Ross watched the torn and crumpled newspaper blow away on the breeze. "She could have left," he said. "She could have written. If she'd told me…"

But she'd chosen her father's anger and contempt—and his threats—over a mate who was, and would never be, good enough.

"No one can make someone else believe something they don't want to," he said bitterly. "Maybe she isn't being coerced into this marriage at all."

Hugh sighed. "She clings to the idea that there are certain civilized standards that few Old World *loups-garous* will violate. She probably hopes that Sir Averil has chosen someone honorable, someone who will be a good father for Toby. But Sir Averil set up this Convocation to support his philosophy. Anyone the old man chooses will be just like him—or worse." He shot a glance in the direction of the limousine. Sir Averil had gotten out and was staring toward the docks.

"We're out of time," Hugh said. "Will you help?"

Ross focused his rage on Hugh. "Why are you so concerned now? You say you're a coward, as if that's an excuse. You could have tried to prevent Gillian and Toby from coming back to England."

"But I did," Hugh said. "She wouldn't listen."

"And you think she'll listen to me?"

"You're the only hope I've got left." Hugh gazed at him with an earnestness that Ross couldn't deny. "I'll do anything to see Gilly happy. And I think you'll do anything for your son."

"Have you forgotten that I'm a criminal?"

"Gilly doesn't believe that, and neither do I. If she ever decides to stand up to the old man, the only ally she'll have besides me is Warbrick. Is that what you want?"

"What do you expect me to do?"

"It's not going to be easy. You need to be at Snowfell during the Convocation. We'll have to give you a new identity and background."

"And hope that Gillian will play along, even though she doesn't want anything more to do with me."

"She won't risk exposing you to the delegates. Not only for her own and Toby's sake, but…" Hugh shook his head. "I won't deceive you. Father may guess who you are. This could be very dangerous."

As if being a cop wasn't. As if he hadn't already lost the things he cared most about and somehow managed to survive.

Gillian might have prayed never to see him again, but Toby had asked for his intervention. Toby needed and deserved to have some say in his own future.

A love twelve years dead had absolutely nothing to do with it.

"All right," he said. "I'm in."

ETHAN WATCHED Kavanagh walk away from the newsstand, his rage slowly giving way to calculation. He had already cursed himself for not having realized that Kavanagh was on the ship; it was scant consolation that Gillian obviously hadn't, either. She would never have faced Sir Averil with such calm if she'd known that the American was observing from a few yards away.

She had no idea at all that her witless brother had been conspiring with her former lover to make her life even more miserable than it had been before. Hugh Maitland had unexpectedly developed a backbone, and Kavanagh was a wild card who could ruin the entire game.

Ethan drew a silver case from his jacket and shook out a cigarette. He had made several errors since he had resolved to be rid of Ross Kavanagh. The first had been assuming that Bianchi would be willing to repay his debts. But the most egregious had been his failure to foresee the extent to which Kavanagh would interfere.

And then there was Gillian herself.

Ethan open a matchbook he'd picked up at one of Manhattan's fashionable nightclubs and struck a light. How was he to have guessed how erratically Gillian would behave after she'd slipped Sir Averil's leash? Certainly he had recognized a few disturbing changes, but he had allowed himself to believe that they were mere aberrations.

Until Gillian had chosen to fight the American enforcers, accompanied Kavanagh to dispose of them and proceeded to ignore Ethan throughout the entire voyage to England.

He tossed the match onto the pavement, ground it under his heel and took a long pull on his cigarette. When he'd renewed his friendship with her eighteen months ago, she had needed him just as much as she had during their shared childhoods, perhaps even more so. She'd given birth to a son, and the boy had become the center of her world, but that world was as miserable as ever. She expected nothing but to live out her days as an obedient slave to her father's tyrannical will…and had clung to Ethan's affection as her sole support.

And then she'd come to New York, where she had contracted an illness…a disease that threatened to steal Gillian away from Ethan as surely as death itself. He had taken the necessary steps, but the incompetence of others had thwarted him. If the New York police had been more efficient, Kavanagh would never have boarded the ship.

By now they would have found Kavanagh's sudden disappearance highly suspect, and a manhunt would almost certainly be under way. He might call the local constabulary and let them know that a criminal was in their midst. But he had no desire to involve the English police. Forcing the issue too soon might backfire. Gillian would certainly be appalled by Kavanagh's appearance and do everything within her negligible power to drive him away without arousing suspicion. Nothing he himself did must cause her to regret the decisions she had reached in New York.

He tapped his cigarette and watched the ash crumble. Kavanagh might bring about his own downfall with no effort on Ethan's part. Whatever his motives, the American had no idea what he would face at the Convocation. And even if he somehow managed to hold his own, he had already burdened himself with a serious misjudgment. He had dismissed Ethan Warbrick as an ineffectual British aristocrat unworthy of his attention.

Ethan smiled, giving free rein to his imagination. The cigarette burned his fingers. He threw it down and smashed it into a shapeless mass. Then he turned and walked in the direction of the train station, thinking how very glad Mother would be to see him again.

CHAPTER TWELVE

NUMBNESS.

It was a state of mind to which Gillian had long been accustomed, and she had slipped back into its familiar embrace long before the Austin Mayfair passed through Snowfell's tall wrought-iron gates. Sir Averil had been largely silent during the long drive, his thoughts no doubt focused on the Convocation now that other distractions had been disposed of. Hugh had assumed a dignified air befitting the favored son, a mask that he had learned to adopt whenever there was the slightest danger that Sir Averil might actually become angry with him.

He had surprised Gillian when he'd tried to defend her by taking the blame on himself. It wasn't like him. But then, none of them had been much like themselves lately. Already the things she'd said and done in New York felt like a dream, a dream in which she had become some other person.

Sir Averil would have been horrified by her behavior. No, not horrified, but incredulous. Astonished that she had relied on her own judgment with regard to Toby's interactions with his father and in her determination of Ross's guilt or innocence, that she'd mingled with common humanity at a vulgar amusement park, made a spectacle of herself by assisting a mere human child in distress.

And what would he have said if he'd seen her turn into a wolf and fight American mobsters? Or if he'd guessed, even for an instant, that she had so thoroughly lost her senses as to lie with the same man who'd ruined his scheme for her twelve years ago?

Gillian covered her mouth, afraid that a laugh might escape. Toby looked at her, an anxious frown hovering over his eyes. He, too, had been silent. Sir Averil's presence was certainly enough of a damper, especially since Toby had reached that critical age when nothing Gillian did or said could shield him from knowledge of his grandfather's views.

Her son gave a quiet sigh and turned to look out the small rear window. He had done it several times during the drive, almost as if he expected to catch a glimpse of what they had left behind. Now that he knew about the marriage agreement, he would naturally balk.

She couldn't expect him to completely understand, of course. She must set an example by maintaining her composure at all times. Especially since Sir Averil had renewed his threat, the one he'd used so often to remind her of her place.

Now that he knew she'd seen Ross, that threat had taken on new life. Sir Averil had the power to make sure she never saw Toby again.

If we had remained in New York…

But such a wild fantasy had never been an option. Not when Sir Averil's reach might very well extend across the Atlantic, just as Hugh had told the American enforcers.

There was no running away. Not with a man whose reputation lay in tatters, a man without prospects, without allies. One who could never teach Toby to be all he was meant to become.

She must continue to believe that, or she might very well go mad.

Her duties at the Convocation would make it easier to forget. She would devote herself to acting as Sir Averil's gracious hostess and an ideal representative of the pure breeding he valued above all else.

And she must stop seeing Ethan.

Snowfell passed in and out of view as the limousine wound between the low, rolling dales south of the park. But Gillian was envisioning the secret place where she and Ethan had always met, a peaceful sanctuary she had treasured as both child and woman.

It had been difficult to face the disappointment in Ethan's eyes when she had failed to invite his company during the voyage. She had been in no state to deal with his obstinate condemnation of Ross, or his satisfaction in her parting with him.

Now she understood that the separation from Ethan must become permanent without delay. A week of solitary reflection had convinced her that Hugh had been right in insisting that Ethan no longer regarded her as merely a friend. As much as she had told him about her people and the meeting about to take place, she hadn't revealed that an unknown werewolf, not Ross, was his true rival.

If he should attempt to interfere with the Convocation, it would mean disaster.

Someday she would make him understand. She had lost that opportunity with Ross. She had left him standing on the pavement outside the Palace Hotel and never looked back. That knowledge, that terrible loneliness, would haunt her to the end of her days.

Gillian closed her eyes, waiting for the numbness to return.

The Mayfair followed the final curve of the circular drive and came to a stop before the house. The day was beginning to wane, and the late afternoon sun turned the limestone of Snowfell's impressive Gothic facade from gray to gold.

Faulder, Mrs. Mossop, Miss Rownthwaite and two of the footmen were already standing outside the entrance court to welcome their employers home. Hopkins slid from the driver's seat to open the door for Sir Averil, while Robert, the senior footman, did the same for Gillian. Hugh went immediately into the house, while Faulder supervised the footmen in removing the trunks.

After the footmen had gone, Faulder returned to the house, while Sir Averil stood gazing at the park with its perfectly manicured lawn and fine old trees, his hands clasped behind his ack. Gillian asked Miss Rownthwaite to escort Toby to his room, then went to stand beside Sir Averil, waiting for him to speak.

"Marcus Forster has arrived," he said without turning. "He will be joining us at table. You shall make yourself presentable. The boy is to remain in his room."

"Yes, Father."

"Nothing is to be said about your excursion to New York. I expect the Earnshaw and Macalister delegations to arrive tomorrow. If the incident should become known among the delegates, I shall offer the necessary explanations."

"I understand."

He glanced at her, and for a moment she was afraid that he could somehow smell Ross on her, though she had bathed many times since they had been together. He made a familiar sound of disgust and strode into the house, leaving Gillian to stand shivering in the warm evening air.

It smelled of growing things, rich earth, the animals that called Snowfell's woods their home. It stank of neither raw humanity nor the pollutants and machinery that she had breathed every minute she had spent in New York. Just beyond the edge of the gravel drive was the fragrance of life and renewal. But within Snowfell's imposing front door, life ended.

She walked slowly through the porte-cochère and into the entrance hall. To her weary surprise, Mrs. Spotterswood was hovering in the hall, her broad face creased with concern.

"Mrs. Delvaux," the cook said, "welcome home."

Gillian summoned up a smile. "Thank you, Mrs. Spotterswood."

"I've just started a fresh pot of tea. Is there anything you might like before dinner? I've fresh cake, and a very nice roast beef for sandwiches."

"No, thank you. We have a guest, and I must make myself presentable."

The cook must have detected the mockery in Gillian's words,

for she glanced about as if she expected Sir Averil to appear in a puff a smoke like some malign spirit. "You always look lovely, Mrs. Delvaux," she said softly. "I shall alert Mossop to send Cora up to you at once."

Cora was Gillian's new personal maid, whom she'd recently hired to minister to her appearance during the Convocation. It hadn't been important for her to look anything but plain and respectable when she was dealing only with the local villagers and household staff, so she had seen to her own hair and clothing. Naturally her efforts would no longer be sufficient.

Feeling stiff and brittle after the long drive, Gillian climbed the staircase to her small suite of rooms. The landing and corridor echoed with an emptiness that would soon be filled for the first time in many years. Snowfell would become, for a brief time, what it had been three hundred years ago, when Sir John Maitland, who had actually liked humans, kept Snowfell's halls alive with laughter and scandal.

But no. It wouldn't be like that at all. The Convocation was serious matter for those werewolves who subscribed to Sir Averil's point of view. Laughter would be rare, and as for scandal…

There would be none unless the servants gossiped, and Snowfell's employees knew the danger in that. Toby was the only other possible source of such ruinous information. As soon as she had done her duty tonight, she would once again impress upon him the necessity of absolute discretion. The stakes were too high to allow even the slightest rebellion.

Gillian entered her sitting room and paused, absorbing its dull familiarity. The curtains were drawn like those of a house in mourning. She removed her pumps and sighed as her stockinged feet touched the worn carpet. She would have liked very much to lie down and close her eyes, but there was always the danger of dreams like those that had haunted her on the voyage. She had woken almost every morning with the belief that Ross was very near, only to find herself alone.

It was a mercy that she would have little time to sleep during the days ahead.

She was removing her light jacket when Cora arrived. The pretty young maid curtseyed and gave Gillian a tentative smile. She'd been at Snowfell just long enough to learn the reserve necessary to any human serving at the estate. She had in fact been hired on Ethan's recommendation. There was no danger that she would ever reveal that her employers possessed the ability to change into wolves.

"Good evening, Cora," Gillian said. "I will need some assistance with my hair, and you may lay out the blue crepe frock."

"Yes, ma'am," Cora said. As she selected the gown from the armoire, Gillian sat at her dressing table and undid the pins holding her simple chignon in place. Her hair spilled down around her shoulders, and she remembered how Ross had touched it when they made love.

As Cora worked on her hair, Gillian began to prepare her mask. From the moment she walked downstairs and into the Red Drawing Room with its red-and-gold walls—until the Convocation ended—she must be the obliging, dignified, unexceptionable lady her father expected. She would greet each guest's arrival with reserved graciousness and then retreat into the background until her services were required again. She would have little or no part in the Convocation itself; a few women might be in attendance, but for Sir Averil and the traditionalists, females had no place in political or marital negotiations. Their sole purpose was to bring more pureblooded *loups-garous* into the world.

By the time the Convocation was over, Gillian would be the mate of a stranger. She would feel his intimate caresses, his body joined with hers, just as she had felt Ross moving inside her....

"Ma'am? Are you quite well?"

Gillian realized she had slumped over the dressing table, half undoing Cora's careful work. She straightened and quickly rebuilt her veneer of tranquility.

"I'm only a little tired, Cora. Please continue."

Cora worked efficiently for another ten minutes, received Gillian's approval for the neat and unpretentious coiffure, and then fetched the gown. Gillian had little interest in keeping up with the latest fashions, which was fortunate, since Sir Averil would never have provided a sufficient allowance for her to do so. This dress was relatively new, having been ordered with the Convocation in mind, but it was modest and almost severe in its lines. Even so, Gillian felt exposed, as if she had been asked to parade naked before leering bidders at a slave market.

It's only Marcus Forster, she reminded herself as she descended the stairs and passed through the entrance hall. She had met him a few times; the Forster family was an ancient once, established in Northumberland for centuries, and it was inevitable that they would associate with the Maitlands.

But some of the Forster clan's less conventional members had married humans. Gillian had presumed that Marcus Forster had only been invited to the Convocation because failing to do so would be too egregious a snub to a family whose wealth and influence was not inconsiderable. But as she paused at the drawing room door to make sure her mask was still in place, she considered a second possibility.

Perhaps Forster was the mate Sir Averil had chosen for her.

Permitting herself a cautious hope, Gillian walked into the room. The high, red-flocked walls engulfed her, reminding her of blood, as did the ugly paintings of slaughtered animals hung above the crimson-upholstered chairs and settees. Forster and Sir Averil were standing beside the enormous mantelpiece, wreathed in an uncomfortable silence. Marcus's pleasant face broke into a smile as she went to greet him.

"Mr. Forster," she said, offering her hand. "How pleasant to see you again."

"Mrs. Delvaux." His grip was firm, making no concession to her gender. "Delighted."

She returned his smile. "I trust that your journey from Northumberland was not unpleasant."

"Oh, I quite enjoyed it. My family are always complaining that I spend far too much time in my workshop."

The warmth in his voice was obvious, and Gillian remembered how much she had always liked him. She looked closely into his eyes, seeking some clue that he regarded her as something more than the daughter of his host. *He would be good for Toby,* she thought. She could respect him, perhaps even come to care for him.

And think of Ross every time he came near her.

"…your son, Mrs. Delvaux?"

Gillian snapped out of her thoughts just in time to catch the gist of his question. "Toby is very well, Mr. Forster. Thank you."

He continued to smile, but there was no particular interest in his manner. Her hope wavered, but she reminded herself that tonight, at least, she would make conversation with a gentleman whose company she actually enjoyed. Then she would spend time with Toby, and give him the attention and explanations he deserved.

And tomorrow… Tomorrow it would be as if New York had never happened.

She accepted Mr. Forster's arm and let him escort her into the dining room.

THE EARNSHAW BROTHERS of Yorkshire and the Scottish Macalisters arrived the following afternoon. Hugh was strangely absent when Gillian came downstairs at the footman's summons; she sensed Sir Averil's annoyance, though he would not reveal any such emotion to the people descending from their motor cars in the drive.

The Yorkshire pair were twins, a little older than Gillian and taciturn to the point of unsociability. Graeme Macalister, as bluff and unpolished as any Scotsman of popular literature, had brought his wife, a timid creature who reacted to Gillian's greeting with vague surprise, as if she had expected no acknowledgment at all. The Earnshaw brothers looked Gillian over with cool speculation in their eyes, and she remembered that one of them was unmarried.

The atmosphere was supremely civilized as the first guests retired to their rooms to dress for dinner, then descended again for preprandial drinks and the obligatory conversation. Mrs. Macalister remained in her room. Sir Averil spoke to his guests of casual matters, ignoring Gillian as he subtly established his dominance over the company. There was an unspoken agreement that no Convocation business would be discussed until all the delegates were present, but Gillian sensed that Sir Averil's anger at Hugh's continued absence was growing.

She was content to retreat into the background while the men conversed. She had spent most of the day supervising the staff in making final preparations for the delegates' arrival, though Mrs. Mossop already had matters well in hand. The long-unused guest rooms were spotless and dust-free. Immense quantities of food, especially meats, had been purchased and stored, and additional staff hired in the village and surrounding areas. No guest would want for even the most insignificant convenience.

Everything necessary had to be present, for Snowfell would be cut off from the outside world for the duration of the Convocation. No humans except the servants would be permitted on the premises—though, in any case, residents of the nearest estates had long ago ceased extending invitations or making social calls on their reclusive neighbors. Villagers and local farmers kept well clear of Snowfell unless summoned. Some knew the truth, but for others, rumors—and Sir Averil's reputation—were more than enough to keep them away.

Hugh had yet to put in an appearance when Faulder announced dinner. Toby was to receive his meal in the nursery, as he would continue to do throughout the Convocation. Gillian would have given much to be with him. Their talk last night had left her unsatisfied; there had been an air of watchfulness about him, a sense of anticipation that was hardly in character, given his resistance to Gillian's forthcoming marriage.

Something beyond the natural tension of the situation was also taking its toll on Gillian. She took her seat between Sir Averil and Mr. Macalister, smiling at both men and asking trivial questions. The cheese course was being served by Faulder and the footmen when the front door opened.

Faulder hurried away to meet the new arrivals. Gillian heard Hugh's voice and glanced at Sir Averil, whose face tightened for an instant before he regained his usual dispassion.

"If you will forgive me, gentlemen," he said, beginning to rise. "I shall rejoin you presen—"

His words were interrupted by Hugh's appearance in the dining room. His face was flushed, and Gillian knew immediately that he had committed some imprudence. That thought had hardly taken hold when she realized exactly what he had done.

Ross strolled in behind Hugh, dressed in a casual suit and wearing a broad-brimmed hat and scuffed leather boots of the sort American cowboys sported in the moving pictures. Gillian almost jumped up in shock, but managed to rein in her emotions just in time. Sir Averil stared, for once unable to contain his astonishment.

"Good evening, Father," Hugh said too brightly. "Gentlemen, Gillian. I am sorry to be so late to dinner." He addressed Sir Averil, his insouciant expression never wavering. "Sir Averil Maitland, may I present Mr. Charles Keating. Mr. Keating, Sir Averil."

Ross swept off his hat and offered his hand. "Sir Averil. So pleased to meet you. Your invitation was greatly appreciated."

Sir Averil stared from Hugh to Ross, momentarily at a loss for speech. "Hugh," he said, "what is this—"

"I happened to pick up Mr. Keating's telephone call from Liverpool last night, and I thought I'd run down and fetch him. This is his first time in England, after all, and I didn't want him going in the wrong direction."

Gillian could see that the volatile situation was about to catch fire. She rose without haste, turned and smiled at Ross.

"Good evening, Mr. Keating," she said. "I am Mrs. Gillian Delvaux. I confess I had not been aware that we were expecting a guest from America."

"It was a last-minute decision on Sir Averil's part," Hugh said, forestalling their father with reckless abandon. "Mr. Keating owns one of the largest ranches in Arizona and has many other interests in America, including oil fields and motor cars. He has been in correspondence with Sir Averil about creating an American version of our Convocation." He paused to catch his breath. "But where are my manners?" He faced the table. "Father, would you be so kind as to introduce us to your other guests?"

A deep hush fell over the room. Faulder, who had followed Hugh and Ross into the room, stood absolutely rigid, as did the footmen. They knew something was badly amiss. The guests showed varying reactions, from thinly veiled contempt on the part of the Earnshaw brothers to Mr. Macalister's frank curiosity.

Sir Averil was clearly at a loss, and Gillian knew why. If he should repudiate Hugh's explanation, he would appear to have allowed his own son and a total stranger to manipulate him, a sure sign of weakness he didn't dare show.

But Gillian was certain that he had already guessed who "Charles Keating" really was. Sir Averil would have to contend with the possibility that his despised American "guest" might reveal that he was the father of Gillian's son.

Oh, Ross, Gillian thought. *What have you done?*

Marcus Forster chose that moment to circle the table and

offer his hand to Ross. "How do you do?" he said. "Marcus Forster."

His preemptive action was just short of rude, but Sir Averil had made his decision. As Forster stepped back, Sir Averil took his place. "Welcome, Mr. Keating," he said, staring Ross in the eye and gripping Ross's hand as if he intended to break it. Ross didn't flinch.

"You have a beautiful place here, Sir Averil," Ross said mildly. "Very different from what we have in Arizona, but most impressive."

Sir Averil dropped Ross's hand without responding. "Allow me to introduce you to our other guests," he said. "Aldous and Kenneth Earnshaw—" he gestured to the twins, who stiffly inclined their heads "—Mr. Graeme Macalister. Mr. Forster you have met."

"Glad to make your acquaintance," Ross said. "Sorry for the bad timing on my part."

Each of the men took Ross's offered hand and, like their host, tested the American interloper for any discernible weakness. Ross grinned imperturbably.

"Never been to Scotland," he said to Macalister, "but I hear you have some excellent elk hunting up your way."

"We call them red deer," Macalister said. "Do you prefer to hunt as man or wolf?"

Ross cocked his head. "I think it's a mite too easy to run a stag down as a wolf. I like bow hunting, myself."

Macalister grunted and waited for Gillian to resume her seat. Sir Averil waved permission.

"Would you care to join us for the cheese, Mr. Keating?" he asked. "Or, if you it is more to your taste, our cook will provide you with a sandwich in the kitchen."

His manner was discourteous, but Ross—or the character he was playing—showed no sign of noticing. He patted his stomach in a flagrantly vulgar gesture. "That sounds mighty good to me,

Sir Averil." He sat in the chair Faulder had belatedly sent a footman to acquire.

Her stomach roiling, Gillian declined the cheese and fruit. She was careful not to look at Ross, afraid her expression would give her away. Disbelief, anger, fear and desire conducted a war within her that left her weak. She continued to smile impartially at the table, refusing to look up when she felt Sir Averil's harsh stare.

He thinks I arranged this, she thought. *I agreed to the marriage, but he thinks I am playing games with him. As if I would dare.*

But he knew she had seen Ross in New York. That would be evidence enough of her duplicity in Sir Averil's eyes. And while he silently condemned her, the other guests responded to the newly charged atmosphere. Conversation faltered. While Mr. Macalister seemed neutral in his stance toward the American and Forster was friendly, the Earnshaws radiated superiority and disdain. Gillian feared that would be the typical reaction as the other delegates arrived. Ross's behavior—his speech, his common manner, even his way of eating—would serve to convince them that he was an outsider who could never belong among them.

And he couldn't. Every werewolf who came to Snowfell would be able to Change, and would prove it during the great hunt Sir Averil had arranged. Ross's defect would become common knowledge, and the other *loups-garous*…were not uncivilized beasts, for all their dual natures. The wolf was in all of them, but surely, even if the Continental delegates followed traditions differing from those of the British Isles, they would not attempt to do more than harass Ross into leaving Snowfell.

And how civilized were you when those gangsters came to the hotel?

She threw off the memory. The greatest danger Ross faced was Sir Averil. She had to discover what Ross intended at Snowfell, make absolutely certain he understood that he must not provoke her father any further.

And she must prepare to endure Sir Averil's furious interrogation.

"So, Mr. Keating," Macalister said, unexpectedly breaching the quiet, "you have no Convocations in America."

Ross paused to swallow. "Not that I've ever heard. I hope that'll change soon."

"And do you subscribe to the necessity of purifying the werewolf race?" Aldous Earnshaw asked, each word clipped and precise.

"We-ell," Ross drawled, leaning perilously far back in his chair, "it's a bit more complicated in the States. It's a big country, and our kind are pretty spread out, not like over here. Might be necessary to let a few mixed-breeds in at first, just to get things going."

Earnshaw's expression of disgust was instantaneous, and his brother slightly bared his teeth. Gillian knew Ross well enough to realize that he was deliberately mocking not only Earnshaw, but the entire purpose of the Convocation.

"Do you know any of these creatures yourself?" Kenneth Earnshaw asked.

"Mixed bloods? I've met one or two." He let his chair fall forward again. "Sir Averil tells me you use the Convocation to arrange marriages. Where are all the ladies?"

Sir Averil, who had been maintaining a dreadful silence, abruptly stood. "Gillian, I believe it is time for you to retire." She obediently rose, pausing to test the steadiness of her legs, and the men stood, as well. She politely made her good-nights, and then, with her head high, she made her way through the entrance hall and up the stairs. She continued to the second floor nursery, tucked away at the end of the corridor with the servants' quarters. She quickly dismissed Miss Rownthwaite, who had been finishing her own meal on a tray.

Toby was sitting straight up in bed, his eyes very wide. He leaped up as soon as Gillian closed the door.

"Father is here, isn't he?"

Gillian didn't ask how he knew. He had always displayed the same keenness of hearing and smell as any full-blooded were-wolf…but then again, so did Ross. What troubled her was how unsurprised he seemed.

She sat on the edge of the bed and concentrated on keeping her voice soft and calm.

"Did you know he was coming, Toby?"

His cheeks reddened, and she could see him weighing a possible lie. After all, she had deceived him more than once, and the old trust between them had been strained.

But he decided against it. "Yes, Mother. I knew. But he had to come, don't you see?"

There had been only a few times in her life when Gillian had felt the desire to take Toby over her knee. This was one of them.

"I see only that Mr. Kavanagh has done a very dangerous thing by coming here at this time, and that he will gain absolutely nothing by doing so." She pushed her fingers into the counterpane and curled them into the thick fabric. "He will not be welcome here."

"Maybe when everyone sees he's just as good as they are, you won't have to marry that other man."

"We have already discussed this, Toby. My commitment has been given, and Mr. Kavanagh's presence will not alter my decision."

"But if he can show the other werewolves—"

"No." Gillian closed her eyes. "I warn you, Tobias. If you allow anyone, especially Sir Averil, to know that you were aware of this—this…" She momentarily lost the words. "Why did Hugh help Mr. Kavanagh?"

Toby lowered his gaze. "He wants to make you happy, just like I do." His head lifted, his expression all defiance once again. "You can't fool me any longer, Mother. I've known for a long time that Grandfather is a nasty old tyrant. You mustn't listen to him anymore."

"Toby…" How could she hope to make him understand now if she hadn't managed it already? "As long as Sir Averil heads this household, we are subject to his will. He won the right to host the Convocation because of his natural ability to command and bring others to support his convictions, but it is likely that the delegates will test his leadership. If your grandfather cannot rule his own family, he will appear weak, and that could lead to confusion. It might even cause trouble for Mr. Kavanagh."

Toby regarded her steadily. "Yes, Mother."

"You will not attempt to speak to Mr. Kavanagh. If he should try to approach you—"

There was a knock at the door. Gillian braced herself and opened it. It was Faulder, his expression just short of grim.

"Sir Averil will see you in his study," he announced.

"Thank you, Faulder. I will be down presently." She shut the door again and looked back at Toby. "Remember what I have said. Mr. Kavanagh's safety at Snowfell may depend upon your obedience."

Toby nodded, looking truly worried for the first time. Gillian left the room, realizing just how completely she had failed as a mother. And a Maitland.

She summoned up her scant courage as she paused at the door to Sir Averil's study. She neither heard nor smelled activity among the other guests; she supposed they had retired to their rooms. With any luck they would not hear her humiliation.

She knocked, and heard Sir Averil's terse "Enter." Her father sat at his immense mahogany desk, his head lowered over a sheaf of papers. Gillian did not presume to sit in one of the armchairs opposite the desk.

"Do you have any idea what you have done?" he asked quietly.

CHAPTER THIRTEEN

THE INTERVIEW was every bit as bad as Gillian had feared. In the end, she succeeded in persuading Sir Averil that she had been unaware of Ross's scheme and continued to remain ignorant of his intentions. Even so, he berated her for lending legitimacy to the "mongrel's" presence by greeting him so warmly, even as he glossed over Hugh's part in assuring Kavanagh's initial acceptance by the delegates. He assumed that Ross had somehow forced the entire charade on her innocent brother.

She knew that any attempt to defend the intruder would only exacerbate Sir Averil's thinly veiled rage. And she could hardly contain her own fury at Ross, though she kept her eyes downcast and accepted Sir Averil's caustic reminder of her unforgivable weakness and stupidity.

"You will not speak to Kavanagh while he is at Snowfell unless you are compelled to do so in company," he said. "Any attempt by Kavanagh to disrupt the proceedings will result in severe consequences for him."

But he hadn't said he would send Ross away. No doubt he wouldn't make a move until he had fully ascertained the American's intentions. But Gillian knew she had to obtain that information first and convince Ross to leave without allowing Sir Averil to suspect her involvement. Afterward, she and Ross must have no further contact—no speech, no glances, no touching....

You fool. You miserable fool.

She had finally escaped Sir Averil's office, scampering back to her room like the hapless coward she had always been. It was gone two in the morning when she crept down the corridor to the area where the male guests were housed, seeking Ross's scent. He had been assigned a room at the very end of the wing, as far from her suite as possible.

Not daring to knock, she opened the door. Ross was lying on the spartan bed with his hands pillowing the back of his head. He was still dressed in the clothes he'd worn at dinner, though he had removed his jacket and boots, and the incongruous hat had been set on one of the chairs in the corner. He must have smelled her coming before she entered the room, but he didn't jump up to greet her. He rose slowly, swinging his long legs over the bedstead, and stood, simply waiting.

She had thought she might rage at him, as inadvisable as that might be under the circumstances. But her anger seemed to retreat in his presence, subdued by the warm, masculine scent of his body and the steady sound of his breathing. The urge to walk into his arms was almost too powerful to resist.

"Why?" she whispered, standing close to the door. "Why did you come?"

She was dreading and anticipating his answer in equal measure. But Ross made no impassioned speeches, no protestations of a devotion so desperate that it had sent him across the Atlantic in pursuit of his lady-love.

"I found out about your marriage," he said simply. "I'm here to make sure that Toby doesn't suffer because of it."

Of course. Once again she'd been utterly stupid. Stupid to actually have hoped, if only for a few illusory moments…

"Who told you?" she asked.

But she already knew the answer. And it didn't really matter. The damage was done.

"You had no right," she said. "You agreed that your circumstances had become a liability to Toby's future. You willingly consigned him to my care."

"When I let myself be convinced that you actually had his best interests at heart."

She came within an inch of striking his expressionless face. She carefully folded her fingers against her palm instead. "And how is my marriage supposed to harm him?"

"You aren't dumb, Jill, so you must still be lying to yourself." A muscle in his jaw twitched. "When you talked about Toby's future, I thought you were only worried about him being half-human. Now I realize the problem goes a lot deeper than I ever guessed."

Gillian began to feel light-headed. "You don't know—"

"I've met Sir Averil now. It explains a lot of things about you I didn't understand."

"You never understood me."

"Maybe not before. You never said much about your family in London. In New York you led me to believe that your father was some eccentric old coot, and you were looking after him, as well as Toby. But now…" He hesitated. "It's so obvious, Jill. It would have been obvious even if Hugh hadn't warned me. I've heard what Maitland thinks about humans. I saw how he behaved toward Toby in Liverpool. He called you a whore."

Coming from his mouth, the epithet was unbearable. "My relationship with my father—"

"Relationship? Is that what you call it?"

"—is none of your concern."

He watched her in silence while the small clock on the mantelpiece ticked out the seconds. "But it is, Jill. You're going to marry some guy you know nothing about, someone chosen by that son of a bitch. Are you going to tell me that our son won't pay a heavy price if you end up with someone like Sir Averil, and Toby can't Change?"

Gillian reeled, feeling like a living insect tacked to a board by an enormous pin. *Toby will Change. He will.*

"I know none of this was your idea," Ross continued. "*He* orced you into it, the way he's always made you—"

"Is that what Hugh told you?" Gillian laughed, though the sound emerged more like a madwoman's cackle. "I would not think that believing everything you hear is a valuable trait in a policeman."

He shook his head. "You can stop pretending, Jill. I won't betray you. I'll do everything in my power to help. You don't have to appease that bastard anymore."

His words hurt, and that made what she said next the tiniest bit less painful. "Don't flatter yourself," she said. "I was not forced into this marriage. Each of us recognizes a duty to a higher cause than our own petty desires."

His expression turned uncomprehending, then incredulous. "Hell. Hugh was right. That's your father speaking. You never had a chance, let alone a choice."

"I had a choice. I simply didn't multiply my mistake by choosing to stay with a man who would always live his life in the Maitlands' shadow."

For a moment she expected Ross to dismiss her claim, secure in his assumption that she was nothing but a helpless pawn—that the girl he had courted in London, the woman he'd made love to in New York, had been so different because she had been temporarily free from her father's malign influence.

But then she realized that she had just confirmed the supposition he'd drawn when she left him twelve years ago. He had lived with that conclusion far longer than he had known her. Something in her voice, her choice of words, had pierced his armor. His brown eyes became hard as agate.

"Yeah," he said. "I guess I was right at the very beginning, before you played all those games in New York. You really do agree with the things those guys were spouting in the dining room—that stuff about purifying the race and referring to part-werewolves as 'creatures.'" He didn't allow her a chance to respond. "They think they're big shots, but they're being played for fools. Just like I was." His empty expression was terrifying. "Funny thing is, I still believe you love Toby. You believe what you're doing is going to help him. But there's one thing I don't understand. Your father knew you had a human lover. He knows Toby might never Change, and that's the thing that matters, isn't it? Why are you going to let the others believe that he's a full-blooded *loup-garou,* when that lie could doom him later?"

Gillian was almost too dazed to speak, horrified at the things she had said but unable to take them back. "You don't…Toby—"

"If either you or your father intended to be up-front about Toby being half-werewolf, Maitland wouldn't be so worried that his guests might find out about me."

"A—a relationship outside marriage is… It is simply not done among…"

"Don't give me that. Averil made it very clear what bothered him about what we did, and it wasn't because you were promised to someone else. For some reason he wants to sell you and Toby as a package deal, and he's lying about the goods."

Gillian shivered. How could he know so much? Had Hugh told him, or had he come to these conclusions entirely on his own?

"My father is—" she began. "He is not a fool, and—"

"He's taking a pretty big risk if his main concern is preserving the illusion of your family's purity," Ross interrupted. "He's supposed to be the high muckamuck. What could he have to gain by alienating his allies and being exposed as a liar?"

Gillian remembered her first discussion with her father on the topic of the marriage, how stunned she had been that he had proposed such a thing when she had passed out of her twenties and had a half-grown, half-human son.

She had been too shocked and dismayed to register everything he had told her. But she knew that he had recently defeated the Russians, the Germans and several other candidates in a contest to become host of the newly revived Convocation, and was compelled to make a contribution of at least one marriageable off-spring. She had accepted his proposal, because the alternative was to lose Toby entirely. That immediate threat had seemed far more real than a future difficulty that might never come to pass.

Now the future was here. And Toby…

"Sir Averil has devised a scheme for dealing with the…issue, should it arise," she said.

"And do you know what that scheme is?" He searched her eyes. "You don't, do you? Maybe he based his original plans on the assumption that Toby would have Changed by now, and he's starting to realize that he made a mistake." His gaze grew even more intense. "Do you really think he'd do anything in Toby's best interest if he can't be sure that his grandson will be an asset to his cause?"

It's a trick, Gillian thought. *A trick. He's trying to confuse me.…*

"Think, Jill. A lot men would rather not be saddled with a marriage that included a kid who's someone else's son. With men like your father, like those Earnshaw guys downstairs, it'll be worse. Would either of them put up a fight if Sir Averil suddenly decided that Toby should have a more extensive education somewhere halfway around the world before he joins you?"

"We had an agreement—"

"And of course you believe the son of a bitch, after everything he's done to you."

"You will not speak of my father in that manner," she snapped, desperate to hold the ground that was rapidly crumbling under her feet. "This is his house. You are here on sufferance."

"Just like you."

"No. This is *my* world. You are a stranger, an outsider, and yet you presume to know everything about us, our way of life—"

"A way of life that's betrayed you. And will go on betraying you."

"As yours betrayed you?"

His lips thinned. "We all tell ourselves lies," he said. "If it weren't for Toby, I wouldn't give a damn if you stuck with yours for the rest of your life." He paused, and his voice softened "Averil obviously figured out who I was as soon as I walked in the door. Why did you cover for me, Jill?"

Somehow she found a reasonable answer. "I could not le Toby's father suffer the consequences of being exposed as a fraud."

He shifted his weight and leaned forward, almost as if he intended to approach her. Touch her, the way her stupid, treacherous body wanted so badly.

"Hugh said he could pull off just about anything without making your father angry. He promised he'd make sure Maitland knew my coming was his idea. Did he?"

Hugh said. Oh, how she had wished, so many times, that Hugh would do the things he said.

"Sir Averil knows I had no part in your arrival," she said. " am certain that Hugh intended to do just as he told you."

Real distress flashed across Ross's face. "I'm sorry, Jill," he said. "I trusted your brother to follow through. I won't make that mistake again."

"You will not make any further mistakes at all," she said. "You must leave Snowfell."

"You know I can't do that. No more than you can stop accepting the ideas your father has beaten into you all your life."

"Whatever Hugh told you…" She inhaled sharply. She could no longer deal with the profound contradictions in her heart and mind, not in Ross's devastating presence.

"Your fears are entirely misplaced," she said. "The longer you remain, the more harm you will do us."

"Maybe you don't want my help, but Toby does. I haven't been much of a father, but I'm not going to let him down now."

Oh, Toby. Toby. "Just what do you propose?" she asked mockingly. "You have no power here, no influence. Or do you intend to abduct Toby, as you once swore you never would?"

He didn't answer. She hadn't thought herself so capable o

ating someone as she hated Ross now. "If you attempt anything of the kind," she said, "I will stop you. Sir Averil will stop you. If you set yourself against him, you will lose."

"I'm not afraid of him, Jill. I know his breed. They always tumble in the end."

"But he will not be alone." She found that her lungs still refused to function as they should, and she paused to catch her breath. "Every delegate at the Convocation will be a full-blooded werewolf, as will my husband. And you—" She broke off in horror, realizing that she was about to confirm everything Ross had said about Toby's status.

"I'm a 'breed' who can't Change," he said without any trace of triumph. "And those pure-bloods will turn against me if they find out what I am."

"Not…not in the way you—"

"Tell the truth for once." He took a step toward her. "How well do you know the people coming here? Had you met any of them before tonight?"

"I have known Marcus Forster. He is a good man."

"But will the rest of them be like him, or like your father? Do you know what they're capable of, or has Sir Averil told you another bunch of lies to make you fall in line?" He moved closer. "They're *loups-garous,* Jill. The wolf is in all of them, and it's the wolf they're so dead-set on saving. No matter what you think about Old World superiority, these guys are probably every bit as ruthless as the Manhattan pack when it comes to getting what they want."

Gillian could no longer breathe at all. She *didn't* know anything about the delegates coming to Snowfell. She had learned what *she* was capable of. She had denied it to herself, but wasn't that what she most feared about Ross's presence at Snowfell? That he—so obviously hostile to Sir Averil, the Convocation and everything it hoped to achieve—would provoke a real fight with someone like the Earnshaw brothers and lose more than his dignity?

"You must go," she said, repeating herself like a scratched record.

"The worst has already happened to me, Jill. I've got very little left to lose. Toby could lose everything."

Her mind went blank. She backed away, brought up short by the door behind her. She reached for the doorknob, but her fingers refused to grasp the polished brass.

"Jill."

The husky warmth in his voice was more deadly than all the accusations, rebukes and tongue-lashings to which Sir Averil had subjected her in nearly thirty years. "Please don't use that name Mr. Kavanagh," she whispered.

He crossed the room and came to a halt less than a foot away. "Gillian, don't fight me on this."

"I must." She gained a grip on the doorknob at last. "I shall do everything within my power to prevent you from interfering."

"You do what you have to do, *Mrs. Delvaux,* and I'll do the same. Toby won't pay the price for your father's twisted ideas. Or yours."

He'd spoken similar words to her when they'd first met in New York, but there, in her desperation, she had found an unexpected strength as ephemeral as the illusion of love. She had no choice now but to conjure up that other Gillian, or else the life she knew—the life for which she had bartered to win herself and Toby some measure of peace—would cease to exist.

She left without saying good-night and returned to her room. No unusual noise suggested that anyone had heard her conversation with Ross. She quickly undressed and slipped into bed, knowing there would be no sleep for her tonight—only the searing memories of what Ross had said to her, the recollection of his touch on her body…and the acceptance that such a miracle would never come again.

ROSS TURNED AWAY from the door, the sound of Gillian's retreating footsteps pounding in his ears. He had never felt so much like putting his fist through the wall, even when he'd been framed for murder. And as much as he would have liked to have gotten drunk, he knew damned well that he couldn't risk even a second of vulnerability in this house.

This house.

Toby's brief comments and Hugh's description of Snowfell hadn't prepared him for the monstrosity that came into view as Hugh drove up the winding road to the house's front drive. Toby had said that the mansion had twice been rebuilt after fires had destroyed the first two versions. The huge stone building was almost a castle, with its multiple turrets, ivy—covered pillars and immense bay windows. Sticking out at an angle from one side was a section built in an entirely different style, the remains of a former house.

Hugh had already explained that Snowfell had been remodeled by the late baronet, Sir Aubrey Maitland, as a combination of historic edifice and a more modern floor plan. Still, he'd warned, there had been few improvements to the place since the late nineteenth century: no bathrooms, few water closets, gas lighting and hardly any of the amenities most people now took for granted. Sir Averil had seen such modernizations as unnecessary and soft.

Ross had kept the warnings in mind as Hugh guided him through an imposing columned porch, and into an entrance hall with gleaming wood paneling and marble statues precisely placed every few feet. The place was cold in spite of the large fireplace and the summer heat outside. The hall opened onto a grand staircase to the left, which Hugh ignored in favor of continuing into a corridor that eventually led to the dining room. Ross had been too intent on his new role to take in all the details.

Until he saw Gillian again. Then it all became real.

He went to the window now and twitched back the curtains. From his room he had a full view of the huge park, with its woods in the distance and the spare, rolling hills beyond. There were ranches all over the west bigger than this, but none were as lush, as brimming with conspicuous life…or as full of secrets.

But the alien landscape wasn't what concerned him. It was everything this house represented. He'd known he would be out of place even before he'd walked through the carved double front doors. Everything here stank of age, money and respectability.

And the so-called guests…

Oh, he'd run into plenty of wealthy snobs during the course of his profession. And he'd certainly met a few in London, officers from privileged backgrounds whose manner of speech and bearing declared them naturally superior to the common run of mankind.

But the guests here, and their host, were of an entirely different order. They were the ultimate aristocrats, and they knew it…except maybe the affable Marcus Forster, who had seemed almost as out of place here as Ross himself. Their eyes had evaluated the crude American and found him badly wanting, though at least they seemed to have accepted his ruse—for the time being, anyway.

As for Sir Averil, Ross had personally experienced the power he'd previously observed only at a distance, that wolfish dominance that compelled others to defer to his authority and watch their host's every move with cautious speculation. He alone had convinced Ross that the Convocation was going to be a nasty affair.

But damn her, Gillian wouldn't see. His argument had only served to harden her position that Toby would somehow benefit from her father's insane ideas.

Her ideas.

Ross left the window and paced the small room. He'd told her that he wasn't afraid of Sir Averil. But he wasn't a fool. It was going to be just as rough as Hugh had warned, and he couldn't count on any allies, least of all Hugh himself. Gillian had all but declared open war, and he'd returned the favor, knowing all the while that she had to live in this house day in and day out, reduced to a shadow under the thumb of a man who despised her for reasons even Hugh couldn't fathom…reasons that had to go well beyond what she'd done in London and New York.

Sir Averil had crushed her so often and so well that she no longer questioned his right to do so, or believed in her own right to challenge the ugly philosophy he had taught her.

Sympathy will have you beat you even before you start, he thought. Sympathy would destroy his focus on the one thing he had to accomplish: saving Toby.

She covered for me when she didn't have to. She cares….

She'd covered for her father, knowing how bad he would look if it seemed that Sir Averil hadn't known the new arrival was coming.

No. It was essential to accept that Gillian *had* made a choice. She'd had at least two chances to escape and hadn't taken them. No matter what Ross did or said, she wasn't going to change.

But he couldn't forget how it had been in New York, with her lying in his arms.

He tried to block the memory, but he was too late to stop his cock from reacting like the traitor it was. Sex was as deadly as sympathy. He would have to try to ignore her, her rich, unconsciously sensual fragrance, the golden hair he could never stop wanting to touch, the slender, supple body that could mold so perfectly to his….

The wall narrowly escaped his battering fist.

He lay back on the bed, returning to his examination of the ceiling as if it were the scene of a crime and someone's life depended on his solving it in the next few minutes. Eventually he gave up and closed his eyes, knowing he would need any sleep he could snatch away from the turmoil of his thoughts.

The thoughts didn't quit. He remained awake, weighing

dozens of half-baked plans and rejecting them one by one. Finally he got up, pulled on his boots and went downstairs.

First light was already brightening the sky, reminding him that the days were longer this far to the north. He considered finding Toby, but instinct told him the time wasn't right. Instead, he pursued the smell of freshly baked bread to the dining room, into a small adjoining room, through a door covered with green cloth, along a corridor lined with rooms of uncertain function, turned left and finally arrived at the source of the fragrance. He opened a plain wooden door and stepped into the kitchen.

The large room was bigger than any kitchen he'd ever seen, but it was warm and pleasant, in marked contrast to the rest of the house. Servant girls in caps and aprons bustled here and there, rushing from one worktable to another, from the open mouth of the blackened hearth to the equally black closed range covered with pots of all shapes and sizes. The aromas of spices and meat and vegetables were like a siren call to Ross's empty stomach.

Several girls came to a halt when they saw him, frozen in the middle of their tasks. The portly woman standing over the range, wisps of gray and brown hair escaping from under her cap, didn't seem to notice. He took a seat at the scarred, unoccupied oak table at the end of the room and simply enjoyed this little slice of blessed normality.

The woman he presumed to be the cook turned abruptly, stared at him and placed one hand on her ample breast.

"Oh, Lord!" she exclaimed. "You gave me such a start, sir. I didn't know any of the guests was round and about at this hour."

Ross stood as a matter of courtesy and smiled. "I didn't mean to intrude on your work, ma'am. My name is Charles Keating, of Arizona, in the U. S. of A."

The cook seemed unable to decide what to make of him. She frowned at the gaping girls, who immediately returned to their work.

"Please pardon me, sir," she said. "I didn't realize the master was to have guests from America." She took a few cautious steps toward him. "Would you be wanting something to eat, sir? I've some fresh bread, currant jam and a very good roast beef, if it suits you."

Ross's stomach growled. He needed food just as much as he needed sleep. "I might just take you up on your kind offer, ma'am," he said, "so long as you don't keep calling me 'sir.' My name's Charles."

Disconcerted, the cook curtseyed, her ungainly body surprisingly graceful. "Spotterswood is the name, si— Mr. Keating. Please do be seated, and I'll see to your breakfast." She went to door that Ross presumed led to a larder, disappeared inside, then returned with a partially sliced roast beef. She set it down on the table, hurried to get him a plate and utensils, then hovered as if awaiting his approval.

"I don't like to impose, Mrs. Spotterswood," Ross said as he stared at the cold beef.

"Oh, no, sir. This is no trouble at all, considering the likes of them staying—" She clamped her lips together, and the healthy flush on her cheeks disappeared. "Forgive me, sir. I spoke out of turn."

Ross waved a hand. "We don't hold with formality in the West, ma'am," he said. "Some of the folks coming here might stay up on their high horses, but I ain't one of 'em."

Mrs. Spotterswood studied him intently, though she tried to conceal her interest. "You're not at all like…like…"

"Sir Averil? I hope not." He speared a slice of roast beef with his fork and set it on his plate. "I'm here to observe, but that don't mean I agree with everything he thinks. Especially about humans. I tend to think we're pretty much all alike, at least where it counts."

Mrs. Spotterswood began to relax. She left to fetch a wooden board complete with freshly baked bread, laid it before him and cut several slices. When she spoke again, her accent was slightly different, tinged with a broad, country rhythm.

"Thoo're dead kind, Mr. Keating," she said.

"And you're a very good cook," Ross said, taking a big bite of bread. "We don't much hold with keeping lots of help where I come from. Does Sir Averil treat you badly, Mrs. Spotterswood? You and the other humans here?"

She froze. "We're only servants, Mr. Keating, and not worth your concern."

"Don't you believe it, ma'am."

"I…" She fled, this time to bring a pot of jam and a plate of little cakes. She set them down with a firmness that suggested that she'd reached some important decision.

"Thoo're a proper gentleman, Mr. Keating," she said. "If all Americans ist like thoo, Ah 'ope ter see yoower country yan day."

"I hope that you shall," a familiar voice said from the door way.

Gillian walked into the room, wearing a loose silk jacket and soft, wide trousers that flowed against her body with her every movement. Ross got to his feet, every girl in the room curtseyed and Mrs. Spotterswood bobbed her head. Gillian smiled at the cook, who grinned in return. Mrs. Delvaux might be the master's daughter, but it was clear that she had gained the older woman's unquestioning trust.

"I see you've met Mr. Keating," Gillian said in a neutral tone that neither approved nor disapproved of Ross's presence in the kitchen. "I trust your work has not been disturbed?"

"Not at all, Mrs. Delvaux," the cook said, reverting to a more standard form of English. "I was only getting him a bit of break fast." She peered at Gillian. "You've grown too thin, if you don't mind my saying so. I'll get you a plate."

Ignoring Ross, Gillian wandered about the kitchen as if she were as much accustomed to the rustic room as she was to the far more elegant quarters she and her kind enjoyed. She hesitated only when Mrs. Spotterswood indicated that she should sit at the table with Ross.

The awkwardness between them was painful. The cruel things they had said to each other weren't likely to be forgotten soon. But an unspoken truce took hold as the cook bustled about, piling ever more food on the table.

"No one shall starve in *my* kitchen," she announced, placing her hands on her hips. "Eat, Mrs. Delvaux, or I'll think you've lost your taste for my cooking."

Meekly, Gillian selected a piece of bread and laid a thin slice of roast beef on top of it. She watched Ross from the corner of her eye as she took a delicate bite.

"Do you come here often?" Ross said without cracking a smile, trying to pretend he didn't see the way Gillian's unbound breasts swayed gently under the silk of her tunic.

She seemed too distracted to notice. "I have always liked the kitchen."

"And the people in it?"

She took another bite—a very small one, like a Victorian girl who had been taught it was unladylike to have a good appetite. "Mrs. Spotterswood has been at Snowfell since I was... Since I returned from London."

"You consider her a friend?"

Ross could see Gillian debating her answer. She glanced over her shoulder, saw that Mrs. Spotterswood was busy chopping vegetables at the work table and lowered her voice.

"There are rules in a house such as Snowfell," she said. "Servants have their own world, and it is not to be intruded upon."

"Or allowed to intrude on yours."

She put down her makeshift sandwich. "Sir Averil knows nothing of my visits here."

"So the obedient Mrs. Delvaux defies the master once again."

Gillian began to stand. Ross got up and circled the table to pull back her chair. Gillian averted her eyes and strode for the kitchen door. Ross let her go, then sat again and looked down at the food spread across his plate.

Mrs. Spotterswood appeared at the table. He could tell from the slight change in her scent that she was upset.

"Is there something else I can get you, Mr. Keating?" she asked brusquely.

"Nothing, thanks." He met her gaze. "Tell me…is Mrs. Delvaux always so friendly to you?"

Her obvious disapproval gave way to a more speculative look. "To all the servants, when the master's not around." She leaned over the table, bracing herself on her sturdy arms. "She's had a bad time of it, if you don't mind my saying so. Raising the boy alone, without even a—" She broke off. "But I think you already know that, Mr. Keating. A blind man could see that you care about her."

Ross was momentarily flustered. If the cook could reach that conclusion after his brief and prickly exchange with Gillian, he was already making some serious mistakes.

"I met her years ago," he said cautiously.

"During the Great War? Were you a soldier, Mr. Keating?"

Swallowing his last bite of bread, Ross got up. "Whatever you may have guessed about me," he said, "I'd ask you to keep it to yourself. Mrs. Delvaux and Toby might get hurt if the others found out we already knew each other."

"Say no more, sir. No word of it will escape my lips."

Ross offered his hand. She took it. "Good luck to you, sir," she said.

"Charles," he said.

She stared at the spotless floor and then met his gaze. "Hazel."

He thanked her for both the food and her promise, carried the plates to the counter beside the sink and left the kitchen. He retraced his steps through the maze of servants' corridors and entered the main part of the house, feeling more perplexed than ever.

Since his arrival at Snowfell, he'd seen three distinct and very different Gillians: the one who rigidly adhered to her father's expectations while denying her own, the one strong enough to stand her ground against a very personal enemy and the woman who contradicted her father's philosophy by treating humans with kindness rather than considering them inferior beings unworthy of notice.

She wasn't fighting the war the way he'd expected. Now he was in very real danger of losing his shaky defenses all over again.

As he walked through the hall toward the front door, he heard faint footfalls on the floor above; the guests were beginning to stir. He continued through the entrance hall, passing Faulder on the way.

"Are you going out, sir?" the butler asked.

"Just for a while," Ross said. "I've already eaten. If anyone asks, I'll be back in an hour or so."

"Yes, sir." He looked Ross over. "Perhaps the gentleman would prefer to select other apparel?"

Ross glanced down at his crumpled suit, remembering he was a rich man now. He had to act like one.

"These boots have seen a lot worse than that tame countryside out there," he said. "I can always pass the suit on to one of the servants if it gets dirty."

"Very good, sir." The butler retreated, his back as stiff as those of the werewolf guests. *He doesn't think much of me, either,* Ross thought. It didn't matter—as long as the guy didn't hear about the conversation that had just taken place in the kitchen.

Ross walked out the door. The feeling of freedom that came over him was immediate. He crossed the park with its formal garden, jumped over the sunken wall that he presumed kept livestock away and continued on to the woods. The trees were old and tall, creating a world of shadow broken only by the occasional shaft of early morning sunlight. Twittering birds fell silent as he passed beneath their perches; they sensed the wolf in him as he sensed the rabbits before they bolted from his path.

The forest wasn't particularly big, but it contrasted sharply with the land on the other side. Here the well-groomed estate ended and the rocky, almost barren hills, the fells, began. Flocks of sheep grazed on the slopes, raising their heads warily as they debated whether or not to run.

Ross climbed the first fell and found a meandering creek on the other side, sparkling with water clearer than anything he'd seen in the West. Successive rows of hills rippled in the distance, climbing higher and higher until they became mountains. A herd of black ponies with sweeping manes and thick feathers adorning their hooves galloped past him. Ross paused to admire them, thinking how long it had been since he'd seen a wild horse.

A long shadow fell over his feet.

"Father. You've come!"

CHAPTER FOURTEEN

WITH A START, Ross realized he hadn't heard or smelled Toby until the boy was standing right next to him. He cursed his inattention, turned and just stopped himself from letting Toby see just how glad he was to see him.

"Toby," he said in his sternest voice. "Are you supposed to be out here alone?

Toby's response was direct and completely unabashed; he flung himself at Ross and hugged him as hard as he could. "I knew you'd come," he said, his words muffled in Ross's jacket. "I knew you wouldn't let us down."

It was all Ross could do not to stroke Toby's fine, brown hair. "You shouldn't have followed me," he said gruffly. "Your mother must have told you that we shouldn't talk to each other where anyone else might see."

Toby drew back and stared up at Ross. "She told me," he said. "I know you're pretending to be somebody you aren't. But Grandfather suspects that you're my father, doesn't he?"

"Yes. And he's very angry at your mother and me right now. We don't want to get your ma in more trouble, do we?"

"You won't let anything happen to her. You're here to help us."

Ross knelt to Toby's level. "It's a very complicated situation," he said. "We have to be careful. No one else can know my real name or that your mother and I…" He gripped Toby's arms. "They need to keep believing that your real father was Mr. Delvaux."

Toby's brow furrowed. "Mother said what Hugh and I did put you in danger."

"It was my choice, Toby. I've been in dangerous situations before. But we have to work together. I'm counting on you to do just what I tell you."

"Yes. But you *will* stop Mother from marrying some other man, won't you?"

Damn it, lying to Toby wouldn't do a lick of good in the end, so he told the truth. "Your mother doesn't agree with us. I don' know if she'll listen to me."

"I can help. I'll talk to her, and—"

"No. You've got one important mission, and that's to keep our secret."

Toby kicked the toe of his glossy shoe against an exposed rock. "I won't tell them, not even if they take me down to the basement and put me on a rack."

Ross wondered exactly what books the boy had been reading. "I know you won't," he said. "Go on back to the house. I'l come along later, so no one knows we've been together."

Toby sighed. "Very well, Father." Very much on his dignity, he clambered back down the fell and disappeared into the woods. Ross sat beside the creek, tossing pebbles into it for a good half hour. He wondered how often the Maitlands took wolf shape, and what their human neighbors thought when they saw a pack o long-vanished predators skimming over the hills.

Sir Averil's ancestors must have dealt with the possibility o exposure ages ago, just like the pack. Ross's father had been ver good at concealing what he was from the humans who weren' privileged to know his secret.

Ross didn't envy the humans unfortunate enough to live nea Snowfell; knowing Maitland, it was probably a matter of threat and intimidation.

The exposure he himself faced was likely to have equally un pleasant consequences.

After another quarter of an hour had passed, Ross returned to the house, approaching by way of the mismatched wing that he now realized contained the kitchen. He caught the fragrance of frying bacon, and then the scent of someone he hadn't seen since his arrival. He stalked around a corner to a fenced kitchen garden filled with summer vegetables. Two figures stood in the shadow of the wall beside the garden.

Hugh was embracing a dark-haired girl a few years younger than he was, so entranced by her caresses that he didn't break it off until Ross was nearly on top of them. The girl sprang away, flushed and breathing hard.

"Ross," Hugh said, smiling nervously. "I didn't expect…that is, I didn't realize you were—" He glanced around, as if afraid that a whole horde of eavesdroppers was about to descend on him and his girl. "You…you won't tell anyone, will you?"

"What will you give me if I don't?" Ross asked. "More promises you don't intend to keep?"

"Oh. Blast it, I'm sorry, old man. I meant to talk to Father, but…" He swallowed. "Is Gilly in trouble?"

"It's a little late to worry about that now."

"I'll go to the guv'nor right away, tell him the story. I—"

"Don't bother. Your sister seems to be in the clear."

"Thank God," Hugh said, sounding as if he really meant it. He glanced at the young woman, who was listening to the exchange with slightly narrowed blue eyes.

Ross took a closer look at her. She was dressed in a servant's uniform of severe black dress and boxy shoes, and her dark hair was tightly confined and topped with a cap, but she was undeniably pretty. And human.

"Cora," Hugh said, "this is, um, Ross Kavanagh, from America. He's on our side, but you must never refer to him as anything but Charles Keating."

"How do you do, Mr. Keating," Cora said, bobbing ever so

slightly. She stared at Ross almost defiantly. "Are you really Toby's father?"

"For God's sake, Cora," Hugh hissed, but Ross held up his hand.

"I am, miss," he said. "And Hugh knows how bad it could get if anyone else found out."

"You can trust Cora," Hugh said eagerly. "We love each other, you see. But you can imagine what my father would do if…" He plucked at his collar. "He has plans for me, you know. I expect that he'll choose a bride for me at the Convocation. But I won't do it." He reached for Cora's hand. "I won't marry some were-wolf girl I've never seen."

A grim conjecture came into Ross's mind. "That's why you wanted me here, isn't it?" he asked. "If Gillian broke with Sir Averil, maybe you'd find the guts to do it, too."

Hugh's skin turned ruddy, and he looked away. "I told you I was a bloody coward."

"And useless to me and your sister."

"You're wrong!" Cora said, pulling her hand free of Hugh's, her striking eyes filled with passion. "He's *not* a coward. He is going to marry me. And no one, not even Sir-bloody-Averil, is going to stop us."

"Cora, go back inside," Hugh said, catching at her sleeve. "I'll see you again as soon as I can."

The girl gave Ross a long, measured look and slipped through a narrow door into the house. Hugh lingered, his mouth half-open, then changed his mind and strode after Cora.

Ross followed slowly. The room he entered was furnished with a large table and plainly decorated, obviously very close to the kitchen. He found the servants' corridor and heard low, harsh voices from a nearby room. Hugh and Sir Averil were arguing, and Ross could guess the reason.

The fortunate son, the heir who could do no wrong, was finally getting the drubbing he so richly deserved. Cora, feisty as she was, might as well kiss any hope of marriage goodbye, unless confronting the end of his own very personal dreams finally turned Hugh into a man. Ross wasn't holding his breath.

A door opened, and Ross ducked around a corner. Sir Averil passed without noticing him, his face blotched with rage. When he'd gone back into the main part of the house, Hugh crept into view. Ross stepped from his hiding place. Hugh looked right through him.

"He knows," Hugh said blankly.

Ross was in no mood to commiserate. "What are you going to do about it?"

"He's never spoken to me that way before," Hugh said, as if Ross hadn't said a word.

"I guess you finally know how it feels to be in Gillian's shoes."

"Poor Gilly. Poor, poor Gilly."

"You're breaking my heart."

"Kavanagh—"

"We're done."

"No. This isn't about me." Hugh held Ross's gaze. "There's something I have to show you."

If it hadn't been for Hugh's strange tone, Ross would have ignored him. Instead, he followed Hugh upstairs to his bedroom suite. With almost furtive movements, Hugh knelt and reached under the cushions of his sitting room. He pulled out a tightly folded piece of newsprint and handed the paper to Ross.

Ross unfolded the paper and saw the masthead of the *New York Sentinel.*

"I got it in Liverpool, at a newsstand that specializes in foreign papers," Hugh said.

Ross glanced down to the blaring headline and froze.

Girl Found Murdered in Hell's Kitchen, it screamed. The extensive story beneath carried the byline of Miles O'Grady. Ross clutched the paper, struck by a grim premonition, and continued to read.

The young woman had been a party girl, a flapper who'd done a stint as a showgirl on Broadway before taking up with various men of dubious moral character. The details of what the cops had found were horribly familiar: the same type and style of binding used on her ankles and wrists, the same pattern of bruises, the same slit throat. The body had been discovered by a hooch hound staggering home from an evening at the speakeasies. The location had been just two blocks from Ross's apartment building.

The tragic event had occurred the very night before he had boarded the ship for Liverpool.

Ross went to the armchair beside the fireplace and sat down heavily. O'Grady had made no effort to avoid speculation as to the nature of the crime, given that it appeared to be nearly identical to the one of which a certain New York City cop had been accused.

"I'm sorry," Hugh said. "I should have shown it to you earlier, but I wasn't sure…"

Ross hardly heard him. If the cops had collected sufficient evidence to consider Ross a viable suspect—an opinion the Sentinel clearly favored—they would have been at his door before he'd left for the docks the next morning. But Ross had no doubt in his mind that they'd have been looking for him by the time the Terpsichore was a hundred miles off shore. They would have thoroughly searched his apartment, eventually discovering, by one means or another, that he'd left the country. It would look as if he had fled in order to escape capture for what he'd done.

In his years on the job, Ross had dealt with a number of murders. None had been anything like these. It seemed possible, even likely, that the same bastard who'd killed Bonita had been responsible for this murder, as well.

But even if Ross had remained in New York, he wouldn't have been free to follow any new leads. He would be in jail, awaiting another hearing. And this time, the people who'd wanted to see him in prison might succeed.

"I haven't told anyone," Hugh said. "My father doesn't take an American paper. Unless one of the guests has run across the story…" He frowned. "Would the American police find out that you'd come to England?"

Ross carefully folded the paper, taking great care to make each crease neat and precise. "If they do their jobs right, they will."

"Then your police might communicate with ours."

Ross deliberately loosened his tight shoulders. "If they had any idea I was here at Snowfell, someone would have shown up by now."

"Then you have time."

Ross almost laughed. "You don't believe I did it?"

Hugh shrugged. "I may be a terrible judge of character, but I stand by my original opinion."

"I guess I ought to thank you for that."

"I know it's not much, but when my father is… When this is over and I come into my inheritance, I'll see that you have the means to travel wherever you must in order to avoid the police, or hire the best barristers in New York, if you prefer."

More promises. Ross got up, feeling stiff and old. "None of that's important now.

Hugh nodded. There was still hope in his eyes. Hope that Ross, the outcast, could save him, his sister and his nephew all at once.

Weary beyond measure, Ross left the room, closed the door and coldly debated his next move. Breakfast was still being served; he should go down and make his presence felt, remind the others that he wasn't someone they could push around.

He met Gillian halfway down the stairs. They both came to a halt.

"Mr. Kavanagh," she said formally.

"Mrs. Delvaux."

They stared at each other, neither willing to make the first move. Ross thought of the incriminating newspaper in Hugh's room.

Tell her now.

But he couldn't. Not when telling her would only give her more ammunition in the war over their son.

And you don't want her to start thinking you were the killer all along.

"Are you going down to join the others?" Gillian asked.

"I don't want to make it look like I'm hiding," he said. "If I've got to prove myself, I'd better start doing it."

"I wish you would not."

That wasn't a repeat of her demand that he not interfere. That was concern. For his safety. He hadn't completely imagined that she was worried about him, even though that kind of emotion could only hurt her cause.

To reach out, to touch her, to hold her again… God, he would have given his life to make things the way they'd been in London.

"They're going to have to accept that I have a right to be here," he said with more belligerence than he'd intended.

She chose not to notice. "More guests will be arriving today," she said, "from northern Europe, Spain and France, and perhaps a few from countries in eastern Europe."

Seething, uncontrollable jealousy drove all the wistful yearning out of his head. "I guess congratulations are in order," he said. "Anytime now, you'll be meeting your new husband."

GILLIAN WAS UNPREPARED for Ross's hostility, though she was well aware that she should have expected something like it. He had made it abundantly clear that he intended to disrupt Sir Averil's plans at any cost to her or himself, and he wasn't about to let her forget.

When Ross had first arrived, she'd been able to cover her shock with private anger and an outward display of perfect manners. But that shield could not possibly endure. Last night, as she'd lain sleepless in her cold bed, she had exhausted the outrage that had sustained her, along with any hope that she could convince him to go.

Oh, she had put on a brave front when she'd found him so comfortably settled in her only true haven at Snowfell, conversing with Mrs. Spotterswood as if he'd known the woman all his life. She thought she'd made a reasonable success of convincing him that his schemes did not have the power to disturb or distract her.

But she wondered how long she could continue, how long before she slipped and the others began to suspect that "Charles Keating" had meant more to her than they could possibly imagine.

She must not slip. She must not weaken, even though she would be spending long, agonizing hours in Ross's company. Concentrating, as always, on what must be done day to day, hour by hour, so that she might banish the most treacherous memories and sensations from her body and mind. But Ross's scent had begun to permeate the house, and his footsteps had become as familiar to her as Toby's or Sir Averil's. She was aroused every time she saw him, and if she were to touch him…

"Yes," she said, as if there had never been a pause in their conversation, "my intended will undoubtedly be among them."

Ross didn't answer. His eyes and his face were as expressionless as the busts in the entrance hall.

Would you care whom I married if Toby were not part of the arrangement? she silently asked the man on the step above. *If I gave you a sign, would you whisk us both away like a knight in a fairy tale?*

Would you love me?

She slipped past him, taking great care not to so much as brush his sleeve, and continued upstairs.

"Gillian…" He pursued her to the landing.

"I would prefer to be alone," she said without turning.

"Is Toby in his room?"

"Of course."

Ross's breath blew gently against the base of her neck, caressing the narrow gap between her collar and her hair. "Are you sure about that?"

Prodded by sudden alarm, Gillian hurried to the nursery. Toby wasn't there, and neither was Miss Rownthwaite. Gillian remembered that she'd asked for the afternoon off to nurse a sick relation, but Gillian had been so absorbed in her own concerns that she hadn't noticed that Toby wasn't even in the house.

"Did you see him?" she demanded.

"He came to find me on the fells, but I sent him back."

His voice held a grim note. He obviously knew as well as she that such disobedience could have unthinkable consequences.

"I think I know where he might be," she said.

"I'm going with you."

She lacked the will to argue. She told him to meet her downstairs, then went directly to her room. She considered locking the door. But Ross had shown no interest in her—not in that way—since he'd come to Snowfell. And why should he? He wouldn't let himself be weakened by lust. It was her own desires she must control.

After changing into a walking skirt and her oldest shoes, she joined Ross at the foot of the stairs and assured herself that no one had observed them together.

"Follow me at a distance," she said, and quickly set off. Only when she was halfway across the park did she hear Ross's shoes brushing the grass some dozen yards behind her.

Much to her concern, Graeme Macalister was also enjoying the fresh morning air. Gillian had no choice but to stop and greet him. He touched the brim of his cap.

"It is a pleasant time for a stroll, is it not?" she asked with forced cordiality.

"Indeed it is, Mrs. Delvaux," he said, unsmiling. "I wanted a good look at the fells. Different to our Highlands, but this bids fair to be a good place for a run."

"My family has found it so. How is Mrs. Macalister? I hope she is feeling better."

Macalister grunted. "We haven't yet seen your son. He's eleven years old, I believe. Has he made the transition?"

"He is a bit young, Mr. Macalister."

"I've seen it happen with boys much younger."

"The transition is difficult enough without asking our children to perform according to a schedule."

Macalister looked at her with faint surprise, doubtless taken aback by her directness. He touched the brim of his cap again. "Good day to you, Mrs. Delvaux."

He walked on, leaving Gillian short of breath. Her fears for Toby had taken hold of her again.

He had shown no signs. None at all.

She broke into a brisk pace, eager to leave Macalister and his questions far behind. Ross had possessed the good sense to keep himself hidden from the Scotsman, but she was very much aware of his nearness. She climbed the low fell to the north of the wood and followed a narrow track that wound for a half mile before it descended into a wide vale defined by a cluster of trees and a small beck. The area was quite level, and from the top of the last fell Gillian could see the remnants of a stone wall, a scattering of crumbled bricks projecting no more than a few inches from the earth.

She made her way down the fell and walked along the beck. She found Toby kneeling in the dirt near the wall, probing at the earth with a small spade. A pair of coins lay on the ground beside him, corroded almost black and crusted with soil. He looked up as she approached.

"Good morning, Mother," he said. His nostrils flared, and a spark brightened his eyes. "You brought Father with you."

Gillian knelt beside him, smoothing her skirt under her knees. "Is there some difficulty with your hearing, Tobias? Did I not make clear that you were to stay in your room?"

"I meant to, Mother, but I had too much to think about, and the ruins always help me make sense of things." He pushed the spade into the soil again. "Don't you agree it's ever so much easier to think here?"

She disregarded her love of his bright spirit and prepared a stinging rebuke. She forgot it completely when Ross reached the foot of the hill and started across the dale.

Toby stood, craning his neck to watch Ross with puppyish eagerness, though he shrank a little when he noticed his father's stern expression.

"Didn't I tell you to go back to the house?" Ross asked.

"Yes, but—"

"Your mother told you to stay in your room, didn't she?" He dropped into a crouch. "Do you really want to make things more difficult for her?"

Toby looked at Gillian with real repentance in his eyes. "I'm sorry, Mother," he whispered. "Can I stay just a little longer and show Father what we've found?"

"Toby—" Ross began.

"Only for a few minutes," Gillian said, wondering what Ross and Toby had discussed on the fells, and why Ross had taken her part. She rose, brushed loose soil from her skirt and nodded to Toby. He shed his remorse as he might kick off the shoes he was well on his way to ruining.

"It's an ancient Roman ruin," he told Ross in a professorial tone. "Mother and I have been digging here. This was probably a garrison where soldiers lived. We've found all sorts of things." He bent to gather up his coins and displayed them on his palm. "These are probably two thousand years old."

Ross took one of the coins. "Romans lived here?"

"Oh, yes. They had a very large empire, you know. They conquered the British tribes, but they married them, too. A lot of Englishmen have Roman blood."

"They didn't mind that their children wouldn't be pure Roman?"

Gillian felt the barb, but she refused to let it penetrate too deeply. "The Romans and Britons had one thing in common," she said. "They were all human."

"Not all of them, Mother," Toby said. "I'm sure some were just like us."

Gillian couldn't argue with his logic. But the werewolf kind would be extinct if even that ancient breed hadn't taken precautions—and paid the necessary price.

Ross returned the coin to Toby. "Maybe not. Maybe we were all human once."

"I think you're right, Father." Toby avoided Gillian's eyes. "Would you like to help me dig? I've found something…" He bit his lip. "I've found something I think you ought to—"

"Not now," Gillian said. "We must all return to the house."

"But I want—"

Gillian's frustration bubbled over like a pot left too long on the boil. "I don't care what you want," she growled. "You will do precisely as I tell you." She loomed over him, the wolf clawing its way to the surface. In another heartbeat she would shed her clothes, right here in front of Ross, and pin Toby to the ground with the weight of her body. He wouldn't be able to ignore that.

But something in her behavior made an impression. Toby cringed and lowered his eyes. He began to tremble. Gillian expected Ross to interfere, but he was silent.

The three of them remained frozen in a rigid tableau. Ross finally picked up the spade Toby had dropped and poked at the hole with far more force than was necessary. Toby continued to shake long after his ordinarily optimistic nature should have overcome his fear.

"Are you all right?" Ross asked him, frowning.

Toby opened his mouth. His teeth chattered.

Gillian fell to her knees. "Toby?"

Perspiration gleamed on his face, dripping off the tip of his nose. "Mother," he whispered, "I feel…rather ill."

Ross reached over her and laid the back of his hand against Toby's forehead. "He's burning up," he said. "I think we'd better get him back to the house."

CHAPTER FIFTEEN

IMMEDIATELY, GILLIAN gathered Toby against her chest. His fever scorched her skin where they touched.

"Give him to me," Ross said. "I'll go around the back. You distract anyone who might see us."

For all his human blood, Ross was both strong and fast, and she didn't trust her body to obey her commands. She passed Toby into his arms.

Ross lifted Toby easily and started for Snowfell at a trot. Gillian waited as long as she could bear and then began to run, taking a different route back to the house. She passed one of the Earnshaw brothers, but she couldn't force herself to stop for the sake of an explanation. She burst through the side door and raced up the back staircase to the nursery.

Toby lay on his bed, eyes closed, tossing and moaning as if ravaged by some terrible disease. Ross paced back and forth at the foot of the bed, his fists clenching and unclenching.

"We have to call a doctor," he said.

Gillian sat on the bed and took one of Toby's hands in his. It was moist and limp. "Not yet," she said. "We must wait."

"Wait? Are you crazy?"

"You have never Changed. You don't know what happens when a child makes the transition."

"What the hell are you—" He stopped abruptly. "Are you saying he's about to Change?"

"I am saying that his body may be altering to prepare for the transition."

"Would it come on this suddenly?"

It was evident that Ross had never discussed this issue with his half-werewolf father. And why would he have, given his breeding?

"Every child is different," she said. "It strikes sometime within the few years surrounding adolescence."

"And how long is this supposed to last?"

"There is no way of knowing. For some it is very quick. For others, it may require weeks."

"Weeks of this?" He stared at Toby, and Gillian could hear the grinding of his teeth. "What if he really is sick?"

"He has never been ill. *Loups-garous,* even children, seldom—"

"I know. But he's almost half-human."

She pressed her palm to her mouth. Had Ross suffered common childhood illnesses because he was more human than werewolf? He had healed quickly in hospital, but...

Could I be wrong, just because I want to believe that this is the sign I've been waiting for?

She rose. "I will inform Sir Averil that Toby is ill, and that I must stay with him. If he is not improved by tomorrow morning, I will request that Sir Averil summon our doctor." She felt dangerously close to tears. "Please watch over him until I return."

They gazed at each other, all hostility set aside, fully united in their concern for their son. Gillian kissed Toby's hot forehead and hurried downstairs. She found Sir Averil in conversation with Macalister and Marcus Forster.

"Your attitude is most unfortunate," Sir Averil was saying to Forster. "You will not find many of the same opinion here."

"I had assumed as much," Forster said, "and yet I have fostered the hope..." He turned as he registered Gillian's scent. "Mrs. Delvaux."

Sir Averil gave Gillian a look that could pierce steel, his gaze taking in her rumpled and slightly soiled clothing. "What is it?" he asked tersely.

"If the gentlemen will be so kind as to excuse us…"

"What is it?" Sir Averil repeated.

"Toby is ill, Father. I must ask to be excused from luncheon and dinner."

Real interest replaced the annoyance in his eyes. He murmured something to his guests and dragged Gillian into the corridor. "In what way is he ill?"

"He has a fever and is not fully conscious. It may be the transition, but if not…" She met his gaze. "If he does not improve, we must call the doctor."

Sir Averil's astonishment was palpable. No one, least of all his daughter, ever used the word *must* to him. But Toby's health was a thousand times more important to Gillian than any humiliation to which her father might subject her afterward.

And Ross was with her. Mad as it seemed, that knowledge made it easier to stand unbowed in Sir Averil's presence. If he refused to request a physician's assistance if and when it became necessary, she would ask Ross to fetch the doctor personally.

You may do with me what you wish, Father. But not with my son. Never with him.

But Sir Averil was no longer staring at her when she completed the silent vow. "I shall look in on him presently," he muttered, distracted as he considered the implications of Toby's condition. "You may remain with him for the time being, but when I require your presence, you will set Rownthwaite to tend him."

"Thank you, Father." She wasted no time in rushing to the kitchen for a glass of cool water and carrying it back to Toby's room. Ross had pulled a chair up beside the bed, gazing at his son with a deeply furrowed brow and a mouth stretched thin with worry. Toby was lying still and breathing steadily.

"He seems to be better," Ross said without looking up. "His fever is going down."

"Thank God." Gillian rushed to the bed. Ross rose to give her his place. She handed the glass to him and touched Toby's forehead. He was still sweating, but a more careful examination revealed no other obvious symptoms.

"It *is* the transition," she breathed.

"So now you don't have to worry that his blood is too human, or that he'll be thrown out by your father or whomever you're supposed to marry."

His blunt cruelty was a shock after the balm of their alliance.

"There may be more episodes like this," she said, disregarding his comment, "but no one at the Convocation will consider his illness a sign of weakness if they know what is happening."

"A sign of weakness," Ross repeated, his voice hoarse. "It's always about that one thing, isn't it? What would you have done if this hadn't worked out the way you were hoping? If Sir Averil was willing to let him die, would you have spat in his face and called the doctor anyway?"

Ross had said many terrible things, but none so terrible as this. Gillian's throat closed. Unable to answer, she lunged at him, fingers curled to tear at any flesh she could reach.

He was not prepared, and stumbled back against the wall. She raked his face with her nails. Gillian had the benefit of her full werewolf blood, but Ross was bigger and had a male's physical advantage. He wrestled with her until he was able to grasp her arms and hold her still.

"Jill," he rasped. "Jill, I'm sorry."

She didn't stop until the smell of his blood penetrated the red haze of her rage, and then she tried to wrench herself free. Ross resisted, but finally let her go.

"I'm sorry," he repeated, ignoring the blood dripping onto his collar. "I know you wouldn't do it, Jill. I know."

Gillian's legs had turned to rubber, useless now that she had regained control. She twisted to look at Toby, and her knees buckled beneath her.

Ross was there again, lifting her, babbling meaningless, soothing words that stole the last strength from her body. She pressed her face into his shirt and breathed him in, letting his warmth seep into her and ease the chills she couldn't subdue.

After a while he stopped speaking, and her trembling ceased. She slipped from his arms, looking for something to staunch his bleeding, and opened Toby's armoire. She pulled out the first shirt she found.

"Don't ruin his clothes," Ross said. "This shirt's done for anyway."

While she stood there with Toby's shirt in her hands, Ross removed his jacket and stripped off the stained shirt. He tore the cotton into a few broad strips and folded them into bulky pads.

"It'll heal up quick," he said, holding the pads to his cheek. "No one will know."

Mechanically, Gillian returned Toby's shirt to the armoire. He hadn't awakened through the conflict or its aftermath. She sank to her knees on the carpet and buried her face in her hands.

"Jill. It's all right. What I said was wrong. Unforgivable." She heard him come nearer, but he didn't try to touch her. "I know you'd give your life for him."

She pushed her palms against her eyes. "What *I* did was unforgivable."

"No, Jill. It was only natural."

His forgiveness was worse than his contempt. She made certain that her tears had stopped, got to her feet and drew away from Ross, flinching from his gaze.

"You must go," she said. "It would…not be pleasant if Sir Averil finds you here when he comes to look in on Toby."

"I guess he'll be relieved that this particular problem is solved."

"Please, Ross." She forced herself to meet his eyes. "After what I did…you have no reason to listen. But I beg you…"

He cut her off with a downward sweep of his hand. "I'm leaving," he said. He lifted the bandage away from his face; the wounds were already beginning to heal and would likely be invisible by tomorrow. "I'll go to my room and change. But I'll be back to make sure Toby's okay."

That was a privilege she couldn't deny him. "Thank you."

"Yeah." He bent over the bed to stroke Toby's damp hair, a tender gesture that Gillian had seldom witnessed from any male, then wadded up his torn shirt and left the room.

Gillian remained by Toby's side, grateful for the ease with which her thoughts faded into emptiness. Sir Averil arrived an hour later.

"How is he?" he asked, examining Toby from a distance.

"He is improving, Father."

Sir Averil grunted and approached the bed, bending to pry open Toby's eyelids and pulling his jaws apart as he might examine a horse. Gillian tensed to knock his hand away.

"The transition," he said with satisfaction, stepping back. "You are excused for the remainder of the evening, but tomorrow…" He sniffed the air, and his eyes narrowed. "Blood." He sniffed again. "Where is Kavanagh?"

"I've no idea, Father."

"Don't lie to me. He was in this room."

He is Toby's father! But she began to fall into the chasm of Sir Averil's implacable eyes, and she couldn't speak the words.

"I drove him out," she whispered.

"You?" He laughed. "The blood was his?" His smile was brief and never reached his eyes. "The boy is well enough. Go to your room and clean yourself."

"Yes, Father."

"And keep him to his room. Macalister said he saw the boy outside. There will be no more such transgressions."

Gillian kept her head low and said nothing. When Sir Averil had gone, she realized how very close she had come to being caught in a lie.

Macalister had seen Toby. He and Earnshaw had both seen *her*. If anyone had seen Ross, as well…

She stretched out beside Toby on the narrow bed. She had lied to her father, something she had done only a handful of times in her life. The illusion had been maintained. She was still the obedient daughter who accepted the master's word as law.

But Ross had held her. He'd held her in his arms, the blood trickling from his cheek, and told her what she'd done was natural.

Just as it was natural that she should feel nothing but self-contempt and yet continue on just as she always had.

Soon it would surely be over. Toby was safe; no one could ever claim he did not belong. Ross's fears for him, like her own, had proven groundless. And when he saw that *she* had not changed, he might finally realize that there was nothing left to fight for.

ETHAN TORE the short letter into several pieces and let them fall to the ground. He stared toward Snowfell, imagining Gillian among all those haughty werewolves with their delusions of superiority.

With Ross Kavanagh.

I cannot come, the note had read. *All the delegates will arrive by tomorrow. If I leave the house to meet with you, we may be discovered. I would not put you at such risk. And Toby is ill...*

There was more of the same delivered by Cora, who had looked more than a little nervous as she placed the note in Ethan's hands. Of course, she'd already informed him of Kavanagh's arrival. She had told him most reluctantly, afraid that he would withdraw his support.

Why should he? She was his foremost spy in the Snowfell household. She was his to use as he chose, as long as she believed that he could help to ensure that she and Hugh would find a safe haven when they escaped from Snowfell.

As if Hugh would dare, Ethan thought. He would never find the courage to abandon his inheritance or defy Sir Averil, even for the sake of the human he thought he loved.

Ethan picked up the fragments of the note and pieced them together again.

Lies, of course. Oh, not the blatant sort. Gillian was not the type. No, these were excuses, and they would not be the last.

Ross Kavanagh.

She had walked away from him in New York. She'd sworn, on one of those rare occasions when she'd spoken to Ethan during the voyage, that she was through with him. And he had been convinced that she meant it. Kavanagh should have received a cold reception from her, especially since she knew how thoroughly he could disrupt her life.

Instead, she had actually taken steps to welcome the American under her father's very nose. And the old wolf had gone along for inexplicable reasons of his own, though Ethan found it impossible to believe that he hadn't guessed at Kavanagh's identity. Gillian had, with her interference, become fully complicit in Kavanagh's game.

There was only one reason why she would make such a dangerous move in Sir Averil's house, one reason that would cause her to so abruptly sever a friendship upon which she had relied so heavily. She might tell herself that her commitment to duty and the werewolf kind had not faltered. But she had become just what Sir Averil had named her at the dock in Liverpool.

Whore.

Yet Ethan still wanted her, more than he had ever wanted anything in his life. She was his greatest weakness, the one he could not overcome. And even this insult of a letter could not alter his plans in the slightest.

He crumpled the pieces and placed them in his trouser pocket, setting off for Highwick. As always, his mother was in the drawing room she had long ago claimed as her domain, holding a glass full of whiskey while Cruthers waited just outside the doorway, ready to refill the glass as soon as his mistress had emptied it.

Ethan intended to pass by without speaking to her, but she had an uncanny ability to sense his proximity. She rose, swaying as she did so, and called his name.

He stopped, smoothed his expression and went into the room.

"Ethan, darling," she cooed, staggering into him and draping her arms around his neck. Her skin and clothing were drenched with the scent of alcohol. He pushed her away, noting that she was wearing another new frock, one that might have looked well on a much younger woman. But Lady Cynthia Warbrick believed she was still twenty-five years old, ravishingly beautiful and sought after by many men.

"Mother," he said coldly. "I was just going to my room."

"Oh, no." She gave him a flirtatious smile. "Stay with me, darling. Tell me where you've been this morning."

Of course she didn't know. He'd never told her about Gillian. Lady Warbrick had hated Sir Averil since Ethan could remember, and he had always preferred to avoid open arguments.

"Sit down, Mother," he said, guiding her toward the threadbare sofa. The whiskey sloshed in her glass as she fell into the flattened cushions.

"Why didn't you send me more funds to repair this wretched place?" she complained, finding her dubious balance as he sat down next to her.

"I give you a generous allowance, Mother. If you choose to spend it on dresses from Molyneux and Chanel, it is none of my concern."

She pouted for a moment and then remembered her original question. "I think you have a lady friend," she said in a singsong voice. "Who is she, darling?"

"There isn't anyone, Mother."

"You think I don't know anything because I seldom leave the house. Well, you're wrong." She smoothed her hand over the upholstery as if she were caressing naked skin. "I know quite a lot even you don't know."

"I don't wish to argue." He made to rise, but she clasped his arm and drew him down again. She thrust her face close to his, bathing him in her foul breath and cheap perfume.

"I'm still desirable, you know," she whispered, pushing a strand of bleached blond hair away from her face.

He shuddered. "You should go up to bed, Mother."

"Only if you come with me."

A wash of memories briefly held him paralyzed. He wanted to strike her. He thought instead of Sir Averil. And Gillian.

Lady Warbrick slumped, still pouting like the spoiled child she was. "Why did you have to go away?" she whined. "I was so lonely. It wasn't right for you to stay in America so long."

"It was necessary, Mother. You won't be buying any frocks at all unless we find new sources of income."

"By working with those awful Americans." Her eyes narrowed. "Is that where you met this girl?"

He wondered if she might have guessed after all. But no…if she had, she would be throwing a terrible tantrum. And she certainly had no conception of his primary reason for going to America.

"You don't really care for her," Lady Warbrick said dismissively. "Whoever she is, she can never compare to me. To what we've had together."

The memories overwhelmed Ethan, and his hands trembled so badly that he was forced to hide them behind his back. "She is nothing like you," he said. "She doesn't bathe herself in whiskey every day, nor spend her time complaining about her life."

As Ethan had grown to expect, Lady Warbrick's mood shifted instantly from seductive to outraged. She grabbed the lapels of his jacket.

"Tell me who she is," she hissed.

Ethan knew she ought not to be told anything. But she was seldom coherent enough to speak rationally, even if there were anyone to listen.

And he would relish the look on her face when she knew the nature of her rival.

"Gillian Delvaux," he said.

Even the streaks of garish crimson paint on her cheeks couldn't conceal her pallor. "Gillian?" she whispered.

"Yes, Mother. We met often as children, and recently renewed our friendship. She is everything that you are not. And I will have her."

Lady Warbrick gasped several times, touching her throat as if she could not get enough air. Then she drew herself up, for a moment reclaiming the elegance and dignity that had won the viscount's heart so many years ago.

"Cruthers?"

The butler stepped into the room. "My lady?"

"You may leave us."

He bowed slightly and retreated. Lady Warbrick listened to his receding footsteps and returned her attention to Ethan.

"I had not meant to tell you," she said in an uncharacteristically steady voice. "It was better that you not know."

Ethan tensed. "Know what, Mother?"

"That you and Gillian are brother and sister."

He felt a brief moment of profound horror. "You're lying."

"No, Ethan. I am not."

The statement was so calm and direct that Ethan knew she was telling the truth. He picked his way carefully to an armchair opposite the sofa and sat down, his hands clenched on the padded arms.

It explained so much—the powerful bond he and Gillian had established in childhood, their easy confidence, the trust Gillian had placed in him when they met again as seasoned adults. It explained his deep attraction to her, his sense that they belonged together.

"How?" he asked Lady Warbrick quietly.

She scraped her hair away from her face, drained her glass and set it down on the side table. "Averil and I were lovers," she said, "while the viscount was in Monte Carlo, losing the rest of his fortune."

Ethan gripped the arms of the chair. Sir Averil. It didn't seem possible. Sir Averil hated humans. He'd ignored Toby for most of the boy's life because he was tainted with human blood. Yet he'd made love to a human woman…one undoubtedly beautiful and capable of great charm, but human nonetheless.

"We met at a party given by Lady Veronica," Lady Warbrick continued in the wake of Ethan's silence. "God only knows why he was there…even then, he seldom visited the neighbors. He was married and had never shown any sign of being a libertine. But something happened between us." She stared at her empty glass. "I had not seen the viscount in two months. I was lonely. Averil was handsome, and had an intensity about him that fascinated me. So we began an affair. It lasted a month. Then he left me." Her face tightened with slow-burning anger. "Before he went back to his wife, he told me that I must rid myself of any issue of our love before it could be born."

Of course. Ethan smiled at the irony of it. Sir Averil wanted no evidence of their affair, knowing that one day any illegitimate son or daughter of his might reveal its mixed blood by showing the ability to Change.

Lady Warbrick touched her slightly rounded stomach, as if she could still feel life moving inside her. "I realized I was with child a month later," she said. "I didn't do as Sir Averil demanded. My husband was due to return presently. I chose to bear my…my children and present them as his."

"The viscount died before I… Before Gillian and I were born."

"It was a terrible accident, and quite inconvenient. I didn't know I was to have twins, you see." She laughed hoarsely. "I was quite alone, of course, with very little income. I discharged what servants remained, except for a maid to help with the babes. And Cruthers."

Ethan's hands had gone numb. "How did my… Gillian and I come to be separated?"

Lady Warbrick got up, wove her way to the sideboard and

sloshed cheap whiskey into her glass. She took a long, fortifying gulp.

"I sent Cruthers to Snowfell the day after you were born," she said, wiping her mouth with the back of her hand. "Sir Averil came to Highwick, furious that I had defied him. He threatened me. That was when I realized what he was capable of. I thought at first he might kill both of you in your cradles."

Ethan had no trouble imagining such an event. He gazed at Lady Warbrick's bitter face. She didn't know the rest of it, didn't know her onetime lover's true nature. She'd been with Sir Averil for a month, and he'd kept it hidden.

"Why didn't he?" he finally asked.

"I don't know. I suppose I never shall." She drank again. "He glared at your tiny faces and said he would send you both to be raised elsewhere. I refused."

Her stark pronouncement briefly startled him. He had never thought her in the least courageous, and Sir Averil would have made a formidable enemy. "How did you stop him?" he asked.

"I threatened to tell his wife what we had done. And as much of the countryside as I could reach." She smiled. "Oh, he raged. He said no one would believe me. He said he would prevent me from ever leaving Highwick." Her hands began to shake, and she dropped her half-empty glass. She stared down at the puddle rapidly soaking into the ancient Aubusson carpet. "Then he offered to take both of you and raise you as his wife's children."

"Lady Maitland agreed?"

"I doubt she had any choice. She was terrified of her husband." Lady Warbrick returned to the sofa and stood over it, as if trying to recall how to bend her body to sit. Then she slowly turned toward Ethan, a strange sort of tenderness softening her face. "I consented to part of his scheme. I could let the girl go. But you...not you, darling. Never you."

Ethan breathed in and out with great care. "He didn't insist on taking us both?"

"He agreed that I might keep you if I swore to inform him at once if you ever showed any signs of a particular illness that might strike when you reached adolescence. Thank God you did not." She found her seat. "He left me with no doubt that he would have something…done to me if I failed him again. But it didn't matter. I would have risked anything for you."

A foul taste coated Ethan's tongue. No wonder Sir Averil had always treated Gillian so poorly, even before she had given herself to Kavanagh. She was a thorn in his side, a reminder of his indiscretion with a mere human.

But why had he taken Gillian at all, and left Ethan behind? He had undoubtedly tried to threaten Lady Warbrick into giving up the twins because he couldn't risk allowing mixed-blood children to run about the countryside unwatched and uncontrolled. But he had done just that with Ethan.

And he'd accepted Gillian as his offspring. A half-blood might or might not make the transition; the odds were even, according to what Gillian had told him. Sir Averil must have been deeply relieved when she had Changed.

If she hadn't, would he have sent her away, as he'd so often threatened to be rid of Toby? Or would he…?

A new thought brought Ethan up short. Kavanagh was mainly human, which made Toby even less than a half-blood. His odds of being able to Change were consequently reduced, a sure disgrace for Sir Averil if the boy failed to make the transition. Why, then, was the old man attempting to present his flawed offspring as a full-blood to the Convocation's delegates? Perhaps he had permitted Toby to remain at Snowfell in order to control Gillian, but any future child, even one sired by a full-blood, would be less than pure and might be unable to Change, revealing at last the secret the old man had sought to hide.

Ethan answered his own question. Having accepted Gillian, Sir Averil was bound to treat her as his legitimate daughter. When he had won the right to lead the Convocation, he could not very well withhold her as a potential mate and still propound his great cause, though the danger of ultimate exposure was great.

The final question remained. Why Gillian? Why not his son?

Ethan closed his eyes, summoning every feature of Gillian's face in his mind. And he knew.

She was the very image of Lady Warbrick in her youth.

The *others* danced through his memories, wriggling their half-naked bodies, laughing, promiscuous—sluts every one. Pretty, as Lady Warbrick had once been. Easy to despise. Easier to kill.

Fair-haired, like Lady Warbrick.

Like Gillian.

Ethan dragged his hands over his face. He had gone a little mad, but his sanity was beginning to return. Gillian was nothing like Lady Warbrick, like those other girls. The resemblance was imaginary. There must have been some other purpose behind Sir Averil's choice.

He condemned me.

Ethan dropped his hands, vaguely aware that his mother was staring at him in confusion. *He knew what I was, even then. He hated me. He left me with this. Poverty. A title that meant nothing. A house hardly worth living in.*

And her.

From the beginning, as soon as he was old enough to understand, he had hated Sir Averil because his mother had hated him, because of what the bastard had done to Gillian, and because of the way he had driven Ethan from the estate when he had realized that his daughter was seeing a human.

But the old man had known the truth. He had *known* that Ethan was his son…and Gillian's brother. He had condemned his own flesh and blood. And now Ethan would condemn *him*. Not as he had originally planned, merely disabling Sir Averil during the Convocation so that he would lose his status among his own kind. No, the punishment must be commensurate with the crime.

And there was Kavanagh, of course. That was one aspect of the situation that hadn't changed. And there was a third, someone who deserved a stronger rebuke than the one Ethan had originally devised as an additional benefit of Sir Averil's humiliation.

You *were the one he favored.* You *were always with her, but you never protected her. You, too, will pay.*

Once Gillian was finally with the one who truly loved her.

CHAPTER SIXTEEN

THERE WAS NO ESCAPE.

Gillian was staying upstairs with Toby, emerging from his room only to make occasional reports to Sir Averil about his condition. By now it had become pretty clear that he was undergoing the transition.

A damned fine time for it, too, Hugh thought. He couldn't begrudge Gillian remaining with Toby during such a crucial event, but it left *him* with the uneasy job of greeting the delegates as they arrived and playing the role of worthy heir to Sir Averil's title, fortune and cause.

There was quite a gathering in the Red Drawing Room when he entered. All but a few of the delegates had arrived, and the smell of tension and suspicion hung in the air like the stench of hot pavement. Hugh tugged at his collar and glanced about with a casualness he was far from feeling.

If he'd ever harbored any doubts that the Convocation was destined to be a most unpleasant affair, such doubts had been thoroughly quashed as soon as the delegates had assembled in one place. Not that he and Sir Averil had ever discussed what might be expected; his father had simply assumed that Hugh would understand.

And now he did. Gillian had clung to her unsupported belief that the delegates, being of the best families and schooled in the finest traditions of aristocratic chivalry, would comport themselves as civilized guests and rational contributors to the cause that had brought them together—even though she'd seen the effects of the War and presumably understood the nature of the powerful men who had begun and sustained it.

Hugh shook his head. There was sense in her willful ignorance, really. Gillian had learned to survive by turning a blind eye to Sir Averil's far-from-honorable behavior and somehow come to accept that she was to blame for his cruelty. Her belief that the Convocation would be a meeting of polished intellect and shared purpose was necessary in order to justify her commitment to her imminent marriage and contend with such an enormous and unpredictable change in her own and Toby's lives.

He had tried to warn her. He'd seen enough of the world, if only from a bon vivant's perspective, to know that even the rich and titled were not what they would have the world believe.

Especially if they were werewolves who put great store in their superiority and right to rule. Put this many *loups-garous* together—creatures influenced by natural lupine instincts to challenge possible rivals and drive away enemies—and there would be conflict, shared purpose or no. Quarrels, maneuvering for position and, to judge by what Hugh had already observed, the very real likelihood of open challenge. Alliances would be forged and matings arranged, but they would not all be achieved with reasonable negotiation and a desire for mutual advantage.

He resumed his surreptitious study of the guests. Over in the cluster of armchairs, next to the enormous hooded fireplace, lurked a distinctly foreign lot in proudly traditional dress, who spoke among themselves in their impossible language and watched everyone else as if they expected imminent attack. Except for the Russians gathered at the opposite end of the room, the Hungarians came from farthest away, and England must have seemed very strange to them.

The Scandinavians, a pair of Viking-tall Norwegians and a laconic Swede, led by one Sigurd Eidhammer, observed, but said little. The Spanish delegation, which consisted of one rather wiry, rustic aristocrat who spoke heavily accented English, glared from his dark eyes as he felt his disadvantage.

Graeme Macalister, as usual lacking his timid wife, stood slightly apart from the Earnshaw brothers, who had lost some of their arrogance in light of the present company and preferred to remain unobtrusive. Marcus Foster appeared perfectly content to observe, a slight and ironic smile on his lips.

The French—along with Marcus Forster—seemed by far the most amiable. The handsome Thierry de Gévaudan and his compatriots, one a very elegant ginger-haired woman of middle years and the other a lean younger man with a serious mien, were clearly more relaxed than their fellow delegates, only occasionally casting the German delegation understandably wary glances. The War hadn't quite been forgotten, even among werewolves who had held themselves aloof from the fields of battle. Certainly the overt hostility brewing between the Russians and Hungarians was proof that nationalistic pride and devotion to ancient grudges were well represented among those whose participation in the War had been minimal.

The French, however, didn't behave as what Hugh had come to think of as typical werewolf supremacists; they were the very picture of Gallic politesse. Hugh wondered if they were going to turn out to be something Sir Averil hadn't quite anticipated.

Yet of all the groups present, none was as imposing as the Germans. They weren't at all ostentatious about it; power radiated from their leader as it did from Sir Averil, a kind of disciplined severity and a ruthless air that would have intimidated anyone who'd stood against the Hun during the War. Not that Hugh had done so. He'd been too young.

But Ross hadn't been. The American stood alone, close to the door—not as if he expected to decamp, but rather because he wanted a strategic view of every guest.

He wants to know which of them is going to marry Gillian.

What he was going to do about it, or even if he planned to do anything at all, Hugh couldn't predict. He knew that Ross and Gilly had quarreled—which was hardly unexpected, given the disruption Ross was bound to create and the danger he presented to Gillian's deeply ingrained habit of unquestioning obedience to Sir Averil. She had not inaccurately concluded that Ross was very much a threat to her control of Toby's future.

But was he still a danger to her heart? Hugh had more than a little hope that he was. And he suspected that he was about to find out just how much of a danger *she* was to Ross's.

The American began to make a gradual circuit of the room, looking around as if he found the grotesqueness of the overblown embellishments quite ordinary, pausing to exchange a word with the Norwegians here and nod pleasantly to the Spaniard there. As on the night when he had first been introduced to the British delegates, he had been subjected to a very pointed inspection by most of the Europeans. None of them had expected a colonial; his manner was too informal, his apparel vulgar, his American egalitarianism distasteful and far too provocative. They might not have sensed just how completely he stood outside their fiercely defended circle, but they recognized him as an unknown quantity, and that made them nervous.

And he, like the Spaniard, was alone. Not that he seemed troubled by his isolation. He smiled and pretended not to notice the probing stares directed his way. His very confidence ensured that Sir Averil would continue to cover for him.

That was the only pleasure Hugh got out of the current situation: seeing Father forced to swallow his bile and support the American's presence.

"Hugh."

Sir Averil's voice pried Hugh from his introspection. The old man had been speaking to the Germans with a hushed intensity that made Hugh's hair stand on end.

It's one of them, he thought. Except for de Gévaudan, Forster and possibly Thierry's younger brother, Yves, Hugh didn't consider any of the delegates remotely good husband material for Gilly. But even if the deal hadn't already been struck, Sir Averil would surely have eliminated them from the list of suitable candidates for their insufficient fervor.

Squaring his shoulders, Hugh went to join his father, putting on the mask of confidence he had devised for just such occasions. As he approached the Germans, they rose with military precision and ever so slightly clicked their heels.

Huns, Hugh thought, doing his best not to let his dislike show on his face. He smiled and returned their nods of acknowledgment.

"Count von Ruden," Sir Averil said, "may I present my son, Hugh Maitland. Hugh, the count."

Hugh offered his hand. "Count."

The dark-haired German's grip was startling in its strength, and he held it a few moments too long. "How do you do, Mr. Maitland?" he said, his English pronunciation almost perfect.

Hugh wrested his hand free. "Welcome to Snowfell, Count."

"Friedrich, if you please. There will soon be no need for formality between us." He gestured to his two companions. "My son, Conrad, and my nephew, Benedikt."

Conrad shook hands, subjecting Hugh to the same test of strength and apparently concluding that he had won the contest. Benedikt, a good deal less handsome and impressive than his fellows, remained in the background, only briefly stepping forward to tend his obligations.

He doesn't want to be here any more than I do, Hugh thought. He smiled a little more broadly. "Good evening, Conrad, Benedikt. I trust your stay at Snowfell will be a pleasant one."

"I am certain it will be most profitable," the count said, speaking for them.

Sir Averil invited the three men to resume their seats. "As you know," he said to Hugh, "I have been seeking to provide Gillian with a mate who shares our commitment to the cause. Count von

Ruden and I have concluded that a closer alliance between our two families will be most beneficial."

So I was right, Hugh thought. "May I ask which of you gentleman is to be the lucky groom?"

The count looked briefly amused. "I am married, and Benedikt is affianced to another. Conrad will be the fortunate one."

But there was nothing in Conrad's manner to indicate that he considered the forthcoming marriage fortunate in the least. His broad face, with its classically square jaw and prominent cheekbones, wore a permanent scowl. He smelled of sourness and foiled ambition. Hugh guessed he was a few years younger than Gillian, and now he was to be burdened with a half-grown son, as well as a less-than-stainless bride.

"I regret that my daughter will not be at dinner tonight," Sir Averil said gruffly. "Tobias is undergoing the final throes of the transition."

Conrad's narrow lips curved downward. "In our family, children are never coddled so."

Neither von Ruden's father nor cousin confirmed or denied Conrad's scornful comment. Hugh sensed that they were waiting to see what Sir Averil would say. His father didn't disappoint.

"The boy has never been coddled," he said, staring into Conrad's eyes. "He is a Maitland."

Conrad shifted in his chair, primed for an argument, but a swift glance from his father silenced him. *Von Ruden's just like Father,* Hugh thought. *No one questions him, and no one disobeys.*

Except for Gillian, twelve years ago.

"I hear that congratulations are in order," a drawling voice said behind him.

Ross joined them, a glass of Scotch in one hand and the other shoved in his trouser pocket. He was still wearing that ridiculous hat and the Western boots, as if he'd just ridden in from the range.

"Charles Keating," he said, thrusting his hand at the Count. "We didn't really get to talk when you first arrived."

Von Ruden looked at the American's work-roughened hand and hesitated just long enough to suggest a deliberate insult before taking it. "Good evening," he said. "I understand that you have come all the way from the American West. A place called Arizona, if memory serves."

Hugh felt the air begin to boil as the two men's hands grew white with strain. They let go simultaneously, neither one the victor.

"That's right," Ross said. "Quite a place, Snowfell. This old cowhand is mighty impressed with everything he's seen so far."

"Oh?" Conrad asked. "Is your country as primitive as I have been told?"

Ross grinned. "Depends on how you look at it. You tend to get toughened up pretty fast where I come from. And that's what matters, ain't it?"

Conrad clearly wasn't certain whether or not he'd been mocked. Von Ruden filled the silence. "You have never been to Europe before, Mr. Keating," he said.

"Sure I have. I was a doughboy back in '16."

Hugh held his breath. Sir Averil quickly stepped into the breach.

"That was many years ago," he said, spearing Ross out of the corner of his eye. "It is of no consequence to us here."

"Maybe not," Ross conceded, "but some things that happened many years ago haven't been forgotten. They can change a person's life forever. Like Mrs. Delvaux's loss of her first husband, for instance."

The Germans exchanged glances. If Sir Averil had told them about Delvaux, as he must have done, he would also have mentioned that he'd died in the War.

"An unfortunate event," von Ruden said, icily enough to wilt all the flowers in the garden.

"It sure is. Let's hope she has better luck this time."

Conrad half rose. "What do you mean by that, Keating?"

"Nothing at all. It's just that we in the States aren't used to arranged marriages. It's one of the reasons I'm here, to see if it'll work for us."

"Very little of our culture has worked for you," Conrad said. "You have left it lying in your prairie dust."

"Some would say we've made a lot of improvements, like getting rid of kings and such."

Conrad's sallow skin turned red. "We also have dispensed with kings."

"We don't have counts, either."

"So you believe all men are equal…even humans?"

Careful, Hugh warned, as if Ross could hear.

"Democracy works pretty well for us," Ross said, "even though we're not all the same."

"You are mistaken in believing that your 'democracy' will survive."

Ross's smile slipped a notch. "I thought you folks had a republic?"

"A failure," Conrad said. "Weak and decadent. When the new order—"

"Sir Averil is correct," von Ruden interrupted. "This talk of politics is of no relevance." He stared at Ross. "You seem much concerned with Mrs. Delvaux. Are you well acquainted?"

"Not very. I admire the lady. She's got class, as we say in the U.S.A."

"I was unaware that an American could recognize such a quality," Conrad snapped.

"Enough," Sir Averil said. The force of his personality was just as effective as the count's at putting Conrad in his place, and the younger man turned his face away. But Friedrich von Ruden didn't like Sir Averil poaching on his territory. He met Sir Averil's gaze and held it, a wolf unwilling to yield to another of equal rank. The atmosphere was poisonous, and Hugh knew it wasn't going to get any better.

"Maybe we can continue our conversation later, in a more private setting," Ross said softly to Conrad, breaking the impasse. "We're all here to get to know each other, after all."

Conrad leaped to his feet. "I shall be most pleased to meet you at your earliest convenience," he spat.

Hugh groaned. For all his pessimism, he hadn't expected a challenge to come so soon. Ross had made a serious miscalculation. Challenge meant fighting it out in wolf shape, and Ross couldn't Change. Hugh wasn't sure that Sir Averil would interfere. He could always claim afterward that "Charles Keating" had lied about his pure werewolf blood.

And look like a gullible fool, Hugh thought. But now, having seen what Ross was capable of, perhaps Sir Averil considered that an acceptable price.

Hugh took Ross's elbow. "I'd rather like a drink, Mr. Keating. Perhaps you'll join me." He nodded toward the Germans. "If you gentlemen will excuse us…?" He led Ross away, and just in time. Conrad's knees were slightly bent, as if he were about to launch himself at Ross then and there.

Hugh was beginning to wonder just how nasty things were about to become when Gillian walked into the room, her long, slim gown adorned simply with Mother's pearls and a pair of tiny matching earbobs. Her gaze immediately fell on Ross, and she stumbled slightly before recovering and going on to greet Sir Averil.

"Father," she said. "Toby is resting. I have asked Miss Rownthwaite to watch him so that I may greet our guests." She smiled at the Germans. "I do apologize for not being present at your arrival."

"My daughter, Gillian," Sir Averil said. Hugh noted how he failed to present her with the fictitious name of Mrs. Delvaux. There was no particular pride in his voice, but surely even he could see that Gillian, with her unexpectedly confident bearing and natural grace, could not help but make a good impression on her future husband.

The von Rudens rose to acknowledge her, waiting while Sir

Averil made the remaining introductions. Ross was watching carefully, his muscles growing tight under the sleeve of his jacket.

"Good evening, Mrs. Delvaux," the count said. He looked Gillian over from her patent pumps to the top of her golden hair in the same manner a farmer might judge the breeding prospects of a good heifer. His son did the same, his expression giving nothing away.

It was possible that Sir Averil had originally planned to introduce Gillian to her husband in a less public place, but he had clearly changed his mind. "Gillian," he said, "Count von Ruden has consented to your marriage to his son. You and Tobias are to accompany the count's family to Germany when the Convocation concludes."

Hugh was half afraid to look at Gillian. She had known what was coming, and she had consented, to a union with a stranger. But now, what had been theoretical was real. She didn't move a muscle, nor did her smile waver. But Hugh knew her too well. She gazed at Conrad as if she were facing her own death.

"Herr von Ruden," she said very quietly. "I am greatly honored."

Conrad said nothing, not even offering the most basic courtesy in return. His snub could not be mistaken. Ross rumbled deep in his throat.

The count addressed Sir Averil as if Gillian weren't there. "I find her acceptable," he said, subtly challenging his host with faint praise. "I am sure that my son and your daughter would benefit by a little time alone."

"That is hardly necessary," Sir Averil said. "Gillian is young enough to produce healthy children for several years, and your son is capable of siring them. That is the only consideration."

"Of course," the Count said. "Conrad knows his duty."

"As does my daughter."

Hugh wasn't certain whether or not the shaking he felt was Ross's or his own. Gillian gazed at the wall above the chimneypiece, as immobile as the useful but unappreciated object her father thought her to be.

Abruptly Ross walked away from the sideboard and stopped behind Gillian.

"You know," he said, "I reckon I don't much like your idea of marriage after all. Duty alone seems a mighty slender thread to hang a marriage on."

"It is more than sufficient for us," von Ruden said. Though he remained seated, Hugh could see that he had began to take more careful notice of Ross: his size, his weight, the muscles flexing under his suit. "Perhaps you Americans know nothing of duty. You are an emotional, immature people, I'm afraid."

CHAPTER SEVENTEEN

"I DON'T KNOW ABOUT that last part," Ross said, smiling to reveal the edges of his teeth, "but we live large in every way, including in our passions." He didn't look at Gilly, but Hugh did. She was holding herself so rigid that she was almost trembling.

Von Ruden pretended to be amused. "I confess I do not understand why you are here," he said. "I doubt your people could adopt our ways."

"That remains to be seen," Sir Averil said, not yet prepared to drop his feigned support.

The rage had become palpable. Gillian broke her paralysis and moved closer to Sir Averil.

"May I bring you gentlemen drinks?" she asked, her voice cold enough to freeze the contents of all the bottles in the room.

"I would prefer to visit young Tobias," von Ruden said.

"I'm afraid he is not up to visitors at present," Gillian said.

"Did you not say he was resting comfortably?" Conrad asked. "You would not perhaps be making excuses, Frau Delvaux? Perhaps the boy is imperfect in some way?"

Sir Averil's chest expanded in outrage, and Ross's face went blank. Gillian spoke before he could move. "He is not perfect," she said. "But neither are any of us."

"We in the Fatherland value perfection and never fail to strive for it," Conrad said. "You and the boy will do no less when we return to my country."

"You will have no cause for regret," Sir Averil said, clinging to his temper. "You may see my grandson now, if you wish."

Hugh was startled. Toby was bound not to look his best in his current condition. But apparently his father felt he had to reclaim the upper hand by any means open to him.

The von Rudens rose and accompanied Sir Averil from the drawing room. Gillian and Ross began to follow, but Sir Averil stopped Gillian with a searing glance.

"They can't stop *me* from going," Ross said under his breath.

Gillian avoided his gaze. "You must cease interfering," she whispered.

"Are you actually going to marry that jerk?"

Hugh was aware that other eyes were beginning to turn toward them. "Keating," he said loudly, "I never did get to show you my new motor car. It's quite the rage. Gillian, will you join us?"

It was exactly the frivolous sort of thing Hugh might say in the midst of a serious situation. The delegates briefly focused on him before losing interest.

"I must go up to Toby," Gillian protested.

"Come on," Hugh whispered. "You've attracted too much attention as it is." He herded her and Ross out of the room and led them to the garage, where the Rolls-Royce and the new Bentley four-seater sparkled like gemstones.

Ross didn't waste any time. "You can't go through with it, Jill," he said.

She stared at her distorted image reflected in the glossy surface of the Bentley. "I have no choice," she said.

"Do you still think Toby will benefit by living with those… those—" He seemed at a loss for an epithet strong enough to use in a lady's presence. "They're no better than your father. They'll never value either you or Toby. They've made that very clear."

"I do not expect affection. Toby will be safe with me and I will do my part to save our kind."

Ross grabbed Gillian's shoulders and pulled her about to face him. "When are you going to wake up?" he demanded. "Your life—Toby's life—will be a living hell. 'Perfection' is what they want. No one could live up to that."

"Listen to him, Gilly," Hugh said. "He's right."

"If I refuse," she said, "our father will send Toby away."

"He can't send Toby away," Ross said. "Not if you two come with me now."

She met his eyes, her face gradually losing the glazed expression she'd worn ever since she'd met the Germans. "What?" she said.

"Marry me, Gilly," he said. "I know I don't have many prospects right now, but I've got some ideas, and we'll find a decent place to live. Maybe Mexico, where my past won't matter. You can live as independently as you want. Even if it's just a marriage of convenience, you know I'd never hurt you or Toby. You'll be safe, Jill. *Safe.*"

Passive in his arms, Gillian looked away. "No need for troublesome emotions," she whispered.

"I won't ask anything of you, Jill. You won't have any duty except to yourself and Toby."

"And he will live apart from his own kind."

"*We're* his kind, Jill. You and me."

She moved away so slowly that she had put several feet between them before Ross realized she had slipped free. "I can't," she said, bowing her head.

"Because you have to save the race? For God's sake, Jill, one person won't make any difference. Whatever those schmucks believe, werewolves aren't in danger of extinction yet. Look at Toby. He'll be able to Change."

"But there was always the risk—"

"And they would have condemned him if he hadn't."

Hugh judged that their previous arguments had followed the same lines and had failed to move either one of them from their entrenched positions. "Gilly," he said, "you've always known that it could have gone either way."

"We don't have to have children, Jill," Ross said, taking advantage of Gilly's bewildered silence. "And if you want a divorce after a few years, I won't stand in your way."

She lifted her head, and Hugh could have sworn he saw pain in her eyes. "My father would never let us go. He would track us down, no matter where we went."

"And I'd fight him. He's not all-powerful, Jill. He never was." He stared at her, merciless. "Maybe I don't hold up so well against all these aristocrats, but I'll be damned if I'll let any of them drive me away. And that includes Sir Averil's daughter."

Gillian held his gaze. "If you fight them," she said, "you will be defeated. Please, Ross. Don't antagonize the count or his family."

But Ross had had enough. He turned on his heel and strode out of the garage. Gillian simply stood there, as puffed up with stubborn and unyielding pride as Sir Averil himself.

"Why do you keep doing this, Gilly?" Hugh asked. "Is it just another way of punishing yourself for failing to be the paragon of ideal werewolf womanhood our father expected?"

She turned on him with a snarl on her face. *"You?"* she said. "You speak to me like that, when you've never had to—" She exhaled and continued in a softer tone. "You have already done quite enough. No more, Hugh."

"Gilly, I only—"

But her expression was so fierce that he instinctively ducked his head, showing submission. She was gone before he realized what he'd just seen.

She's still here. The Gillian from New York is still alive.

After a moment he followed her, pausing at the open drawing room doors as she continued up the stairs.

You're changing, Gilly, he thought. *Ross has begun to peel away those layers of armor you've worn so long. Pretty soon you'll be forced to acknowledge that you aren't who you used to be.*

And she'd damned well better realize it before she ran out of time.

Though he knew that Sir Averil would be furious that he'd abandoned the guests, Hugh deliberately turned in the opposite direction and went through the green baize door. He passed by the butler's rooms and found Cora in the servants' hall, nursing a cup of tea.

She leaped up from her chair and flung herself into his arms. "Oh, Hugh," she said. "I thought you'd never get away."

"Neither did I. And I can't stay long."

She smoothed his hair away from his forehead. "What is it? Something's wrong."

"It's only that Ross proposed to Gilly and she turned him down."

Cora's intelligent eyes narrowed. "Then *you* won't defy your father, either."

They'd discussed the issue a hundred times, and Hugh never had a different answer to give her. "You have to be patient, Cora. It's not as simple as you think, but I know our time will come."

"Yes. I know it, too." She stood on her toes and kissed him, grazing the inside of his lips with her tongue. "We won't have to fight this battle alone."

Hugh was about to ask what she meant when Faulder entered the room. He stopped, took in the scene and glared at Cora. Human though he was, he was just as opposed to their affair as Sir Averil. Hugh wouldn't have been surprised if he turned out to be his father's informer.

"It would be unfortunate if you mentioned anything about this to my father," Hugh said in his most authoritative voice.

Faulder bowed. "Nothing will be said, Mr. Maitland."

"Cora," Hugh said, "maybe you should go upstairs and see if Mrs. Delvaux needs you."

Chin high, Cora brushed past Faulder, leaving the scent of scorn behind her. Faulder came as close to a grimace as he ever had in twenty years of service.

"Sir," he said, "that young woman is not to be trusted."

"If I wanted advice from you, Faulder, I'd ask for it."

"I believe she is involved with another man, Mr. Maitland."

Hugh froze. "What are you talking about? What other man?"

But Faulder beat a hasty retreat, and Hugh was left wondering if the butler was simply discouraging him or really knew something he didn't.

Cora would never betray me, he told himself, and quickly put the thought from his mind. He knew he'd better get back to the drawing room before Sir Averil returned. Maybe he could still prevent Ross from going after Conrad von Ruden.

And maybe the sun would rise in the west tomorrow morning.

With a sigh, Hugh marched back to the drawing room like a deserter on his way to meet a firing squad.

"THE BOY IS SMALL for his age," Count von Ruden said, his voice carrying through the half-open door. "Look at him. Scrawny and weak."

His son didn't answer immediately. Gillian could hear his footsteps as he moved around the bed for a closer look. She could imagine him gazing down at Toby, weighing him against the "perfection" he and his family valued so highly.

"He is ill," Conrad said at last. "We can make no judgment until the boy has recovered."

"It is only the weak ones who suffer during the *übergang.*"

"At least he appears Aryan."

"Which means nothing if he retains his English softness. Why are you so anxious to defend the boy, Conrad? You revealed no such womanish feelings when you met Mrs. Delvaux."

"He is part of our agreement, is he not?" He paused. "Having been sired by a Belgian, he is not likely to represent the children he will produce with the proper mate."

"But he will naturally compete with any future offspring."

"He will not compete. Our children will be German."

The count chuckled, the sound like icicles clashing. "I believ
you have developed quite an infatuation with the girl, *mei*
Sohn."

"No infatuation, *mein Vater,*" Conrad said, too hastily for a
effective denial. "She is healthy and strong and of excellen
breeding. This boy means nothing to me. But the woman ha
about her a certain rebelliousness that is not apparent in he
manner."

"You surprise me again, Conrad. Your insight in such matter
had never been noteworthy."

"But you agree."

"I do. She presumed to contradict her father and argue wit
us. Her greatest weakness is this boy. If our control of him make
her more obedient, he must come with us." Another pause. "Wha
of Keating?" he murmured. "His interest in the woman—"

"*Der Amerikaner?* I shall deal with—"

"Patience. The time will come when he will cease to be
problem."

Gillian tensed as someone moved toward the door. She knew
they would smell that she was standing in the corridor. The
would know she'd been listening. And they wouldn't care. Jus
as they wouldn't care if Toby had heard them.

She would go to him again as soon as the Germans had lef
She knew what he would say. She knew that he would spea
every treasonous thought in her own head.

The Germans didn't want her son. They had made that ampl
clear.

But there was someone who *did* want him.

Ross offered to marry me.

And he had made it absolutely plain that he had done so out o
concern for Toby and some sense of lingering obligation to Gillia
entirely without the troublesome complication of desire for her.

She walked toward the second-floor landing and descende
to the first, her ears alert for sounds behind her. How was she t

expect otherwise from Ross? When he had held her after her loss of control in Toby's room, when he had apologized so sincerely for implying that she would sacrifice Toby to her pride, it had merely been out of misplaced pity for Sir Averil's downtrodden daughter. And as for the apparent jealousy he'd displayed when he'd spoken to Conrad, Gillian wasn't deceived. Ross had his own motives, among them to prove that he was the equal of any European aristocrat and could meet them on their own terms.

To marry him would be yet another lie. But he had been at least half-right when he had made his proposal. The Germans would never value Toby. They would push him aside even if they didn't openly revile him.

She, however, was of use to them. Apparently Conrad wanted her, as fantastic as the prospect might seem. If she made it clear to him that she could defy Sir Averil if she chose, but that she would renew her pledge of marriage if Toby were removed from the agreement...

Father would never permit it, unless I—

A shout interrupted her thoughts. Hugh was standing at the foot of the stairs, beckoning wildly. Gillian glanced once over her shoulder and descended as fast as her gown allowed.

Immediately she noticed the commotion near the open doors of the drawing room. Faulder, forbidden from entering, fluttered about in distress. Mossop was there, as well, craning her neck to see over the butler's shoulder.

"It's Father," Hugh said in a near-whisper. "Something's wrong with him."

Gillian pushed past Faulder and stepped into the room. Her father was kneeling on the carpet, one hand braced against an armchair as he gasped and clutched at his chest. Beside him were Messieurs Thierry and Yves, Mademoiselle Dominique de Gévaudan, Marcus Forster and—to Gillian's surprise—Benedikt von Ruden. They were hovering over Sir Averil, hesitating to touch him as he struggled to rise.

The Frenchwoman looked up as Gillian rushed toward them. "Madame Delvaux," she said, pronouncing Gillian's fictitious surname with the lilt of a native, "it appears that Sir Averil is very ill."

Gillian knelt, aware that any attempt to help Sir Averil would only add to his apparent weakness. "What happened?"

"He fell," Marcus said. "He appears to be having difficulty breathing."

"I am perfectly well," Sir Averil growled, still gasping as he worked his way to his feet. But no one in the room could possibly believe his assertion. Gillian took note of the delegates, many of whom had not even bothered to rise from their chairs. They studied Sir Averil with wolfish intensity, especially the Russians and Norwegians, who last year had competed with her father for leadership of the Convocation.

Sir Averil swayed, clearly distressed and about to fall again. He turned to face the delegates, to prove there was nothing wrong with him. But his face was pale and moist, and every breath caused his body to shudder.

Gillian finally dared to touch him. "Perhaps it was this morning's breakfast, Father," she said. "I thought I tasted something amiss."

He glared at her. He knew full well that he was incapable of continuing to preside over the gathering, and she had offered an excuse that—while hardly plausible, given most werewolves' superior constitutions—was preferable to any other.

"I will…speak to Spotterswood," Sir Averil said. "Inform me at once should anyone else become ill."

"Of course, Father." Gillian glanced at Hugh, giving him a silent message she hoped he understood.

Hugh nodded slightly. "One should always rest in such cases, to allow one's body to rid itself of the poison," he said wisely.

As Gillian had expected, Sir Averil was much more inclined to listen to Hugh than to her. He stood upright and walked across the drawing room, refusing to reveal any pain until he was at the foot of the staircase. Only then did he permit Hugh to help him up the stairs and to his room.

It was very near dinner, and Gillian was left to handle the guests alone. There was no question of going up to see Toby; she hoped the Germans had by now left him in Miss Rownthwaite's care. She wished for Ross and quickly cast that thought aside.

"Ladies and gentlemen," she said.

They all stared at her, and she wondered how many had guessed how little suited she was to take the lead. In a true wolf pack, she would be the one whom the other wolves teased and tormented, the one who slunk around the fringes with her tail between her legs.

She could not afford to be that lowly creature tonight.

"Dinner shall be served presently," she said, taking care to meet every gaze just long enough to establish her lack of fear. "I will personally inspect and taste each dish to ascertain that it is safe."

"There was nothing wrong with the food," said the sandy-haired Russian leader, Prince Vasily Arakcheyev, his posture belligerent. There were murmurs of agreement.

The Hungarian delegates moved restlessly in their chairs. "What is really wrong with him?" János Károly asked.

"Nothing." Ross walked into the room and stood at Gillian's shoulder, granting her the dominant position. "Sir Averil's a tough old bird. He'll be on his feet again in no time."

Gillian fervently wished that Ross had remained silent, even as she felt a rush of relief. "I am certain that Sir Averil will be fully recovered in a few hours," she said. "He would not desire any of you to be concerned on his account." She heard Faulder's footsteps in the corridor. "Shall we proceed to the dining room?"

For a moment no one stirred. Then Thierry de Gévaudan got to his feet. "I, for one, am quite peckish, as you English say." He offered his arm to Mademoiselle Dominique. Marcus Forster joined them, and slowly the other guests followed suit. There was jostling at the door as the delegates maneuvered for precedence; Gillian held a brief conference with Faulder and Mossop, who hurried off to resume their duties.

In the entrance hall she and Ross met the Germans, who had apparently been holding their own conference since Gillian had left her position outside Toby's door. Conrad blocked their way to the dining room.

"You have something that belongs to me," he said, baring his teeth at Ross.

Ross grinned. "I reckon I don't know what you're talking about, von Ruden."

The German seized Gillian's arm. Ross swung around and pushed Conrad away. Everyone else stopped where they were. Conrad, breathing hard, lifted his fists.

"Now," he said. "Outside."

Count von Ruden made no effort to interfere. Gillian held absolutely still. She had finally acknowledged to herself just how wrong she'd been to believe that a gathering of foreign werewolves from disparate homelands, few of whom knew each other, would restrain their bestial natures for the sake of peaceful negotiation.

Sir Averil had known better. He'd dealt with these men before, when the representatives of various nations had met to determine the venue for the Convocation. She had never asked what form those negotiations had taken, assuming that it had been a test of will that her father had easily won.

Hugh had tried to open her eyes, and so had Ross, even if Sir Averil hadn't seen the necessity of preparing her. He had clearly expected to maintain dominance over the others, ensuring that any quarrels or challenges among the delegates would take place only under his authority.

Now he had lost that advantage by falling inexplicably ill. But Gillian had seen enough to know that if a Maitland didn't take command, someone else—the count, or perhaps Arekchayev—

would certainly do so, and then matters would soon spin out of control. A single incident, such as a scuffle between Conrad and Ross, would open the floodgates to other disputes and altercations that could tear the Convocation apart.

And Ross would be exposed for the fraud he was.

She turned to face Conrad and stared into his eyes. He would not give ground, but neither would she.

"There will be no duels tonight," she said, matching Sir Averil's tone as best she could. "We are not children to fuss over trifles."

Conrad gaped at her for a few seconds, then abruptly shut his mouth. The rest were watching her the way they'd watched Sir Averil when he'd fallen, waiting to see if she could maintain her show of strength. Only Ross was looking at her in a different way. As if he almost approved. As if he were, however grudgingly, proud of her.

She would have to rebuff him now for the sake of peace.

"Herr von Ruden," she said to Conrad, "You may escort me to the dining room, if you please." She nodded to Ross. "I thank you for your assistance, Mr. Keating."

He inclined his head. "I understand that sometimes we have to do things we don't like."

Conrad's face reddened. Gillian stepped smoothly to his side as he offered her his arm. She slipped her hand through the crook of his elbow, struck by a chill at the contact.

You will own me soon enough, she told him silently. *But you will never have anything but my body, and if I can somehow deny you the Aryan children you desire…*

She heard Ross's tread as he fell into step behind them. He was a warmth at her back, a steadying presence, a safe harbor in dangerous waters. A harbor she didn't dare enter.

Faulder, having recovered his usual aplomb, stood beside the dining-room door and bowed as the delegates entered. Several additional footmen had been employed to serve the visiting dignitaries. They were nearly shaking in their shoes.

Without thinking, Gillian proceeded to the head of the table. She almost corrected herself and chose the chair beside it, but such hesitancy would undermine her assumption of leadership, however temporary it might be. While one of the footmen pulled out her chair, Conrad claimed one of the seats beside her. Ross grabbed the other one, upsetting her father's strategic arrangements. Ross's scent enfolded Gillian, bolstering her courage even as she recognized that his actions would only make the evening that much more difficult.

The remaining guests chose their own places at the table, clumped together by group, with Macalister and the Earnshaws keeping very much to themselves, while the Russians and Germans stalked around the table, settling after a great many glares and nearly soundless growls. De Gévaudan sat next to Marcus Forster, and Mademoiselle Dominique swiftly moved into the seat on Ross's other side.

When Hugh failed to arrive after fifteen minutes, Gillian signaled that the serving of the meal should commence. A nonplussed Faulder, lacking any alternative, deferred to her. There was little conversation. Conrad continued to scowl at Ross, who ignored him and ate with gusto as each course was served. Rather than pick at her food with proper female delicacy, Gillian followed his example. She was distracted by the low exchanges between him and Dominique, who obviously enjoyed his company.

After dinner was completed, Gillian rose. Many of the men kept their seats in direct violation of the most common courtesy.

She took particular care to stare directly at each of the men who had continued to sit. There was no question of leading Dominique to the Yellow Parlor while the men brooded over their port and cigars—if any of them smoked—and glared at each other. "Drinks will be served in the drawing room," she said, and walked out without looking back.

The footsteps were somewhat delayed, but they came. Once everyone was seated in the Red Drawing Room, Gillian took up a position beside the fireplace. Ross had taken one of the chairs closest to her, but he kept his distance, as if he realized how fragile a hold she had over the delegates.

"Ladies and gentleman," she said, "tomorrow Sir Averil will convene the first formal meeting of the Convocation. Each of you will have ample opportunity to address your fellow delegates, and make known your needs and intentions regarding the purpose that has brought us together."

Vasily Arakcheyev started from his chair, practically bristling. "What if Sir Averil is unable to preside?"

"I am certain he will be," she said.

"Do *you* intend to take his place if he is not?" challenged Sigurd Einhammer. "Where is Sir Averil's son?"

That was indeed the question. Gillian doubted that he would have remained solicitously by Sir Averil's side. He was deliberately avoiding the guests, and she knew why.

"My brother is consulting with Sir Averil," she said. "He will join us presently."

Muttering in his guttural language, the Norwegian resumed his seat. Arakcheyev finally subsided. Gillian permitted Faulder to enter and inquire about drinks. Most abstained, undoubtedly determined, as Gillian was, to remain clearheaded in the midst of uncertainty.

She made the rounds among the guests, all the while behaving as if she were completely unfazed by the current situation. She could not mistake the speculation in the eyes of the Russians, the Hungarians and the Scandinavians. The Earnshaw brothers were chilly, and Macalister clung to his aloof neutrality. The French, the lone Spaniard and Marcus Forster deferred to her graciously. The von Rudens merely observed, their silence more telling than any overt hostility.

Gillian had nearly reached a state of utter exhaustion when the delegates began to disperse, most simply leaving without comment. Conrad lingered, clearly hoping to engage Ross in another round of insults. Gillian intercepted him and led him out of the room, questioning him about the ancient castle on the Rhine where the von Rudens made their home.

He was not so easily pacified. "You will not speak to Keating again," he said.

They were almost the same words Sir Averil had used. Gillian's temper flared.

"I do not understand you," she said. "He is merely one of Sir Averil's guests and of no special interest to me."

"He wants you. He will not have you."

So the count had been right. Conrad *was* infatuated with her, contrary to all expectations and his previous behavior. She must encourage him.

"I fear you are mistaken, Herr von Ruden," she said, leaning closer. "Mr. Keating will return to America soon enough."

"And you will come to Germany."

"That is my father's wish."

"And yours."

"Indeed." She breathed gently against his ear. "But I think that you and I ought to reach a more *private* agreement, Herr von Ruden."

He searched her eyes, suspicion giving way to anticipation. "My father—"

"Are *you* under the thumb of your father, Conrad?"

Teeth glinted. "I will soon show you."

"Then we must discuss what we might do for each other. Soon."

Conrad would have pressed the issue then and there, but Gillian persuaded him to wait until later the next morning, when they could speak, before the Convocation began. When she left him at the foot of the staircase, he had the look of a man who was quite thoroughly lost. Perhaps he regarded her apparent strength as an intriguing challenge, one that would make her ultimate conquest all the more satisfying.

But what he had seen tonight was only another mask. Soon enough, it would begin to crumble.

Gillian knew she would find Ross waiting when she sought the comfort of the kitchen. The tables and worktop were piled high with dirty china and cutlery, but she welcomed the warmth of the room.

Mrs. Spotterswood gave her an assessing glance, dismissed the exhausted scullery maids and then returned to her work of preparing the excess food for storage. Ross was standing at the end of the table, and he gazed at Gillian as if she were a goddess come to earth.

"You did it, Jill," he said. "I've never been so proud of anyone in my life."

His words undid her. She collapsed into the nearest chair and let the waves of suppressed fear wash over her.

"I had no choice," she whispered.

Ross circled the table and crouched beside her. "You had a choice," he said. "You could have backed away. You could have stayed what your father made you."

"And let the Convocation descend into chaos?" She began to shiver, though the kitchen was warm. "I pray I'll never have to do it again."

Before she could prepare herself, he put his arms around her. She sank into his heat and strength, letting herself be weak for a few desperate seconds.

"You don't have to," he said. "You and Toby can still come with me. Your father can't hunt us down if he's sick in bed."

She could hardly bear to leave his embrace. "I have even less excuse to abandon Snowfell now," she said, her voice unsteady. "I was naive to assume that the delegates would conduct themselves as if they were human."

Ross's eyes were so dark that she could see nothing beyond their surface. "You think one of the delegates will try to take over?" he asked.

"It would not surprise me." Not any longer. "Several of the

delegations were eager to claim the prestige of presiding ove the Convocation before Sir Averil prevailed, and they may nov see their chance to take back the prize."

"And you think you should assume control until the old mai recovers?"

"If I were to leave the Convocation to Hugh, he would no last the day."

"Yeah." He leaned closer. "What about you?"

He was asking if she, too, might be in danger. "It will not b necessary for me to continue this charade much longer," sh said.

He let her evasion pass. "What would happen if the Maitland lost control?"

"Would you have someone like von Ruden set the course fo the future of our kind?"

She knew instantly how great a mistake she had made in ex pressing her true opinion of the Germans, but Ross only stare at her without any show of triumph at her admission.

"Are you saying that you disagree with what they believe even though it's exactly the same thing your father wants?" h asked softly. "Or did you just decide that they're only a littl worse than the rest of the purists?"

She wanted to tell him that she despised the von Rudens hated what they had said about Toby. But Ross would seize o that doubt and expand it until it became a chasm wide and dee enough to swallow her whole.

Perhaps that was exactly what she deserved. But she ha begun to make provisions for Toby's welfare, and only when sh was certain of her success would she reveal the plan to Ross. I she were honest now, his chivalrous instincts might interfere wit achieving the one thing they *both* wanted.

She would have very little time to play out the game. An everything would hinge on her ability to maintain a facade o absolute confidence.

She pulled free. "I cannot permit our family to surrender leadership," she said, as cool and self-possessed as any impostor could be. "The Convocation officially begins tomorrow. If my father is not out of his sickbed by morning, Hugh and I will jointly preside."

His eyes told her that she had succeeded in obliterating his ephemeral pride in her supposed courage. "What if the others demand that Hugh take over?" he asked in a voice utterly devoid of emotion.

"Sir Averil will recover. There is no other possibility."

"Because you can't imagine life without him, can you? You can't imagine yourself completely free."

"No one is completely free. Not even you."

She rose and walked out the door, her footsteps ringing as hollow as her heart.

"You can't imagine yourself completely free," he'd said. He was wrong. She had imagined it often in her childhood, before constant humiliation and defeat had smothered such ridiculous ambitions.

True freedom would never exist for her, for Hugh, for anyone within the circle of Sir Averil's influence.

Unless he were dead.

CHAPTER EIGHTEEN

GILLIAN CAME TO A halt halfway up the stairs.

A world without Sir Averil… She glanced up in the direction of his rooms, her heart racing. His constitution had always been unbreakable, even beyond that of most werewolves. In his younger days he had endured severe injuries and had healed without a mark. No minor illness could lay him low.

And what if what he suffers from now is not *minor?*

She nearly ran the rest of the way up to the nursery, where she checked on Toby. Then she returned to her room, undressed and lay on her bed, Ross's final accusations still ringing in her ears.

What would you do with freedom if you had it? Once Hugh inherited, the tyranny at Snowfell would cease. Hugh might very well live even more profligately than he already had, but he could scarcely use up all of Sir Averil's massive fortune.

And he would never continue Sir Averil's work. It was nothing to him but an obstacle to the hedonistic life he wanted.

Gillian realized that she hadn't answered her own question. What would she herself do?

Employ tutors of every description to provide Toby with a broad education. Take him to a thousand different places in England and on the Continent, where his hungry mind would absorb everything put in front of him. Remove the heavy drapes that blocked the light in every room. Fill the house with flowers and bright colors. Let the servants understand that they no longer had anything to fear.

Everything that came to mind required that she and Toby stay at Snowfell. Sir Averil's cause was absent from the scenario. Conrad von Ruden made no appearance.

But there was another who did.

Ross, striding over the fells with Toby at his side. Ross, caressing her naked body. Ross, the harsh lines about his eyes and across his forehead eased with the hope of peace.

Ross, loving her.

She sat up, stunned by the knowledge she had struggled again and again to reject. She had asked herself—oh, forbidden thought—if he could still have loved her had she been free. But she had refused to admit that the reverse was just as true as it had ever been.

The truth was that she had never stopped loving Ross, not in all the years since she'd left him in London. She had tried to forget her feelings in order to survive at Snowfell, and again in America, so that she could win the battle with him over Toby's future. She'd thought that sex would be enough to rid herself of the old attraction, that what lingered was only physical.

But lovemaking had not eliminated her desire or released her from the chains of emotion. She might have continued to pretend if Ross had remained in America. Not anymore. She was forced to admit that he had a permanent and indelible place in her soul.

She lay back again, wrapping her arms about herself. No wonder she had refused him in the garage. She could accept nothing less than his love in return for hers, even before she had recognized the full depth of her feelings.

At least Ross had not recognized them, and that was a blessing. Now, more than ever, she must make absolutely certain that no one sensed her weakness, especially Ross. She must fight for every ounce of fortitude she possessed. Nothing must interfere with her resolution. From this moment on, her dealings with Ross must be no more than civil. There would be no more arguments, no seeking of comfort, no further explanations.

Gillian closed her eyes. The clock chimed midnight. Someone tapped on the door.

She was on her feet and nearly to the door when she recognized Hugh's scent. He peeked in, the tight expression on his face demanding all her attention.

"What is it?" she asked as she gathered up her dressing gown from the foot of the bed and draped it around her shoulders. "What has happened?"

"You'd better get dressed," he said. "Father wants to see us both."

"Why? Is he—"

"He's not getting any better." He began to close the door. "Hurry up."

She hurried, twisting her hair into a knot at the base of her neck and leaving off her stockings. She smelled sickness in the air long before she reached Sir Averil's rooms.

Hugh was waiting for her. His eyes were anxious, his nervousness apparent in the clenching and unclenching of his hands.

"Prepare yourself," he said, and opened the door.

Sir Averil lay on his enormous half-tester bed, a teapot and half-empty cup on the tray beside him. His eyes were circled in deep shadow, his face sallow and his whole body somehow shrunken. It was evident that he had recently expelled the contents of his stomach. He focused slowly on his son and daughter, squinting, as if the room's meager light was too bright for his eyes.

"Hugh," he said. "Come closer."

Hugh obliged, creeping more than walking to the far side of the bed. Gillian stayed where she was, shocked in spite of Hugh's warning by their father's deteriorating condition.

Sir Averil never changed. He never faltered, never yielded to anyone or anything. Yet now he was withering before her eyes, a relentlessly powerful man reduced to helplessness.

"Gillian," he said, his voice cracking on the word. Gillian

moved to his side of the bed, a strange and unfamiliar pity welling up in her throat.

"Do not..." Sir Averil croaked, trying to sit up. "Do not presume to—" He fell back, his chest heaving for air. "Do not think that I have no knowledge of what you attempted this evening. Your unconscionable actions have called Maitland honor into question. As if any female..." He coughed, unable to speak for several seconds. Gillian made a move to help him, but he held her away with a stiffened arm and turned his head toward Hugh. "Listen to me. I may require a few more days to recover from this—this ailment. While I am indisposed, you are to assume leadership of the Convocation."

It was exactly what Gillian would have expected, but the command still came as a jolt. Who had told her father what she had done? It must have been Faulder, who was blindly loyal to Sir Averil. Or had one of the delegates, perhaps one of the Russians or the Germans, managed to speak to him?

The von Rudens must put me in my place. Even if Conrad prefers to maintain a truce, the count has no such compunction.

She glanced up at Hugh. He was pale, but managed not to reveal his fear when he spoke. "I understand, Father," he said.

"You will begin by affirming our leadership. There must be no doubt—" He coughed sharply. "Do whatever you must to maintain it."

"Yes, Father."

Sir Averil reached for his teacup. Gillian touched the teapot. "It's cold, Father," she said. "Let me bring up a fresh pot."

Sir Averil lifted the cup to his mouth and swallowed the cold tea, as if to prove he could endure any unpleasantness. "You are to support your brother in all things," he said without meeting Gillian's eyes. "Under no circumstances are you to repeat what you did this evening."

She didn't answer, but her father seemed not to notice. His eyes were beginning to close.

"The contract stands," he said. "We will sign the agreement with the von Rudens tomorrow." He sighed as he sank among the pillows. "Now go."

He said nothing further. No admonitions about her speaking with Kavanagh, or Ross's interference between her and Conrad. He could not have dismissed Ross's actions unless his mind, as well as his body, was profoundly affected by his illness.

She and Hugh were at the door when Sir Averil called out.

"Hugh, come back. I have more to say to you."

With a worried glance at Gillian, Hugh returned to Sir Averil's bedside. Gillian left the room and hesitated outside the door, tempted to listen. Instead, she went to her own room and waited, knowing that Hugh would come to her when he could.

He arrived fifteen minutes later, face flushed and eyes wild.

"You know I can't do it," he whispered, leaning against the inside of her door as if to physically bar potential intruders. "What he wants…you know it's impossible, Gilly."

Gillian sat on the sofa. "What did he say?"

"He made me swear. On the Maitland name. He said if he died…" He rubbed at his mouth. "*Can* he die, Gilly?"

"I don't know."

"The man has been living in a dream. What's the old cliché? All our chickens have finally come home to roost."

His bitterness reminded Gillian of every time she'd let Hugh take credit for something he hadn't done, deferred to him in their father's presence, or covered for him when he'd committed some reckless action that didn't suit Sir Averil's ideal. She'd meant it for the best, to spare Hugh the humiliation and contempt their father had saved for her.

Now she understood how mistaken she had been. In her desire to protect him, she'd set him up to fail…

"Hugh…"

"I'm no leader, Gilly. The delegates will discover that soon enough."

She twisted a bit of her skirt between her fingers. "I'll be by your side every moment."

"So you're defying Father again?"

"There is little he can do to me that he has not already done."

Hugh knelt at the foot of the bed and took Gillian's hands in his. "I won't let him hurt you again, Gilly."

She freed one hand and cupped it around his cheek. "I have always believed that there is more to you than what you see in the mirror. We will hold the Convocation together. That is all that matters now."

His expression hardened in a way as foreign to him as Sir Averil's ambition. "'All that matters,'" he repeated mockingly. "I despise him. I hope he snuffs it."

They froze in place simultaneously, like blasphemers awaiting the wrath of God on Judgment Day. But no one had heard. No one knew that Sir Averil had fathered a pair of fratricidal traitors.

Hugh sighed, and the look of hate slid from his face. "It'll never happen," he said. "But he's made a mistake about you, too, Gilly. He doesn't rule you anymore."

She lacked the heart to contradict him. "We should both try to sleep. We must rise early to prepare."

Hugh rose and waited for her to precede him to the door. "You'll have someone else at your back, Gilly. Someone who will never abandon you."

She could not fail to understand him. But he was wrong. When the agreement with Conrad was finally settled, Ross wouldn't hesitate to take Toby and leave her behind.

Gillian visited Toby's room again before she retired. He was deeply asleep in the way only children can be. She sat beside the bed and watched his beautiful, innocent face until the dawn came and it was time to meet with Conrad. She crept from the room, promising herself that she would survive their parting. Just as she would survive never seeing Ross again.

GILLIAN HAD CHANGED.

Ross watched from a distance as she and Hugh took command of the delegates who gathered in the Great Hall. He'd known last night that the difference wasn't only skin-deep. Tonight, when the first official day of the Convocation was over, she wouldn't come running into the kitchen to confess her fears and let him hold her. Tonight she was everything Ross had believed she could become. And it was all wrong.

Last night she'd said a lot of things about carrying out a charade and hoping she would never have to do it again. Even when her tone had changed and she'd slipped back into that familiar litany of duty and obligation—of saving Hugh from his own stupidity and carrying on like a good soldier until Sir Averil was back on his feet—there had been a moment when he had actually thought she might give in.

That had been just another stupid piece of self-deception on his part. She was willing to admit that the delegates could behave like animals and that she wouldn't want the von Rudens in charge, but that was as far as it went. The only thing that might make her give up this life was the one emotion she obviously couldn't feel. Not for him.

"No one is completely free," she'd said. *"Not even you."*

She'd been more right than she knew.

Ross allowed his gaze to wander over the hall, with its towering vaulted ceiling, stained-glass windows and gaping fireplace. He didn't have to be told that this room didn't match the rest of the house; it was as if the designer had deliberately set out to create something from the Middle Ages, with mounted animal heads, ancient weapons and martial banners.

Most of the delegates seemed to fit right into the warlike setting. He continued to observe from the back of the hall, listening to the opening speeches of the delegates and noting each feint and riposte as the werewolves continued to assess one another's strengths and jockey for position. Sometimes he felt as if he were watching a posse of pack enforcers squabbling over who was going to earn the most glory in the next assault on a rival gang.

But he didn't underestimate the Europeans. And neither did Gillian. No one with any brains could help but admire her. Hugh was only a pale figure crouching in her shadow. Her voice carried over the arguments of the others, never shrill or hurried. She easily deflected questions about Sir Averil and answered every subtle challenge with unflappable composure.

Just as she'd done in New York, she'd convinced herself that she could do whatever she had to. The confidence she'd lost at Snowfell was back with a vengeance. If Ross had thought it was worth the effort, he would have bet his hopes for justice that she wasn't going to lose it again.

The morning passed without open conflict, though the Russians, Norwegians, Hungarians and Germans—and occasionally the Earnshaws—continued to scrutinize each other in a way that had both Ross's cop and wolf instincts constantly on edge. In their minds, there was still a very real chance that one of them might succeed to Sir Averil's position if—unlikely as it seemed—he remained disabled. But when they broke for lunch and Ross joined Gillian, Hugh and the other guests at the table, he couldn't help but see a grudging respect for Sir Averil's daughter growing in the eyes of even the most skeptical of the delegates.

Respect wasn't going to be enough if Gillian made a mistake. She had left the head of the table to Hugh in an attempt to maintain the fiction that he was leading the Convocation in their father's absence, but Ross didn't think many of the delegates were buying the act. Hugh kept up the pretense, but most of the delegates ignored him.

That still left Gillian the object of most of the digs and probing comments. Ross had finally been forced to accept that she didn't want his help, that maybe she was right in implying that he could only make things worse for her. He didn't speak up when

Arakcheyev made some remark about English habits designed to provoke her, or when Kenneth Earnshaw opined on the necessity of females remembering their true and only duty. He bit his tongue when Conrad von Ruden sat next to her, alternately purring in her ear or touching her arm like a proprietary husband, while she did nothing to discourage him.

If Gillian was aware of Ross's restraint, she didn't show it. She paid him no attention at all. To her way of thinking, treating him like a stranger was necessary to fend off any doubts about her loyalties or possibly dubious former relationships. He couldn't disagree. The more firmly she established her position, the safer she would be. And the closer he himself came to being able to rescue Toby from her.

Because there was no further doubt in his mind that she was going to marry Conrad von Ruden, fulfilling her father's expectations and her own conviction that she could make a difference.

While Gillian and Hugh oversaw the afternoon meeting in the Great Hall, Ross cautiously made his way up to Toby's room. The boy hadn't emerged since the guests had arrived; he was on the mend, but Ross knew that Gillian had been warned to confine Toby during the Convocation, and she wasn't prepared to break that rule.

Toby's governess, the rather prim Miss Rownthwaite—whose unremarkable face was beginning to surrender to the inevitable pull of middle age—was reading to him in a voice touched with the distinctive Cumbrian accent. She glanced at Ross, startled to see him at the door.

Maybe she knew who he really was. Maybe she didn't. Either way, Ross was in no mood to explain. "If you don't mind," he said, "I'd like to speak to Toby alone."

She swallowed several times. "I was told… I was told to stay with him, Mr. Kavanagh."

"I won't be more than a few minutes."

Accustomed to obedience, but plainly reluctant, she closed her book and looked at Toby. He had pushed himself erect against the pillows and was staring at Ross with an intensity that barely dammed a flood of questions. Miss Rownthwaite rose, smoothed her gray tweed skirt and gave Ross a brisk nod.

"I shall be right outside the door," she said to the room in general, and marched out with an elaborate show of dignity.

Toby hopped out of bed and ran to Ross with outstretched arms. Ross gave him a hug and sat him on the edge of the mattress.

"You shouldn't be up," Ross said, sitting beside him.

Toby rolled his eyes. "I am perfectly well. Mother has said that the Convocation is a meeting of adults and I should stay in my room, but I think she's just afraid of what I'd do if I went downstairs and met the other werewolves."

"What *would* you do?" Ross asked.

"Help Mother, of course."

Toby's light tone was a good indication to Ross that the kid didn't know just how much help his mother might require. And he wasn't going to find out, not if Ross had anything to say about it.

Still, one thing had to be discussed. "Do you know what's happened to Sir Averil?" he asked.

He frowned a little. "I know there is something wrong. Mother came in and sat with me for a long time last night. She didn't know I was awake." He picked at the weave of his bedspread. "It's very odd. Grandfather has never been ill. What is wrong with him?"

"We don't know. He hasn't come out of his room yet." He laid his hand on Toby's shoulder. "The thing is, your grandfather's illness has confused a lot of the guests. They're not sure who should be the leader until Sir Averil is better."

"Ah, I see." Toby nodded sagely. "Well, Mother will take care of it."

"Why do you think that, Toby?"

"She's always been very good at taking care of things, not like

Uncle Hugh. But she's been different, too, ever since we went to America. Haven't you noticed?"

Ross didn't point out that he hadn't been at Snowfell before she'd gone to America. "What have you noticed?" he asked.

"Oh, just little things. When I was small, I didn't realize how nervous she was. She didn't want me to know. But now she walks almost like Grandfather, and her voice isn't nearly so quiet, and…oh, lots of stuff." His hazel eyes gleamed. "It's all because of you, Father."

A subject he didn't dare touch with a pole the length of the Woolworth Building. "Maybe she's always been that way inside, Toby," he said.

"Then she had to hide it," Toby said. "Because of Grandfather." His upper lip lifted in a perfect imitation of an adult werewolf showing his teeth to a rival. "Well, at least she isn't going to marry that Hun."

Ross found himself squeezing Toby's shoulder a little too hard and let his hand fall. "How did you know…who she was supposed to marry?"

"I can't tell you. I promised to keep it a secret. But it doesn't matter, because she would *never* go with them to Germany, even if you weren't here." He tipped his head toward Ross with a confidential air. "The Huns came in to inspect me, you know. They said a number of very nasty things." He swelled with indignation. "Scrawny! Ha! They thought I was asleep, but I heard them, and Mother was outside listening. She'd never marry someone who wanted to get rid of me."

A roaring started in Ross's ears. "What do you mean, get rid of you?"

"Well…perhaps not in quite in those words. But that is what they meant."

What Conrad *meant*, Ross thought, his ears still ringing. He wanted Gillian, but not Toby.

And Gillian had overheard. She *knew* what her husband-to-be thought of Toby. She *knew* the von Rudens would treat her like a broodmare, and would, at best, ignore Toby the same way his grandfather had.

Anger forced Ross to get up and walk away from the bed so that Toby couldn't see his face. The last of his reluctance about taking Toby was gone. The Germans' attitude was actually to his benefit; if they weren't interested in Gillian's "scrawny" son, they wouldn't protest too loudly or look too closely when the boy disappeared.

"Father? Did I say something wrong?"

He should have known better than to think he could fool his son. *His* son. That was what Toby would be from now on.

He turned around and knelt before Toby. "You didn't say anything wrong. I'm just very mad at the Huns."

Toby scowled in agreement. "I wish I were bigger. I'd make them take back everything they said about…" He trailed off, gnawing on his lower lip. "They talked about you, too, Father. They said you would 'cease to be a problem.'"

"Did they?" Ross said grimly. "Mighty brave of 'em."

"Will they try to fight you?"

Ross knew very well that Conrad was straining at the leash to teach his presumed American rival a lesson. And he knew what that would mean, even if he wanted a shot at the German just as badly.

"If they do," he said, "they're going to regret it."

"I know you won't let them beat you," Toby said with a gallant show of confidence.

"I don't plan to. You're not to worry about it, Toby."

"Oh, I shan't. I can't wait to see them all run crying back to Germany, the cowards."

He grinned, forgetting his previous concern. He didn't ask if his mother had agreed to leave Snowfell. For him, it was a given.

"I think we've talked enough for now," Ross said. "You have to concentrate on getting better."

"I *am* better. And I'm not going to do it."

"Do what?"

"I'm not going to Change."

Ross swallowed a curse. "Why, Toby?"

"Because *they* all think it's so important, and I don't want to be like them. I want to be like *you*."

Damn it, a man didn't bawl in front of his kid. "I'm flattered," Ross said thickly. "But you can't stop what's going on inside you."

"Mother has been worried that I wouldn't fit in. She needn't have. You don't fit in, either, and you're as good as anyone here. Better."

Ross wanted to contradict him, wanted to admit that he was playing a role at Snowfell that demanded more from him than anything he'd ever had to face in New York. But Toby needed his illusions. They would have to sustain him through some hard times ahead.

"You can't run away from what you are," he said gently. "None of us can."

But wasn't that what he was going to ask Toby to do when they left Snowfell? Wasn't he lying with every breath he took? Would Toby come to hate him, knowing that his father hadn't fought hard enough to convince Gillian that she belonged with him?

Would Gillian let Toby go? Or would maternal love overcome her irrational obsessions? Would she abandon the Convocation and all it represented to follow and find them, realizing at last that she had been wrong?

Wasn't that what he was counting on?

No more hope. It's finished. Over.

Ross gently nudged Toby back under the covers. "You sleep," he said, pulling the blanket up to Toby's chin.

"But I'm not…" Toby yawned. "You *will* tell me everything that happens?"

"As much as I can."

"But…" Toby's protest dissolved into muttering, and he snuggled under the sheets.

"Good night, son," Ross said, then kissed Toby's forehead and left the room as quietly as he'd come. He nodded to Mrs. Rownthwaite, who was still standing a few feet from the door. Ross knew from her bored expression that she hadn't heard any of his conversation with Toby…which he'd counted on, knowing she was human.

He went down the back stairs near the nursery and paused in the first-story corridor. The smell of perfume was so overwhelming that he couldn't help but notice that someone had raced down the next flight of stairs ahead of him and disappeared before he could identify her.

Definitely not Gillian; no werewolf could stand perfume, and he was surprised that any human at Snowfell was permitted to use it. He backtracked the flowery odor to Sir Averil's door and listened through the heavy wood for Sir Averil's loud breathing.

There was nothing. No movement, no suggestion that someone occupied the room. Ross cracked open the door. The stench that crashed over him cut through the perfume like a prohibitionist's axe through a bootlegger's crate of forbidden alcohol. He'd smelled it before a hundred times, and he could never mistake it.

Sir Averil was dead.

Stepping into the room and closing the door behind him, Ross went to the old man's bedside. He lay in a relaxed position that suggested a peaceful death, hands folded too precisely over his chest, his old-fashioned nightshirt suspiciously smooth.

The bed itself told a different story. The sheets were twisted as if by thrashing limbs; a cup that had once held tea lay overturned on the carpet, leaving a dark stain that had soaked into the weave. The teapot on the tray beside the bed was poised on the very edge of the table on which it had been set.

Ross leaned over the bed and pried Sir Averil's eyes open. The pupils were dilated. Ross detected the smell of tea on the old man's lips, mingled with something else he had just begun to recognize. He circled the bed and crouched beside the fallen teacup. Without touching it, he put his nose to the ground where the tea had disappeared into the carpet.

The other case had happened long ago; Ross had been only a rookie beat cop when he had been called to the site of the murder. He remembered avidly watching the detectives as they analyzed the scene and collected evidence. Even when he returned to his regular duties, he'd followed the details of the case.

The victim had died of poisoning. It wasn't a type of poison the detectives had encountered before, and it had taken some time to identify it and find the man responsible.

Aconitum, the stuff was called. Monkshood.

Wolfsbane.

Ross got to his feet and stared at the teapot. The lid had been knocked off, and Ross could see that it was less than half-full.

Someone had poisoned Sir Averil with enough Aconitum to kill a strong, healthy werewolf within two days.

Ross stood very still, his mind working at lightning speed. Who had a motive for killing the bastard? Just about everyone at Snowfell.

But that wasn't quite true. None of the servants would dare to try it, even if they harbored a serious grudge. Any number of the current guests might kill him in an effort to take control of the Convocation—leaving out Marcus Forster and probably the de Gévaudans, as well. Sir Averil stood in the way of Hugh' romance. And Gillian…

She wouldn't do it. Nothing could have driven her to commit patricide now if she hadn't found cause for it during the past thirty years.

Unless the old bastard had threatened her with Toby's exile one too many times…

Hell. Sir Averil would be pleased that Toby was going through the transition. He wouldn't have any reason to repeat the threat. *So it can't be Gillian. And Hugh wouldn't have the guts.*

Ross laughed. *He* had as much motive as anyone. With one act, he could free Gillian and Toby from their bondage.

And bring down a rain of consequences that would only confirm his roll as prize idiot.

The others think the old man's only sick. They've been convinced that he's going to recover and take charge again.

Ross looked at Sir Averil's lifeless face with contempt. Whoever had killed him had done the world a favor. But the fact was that his death would send a ripple through the Convocation that could seriously weaken Gillian's grasp on leadership. *His* reputation had assembled this group. *His* power and charisma had won him the Convocation, not Gillian's.

And she'd refused to believe that he could die.

One thing was certain: the truth had to be hidden until Gillian had time to absorb the implications. She would have to pretend that Sir Averil had died of natural causes. And someone would have to find out who'd done it, or the assassin might strike again at the surviving Maitlands.

It could still be someone with a private grudge. But Ross didn't believe it.

The main thing he had working in his favor was that the last person in the room had made the stupid mistake of using that ghastly perfume. It permeated the air as if it had been liberally and deliberately sprinkled on the carpet and bedding. The only reason someone would do that was to obscure his or her own scent. But the ploy would backfire, since the smell would follow that person wherever he or she went, even outside the house.

A werewolf wouldn't make that kind of mistake. That left a human as the prime suspect. Or someone who wanted everyone to *think* the killer was human.

Leaving his mind open to all possibilities, Ross began a more thorough search of the room. He found a lot of little things that didn't add up to any real evidence; the intruder, in spite of his or her mistakes, had taken at least *some* basic precautions.

He checked his wristwatch. The meeting should be winding up in a few hours. He had to find a way to keep the delegates from attempting to see Sir Averil. The reek of perfume wouldn't last indefinitely, and it wasn't enough to mask the other scents. Sir Averil's chamberpot was full nearly to overflowing, and whoever had tried to clean up the vomit hadn't done a very good job of it.

Closing his nostrils, Ross poured the contents of the chamberpot around the body. The smell mingled with the perfume in a blend as unpleasant as the odor of death itself. Any werewolf passing by would assume that Sir Averil had lost control of his bladder and avoid the place out of sheer disgust. But someone would come to check on him soon enough.

Ross left the room, closed the door and went downstairs. If he'd had a choice, he would have gone straight after the person with the perfume. But there was something else he had to do first.

As he was about to enter the Great Hall, Hugh came out.

"Ross," he said. His hands were shaking as he pulled a cigarette from a monogrammed case and put it between his lips. He fumbled in his pocket, presumably looking for a lighter, but came up empty.

"I say," he said, "you don't have a match, do you?"

Ross shook his head, wondering how any werewolf who acquired the habit could bear the stench of smoke. "How is she?" he asked.

Hugh removed the cigarette from his mouth and let it dangle between his fingers. "She's got them under control," he said in a low voice. "No one's challenged her yet, though a few…" He filled his lungs and expelled the air sharply. "It's a near thing. I don't know if she can keep it up until Sir Averil is recovered."

"He isn't going to recover."

Hugh blinked. The cigarette slipped from his fingers.

"What…what do you…?"

"He's dead." Ross tugged Hugh away from the door. "I found im that way. I think he was poisoned."

"But that's…" Hugh's eyes darted in every direction as if he vere chasing thoughts around inside his brain. "Good Lord. The ld man's finally gone."

"And you inherit everything he has."

Hugh shook his head. "I…can't believe it."

Ross watched his face. Though Hugh hadn't spared any grief or his father, he'd seemed genuinely surprised, even dazed, by he news, and Ross knew the other man wasn't very good at ying.

"We have to tell Gillian right away," Ross said.

"Yes. Of course." Hugh shook his head again. "This changes verything."

"Yeah." Ross paused to listen for movement or voices near he other side of the door. Nothing so far. "Do you have any idea vho might have done this?" he asked.

It was obvious that Hugh hadn't even begun to think of that spect of Sir Averil's untimely death. His brow creased.

"The Germans," he said slowly. "The Russians, or—not very ikely, in my opinion—the Norwegians or the Earnshaws. They're the ones who've shown the most signs of wanting to ispute our…Gillian's leadership."

"That doesn't leave many delegates above suspicion."

"I can't see the Spaniard doing it. He's been pretty quiet, and vhen he's spoken up, it's always been to dispute Gillian's deractors. The Hungarians are all bark and no bite. De Gévaudan nd his lot are good eggs. Marcus Forster…he's incapable of urting a fly." He stared down at the cigarette lying at his feet. 'I suppose you really can't rule out anyone, can you? Not ven…" He stopped before he finished and choked on a laugh. 'Well, I suppose I ought not to leave the premises, eh?"

Ross hesitated, considering how much to reveal. "I think the last person to see Sir Averil alive was wearing perfume. A lot of it."

"But no werewolf…" He noticed the look in Ross's eyes. "Of course you've thought of that."

"Whoever did it, we have to act quickly. You know what's at stake."

"It's not just a matter of keeping them here. Once they find out that Sir Averil's dead, as they eventually must, the worst of the lot—and I'm not counting the murderer, of course—won't be held back by the uncertainty that's been keeping them in line."

"The thought had occurred to me." Ross looked toward the door again. "Is the meeting almost over?"

"As a matter of fact, a few of the delegates have become a bit of a bother, so Gillian decided to cut it short today. They should be out at any minute."

"Who was causing trouble?"

"The usual suspects." He blanched as he heard his own words. "Actually, the Huns have been rather quiet, though Conrad's been buzzing around Gilly like a carrion fly."

Ross stared at the door, wishing that Conrad would walk through it and into his fist. "I have to talk to Gillian alone."

Hugh's mouth twisted in self-mockery. "I think I can manage to lead them into the drawing room for drinks."

"Good. Ask her to come out."

Squaring his shoulders, Hugh obliged. A few minutes passed before Gillian emerged.

"Ross?" she said, meeting his gaze for the first time that day. "Where have you been? The others have been asking—"

No use beating around the bush.

"Jill. Your father is dead."

CHAPTER NINETEEN

ROSS HAD EXPECTED the news to hit her much harder than it had her brother, and she didn't surprise him. She took an involuntary step backward and reached for the wall. Her breath came in short bursts, and her skin lost its color. He just barely stopped himself from catching and holding her against his chest.

"Dead?" she whispered.

He took her gently by the arm and led her away from the door. He repeated what he'd said to Ross, not mentioning the smell of perfume, or the initial speculation about the murderer's identity that he and her brother had shared.

"I'm sorry," he said, though the words were just a formality. Gillian blinked. Her eyes were perfectly dry, and the color was gradually returning to her cheeks. But Ross knew she was holding herself together with spit and baling wire.

"I must see him," she said, turning toward the stairs. Her stride was uneven, and Ross stayed close behind her in case she should fall.

She didn't. She approached Sir Averil's room step by deliberate step, her body growing more and more rigid as she smelled the stench creeping out from under the door. Ross blocked her way.

"It's pretty bad," he said. "I had to make sure no one would be tempted to go in there until—"

She shoved past him and opened the door. The odor was strong enough to make Ross gag, but Gillian hardly seemed to notice. She stopped just inside, staring at the motionless figure on the bed.

"Are you all right?" Ross asked.

"Yes." She continued on to the foot of the bed, never taking her gaze from her late father's face. "Did he suffer?"

It would be no less than he deserved, Ross thought. "I don't know," he said, sparing her the truth. "The stuff he was given probably works differently on werewolves than on humans."

Gillian bent her head. "I thought he was invincible. I couldn't imagine he'd ever allow death to defeat him."

"He didn't have much choice."

Ross immediately regretted the harshness of his words, though Gillian showed no signs of having heard him.

"Who could have done this?" she asked. But Ross could see she was already running the possibilities through her mind. "I never thought they would go this far," she said, as if to herself. "Threats, perhaps. Obstruction, certainly. A few challenges seemed inevitable. But to kill in this…this…" She straightened. "Someone did this in order to assume control of the Convocation."

"It looks like the best theory we've got right now. But the killer has rolled some pretty risky dice to get what he's after. I'm guessing that direct assassination is breaking all the usual werewolf rules."

"Yes." She pressed her lips together. "It's considered a supreme act of cowardice. Such a person, if exposed, would be driven out and ostracized from all future contact with our kind, if not worse."

"Then he's got an unpleasant future ahead, because I'm going to expose him."

Abruptly she swung toward him, bewildered fury in her eyes. "Why should you care?" she asked, her voice rising. "You hated him. Now you have what you wanted."

"Is that really what you think?" he asked. "That I have what I want?"

She stared at him and finally looked away. "You have no reason to look for his murderer."

He could feel himself about to make the same stupid mistakes as always and stopped himself. "If the killer is really after control of the Convocation," he said, "and he was willing to go this far to get it, there's likely to be a lot more trouble than anyone could have predicted. Toby could be caught right in the middle of it."

Her anger gave way to comprehension and then fear. "If they think Hugh and I stand in the way of their ambitions, they might…" She put her hand to her throat. "Toby must leave Snowfell at once."

And there it was. The opening he needed, the chance to take Toby away with Gillian's blessing.

Even letting the idea pass through his mind filled him with self-disgust. "That might not be a good idea," he said. "Not until we know more."

He paused to gather his thoughts, realizing he was on the verge of falling into yet another dangerous trap. His dislike of most of the delegates, especially the Germans, was clouding his judgment. He'd rushed headlong into assumptions he shouldn't have made in the first place.

"I think you'll agree that we can't get anyone else involved," he said carefully. "Least of all the local police."

"Certainly not!"

Because no one at Snowfell would want human cops digging around…and that went double for him. He was going to have to tell Gillian about the second murder in New York, and soon. But these were the worst possible circumstances for informing her that he was a murder suspect all over again.

"We have a good shot at finding the murderer on our own," he said. "Whoever killed Sir Averil did something incredibly stupid."

"The perfume," she said, calm again.

"That's right. But there's a probability that the perfume was a deliberate ploy to mislead any investigation and direct suspicion away from a werewolf as the killer. And I don't think the poisoning happened all at once. Someone was putting it in his tea several times a day, and someone had to smooth out his nightclothes and…well, humans may also be involved."

"Humans?" Her eyes widened. "The servants?"

"Maybe someone's being used, or getting very well rewarded. Unless you think one of the servants would have a good enough reason to do this on his or her own."

"No," she said. "It isn't possible."

"Maybe not. But whatever's going on, I'll be able to find the owner of the perfume pretty quickly, unless they've arranged a fast getaway." He glanced at his watch again. "Get a couple of footmen to watch Toby's door. The killer would have to be crazy to pick an open fight with them with so many witnesses around."

"He killed my father without attracting attention."

"But I don't think there was any direct confrontation involved. Sir Averil never knew he was being poisoned." He watched Gillian's face to make sure she'd accepted his argument. "Hugh knows what's going on, so the two of you will have to keep the delegates from finding out Sir Averil is dead. Keep a close eye on the Germans."

"Are they your primary suspects?"

He couldn't miss the layers of meaning behind the question. Gillian knew he would like nothing better than to pin the crime on the von Rudens.

"If the murderer *is* one of the delegates," he said, "he probably intended your father's death to serve more than one purpose— removing the main obstacle first, and also creating chaos to disguise his plans until he's ready to make his next move."

"Then I must prevent chaos."

With only Hugh and maybe a couple of the more decent guests to help her.

Leaving her now was crazy. Not finding Sir Averil's unknown visitor was worse.

"Don't push it, Jill," he said. "Give ground if you have to.

Show no suspicion. Let the bastards think you won't be too hard to dislodge."

Which meant losing a lot, maybe most, of what she'd won. But she didn't protest. She understood that her behavior could determine the murderer's next move.

"I shall do what is necessary," she said.

Worry began to chip away at his resolve all over again. "If they ask where I am, play up the fact that I'm American and not very reliable. If you're in a tight spot, look to Forster and the de Gévaudans. Use any allies you can get if someone leaks the story and things get rough."

He headed for the door before he could change his mind. Gillian caught up with him. Her fingertips brushed his sleeve. "Ross…"

"Don't," he said without turning. The last thing he wanted to hear was her gratitude, and the last thing he wanted to see was the grief in her eyes when she let herself remember what she'd lost today. "Be sure to lock the door."

"Yes."

He opened the door, looked up and down the corridor, and strode along toward the landing. Macalister was about to climb the stairs as Ross came down; his nose was wrinkled in reaction to the smells spreading throughout the house. Ross gave a terse greeting and hurried on to the servants' area. Just before he went through the green door, Thierry de Gévaudan emerged from the stuffy billiard room opposite the dining room and lifted a hand to beckon him over. Ross pretended not to see.

The scent trail was still violently fresh throughout the corridor leading to the kitchen. Ross decided to have a quick word with Mrs. Spotterswood. The cook wasn't there, but two scullery maids and several extra girls hired to help cook, bake and clean were all hard at work preparing supper. They froze when they caught sight of Ross.

"Where can I find Mrs. Spotterswood?" he asked them, keeping his distance.

The oldest girl dried her hands on her apron, dipped a curtsey and approached him cautiously. "Mr. Keating?" she asked in her country accent. "Mrs. Spotterswood has gone into town. I am Denise. May I help you?"

He drew her aside. "Do you know who's been serving Sir Averil his tea over the past few days?"

Denise averted her face. Ross sensed that she was afraid that one of her fellow servants was about to get into trouble.

"It's important that I find out, Denise," he said. "Someone's life may depend on it."

The girl jerked up her head. "Whose life, sir?"

"Someone you wouldn't want to see hurt."

Denise shifted from foot to foot and twisted her hands in her apron. "Well," she said, "it's usually Mr. Faulder who brings the master's tray to him when he's in his room or study."

"But he hadn't been doing it lately?"

"He's much too busy now, sir." She lowered her voice. "Sarah has been serving the master since the meeting started."

Ross remembered Sarah as a very quiet girl who, like most of the maids, tended to fade into the background. "You're sure she was the only one?"

"Well…" Denise took a deep breath. "Once I saw Cora—Miss Smith—take the tray from Sarah on the way up the back stairs."

"Cora took it?"

She nodded. "I didn't know why she did it, sir. I know she doesn't like—" She broke off, biting her lip. *Don't worry, kid,* Ross thought. *Nobody liked the son of a bitch.*

"Who prepared the tea, Denise?" he asked.

"Mrs. Spotterswood." The girl was very close to tears. "Is she in trouble, sir?"

Not Mrs. Spotterswood. "No one's in trouble, Denise. Where is Cora now?"

"She—she was in the servants' hall, taking tea."

"Thank you, Denise. You've done very well."

Denise smiled tremulously, curtseyed and rejoined the other girls. Ross returned to the corridor and followed his nose to the servants' hall. It was deserted, though Ross could pick out the scents of most of the servants he'd met...overlaid with the fragrance of perfume. He looked in quickly and saw Mrs. Spotterswood, then kept moving.

He climbed the back stairs to the second floor, where the servants' rooms opened onto a corridor near the nursery. He ended at the room whose occupant couldn't possibly be mistaken.

A direct trail, he thought. *No one is that stupid, certainly not a girl with as much spirit as Cora.*

Ross didn't knock. He walked into the small room and stopped inches from the bed where Cora sat, her face cradled in her hands. The perfume blotted out all the smells that should have filled a room occupied by the same person day after day, and Cora was drenched in it. She looked up, and a flash of horror swept over her pretty features. Her eyes were red from weeping.

"Mr.—Mr. Keating," she stammered, rising to her feet. "I..." She straightened and met his gaze as if she had nothing to hide. "How may I—"

"Why did you do it, Cora?" Ross asked casually, crossing his arms over his chest. "Was it because of Hugh? Did you think getting rid of Sir Averil would make it easier for you to marry him?"

Ross had seen every possible reaction from suspects who'd just been nabbed, and Cora's was a classic. Her eyes widened, and she placed one slender hand over her heart. "I—I don't know what you're..."

Her knees buckled, and she plopped back down on the bed. Ross moved closer, letting her feel the threat of his much larger body.

"Sure you do," he said harshly. "You just didn't know there might be someone in the house who would know what Aconitum smells like."

She swallowed and raised her head. He could only admire her continuing attempt to appear shocked. "Has…something happened to Sir Averil?"

"No more games, Cora. I *know.*"

Her hands began to shake. "No one will believe you."

"Because they're too arrogant to believe a human would be capable of such an unthinkable act against a werewolf?" He laughed. "You had motive, Cora. Motive and opportunity. You brought the tea up to Sir Averil's room, though you obviously started before he showed the first signs of poisoning."

"No! No, you're wrong. I—"

"The thing I don't understand is the perfume. Even a human could easily have followed the smell right back to you. I don't believe you're that stupid, Cora. So…why?" He leaned so close that she had to fall back onto her elbows. "It would be better for you to tell the truth now," he said more gently. "Maybe I'll be able to help you." He posed the question he least wanted to ask. "Was Hugh in on this?"

"No!" Her denial was so unthinkingly automatic that Ross knew she was completely sincere. "Hugh didn't know anything about…about what happened. I swear." Her eyes flooded with tears. "Please don't tell him. Not until I…" She sobbed into her hands. "You have it all wrong. It was the Germans. They *made* me do it."

Suddenly the air in the room seemed far less smothering. Ross released his breath. "What did they tell you to do?"

"To—to put the poison in Sir Averil's tea."

"Did they give a reason?"

Cora glanced around the room as if she expected listeners behind every wall. "Soon after they first arrived, I heard them speaking privately with Sir Averil in his study. They said they wanted him to join something they called the—the National Socialist Party. They said many German werewolves were with the party, even though a human was the leader." She scrunched up her face. "I think they called him Hitler."

Ross wasn't sure he'd ever heard the name, but there was something familiar about this National Socialist thing. "Why did they want him to join?" he asked.

"They said the party was dedicated to the purity of the race, just like the Convocation. They said they could use the humans to forward their goals."

Her words were too smooth, too easy, the explanation too rehearsed. But at the same time, it all sounded exactly like the Germans. "What did Sir Averil say to their proposal?"

"He said no. He said no true werewolf would join with humans for any reason. He said he might not let Gillian marry into their family after all. The Huns left in a fury."

"Did they threaten Sir Averil?"

"Not then. But they caught me…they found me listening and said if I didn't do exactly as they told me, they'd kill me and make it seem like an accident." She shuddered. "You must believe me."

Ross would have loved to accept her story hook, line and sinker. But everything she'd said and done so far could just be a very good act. He'd seen it before.

"None of that explains the perfume," he said, easing back.

"It was a mistake. I thought, just a little, and not even a werewolf would…" She wiped her eyes with her fingertips. "I was so careful. But I spilled it on my clothes. I knew someone would find me. I knew it wouldn't do any good to run. I prayed…" She reached out with pleading hands. "Please, don't tell the Germans! I'll do anything, just don't let them kill me!"

She was pretty damned convincing. And Ross couldn't discount the possibility that she really was at risk.

"Listen to me, Cora," he said. "You may be lying, and if you are, I'll find out. In the meantime, you're not to leave the house for any reason. I don't think the Germans will try to hurt you as long as you stay in your room or with the other servants. If you leave, I can't speak for the consequences."

"Do they…do they know Sir Averil is…?"

"Not yet. It would be a bad thing if any of the delegates knew before I— Mrs. Delvaux is ready to tell them."

A single tear trickled down Cora's smooth cheek. "I won' leave," she whispered.

"A wise choice. If your story is true, you may get off easy." H went to the door, throwing one final warning glance over hi shoulder. "Get rid of those clothes, and wash yourself thoroughly. He paused. "I'll see if I can get someone to stay with you."

She stared bleakly after him as he walked out the doo Though he'd known no one was nearby, he was relieved to fin the corridor empty. He descended the main staircase and heade straight for the god-awful monstrosity known as the Re Drawing Room.

To his surprise, Gillian wasn't there, though Hugh and mos of the delegates were present. Count von Ruden, Conrad an Benedikt were off in their usual corner, taking slow sips of thei brandy and observing the others with predatory gazes. Ros poured himself a bourbon and strolled over to the Germans wit a bland smile on his face.

"So," he said in his Western drawl, "what is this National So cialist Party I've been hearing about?"

It was obvious from their reactions that they hadn't expecte such a question coming from an American. Conrad began t speak, but Friedrich overrode him.

"You are quite knowledgeable, for an American," he sai leaning back in his chair.

"Some of us are interested in what goes on outside our country, Ross said, sipping his drink. "Who's this guy Hitler, anyway?"

"A great leader," Conrad announced belligerently. "One wh will carry us to the ultimate victory."

"I've heard that somewhere before." Ross pretended to ex amine his glass. "Is he a werewolf?"

Friedrich waved his hand as if to dismiss Ross's questio

onrad fumed silently. Benedikt, who never spoke, shrank like dried-out sponge.

"He believes in purity and strength," Conrad snarled. "In eeding out the inferior races."

"Then Sir Averil must like Hitler, too."

As one, the Germans rose and walked toward the French del- ;ates, for whom they'd previously showed nothing but con- mpt. Interesting. They couldn't handle questioning, even from stupid American.

It still wasn't proof. But Ross hadn't given up, not by a long shot.

He left the room and looked for Gillian. He found her alone the Great Hall, standing at the podium above the empty rows chairs.

"Are you all right?" he asked, not letting himself get too ose to her.

"Yes." And at first glance she seemed to be, though the little gns of shock and grief were still evident in her face. She arched his eyes, but she didn't leave the podium. "Have you und something?"

Ross's feet were on the verge of disobeying his orders, threat- ing to carry him across the room so that he could hold her in s arms. "I have a suspect," he said.

"Who killed him?"

The tonelessness of her voice told him how much emotion she as still keeping in check. He decided not to reveal Cora's part the murder. At least not yet. In this state, Gillian might do mething she would come to regret.

"My best bet," he said, "is still the Germans."

"Based upon what evidence?"

"A source I can't reveal yet. You can trust me, Jill."

She grabbed the edge of the podium with one hand, but Ross dn't think she needed its support. "Are you certain that your vn prejudices aren't at work?" she asked.

"I don't condemn anyone until I can prove it."

"Even if you hate the suspect?"

"I believe in the law."

"Werewolf law, or human?"

"Whichever one is most likely to uncover the truth."

Gillian glanced at her hand on the podium. Ross swore h could hear the wood begin to crack.

"Under no circumstances are you to harass the von Rudens she said. "If you offend them and they are not guilty…"

"A guy might think you can't wait to get to Germany." H tried to swallow his anger, but it was sliding out of his contro "Why don't you ask them about their new leader—Hitler? He all for the same things you and Sir Averil believe in. *He* probab wouldn't have much use for Toby, either."

Her face flushed and then blanched in the space of a fe seconds. "You heard?"

"I know what the Huns think of my son. The way you Conrad crawl all over you, you don't seem to care if they end treating Toby the same way Sir Averil treated you. Or has the fa that they probably killed your father changed your mind?"

She didn't offer any rebuttal. She simply looked through hi a creature that wore Gillian's skin but was empty inside.

"You must take Toby away tonight," she said. "I have call the Grand Hunt for tomorrow morning."

At first Ross heard only the first part of the sentence. *You mu take him away. You.*

She'd given up. Given up trying to defend herself, to count the unfounded accusations he'd never stopped making sin he'd found her waiting in front of his apartment. She was letti him win.

Ross knew what it was like to feel hollow and defeated. H skull was as light as a dirigible, and there was nothing under ribs but air.

An apology now would mean nothing. He'd savaged her o too many times. Because *he* was afraid.

"Hugh and I have called the Hunt earlier than planned to distract the delegates from questioning Sir Averil's continued absence," she went on. "It will be conducted entirely in wolf shape. If there is to be any direct conflict among the delegates, it is likely to occur then."

When any lingering inhibitions would be shed along with the semblance of humanity. "That includes attacks against you and Hugh," Ross said.

"You may not have another chance to take Toby once the Hunt begins."

Because then Ross, who couldn't Change to save his life, would be faced with a bunch of purebloods during the event that was supposed to display every delegate's right to his or her place at the Convocation.

He'd been prepared to deal with that danger when it arose, but not so soon. And not with the additional complication of murder.

What if the Germans decided to make their big move during the Hunt itself?

"You need not be concerned about what occurs after you are gone," Gillian said. "I believe I have sufficiently proven that I am fully capable of doing what must be done."

Which meant she would try to stop the Germans if they attempted a coup. Once she had proof that they were the killers, she would finally have to break with them completely. She would become the Huns' deadly enemy, fighting in Sir Averil's stead to hold the Convocation and punish his murderers. And she would be up against people with no morals and fewer scruples. Her chances of winning were slim to none.

Gillian knew him well enough to guess his thoughts. "You *will* leave with Toby tonight," she said. "Hugh has access to monies Sir Averil kept on the premises. He will advance you sufficient funds now and send more when his inheritance is confirmed."

"I don't want your damned money," Ross snapped. But he felt the panic she was barely holding in check and softened his tone. "What do you expect me to do? Do you actually trust me enough to take Toby and bring him back when you have everything settled?"

"I trust you to take him with you to a place where he can be happy. That is all that—"

"I'm not going!"

The drumming of bare feet jerked Ross's attention across the room to the side doors leading off the Great Hall. Toby skidded to a halt halfway between Ross and Gillian.

"Is it true that Grandfather is dead?" he demanded.

GILLIAN RUSHED to cover Toby's mouth. "Be quiet!" she snapped. "How did you get past Robert and Peter?"

Toby wasn't distracted by her question. "I heard you," he whispered loudly. "You want to send me away just because the Huns killed Grandfather. You think they might do something to me, but I'm not afraid of them any more than you and Father are."

Toby was so dismissive about Sir Averil's death that Gillian was momentarily at a loss for words. "You have no conception of what has happened," she said, drawing on the anger and fear that had driven her through the day.

"Yes, I do. And I'm *glad* Grandfather is dead."

His childish candor was just as devastating as anything Ross had said. "You should not be," she said, giving him a little shake. "The people who killed your Grandfather are not characters in a book. They are going to hurt someone else sooner or later. And I will not let it be you."

Toby looked at Ross, an appeal in his eyes. "Father and I won't leave you here to fight the Huns alone."

"You can be of no possible help," she said, as Ross opened his mouth to speak. "I want you gone before the Hunt begins."

Toby pulled free. "We won't go, Mother. It is out of the question."

She could have wept at the loyalty and courage in his unyielding face. "This time you *will* obey," she said, reaching for him again. "Your father will take the Bentley, and—"

"No, Jill. I can't."

Given Ross's natural sense of chivalry, his refusal was not a complete surprise to her, even though it seemed to surprise *him*. She still flinched at the betrayal. "You must—" she said.

"Stop!" Toby pressed his hands over his ears and squeezed his eyes closed. "I won't listen. All you do is argue when there are important things to do."

Ross stared at Gillian over Toby's head, and she stared back, as speechless as he. Then they turned together to look at the doors. Someone surely must have heard. A fresh disaster was in the making.

"I agree that Toby has to be made safe," Ross said, very quietly. "But he's too smart and brave for his own good. As long as there's a killer in this house, he isn't going to leave you here unless someone he trusts stays to help."

Gillian extended her arms to gather Toby up, but he had uncovered his ears and was listening intently.

It was quite possible—even probable—that Ross was right, though Toby had no idea what his father was risking. Even so, Ross's argument was strained, as if he didn't truly believe it himself.

He will not leave you.

"There must be somewhere you can send him," he said. "Someone you can trust to look after him for the next few days."

She took in a slow breath and let it out again. "The Forsters would welcome him."

"Then we'll get Marcus to take him."

"It would be better not to involve them if there is another alternative," Gillian said. "I will make inquiries tonight."

He might have asked for details if Robert and Peter hadn't

burst into the hall at that very moment. They lurched to a stop when they saw Toby.

Robert bobbed his head. "We—we beg your pardon, ma'am." He flushed, his face matching his ginger hair. "Is Master Toby…?"

"You are not at fault," Gillian said, speaking as if she had not just taken part in a very unpleasant argument. "Toby will apologize to you presently. Won't you, Toby?"

He ducked his head. "Yes, Mother."

"You will return to your room. You are not to attempt another escape, or give Peter and Robert any further trouble. If necessary, I shall ask Faulder to sit with you."

Toby shuddered and shook his head. With a heavy tread he accompanied her and the worried footmen upstairs, but not without a final beseeching glance at Ross.

Gillian saw her son settled with Mrs. Rownthwaite installed at his bedside, satisfied herself that the abashed footmen would not permit Toby to escape again and descended the stairs to return to the drawing room.

Ross was staying at Snowfell. She could not have conceived of a more terrible situation, far beyond the shock of Sir Averil's death.

She had known from the beginning that Ross would eventually be exposed as an impostor, but now there was no more pretending that some miraculous solution would present itself just in time. He was soon to become the center of a new and dangerous storm. Once his ruse was uncovered, he could be of no help to anyone, least of all himself. She would be faced with the impossible choice of attempting to shield him or disowning him entirely to prevent the murderers, or the other potential troublemakers, from exploiting a new opportunity for deadly mischief.

And how was she to forgive him for what he had said? *"You don't seem to care if they end up treating Toby the same way Sir Averil treated you."*

How many times had he made such accusations, cruel conjecture driven by his utter lack of trust in her love for her son?

I could have told him about the new agreement with Conrad. Then he would see how much I care for my son.

Be damned to that. She was done with explanations. She would not justify her actions to a man whose behavior toward her changed by the hour.

Let him go on believing the worst. Then he wouldn't evoke his misplaced and grudging chivalry on her behalf, destroying any remaining hope of holding the peace.

Deliberately, Gillian paused at the foot of the stairs and took a few moments to tidy her hair, and ensure that her skirt and blouse were smooth and neat. At least Toby, once he had fully accepted the facts, would be happy with a father whose complete acceptance of him wouldn't be in doubt for a single moment.

She waited a little longer to be sure that her heart was beating at a normal pace. Voices in the corridor—the Hungarians speculating on what had become of their hostess—restored her common sense. She walked toward the Great Hall, her shoulders aching as if her entire body wanted to weep.

I'm glad he's dead. Glad. Glad. Glad.

"Gilly."

Hugh stepped into her path, blocking the doors. She would have warned him that he should not have left the guests, but there was an unfamiliar air about him that silenced her.

"You were fighting with him again," he said.

"It's none of your concern, Hugh."

"Was it about Toby? Or was he asking you to marry him again?"

A single step to the side and she was almost to the door, but Hugh laid his hand on her shoulder, and when she tried to shake him off, he held firm.

"I have something to say, Gilly, and you're going to listen to me this time." He jerked up his chin. "You're going to throw over the marriage with Conrad, hand the Convocation to me, and leave Snowfell with Toby and Ross. And I won't have any argument."

She hadn't enough humor left in her to laugh. "I appreciate the offer," she said wearily, "but I am in no mood—"

"This isn't a joke, Gilly. It's not an empty promise like all the others. I know what I'm doing, maybe for the first time in my life."

"Only yesterday you were telling me how impossible it was for you to become the leader Father wanted," she said. "What has changed your mind?"

"Maybe I didn't show it," he said slowly, "but the old man's death really threw me for a loop. I started to think about what he always wanted me to be, and how hard you tried to create the illusion that I had succeeded." His expression was so grave that she had difficulty accepting that this was her brother, her Hugh. "When I asked Ross to come to Snowfell," he continued, "I told him I hadn't been much of a brother. I've never deceived myself about that, Gilly. But whenever I swore to do better—and I've done that a thousand times—I'd never follow through."

"Hugh, I never expected—"

"But I *do*. At long last, I understand completely. I'm a Maitland. And somewhere in this formerly empty head of mine, there may still be a few shreds of honor left." He offered a smile, but there was nothing the least conciliatory about it. "I'm asking you to give me a chance, Gilly. Let me prove myself. I'll manage the Hunt. Don't interfere."

Tears, which Gillian had so seldom indulged in for the first thirty years of her life, now seemed a constant threat. "They won't let up, Hugh," she said. "You may think they'll accept you because you're male, but they've seen…" She glanced away, but Hugh had understood her well enough.

"They've seen who's really leading the Convocation," he said. "They've been right until now. But you've carried the burden too long." He read her face with an expertise as astonishing as his confidence. "You think I'm doing this so you can be free. But that's only part of it, Gilly. And it isn't any lingering devotion to Father, either. It's my last chance to stand among our kind and prove that *both* Maitland heirs can give them a run for their money."

"The Germans—"

"I'm still not convinced they're guilty. I can't tell you why. It's just a feeling." He half grinned. "Not something to inspire confidence, eh? But we can't borrow trouble." His smile slipped away. "I'm not asking you to fade into the background. You can always come to my rescue if I make a shambles of it. But I don't think I will."

Gillian could find no words to discourage him. She had despaired of having unwittingly contributed to his inability to stand firmly on his own two feet. Now he was ready to try, and he'd convinced her that he really meant it.

But she wouldn't allow herself to dream too far. Only exposure of the Germans as murderers would save her a permanent relocation to Germany.

"What about Father?" she asked.

He didn't have to ask what she meant. "We'll move the body to the ice house," he said, "and save explanations until after the Hunt."

Provided everyone emerged unscathed.

"Are we agreed, Gilly?" Hugh asked solemnly, and extended his hand.

Gillian took it. His grip was firm. She might have believed she held the hand of a stranger.

With a brief, determined nod, Hugh turned and left. Gillian forced a smile onto the rigid muscles of her face and opened the door. Tonight she would help Hugh deflect inquiries as to Sir Averil's health and support her brother as he presided over dinner. And when everyone else had retired, she would write the letter she hoped would remove Toby from any danger of paying for her unforgivable mistakes.

CHAPTER TWENTY

TOBY WOKE from a light sleep and sat up in bed. He strained to hear over Miss Rownthwaite's abominable snoring, cocking his head to make sure he hadn't imagined the sound.

There it was again. Someone was walking on the lawn below his window; he could hear the very faint shuffling of shoes on grass. Carefully, Toby got out of bed and crept past the governess. She didn't stir as he went to the window and opened the sash.

The air was damp and cool. He could smell the roses in the garden, bird droppings on the roof and freshly turned earth. Beyond that were the pungent odors of the woods, and the scent of someone he knew.

The Germans weren't talking. They were walking away from the house very quickly, probably going into the wood, where they thought no one would hear them.

Toby bared his teeth, something he did without even thinking now that he was nearing the Change. He knew, from what he'd overheard of his parents' conversation, that Father thought the Germans had killed Grandfather. And though Toby wasn't at all sorry the old man was gone, he also knew that a lot of problems would be solved if someone could prove what the Huns had done.

A rook called once from the wood. Toby remembered hearing Mother and Father arguing about the Germans and whether or not Father should take Toby away from Snowfell. Father had said some dreadful things that Toby knew he didn't mean, things that must have upset Mother terribly. They had barely looked at each other afterward, and their voices had been like those of strangers.

That was bad enough. But Toby had come to realize that Mother was having a much rougher time of leading the Convocation than he'd suspected. She'd said that the Hunt would make things even worse. That the Germans were out to cause as much trouble as they could. And though no one had mentioned it, Toby knew that the other delegates would not be happy with Father when they found out he couldn't Change.

Something must be done before the Hunt, before Mother could send him away. If he could prove how much he really could help, they would see how foolish it was to make him go.

Toby cast a quick glance at Mrs. Rownthwaite and leaned out the window. It was pretty far down to the lawn, but he'd done it before. He sneaked to the armoire where his clothing was kept, shimmied out of his pyjamas and quickly put on a shirt and the short trousers he wore when he was digging at the ruins. He thought about shoes and decided against them; they might make too much noise.

Once again he went to the window. He could no longer see the Germans. He clambered over the windowsill, clung to the edge and eased himself down, gripping the stone wall with his toes. He grimaced and let himself drop, landing neatly on his feet and catching himself before he could fall.

He crouched to examine the lawn, sniffing and picking out the indentations where the Germans' shoes had pressed down on the grass. He had no difficulty in finding the trail; whatever the Huns were about, they weren't trying very hard to cover their tracks.

A shivery sensation, quite unlike anything he'd experienced before, distracted Toby as he was about to begin his pursuit. Prickles ran up and down under his skin, and he suddenly felt as if he ought to run about on all fours and howl at the moon.

The Change. It was trying to take over, telling him to become a wolf and show the Germans just what he could do.

I won't, Toby vowed. *I don't have to. I will be like Father.*

He shook himself very hard, crouched low and followed the scent path across the lawn and into the woods. He heard distant voices, too soft for him to quite make out what they were saying. He had to get a lot closer and hope the Germans wouldn't hear or scent *him.*

But as he moved in their direction, he realized the voices didn't belong to the Huns at all. And the scents he smelled were those of Cora, Mother's maid, and Uncle Ethan. He'd stumbled on a different quarry.

Toby hid among the trees, unable to decide which way to go. He ought to follow the Germans. That was why he'd come. But a feeling in his chest—what he supposed others called instinct—made him turn toward Ethan. He went on, ears pricked, still moving very quietly.

Ethan was standing in a little clearing among the trees, completely invisible from the house. Cora was with him. She glanced around nervously, clasping and unclasping her hands.

"Luckily for you, they've gone away," Ethan said. "It was very foolish to insist on meeting so near the house, Cora."

Toby realized that if he had been younger, he might have walked right out and asked Ethan and Cora what they were doing in the woods so late at night. But every hair on his body was standing straight up, and he knew without thinking that it would be very stupid to leave his hiding place. Ethan was paying close attention to everything around him. As if he didn't want anyone to overhear.

Why am I afraid of Uncle Ethan?

Toby couldn't answer his own question. That strange feeling under his ribs only grew stronger. He bent his head and listened.

"Is it finished?" Ethan asked.

Cora shivered, her arms wrapped around her chest. "Yes Lord Warbrick. I did just as you said. I didn't…" She gulped loudly. "I didn't know it would happen so fast."

Ethan waved his hand. "I would have preferred a more gradual decline, but such things are never completely certain. He is dead and will no longer stand as an obstacle to me…or to you and Hugh." He narrowed his eyes. "You should be pleased, Cora."

Cora looked everywhere but at him. "Kavanagh came after me, just as we planned. But I'm not sure…" She gulped again. "I'm not sure he believed my story."

"Did you tell it precisely as I instructed?"

"Yes. He hates the Germans. I am certain he wished to believe me."

"But he has doubts."

"He didn't threaten to expose me. He thinks I'm too frightened to run away while he is searching for evidence against the Huns."

The glance Ethan gave Cora was very cold indeed. "Mrs. Delvaux must know of Kavanagh's suspicions by now. Has she continued to keep the delegates in hand?"

Cora hesitated. "Yes," she said. "They listen to her. No one has offered any sort of challenge."

"And the boy?"

"He has improved."

"What of Kavanagh?" Ethan asked.

"He… I believe that he and Mrs. Delvaux have spent little time together."

Ethan's lips curved up as if he intended to smile, but didn't want Cora to see. "Have there been any additional conflicts between him and the Germans since Sir Averil's death?"

"I have been in my room most of the time, your lordship. There have been no open rows. But I have heard that Hugh has announced the Hunt for tomorrow at dawn."

Toby almost imagined he could see the thoughts spinning around inside Ethan's head. "That will put Kavanagh at greater risk."

"I cannot say, your lordship."

"Has Mrs. Delvaux confided anything to you, however trivial it might have seemed?"

"No. She has been very quiet."

Ethan toyed with the chain of his pocket watch. "Well, everything is likely to work to our advantage, in any case. Kavanagh may have ceased to be of concern to us by this hour tomorrow."

Cora didn't seem to be listening. She opened and closed her mouth several times and then pulled a folded newspaper from the pocket of her dress. "I found this in Hugh's room," she said, extending the paper toward him.

Taking the paper from Cora's hand, Ethan skimmed over the words. There was some sort of picture, as well, but Toby couldn't make it out.

"Is it true?" Cora asked.

Toby rather thought that she was expecting Ethan to be shocked by what he'd read, but he simply refolded the paper and returned it to her.

"As I am not conversant with the details of this particular case," he said, "I am reluctant to hazard a guess."

"But you hate him!"

"For reasons entirely unrelated to these charges. I have observed that the American police are often mistaken in their assumptions. Nevertheless, you were wise to show this to me, Cora. It may provide yet another means of throwing Kavanagh off the scent. Return this to its hiding place, but be prepared to use it."

"How?"

The next part of their conversation dropped to a murmur, though Toby couldn't imagine that whatever they were saying was worse than the rest. Cora nodded several times, her lips tight. When Ethan had finished, she swallowed several times and looked even more frightened than before.

"You—you will help me get away if the Germans find out?" Cora asked.

"As I promised. You will be completely safe."

"But if Kavanagh—"

"Don't be foolish, girl. He would scarcely attack you in a

house full of guests. And he certainly won't involve the police under the circumstances, even if Mrs. Delvaux were to permit it."

"Shouldn't I warn her?"

"No." She flinched, and he lowered his voice. "She is in a delicate position. As long as Kavanagh believes his secret is safe—if indeed he *is* guilty—he will not do anything to endanger his precarious position."

Cora's knees bent a little, and she swayed from side to side. "I am sorry, Lord Warbrick. Of course you're right." Her eyes were so very big that Toby could see moonlight shining in them. "If you hadn't suggested a way to get rid of that horrid old man so I could marry Hugh…"

Ethan raised his hand. "The long wait is almost ended, Cora. Soon Hugh will know what you've done to end Sir Averil's tyranny, and you will both be free. All you need do is continue to follow my instructions and keep me informed." He cocked his head and stared in the direction of the house. "Come to the usual place tomorrow night."

"I—I will try."

"Trying is not sufficient. You *will* be there."

"Yes, Lord Warbrick."

"Ask Hugh to join you there an hour later, after you and I have talked. But do not mention your meeting with me beforehand. We must continue to act with the greatest discretion. Do you understand?"

"I understand."

"Then you may go. Remember, avoid any temptation to embroider on your story or approach Mrs. Delvaux regarding that article. Continue to play the humble servant who had no choice but to obey the foreigners." He reached inside his jacket and produced a single folded sheet of foolscap. "Take this to Miss Rownthwaite first thing in the morning. She will assist you should the situation deteriorate."

Cora clutched the paper tightly. "I will." She made a low curtsey, turned and began walking toward the house. Toby waited. Uncle Ethan still hadn't noticed him, but he seemed in no hurry to leave, and Toby knew he couldn't get away without attracting Ethan's attention.

What would happen if Uncle Ethan knew he'd been listening? The Germans hadn't killed Grandfather...*he* had. Cora had helped him, but it had been Ethan's idea. And he didn't want anyone else to know.

But why had he done it? Cora thought he had done it to help her marry Hugh. Toby didn't believe it. Uncle Ethan had never liked Grandfather. *He* wanted to marry Mother, and Grandfather had stood in the way.

Even that didn't make any sense. Surely Uncle Ethan must realize by now that killing Sir Averil wouldn't help him with Mother. She loved Father. She could never love anyone else.

And if Ethan knew that, wouldn't he want to get rid of Father, as well?

To make things even more confusing, there was all the talk about Father's "secret" and the police. But Ethan had already known about the murder in New York, and Mother hadn't believed it was true. Perhaps Ethan was planning to tell everyone at the Convocation, and some of them *would* think Father was guilty.

I have to get home. I have to warn them. But there was only one way to get back to the house without Ethan thinking he'd been eavesdropping. He counted to one hundred and then deliberately moved the shrubbery around before walking into the little clearing.

"Uncle Ethan!" he said. "I didn't know you were here."

The viscount's eyes narrowed, and Toby knew he was wondering how long he had been nearby. Toby did his best to look very young and stupid.

"What are you doing here, Toby?" Ethan asked softly.

Toby decided that at least part of the truth was best. "I was following the Huns," he said.

"Why?"

"Because..." He looked right into Uncle Ethan's eyes. "Grandfather is dead, and Mr. Kavanagh thinks they killed him."

He tried to keep breathing normally, hoping that he sounded convincing enough. He would have to run very fast if Ethan decided against him.

But he was in luck. Ethan made a face, pretending to be shocked. "Sir Averil?" he said in a choked voice. "Dead?"

Toby thought Ethan looked just like one of the actors in the moving picture mother had taken him to see a year ago in London, especially the one who liked to throw his hands around in the air every time he spoke his silent words.

"The Huns are very bad people," Toby said seriously.

Uncle Ethan rubbed his hand over his face. "My God," he said. "You say Kavanagh believes he was murdered?"

"He smelled something strange in Grandfather's room. He said it was some kind of poison."

"He told you this?"

Toby shuffled his feet. "I...happened to hear about it."

Once again he felt Ethan's suspicious eye cocked in his direction. "Poison," he muttered. "How extraordinary." He frowned deeply. "Is your mother well?"

Toby knew he ought not to upset Uncle Ethan by saying anything he wouldn't want to hear. "She was upset, of course. But she's very brave. Did you know that she has taken Grandfather's place as the leader of the Convocation?"

"No. Your mother has not had time to speak to me since it began."

The anger in Ethan's voice was obvious, but Toby pretended not to notice. "Well," he said, "she's doing a corking good job. And she has lots of people on her side."

He didn't have to say Father's name to see that Ethan knew

exactly what he meant. The viscount's breath hissed through his teeth. "The situation must be highly volatile at Snowfell," he said. "You should not be out here alone at night."

Toby hung his head. "I know. It's just...I want to help."

"You will not help your mother by putting yourself in danger."

"Mr. Kavanagh still doesn't have evidence that the Huns poisoned Grandfather. I thought if I followed them, they might say something that would prove they did it."

"An overheard conversation is hardly evidence." Ethan gazed into the wood, toward the fells. "Where are the Germans now?"

"I don't know. I lost track of them, and then I smelled you." He decided to take another risk. "I saw Cora going toward the house."

Ethan focused on Toby again, and Toby understood just how it must feel to be an insect in a jam jar. "Yes," Ethan said. "I was out walking when I found the girl weeping. She confided to me that she is in love with your uncle Hugh. She seems to have taken some comfort in telling me the story."

And *that* would have been very hard to believe if Toby hadn't already known that Uncle Ethan could make ladies—like Mother—trust him much more than he deserved. "Is she really in love with Hugh?" he asked, opening his eyes very wide. "But Cora is human. Grandfather would never let them marry."

Ethan didn't answer. "It's time for you to go back to the house, young man."

"Yes, Uncle Ethan." Toby began to back away.

"I will accompany you as far as the garden."

It was the last thing Toby wanted, but he didn't have any choice. He walked back to the house, Ethan's stare burning into the back of his neck like one of H. G. Wells's Martian heat-rays.

Once he reached the edge of the garden, Ethan stopped and let Toby climb back into his room. Toby pulled himself through the half-open window, turning once to see if the viscount was still watching.

But he was gone. Miss Rownthwaite, to Toby's great relief, was still sleeping, her head lolling on her chest. Toby crawled into bed and pulled the counterpane up to his chin. His heart was beating annoyingly fast.

Ethan had believed his story. If his luck held, he might sneak past Mrs. Rownthwaite and get to Mother's room before anyone else woke up.

He threw off the sheets and put one foot on the ground.

"Do you think I don't know you've been outside?"

Miss Rownthwaite was glaring at him, fully awake now. Toby shrank back under the covers.

"I did not hear you slip out," she said with a rather unpleasant smile. "But you have left a trail that even I can follow."

She pointed at the floor, revealing the dirt and bits of grass he had brought with him. Toby wanted to curse just like Father, but he held his tongue.

"I've been in my room so long," he whined. "I *had* to get out."

"Mrs. Delvaux has forbidden it." Miss Rownthwaite rose, moving stiffly, and went to the window. She put her hand on the sash and closed the window firmly.

"This is to remain locked," she said. "If you fail to stay in this room, I shall inform your mother of your disobedience."

"Yes, Miss Rownthwaite. Perhaps you ought to tell her right now."

The governess's face was so stern and sour that Toby knew he had no chance of getting around her. For the rest of the long night, she sat up in her chair and watched him with dark, glittering eyes as he lay there, unable to sleep. When the first light of dawn spilled through the window he was still awake, and Miss Rownthwaite was still staring. She got up, stretching her back until the bones cracked, and went to the door.

"I shall see if there is something for you to eat," she said, and left the room. Toby heard the key grate in the lock.

He threw himself back onto the bed, muffling his yells in his pillow. He *had* to talk to Mother and Father. But it didn't look as if it would be easy.

ETHAN STRODE ACROSS the park toward the wood and home, alert for any sign of the Germans. On that subject, at least, Toby had been truthful. They *had* been out tonight, and Ethan had no desire to confront them.

The mingled fury and elation he'd felt after his conversation with Cora had settled into a steady, grim resolve. He had not intended to initiate the next phase of his scheme quite so soon, but she had bungled the dosage, and now it would be necessary to act quickly. The girl had been a useful tool, but tools could turn in the hand that wielded them.

Before he'd been compelled to go to America, he had already recognized the need for having his own agents in the Snowfell household. His first opportunity had come when he'd observed Hugh meeting with a pretty young girl in the dale that marked the border between Highwick and Snowfell. Her name, he had learned, was Cora, and she was a local girl who had recently returned to Cumbria after two years of attending secretarial school in Liverpool. She had put on airs above her station, and it seemed that she and Sir Averil's son had begun to enjoy a friendly but clandestine relationship. She was also seeking steady employment.

Beguiling girls of Cora's persuasion had never been a difficult prospect for Viscount Warbrick. He had "chanced" to meet her in the village and, with a brotherly air, had persuaded her to pour her troubles into his willing ear. A little prevarication—and a sad tale of his concern for Mrs. Delvaux, a dear childhood friend—had convinced Miss Smith that he was a great egalitarian who only wished to encourage her ambitions and protect a lady who had suffered much from the overweening arrogance of the male sex.

As it transpired, he had not needed to make much effort toward installing Cora at Snowfell. Twelve weeks ago, when he'd been in New York for the better part of eight months, he had learned from Gillian that she was in need of a personal maid. He'd suggested Miss Smith for the position, and Gillian had accepted his recommendation. By the time Cora had taken up residence at Snowfell, she had more than one employer and extra money in her pocket.

Soon afterward, while he had continued to languish in America, Ethan had determined that the forthcoming Convocation was an ideal backdrop for his scheme of revenge against Sir Averil. And Cora would provide a convenient means of carrying it out. He had received regular reports from her by mail, and over time he had convinced her that she would have Hugh only if she were willing to commit an act that would serve to free every oppressed soul at Snowfell.

Through Cora, he'd bought the cooperation of Rownthwaite, who was greedy enough to accept his bribes without compunction.

Ethan strode across Highwick's overgrown lawn and entered the house. Cruthers didn't hear him; the old man was nearly deaf and long past his usefulness. Ethan paused in the entrance hall and glanced up the stairs. Lady Warbrick would have fallen into a drunken stupor hours ago. He continued to his study—his cuckolded father's study, which he so seldom visited—and sat in the vast leather chair behind the desk.

The letter was still lying on the polished mahogany surface where he had left it. He spread his hands to either side and stared at the foolscap without rereading the words. It was only the second communication from Gillian since the Convocation had begun, but matters seemed to have altered since he had received the first.

Or had they? Ethan closed his eyes. Gillian had done nothing he had expected. She had not rebuffed Kavanagh when he had arrived at Snowfell, yet she had failed to rebel against her arranged marriage. When Sir Averil had first become ill, she had defied his wishes and stepped into the leadership role that should have been her brother's, focusing dangerous attention upon herself, instead of withdrawing into the shadows where she and Toby would be safe. She had been seen speaking intimately to Kavanagh, and yet they had been at odds over Toby, and she had shown the American no public favor.

Now she had called the Hunt on the very heels of Sir Averil's death. Kavanagh would be shown to dangerous disadvantage during the event, whatever other benefits might accrue from the distraction. If Kavanagh's well-being were vital to her, why would she take such a risk? Did she plan to ensure his departure from Snowfell before the Hunt took place?

Ethan laughed and pressed his palms against his aching forehead. Cora's observations were of limited value. Gillian had certainly not confided her true feelings in this brief missive she considered sufficient to command her old friend's unquestioning assistance.

He picked up the letter. *I can trust no one but you,* she had written. *Come during the Hunt tomorrow morning. You will find Toby in the old gardener's shed. No one will be at Snowfell except the servants.*

Oh, she had finally turned to him, yes, but only because he could be of some use to her. Still, she might, as he had hoped, reject her father's schemes of marriage now that he was no longer alive to enforce them. She would certainly despise the Germans for what they believed they had done.

But had Cora had been telling the truth and not what she thought Ethan wanted to hear? Was it possible that Gillian had finally recognized how great a liability Kavanagh was to her and her son? Had an unbridgeable rift developed between them, one that had convinced her that the American's welfare was no longer of paramount importance? Was it possible that she had abandoned any affection she had once held for her American lover?

Even if she had, she would never come to the one who had always been her other half, her salvation, her very blood.

So she must be humbled. She must lose every support she imagined she possessed. She must be deprived, not only of her former lover and her useless brother, but of the thing she valued far above her own life.

And with this letter she had given him the very means to do it.

Ethan rose, folded the letter and locked it in the desk drawer.

There was still a chance that Toby had been lying. The brat was clever enough. But as there was no immediate way to send further instructions to Mrs. Rownthwaite, Ethan was compelled to trust his own judgment.

Judgment that had failed him too many times since he had walked into Kavanagh's apartment.

But not now. Now when victory was nearly within his grasp. Destiny had brought Gillian to him. Destiny had laid out his inevitable course, and it would not betray him again.

CHAPTER TWENTY-ONE

THE HUNT began before sunrise.

The delegates came to the border of the park, singly and in groups, each one of them naked to the skin. Here every flaw was exposed, every *loup-garou* subject to the scrutiny of the others. Here alliances would be forged or broken, dependent upon the strength and swiftness and skill of each participant.

Gillian and Hugh, having claimed pride of place on a low rise above the guests, remained clothed. As leaders, their Change would have a greater significance, almost ceremonial in its nature.

Hugh was behaving exactly as he had promised. Like her, he had never particularly enjoyed Changing; he'd spent so much of his "education" away from Snowfell associating with humans that he'd lost the habit. But now, observing him with his head held high and his eyes gleaming with anticipation, anyone would have thought he had Changed a thousand times with ease and was looking forward to the Hunt with unbridled enthusiasm.

And his sister? Gillian filled her lungs, feeding her body with oxygen as if it contained all the courage she would require during the next few hours. In America it had been so easy. The most natural thing in the world.

She clung to that memory as she looked down on the delegates. Ross was nowhere to be seen. Gillian gave a silent prayer of gratitude that he had finally listened to her, if only because she had reminded him of the suffering Toby would endure if his father were injured during the Hunt.

Injured or worse. Men who had murdered once could easily do so again, and they would find no better opportunity than this.

Her gaze swept over the Germans without stopping, and she met Marcus Forster's encouraging, if nervous, smile. How good he was, and kind. If only she might have sent Toby with him.

But no one could care for Toby better than Ethan. And it would only be for a little while. When this was over, Ross would have no further reason for refusing to take Toby away.

She glanced toward the house, seeking the small window that marked Toby's room. She regretted not having spoken to him after he had gone to bed last night, but she hadn't been able to face him, knowing how betrayed he would feel when Ethan came to fetch him. Only an hour ago she had given Miss Rownthwaite strict instructions to keep Toby confined to his room until the delegates had left the vicinity. She was then to escort him to the gardener's cottage, where she and the footmen would await Ethan's arrival.

Gillian jerked her attention back to the present. She purposefully studied each of the guests in turn, surveying them as if she weren't made in the least uncomfortable by their nudity. At the fore were the Russians and Germans, eying each other covertly. The Germans were muscular and well-proportioned, though Benedikt, the quiet one, was a few inches shorter than the others and appeared self-conscious. The Russians were leaner, but hardly weak; Arakcheyev smiled at Gillian with a great deal less then friendliness.

The French, including Mademoiselle Dominique, were all very fine-looking. Dominique's body was richly curved, a painter's ideal. The Scandinavians towered above the rest; the Hungarians and the Spaniard tended toward wiriness, while the Earnshaws were stockier. Marcus Forster, aside from his obvious desire to support Gillian, had the look of one who would rather be anywhere else. Macalister was older, but it was evident that he'd walked a great deal among the mountains of his Highland home. His wife, so long confined to her room, had joined him at last; she had a sickly appearance, and Gillian pitied her deeply.

In her mind, Gillian compared each of the men to Ross. The Germans were broader through the chest and shoulder, the Russians more graceful. Thierry de Gévaudan was more handsome, as was Señor Tovar. Even the Earnshaws had a certain brooding attractiveness, if one could disregard their disagreeable personalities.

But not one of them could hold a candle to Ross. Not in any respect.

She shook away the thought and waited until all the guests were focused on her and Hugh. Without a glance in her direction, Hugh began to unfasten his shirt and waistcoat, his fingers only fumbling once on the buttons.

Gillian managed to keep her hands from trembling as she removed her shoes, stockings, jacket and skirt, setting them on a large rock beside her. She held her head high as she unbuttoned her blouse and slipped her chemise over her head. The bloomers came last. Cool early morning air swept across her skin, raising gooseflesh on her arms and tightening her nipples.

No one made a sound. She and Hugh stood quietly while the others examined them, searching for any faults or imperfections. They would find none, just as they would have found none in Sir Averil.

You must not think of him now, or who killed him. The murderer or murderers would be exposed soon enough.

Friedrich von Ruden stepped forward and made an ostentatious show of puzzlement, spreading his arms wide. "Where is Keating?" he asked.

Hugh was almost regal as he answered. "I asked him to attend to a pressing matter for me," he said.

Conrad stared past him at Gillian. "What matter?" he demanded.

"Perhaps it is none of your concern," de Gévaudan said in a light tone, as if he were relating a joke.

Conrad growled. "All delegates must attend the Hunt. Does Keating have something to hide? Why are you protecting him?"

"All will become clear, but not until after the Hunt," Hugh said. Gillian, well aware of Conrad's real concern, forced her mouth into a secret smile intended only for him. Hugh cleared his throat.

"A herd of red deer has been sighted less than a mile from Snowfell's borders," he said. "Remember that humans inhabit most of the surrounding farms and lands. We do not wish to unduly disturb their owners and tenants."

The guests made no protest. Contempt for humanity did not abrogate the need for discretion among beings that far outnumbered the werewolf kind. There was always a risk of exposure with a public Changing such as this, and any *loup-garou* would be a fool to tempt fate.

Hugh, who knew he had a great deal of lost ground to make up for, wasted no time on unnecessary speeches. He Changed. The air around his body shimmered and blurred, as if he had turned to smoke. The transformation itself was too swift for even his fellow werewolves to observe, and in moments he stood on the rise in wolf shape, his light brown fur ruffling in the morning breeze. He immediately assumed a dominant posture: ruff full about his neck and shoulders, tail lifted, head high and ears pricked forward.

Taking his cue, Gillian willed the Change. The world took on a different shape as she found her new orientation on four legs, but her senses of smell and hearing became even more acute. The scent of the Germans fouled the air. Her fur bristled up in a defensive display; her upper lip wrinkled away from her teeth, reminding potential rivals of the weapons at her command. She continued to stand behind Hugh, lingering human restraint battling with the instincts that urged her to push him aside.

One by one the others abandoned human shape, the colors of their fur ranging from nearly pure white through grays, silvers and golds for the lighter-haired delegates and russets, browns and blacks for the darker. Eyes were amber and green, sometimes touched with blue or brown.

Gillian's thoughts were muted now, less guided by words than emotion and sensation. More than ever she felt the potential danger emanating from the Germans, huge shadow-colored wolves who had already worked their way to the front of the makeshift pack.

Hugh didn't move for a good half-minute, and Gillian knew he was realizing again the enormity of what he and his sister faced without Sir Averil's charismatic power behind them. Then, suddenly, he wheeled about, nimble in his lupine body, and set off into the wood at a run. Gillian fell into position behind him, half her attention focused on the rising ground ahead and half on the wolves racing at her heels. There was an empty space at her side where Ross should have been. Ross, who would have made such a glorious wolf…

She freed herself of the burden of thought and bathed in the new, still unfamiliar joy of being a wolf on the Hunt—the strange joy she had first felt in the fight with Jaime and Rutger—muscles working with perfect grace and efficiency, the wind in her fur, her paws barely touching the rough and rocky soil. Doubts fell away like her human skin. Let any of the others dare approach her and she would show them who was to be feared.

A familiar scent raised her hackles as Vasily caught up and ran beside her. His followers, Pavel and Yuri, flanked her on the other side. They meant to intimidate her, and she would not permit it. She turned and snapped at Vasily, a deep growl rumbling in her throat. He lost his footing as if he had not anticipated her attack and slowed just enough for her to surge ahead. Pavel bared his teeth, but he and his cousin made no attempt to confront her.

She burst free of the trap, silently urging Hugh to keep up the challenging pace. Briefly Sigurd leaped to the fore. Hugh shouldered him aside in a rare act of open aggression. The others kept formation in their own individual packs, choosing not to upset the established order.

They had caught their first whiff of the red deer's scent when the trouble began. The sounds of snarls and scrabbling claws brought Gillian to a trot and then a stop. She let Hugh run on, carrying most of the delegates with him, while she reversed course.

The Germans and Russians were squabbling, the flash of teeth and a yelp of pain telling Gillian that they were not merely testing this time. The count had Vasily by the throat, while their subordinates feinted and lunged at each other, teeth drawing blood with every third strike.

She plunged among them like a rutting stag charging its rival, snapping indiscriminately right and left. She careened into the fighters, driving them apart. Though she was two-thirds the weight and size of any of the males, they immediately scrambled out of her path.

Any one of them could have attacked her then, for she was alone. The Russians circled and snarled, but even Vasily's tail was low and his body hunched. The Germans withdrew, but did not retreat. Conrad stared at her with hungry eyes. She stared back, and he looked away.

Triumphant, Gillian wheeled to follow Hugh's path, her ears cocked back to listen for the Europeans. Presently they, too, began to run again, the Russians lagging, while the Germans drew close to her, only a muzzle's length behind. Within minutes they found Hugh, loosely surrounded by the Earnshaws, the French, the Hungarians, Forster and Macalister, the Norse and the Spaniard, positioned on a fell overlooking a deep, narrow dale graced with a beck and a meandering line of alders. A magnificent stag was poised on the upper slope of the opposite fell, ears flared and nostrils open wide. The mingled scents of his harem rose from among the trees, and Gillian heard the rustle of leaves and the shuffle of numerous hooves.

Hugh turned his head to acknowledge her, eyes bright with excitement, his body taut and ready. Gillian joined him on the rise. The others watched the stag as he recognized the danger to his females and himself.

With a defiant flourish of his tail, Hugh plunged down the fell. He jumped the beck as the stag gave a warning cry and the hinds raced out of the trees. Gillian clung tightly to his right flank, and soon Thierry, Yves and Dominique, dark and russet, claimed the place to his left. Those who came after shifted from position to position, some temporarily winning a coveted spot near the leader only to be displaced by a more aggressive challenger.

The hunt was in Gillian's blood now, and the human world faded from memory. Only a single image remained to haunt her: the shape of the one who could not be with her, the one who was wolf and not-wolf, sire of her cub.

Ross.

Hugh brushed against her, and she ran on. The stag and his harem kept just ahead of their pursuers, bravely defying impossible odds, until the weakest hinds began to falter at last.

It was an unspoken understanding among the werewolves that the hinds with young still in tow would be spared. When one young female came to a trembling halt, desperately shielding her nearly full-grown calf, Hugh continued past. More hinds fell back in exhaustion. The stag turned and circled the stragglers, putting himself within range of the wolves.

Hugh charged the stag, which shook its impressive rack of antlers. Gillian dashed to the right, drawing the stag's attention while she tracked the other wolves' movements. The Spaniard joined her, while the French formed a wide arc around the herd. The Norse and Hungarians loped about, looking for an opening, while the Germans stood still and watched, heads lowered and muscles quivering. Gillian couldn't see Benedikt von Ruden, Marcus Forster, Mr. and Mrs. Macalister or the Earnshaw brothers.

Unaware of her observations, Hugh feinted at the stag and immediately leaped back from the threatening antlers. The hinds cowered in a tightly packed bunch, afraid to renew their flight. Every werewolf knew that the stag might fend them off for a time, but his death, and that of many of his harem, was inevitable.

Hugh lunged again, the Hungarians on his heels. The Germans burst into motion from the opposite side of the herd. Gillian smelled blood as one of the hinds fell to Friedrich von Ruden's attack. Hugh snarled and shoved von Ruden aside in an explicit warning for the German to await the leader's permission. Panicked, some of the hinds lunged past the lupine wall and galloped toward the crest of the fell. While Hugh and half the others remained with the stag, the remainder, led by the Russians, chased the escaping hinds until they disappeared from view.

Gillian stared after them. She might have followed to keep an eye on the Russians, or joined Hugh to bolster his newfound confidence. But he was doing very well on his own, discovering a source of strength in his wolf-self he had never quite grasped in human form.

It was a turning point for him. Gillian wondered if he might actually become secure and resolute enough to assume Sir Averil's mantle.

She retreated from the killing ground, searching for the back-trails of those who had already left. She smelled Macalister and his wife first. The scent path led her to a rocky sandstone outcrop, where a naked Graeme Macalister was comforting his shivering and obviously unfit wife. They looked up. The expression on Macalister's face was stoic, as if he expected Mrs. Macalister's frailty to be exposed for all to see.

Gillian left them alone. Marcus Forster's path moved in almost a straight line across the fells and back to the house, his scent interwoven with Benedikt von Ruden's. Whatever their reasons for abandoning the Hunt, Gillian felt no need to disturb them. Marcus she trusted implicitly, and Benedikt had never offered a single aggressive word on those rare occasions when he spoke at all.

It was the last trail that interested Gillian most. The Earnshaw brothers had retraced a part of the delegates' original path away from the house and then broken off to the west. Puzzled, Gillian dropped her nose close to the ground and set off in pursuit.

The abrupt materialization of a completely unexpected scent almost stopped her. *He* should not be here. *He* should be out of sight and smelling distance, down in the village where he would not be noticed.

She ran, skimming over the earth with her breath rasping in her throat. On the slope that dropped steeply down to Snowfell's wood, the Earnshaws confronted Ross with bristling fur and bared fangs. Gillian had no doubt that their hostility was very much in earnest and intended to cause the greatest possible harm.

Ross held a shotgun in his hands, steady and alert despite his clear disadvantage and the blood dripping from his right arm. He deflected each darting attack with a swing of the gun, but he must have known that even a shotgun blast would do no more than slow a werewolf.

If the Earnshaws meant to kill him, they would eventually succeed.

CHAPTER TWENTY-TWO

WITH A ROAR of rage, Gillian plunged down the fell. She aimed at Kenneth Earnshaw first, reaching him before he had become fully aware of her approach. She knocked him to his side with the weight of her body, and he collapsed with a yelp. Aldous rushed to his aid, striking at Gillian's foreleg with slashing fangs. Ross's shout was unintelligible to her ears.

The shotgun went off, spraying shot into Aldous's hindquarters. He shrieked in pain and whirled to leap at his tormenter, knocking the shotgun out of Ross's hands. Gillian sprang up, favoring her injured leg, and sank her teeth into Aldous's haunch. Instantly Kenneth was on her, but Ross hadn't finished. He had withdrawn a pistol from his trousers and was taking careful aim at Kenneth. Aldous, his rear legs sagging, scrambled backward.

Ross stood over his enemies with the pistol in his hand, staring down at them with no expression on his face. Aldous was breathing heavily, blood soaking the fur of his hindquarters. With a howl, Kenneth streaked past him and jumped at Ross, his front legs stiffened. Ross staggered under the weight, but kept his grip on the pistol and shot Kenneth point-blank in the chest. In moments the brothers fled, Aldous limping heavily.

Ross made no effort to interfere with their flight. He merely watched as they disappeared over the crest of the fell. Gillian followed them to the top. They were headed away from the house. Neither of them looked back.

Gillian returned to Ross, enraged by the thick, acrid odor of his blood. She Changed. The air, just beginning to warm with the rising of the sun, chilled her naked skin before her body adjusted. Ross stared at her as if he'd never seen her naked before. He quickly removed his jacket and draped it over her shoulders.

"Ross," she said hoarsely, "what the bloody hell are you doing here?"

He blinked in shock at her language, his hands shaking slightly as he pushed the pistol into the waistband of his trousers. "I could ask the same of you."

She wished a human body could express anger as well as a wolf's. "*I* have been doing what was expected of me."

"You expected *me* to leave you out here alone."

His quiet tone didn't assuage her fury. "You could have been—" The words wouldn't come. "How badly are you hurt?"

He glanced dismissively at the laceration on his arm. "I've had a lot worse. Sharp teeth, bad aim."

Gillian winced as she remembered the way she'd scratched his face with just as much viciousness and intent to harm. "You would not have escaped so easily had you not been armed," she said.

"That was the idea," he said. He bent to recover the shotgun. "But I sure as hell hadn't expected *those* guys to come after me."

Nor had Gillian. She had thought him in potential danger from the Germans or even the Russians, who were the second most likely candidates for the murder and the most openly hostile. But never from any of the British delegates.

"Why did the Earnshaws attack you?" she demanded.

"They weren't exactly talking when they started." Abruptly Ross sat down on a jutting shelf of sandstone. "They've never liked me. That could have been enough reason. Or maybe we've been barking up the wrong tree. The murderer could just as easily be someone we'd never suspect."

He wasn't wrong, but the Earnshaws, odious as they had been at times, had never shown any ambition to assume control of the

Convocation, and Gillian couldn't imagine the sullen brothers capable of such a rash act against a fellow Englishman.

"We can't assume anything at this point," Ross said. "Whatever the bastards intended, they played their hand and lost. I have a feeling they won't be coming back to Snowfell anytime soon."

Indeed…unless the brothers had allies Gillian knew nothing about. They had been thoroughly routed by a female and a man they might very well have realized could not Change.

But if they did rejoin the Convocation, it was almost guaranteed that they would expose Ross.

If Ross had considered that complication, he didn't seem in the least concerned. He looked closely into her eyes. "What about the Germans? They didn't try anything?"

"No. I found them fighting with the Russians, but they were discouraged from continuing their misbehavior."

"Discouraged by you?" He frowned. "Conrad isn't going to be so anxious to marry you now, even if he thought he could kill Sir Averil and still carry you off."

She offered no explanation, and Ross didn't press. "I've got to talk to the Russians," he said. "I would have done it earlier, but—"

"That is out of the question. The Earnshaws' behavior makes it even clearer why you must leave immediately." She gestured at the shotgun. "You will not be able to use your weapons when the others return and begin asking questions about your absence, for which we have only the most tenuous explanation. Driving the Earnshaws away and conducting the Hunt without undue interference has won us only a brief reprieve, not a pardon."

"If they come after me, I'll give them reasons for not Changing that leave you completely out of it. You'll be safe, Jill."

"This is no longer a question of my safety or yours. You must be fit to go to Toby when the time comes."

"You said you had a secure place to send him until we identified the murderer."

Gillian had no desire to discuss the subject when she knew

Ross's likely reaction. "It is more urgent than ever that we find the parties responsible. I shall question Cora myself."

"She won't tell you the truth if she didn't tell me."

Her anger flared again. "Do not be so sure."

"I'm not. I'm not sure about a damned thing."

The anger died. "Did anyone else see you?"

"I thought I saw Forster and one of the other delegates headed toward the house in human form, but they didn't notice me." He looked up at her, and she noticed the dark circles under his eyes, the deeper lines engraved around his mouth, the weariness in the set of his body.

He had suffered, too, in ways she was quite possibly incapable of understanding. She had doubted his judgment, his motives, his honesty, even his ability to care of anyone except the son he had known for less than three weeks. But she had never doubted his inner core of unshakable strength.

Half-unwillingly, she moved closer to him. "You must rest. Go back to the village inn, at least for a while."

"I couldn't sleep even if I wanted to." He scrubbed at his unshaven chin. Gillian stopped his hand with hers.

She should have known better. Suddenly she was overwhelmed by other smells beyond the blood…the earthy scent of his skin, the faint tang of perspiration, the unmistakable savor of arousal.

Perhaps it was the fight and the blessed stroke of luck that she had found him in time. Perhaps it was their joint victory over the enemy. Perhaps it was the wolf giving over to the oldest instinct in the world.

Or perhaps it was simply because he was with her, and the wanting would never go away.

She leaned forward and kissed Ross's mouth.

He responded instantly, leaping up and taking her in his arms with a hunger that matched her own. It was difficult beyond measure to pull away.

"Your arm…"

She would have had better luck stopping a locomotive with a handkerchief. He grabbed her and kissed her again, pushing his tongue between her lips. She was scarcely able to speak the necessary words.

"Not here. The others might see us."

Breathing heavily, he loosened his grip. "Are they coming back?" He looked over her shoulder toward the fells. "Will they be looking for you?"

"They won't even notice. But we must find a safer place."

"Where?"

She showed him, taking his hand and leading him down the slope to the woods below, following the beck for half a mile until she reached a place where the fell ended in a rocky overhang projecting above a small, deep cavern. The inside was littered with a blanket of old leaves, and it was just large enough to hold two people who had no qualms about sharing close quarters.

Ross removed his shirt, moving his injured arm gingerly. The wound had begun to heal, but it would still cause him discomfort. Gillian took the shirt from him, tore the cleanest part into strips and bound his injury. He gazed at her steadily all the while. When she was finished, he shed the rest of his clothes and folded them slowly, almost as if he'd had second thoughts. His eyes told a different story, and so did his impressive erection.

As Gillian had observed when the other werewolves had gathered in the park, Ross outshone them all. Her breath caught on a surge of desire so powerful that she had to take a step backward to catch her balance.

Ross reached for her, laying his warm, calloused hands on her shoulders. He didn't ask her why she had decided to take this risk, why she was willing to give herself to him again after all that had passed between them. He simply drew her close and caressed her back, his member hard and high against her stomach. They kissed, and Gillian knew this time wouldn't be like the last, when she had been like a virgin again and he had been so gentle.

This time they remembered each other's bodies, and their mouths fit together like two lost pieces of a beloved puzzle. She laced her fingers in his hair, compelling him to deepen the kiss, her tongue dueling with his. Her nipples hardened against his chest; she wasn't sure if the heartbeat she felt was hers or his. The state of his cock gave her no doubt that he wanted to be inside her as quickly as possible, and she was hungry for the feel of him possessing her body.

But he knew as well as she that there might not be another opportunity. He kissed his way down from her mouth to the hollow of her neck and the upper slope of her breasts, stroking his tongue to the edge of her nipple and no farther. She clutched at his shoulders, her nails digging crescents into his skin. He tormented her by deliberately avoiding what she so badly wanted him to do.

Only when she was ready to pull his head down herself did he flick his tongue over one aching nipple. He circled it teasingly, sipping at the tip before taking it fully into his mouth. He suckled her, making her feel every pull of his lips and tongue as if he were tugging at a string connected to the swollen flesh between her legs.

She almost begged him to take her then, but the wolf who had so recently conquered her enemies would not beg. She pushed him away, ignoring the bewilderment in his eyes, and herded him toward the cave wall until it sloped too low for him to continue to stand. His knees bent, and she went down with him. He opened his mouth to speak. She placed one finger across his lips, continued to push until he was flat on his back and stretched out beside her.

Ross was not, she was sure, as inexperienced in the ways of love as she was. He must have had many women after her. But he gasped when she stroked her tongue across his nipple. She gave him the same attention she had enjoyed from him and began working downward, pausing to kiss the slight hollow of his ribs, the ridged muscle of his stomach, the vee of his groin.

There she hesitated. She had never done what she was about to do now. She had only heard about it, with no memory of where or how, but she knew exactly what would pleasure Ross beyond anything else she could give him.

She started at the tip. It was smooth, almost silky, with a flavor all its own. He went rigid, his back arched as if he were urging her to take him all the way. But she was not yet done tormenting him. She swirled her tongue around and around the head, making occasional forays along the ridged underside of his erection. His breathing was rapid and harsh. He tangled his fingers in her hair.

"Jill," he groaned. "God, Jill…"

She took mercy on him at last. She slid her tongue and then her lips over him until he filled her mouth, and she suckled. He groaned again, completely in her thrall. He lifted his hips in time to her rhythm, mimicking the act of love, his cock becoming harder and thicker with every stroke. He didn't have to tell her when he was close to completion; she withdrew just in time, straddled him, and eased down on him with a sigh of satisfaction.

There was a glory in being in control, in guiding the speed and depth of their joining. He grasped her waist, trying to hold her in place so that he could set the pace, but she was strong enough to gainsay him. At last he closed his eyes, his head thrown back, and let her do what she would. In only a matter of minutes he stiffened, gave a brief cry and thrust up inside her very fast. She expected nothing for herself, but just as he reached his peak she did, as well, and she gasped his name in joyful abandon.

Afterward she lay atop him, kissing the perspiration from his chest and face. But he didn't grow soft and slide free of her. When he looked into her eyes, he smiled with such wicked triumph that she knew this was far from over.

She never knew quite how he managed it. One moment she was on top, and the next she was on her hands and knees and

Ross was lifting her hips high as he knelt behind her. She trembled with anticipation as he caressed her hot, wet lips with the tip of his cock, rubbing, bathing in her juices. Then he withdrew completely. She was ready to beg when, without warning, he unerringly found his target, thrusting into her almost savagely.

Now he was the dominant one, controlling her, holding her firmly as he impaled her again and again. He came hard and fast and she followed within seconds. He bent over her, resting his cheek against her back. She longed for more, but she dared not begin what she had no time to finish.

Eventually he pulled away, seated himself against the curved wall of the cave and held out his hand. She took it and sat beside him, still warm and wet and throbbing. It was a sensation she would gladly have enjoyed as long as it lasted, but she faced a dilemma that quickly sobered her.

"There was no Mr. Delvaux," she said.

He gave her a peculiar look, and then he understood.

"You were never married," he said.

He didn't sound surprised. She wondered if he'd already guessed.

"It was necessary," she said, over the noisy drumming of her heartbeat. "To bear a child out of wedlock…"

"I know. You had to save your reputation." He stared at the daylight framed by the cave mouth. "Guess that's the same for both humans and werewolves."

"I'm sorry, Ross. I should have…I should have told you before."

He lifted one shoulder. "Toby suspected it all along. He told me the first time we met."

She wasn't nearly as surprised as she should have been. "I must continue to maintain the fiction during the Convocation."

"Sure. I'll keep your secret."

After a while, when he said nothing more, she rose and went to the cave entrance. The morning was growing warmer, but she didn't feel the sunlight. When she walked out of this little world, it would be as if the past hour had never happened.

ROSS PULLED ON his clothes, his body aching as if the wound in his arm had spread to every bone and muscle. He tried to ignore the beautiful lines and curves of Gillian's form silhouetted against the light, and the desire that was making him hard all over again.

She'd finally told him the truth, finally decided it was important for him to know she hadn't belonged to some other man, if only for a week.

It didn't matter. Nothing was going to be resolved by what they'd just done. He knew he'd said the wrong things too often, pushed Jill to the limit of what she could endure. And she'd lied to him over and over again.

She glanced at him over her shoulder, her face revealing nothing, and walked out. She waited for him outside, rubbing her upper arms as if she couldn't feel the warm sun washing her skin with streaks of gold. He tried to give her his jacket again, but she refused with a shake of her head. She opened her mouth, gave a strange, muffled cry, and broke into a fast walk in the direction of the house.

The jacket hung in Ross's hands like a shroud. He sat down heavily and stared at the ground, watching a small insect scurry across the dirt. He'd never envied a bug before, but now...

Approaching footsteps interrupted his weary observation. Gillian was returning to him, her feet light over the rocky ground. He stood, letting his jacket fall to his feet.

"I will go with you," she said.

CHAPTER TWENTY-THREE

ROSS'S HEART DID what hearts were apt to do in the dime novels he'd read as a kid. He didn't dare speak, afraid that the moment would shatter like the stuff of dreams he'd left behind.

Gillian met his gaze and then looked toward the fells where the Hunt had begun. "Last night," she said quietly, "Hugh came to me and said he wished to lead the Convocation."

Her statement would have struck Ross as humorous if he hadn't already been so stunned. "What are you talking about?"

"He wasn't joking, Ross. I've never seen him so serious in my life."

Funny how that fickle bitch called hope always turned out to be about as reliable as tin Lizzie. "He wants to take your place?"

His voice gave him away. Gillian folded her arms, covering the breasts he had so recently caressed.

"He needed his chance," she said. "And I had to give it to him." She continued to stare out at the fells, as if she expected her brother to appear over a distant hill with the delegates trotting along behind him. "I prayed that he would succeed, for his sake. He has lived without purpose too long. But I didn't truly believe…" Her breath hitched. "Such a change would require a miracle. Sir Averil's death was that miracle."

To hear her speak about her father's death in that way almost distracted Ross from the point of her explanation. "You're saying you think Hugh will do what he says this time?"

"He *has* done it. Something remarkable happened when he

became a wolf. He led the others just as he should, without doubt or hesitation. He didn't need my help."

Ross might have clung to his skepticism if it hadn't been for the fact that Gillian had been willing to leave the Hunt and spend time with him instead of keeping track of the delegates. She never would have left if Hugh hadn't really done what she claimed.

But there was still a very major problem.

"How long can he keep it up?" he asked.

She was quiet for several minutes, which was enough for Ross to know that she wasn't nearly as confident as she pretended. The likelihood that Hugh really had changed overnight, and that the change would stick, was next to nil.

Yet she'd offered his behavior as a reason for her willingness to leave Snowfell with Ross. A reason that had the power to outweigh her senseless commitment to Sir Averil's cause.

Don't. Don't even start.

"I truly believe," she said, her voice barely above a whisper, "that this will last." She finally met his gaze. "Of course there would be no question of leaving until Hugh…until he is well established as leader and is fully committed to carrying on what he's begun."

Naturally. Same old story. "How long?" he asked.

"As soon as the Convocation is over."

Right. A helluva lot could happen in a few days. Hundreds of opportunities for Gillian to give up on the idea and for Hugh to fall back into his old ways.

But what was he thinking, anyway? It wasn't for *his* sake that she was willing to leave.

"How will you break it off with the Huns?" he asked.

"I will not break it off immediately. That would be most unwise." She hugged herself more tightly, the only indication that she was less than composed. "I have renewed my pledge to the Germans in exchange for excluding Toby from the agreement."

Had that been before the murder? he wondered. Either way,

it had not been for any reason other than protecting their son. A yoke of misery lifted from Ross's shoulders. "You didn't tell me."

"I could not find the right moment."

"Why would they care whether Toby—"

"They do not. They believed it was necessary to keep him in order to control me. I convinced them otherwise."

"And all that posturing by Conrad…?"

"I believe it was sincere. But that is of no moment. They must continue to believe that I will not interfere with their plans."

Exasperation proved stronger than anger. "For God's sake, Jill. They'll get wise that you know, and you'll be at their mercy." A fresh thought chilled his bones. "What if they aren't the murderers?"

Her resolute expression didn't waver. "It doesn't matter. The Germans may go straight to hell."

He should have let it go at that, knowing what it meant for her to say those words. He should have shouted hallelujah and accepted what she was willing to give. He couldn't.

"You sure you don't want to stick around and find some other guy with pure blood to marry you?" he asked bitterly. "Someone like Forster or de Gévaudan?"

"Is it that you don't wish me to come?"

He couldn't bring himself to be vulnerable again. "I'll leave that up to you, Jill."

The temperature dropped about twenty degrees. Her face had become an exquisite sculpture made of ice.

"Toby needs you," she said. "But he also needs me."

"Yeah." Ross pushed his hands into his pockets. "Maybe you should be getting back to the Hunt. No point in borrowing trouble."

That quick, and it was as if the passion they'd shared had never happened. "You're quite right," she said with that distant formality she was so good at. "I shall bathe in the beck and then rejoin them. You should bathe, as well."

To get rid of each other's telltale scents and the smell of sex. Made perfect sense. "Don't worry about the others confronting me. I've got a plan, and you'll have to trust me."

Gillian stared at him a moment longer, then turned and descended the hill. She disappeared into the trees and crouched over the little stream. Ross listened to the sound of splashing water as she bathed, wanting her all over again.

She'd said nothing to suggest that she hoped he would renege on his original offer of a marriage in name only. To the contrary, she'd been completely matter-of-fact about the whole thing, including her reasons for changing her mind.

He wouldn't give her any grounds to think he was a liar. He would follow through on whatever terms she chose.

Even if he loved her.

The muscles in Ross's legs threatened to give way.

He'd been so sure that that particular emotion had been burned out of him for good. It hadn't. The ashes had been rekindled and burst into flame, and the fire had been feeding on his heart since he'd found Jill waiting on his doorstep.

And if the flames hadn't been doused by the cold water she had just dumped all over him, *he* wasn't going to put them out anytime soon. All he could do was keep his mouth shut. Gillian had found the courage to turn her back on her past. He couldn't very well balk at making sacrifices of his own.

Disgusted with his stupid sentimentality, Ross descended the hill to the beck. He could wash his skin, but his clothes would retain Gillian's scent. He spent some time looking around for something to disguise the offending smell and found a weed with a potent enough aroma to set him sneezing. He rubbed a handful of the stuff all over his clothing, washed up and dressed again, still sneezing.

He'd reached the woods bordering Snowfell's park when Hugh came charging down from the fells with the full complement of delegates behind him. If it hadn't been for the light brown pelt and the color of the eyes, Ross wouldn't have guessed that this powerful, confident creature was Gillian's brother.

Jill hadn't been exaggerating. This was a different Hugh.

Ross waited and watched while the werewolves gathered near the house, where they were met by footmen bearing thick, fur-trimmed robes. They all Changed together and put on the robes while the servants averted their eyes. Except for the Germans and Russians, who carefully avoided each other, the delegates seemed in good spirits. Hugh led them inside, grinning at some remark that Dominique de Gévaudan had made.

Rejecting his urge to run in after them and check on Gillian, Ross lingered at the edge of the woods while he considered whether to return immediately to his room or go straight to the gardener's cottage where Toby was being sequestered. The boy might already be gone, of course; Gillian had put off telling him exactly where she was sending Toby, promising to inform him once she had confirmed the arrangements. After what she'd just said to him, he was glad he hadn't implied that he didn't trust her by questioning her about her decision.

A sudden and very audible commotion from the house erased any indecision from Ross's mind. The swell of raised voices subsided as he strode through the door and toward the drawing room. The delegates, many still in their dressing gowns, had frozen in position at various points around the room, their gazes fixed on a fully dressed Friedrich von Ruden. Gillian and Hugh stood together near the door. Ross moved silently up behind them.

"It is true, is it not?" Von Ruden said to Hugh, the very softness of his voice working on his audience like the boom of a thunderclap. "Sir Averil is dead."

Ross had been in courtrooms this quiet, just before the judge was about to pronounce sentence. The first thing that entered his mind was that the von Rudens no longer appeared to value Gillian's agreement to "cooperate." The second was that they had just confirmed his suspicions by making the preemptive strike of announcing their host's death.

He searched the hostile, shocked and bewildered faces, wondering why the Huns had waited so long. Had fear prompted Cora to confess Ross's visit and interrogation, even though she might face punishment from her foreign masters? Had the Germans recognized the imminent danger of exposure and decided to bluster their way through?

It was a bold and risky move. If Ross tried to undermine them by telling the delegates what he'd learned from Cora, it would still be his word against theirs, and Cora might very well pay the ultimate price.

Hugh cleared his throat. "It's true," he said in a surprisingly steady voice. "Sir Averil is dead."

Angry cries broke out among the Russians, echoed by the Hungarians. The Norwegians bared their teeth. Macalister, once again without his wife, frowned deeply. The Germans were infested with satisfaction like fleas, knowing perfectly well what they'd unleashed.

Hugh raised his hands. "Please," he said. "Sir Averil has been gone a very short while. You were all to be informed today, after the Hunt."

"Were we?" Vasily demanded. "Or were you hoping to conceal it from us until the end of the Convocation?"

"I'm sure that was not the case," Marcus Forster said from the rear of the room. "It was undoubtedly a great shock to the family."

"And to us all," the Scandinavian leader said. "How is it that Sir Averil came to expire so suddenly?"

The guests stared at Hugh—except the Germans, who looked at Gillian. Conrad had a nasty expression on his face, suggesting that he'd either thrown off his newfound affection for Gillian or had been shamming all along.

"We believe..." Hugh cleared his throat again. "We believe that he was given poison."

Ross cursed under his breath. Hugh had made a big mistake by admitting the real cause of Sir Averil's death. He'd just warned the killers, whoever they were, that he and Gillian knew there was some a plot taking place at the Convocation.

"Poisoned?" Señor Tovar said, breaking the shocked silence. "Surely that cannot be."

"Have you proof?" János Károly demanded.

"Proof enough," Gillian said, stepping forward before her brother could speak. "But we have not determined—*yet*—who did it."

There was a ripple of hushed murmurs as the delegates understood what she was implying. The Hungarians looked affronted, the French speculative, the others puzzled or wary as they eyed their neighbors with fresh suspicion. No one asked why one of them would have a motive to kill Sir Averil.

Count von Ruden must have recognized that he could easily lose the advantage he'd gained with his accusation. "Perhaps," he said, addressing Gillian, "you should search…what is the phrase? Closer to home?"

Hugh flushed, wrecking his otherwise convincing air of authority. "The murderer is close enough."

"Then what will you do?" the count asked pleasantly. "Call the human authorities?" He glanced at Hugh. "Will you summon us into your father's study one by one and interrogate us until you obtain a confession?"

"There will be no police," Gillian said. "This shall be dealt with by our own kind."

"Do you agree, *Sir* Hugh? Or does your sister still speak for you?"

Ross walked past Gillian and stood slightly in front of her. "Maybe you should be asking *me* the questions," he said. "Mr. Maitland was the one who invited me to the Convocation. He had information that there might be some trouble planned by certain delegates, but he knew Sir Averil wouldn't admit that the people he'd chosen could betray the principles he lived by." He let his gaze sweep the room. "I've had a little experience catching criminals in Arizona. And that's what Mr. Maitland and I are going to do."

He didn't turn to see Gillian's reaction, but the others' responses were loud and immediate.

"Who are you?" one of the Károlys cried.

"My name hasn't changed," Ross said, meeting the Hungarian's hostile stare. "Neither has anything else, except my purpose here."

"Indeed?" von Ruden said, his teeth glinting beneath his moustache. "Is that why you were seen coupling with Mrs. Delvaux?"

"That's a damned lie!" Hugh shouted. He advanced on von Ruden with raised fists. "You take it back, von Ruden, or I'll—"

"You'll what, boy? Challenge me?"

"Not him," Conrad snarled. "Keating! He's the one—"

"Shut up," Ross said, hardly raising his voice.

Conrad's eyes bulged. If it hadn't been for his father's restraining arm, he would have attacked Ross on the spot.

"I don't know who's giving you your information," Ross said to the count. "Could be the murderer, trying to cause more trouble. Or maybe you observed this indiscretion firsthand?"

"Do you deny it?" von Ruden asked. He sniffed. "You are so covered in that herbal stench that one might be convinced that you were attempting to disguise another smell entirely."

"Occupational hazard," Ross said. "Guess I chose the wrong place to watch you fellas chase those little deer around."

"Yes," Hugh said, taking up the thread. "That is why Mr. Keating wasn't at the Hunt. I asked him to observe any questionable behavior that might assist us in determining the identity of the killer."

"And what did you learn?" von Ruden asked Ross in that dangerously conversational tone.

"I have a few ideas," Ross said. "One of them is bound to pan out before this day is over."

"You will not be here when this day is over!" Conrad said. "I challenge you, Charles Keating!"

Gillian moved to join Hugh. "You have no basis for a challenge," she said. Not so much as a quiver in her voice gave her away. "You have issued an accusation which both I and Mr. Keating deny."

"And that gives my son every right," the count said. "Ancient law permits us to offer challenge when our honor is questioned."

"Your *honor*—" Hugh began contemptuously.

"Also compels me to challenge *you*, Sir Hugh Maitland."

Hugh was well beyond either commons sense or discretion. "I accept!" he snapped.

"No," Gillian said. "This is *not* acceptable."

"The law is clear," Vasily Arakcheyev said to murmurings of agreement. "Trial by combat is permitted under such circumstances."

"You are forgetting the issue of greatest importance," Thierry de Gévaudan said, drawing all eyes to him. "As Mr. Keating so reasonably suggested, this conflict may be exactly what the murderers intended when they poisoned Sir Averil."

Conrad rounded on de Gévaudan. "Do you dare to imply—"

"Until the murderer is identified," Gillian said, "there will be no challenges."

The Hungarians and Norwegians protested. To Ross's amazement, Benedikt von Ruden raised his hand. "Perhaps we ought to put it to a vote," he said softly.

The other von Rudens' astonishment was almost laughable. "This is no puerile democracy," Count von Ruden growled.

"Your motives are not clear, Count," Tovar said. "How are we to know *you* will behave honorably?"

"You'll be next, Spaniard," Conrad hissed.

Graeme Macalister, who stood at the back of the room with Marcus Forster, spoke in his thick Scottish burr. "You may only challenge one man at a time, Herr von Ruden. The fight must end when one submits or is clearly defeated."

"In other words," Forster said, "there will be no medieval battles to the death."

Tovar nodded. "There shall be no killing."

Ross didn't have to search the room to know which delegates would have liked to nix any such restrictions. Even Ross found himself rebelling. He couldn't think of anything he would like to do more than get rid of the bastard who was so obviously intent on humiliating Gillian.

And how will you do that? With your bare human hands?

He'd hardly finished the grim thought when von Ruden spoke again. "It is acceptable," he said slowly.

"Then let's finish this travesty," Hugh said.

Gillian's fear seeped into Ross's skin, as tangible as the fierce tension in the room. She dropped all pretense of submission to her brother and stepped in front of him. "These games deceive no one," she said, staring at von Ruden. "I also called you liar. *I* challenge *you.*"

"No," Hugh said. He faced the count again. "Fighting her won't do you any good if you're after Sir Averil's position."

There. It was out in the open, and there was no putting the genie back in the bottle.

Ross raised his voice. "Von Ruden challenged *me* first," he said. "And I accept."

Conrad's lips curved into a baleful smile. "Excellent. As Sir Maitland said, let us waste no more time."

"Away from the house," Ross said, staring at the German's smugly confident face. "And in private. Just you and me."

"All delegates are permitted to observe any challenge," Vasily said.

"This is true," Macalister agreed. "There can be no secrecy."

"Do you not know why he wants such secrecy?" a voice said from outside the drawing room.

Ross stiffened. He glanced at Gillian to gauge her reaction, but no warning would change what he knew was about to happen. Kenneth and Aldous Earnshaw strode through the door, ignoring Ross as they came to a halt in the center of the room. Aldous held something up in his hand, a scrap of paper dense with writing. A fragment of newsprint, torn from a larger sheet.

"His name is not Charles Keating," he said. "And he is not one of us. He never was."

A smothering weight pressed in on Ross's chest. He faced Aldous and looked him over with blatant contempt. "You want to explain that remark?"

"He is *human*," Earnshaw snarled. "He is no wealthy rancher from Arizona. He is a common criminal by the name of Ross Kavanagh."

Ross remembered the newspaper Hugh had hidden in his room. Had the Yorkshiremen found it, or had they come upon another source?

He had no time to think through the possibilities. Thierry de Gévaudan spoke, one dark brow arched as if he found the accusation highly amusing. "I do not believe it," he said.

Earnshaw snorted and handed the Frenchman the paper. De Gévaudan scanned it, his skeptical expression unchanging.

"Are you convinced now?" Earnshaw demanded, snatching the paper back. "All of you may read it. It is from the front page of the *New York Sentinel*."

Gillian was so still that Ross could hardly hear her heartbeat. He would have sold his soul to the devil rather than subject her to this.

"I was falsely accused," he said. "I had nothing to do with that girl's death."

"Then why do the police of New York, your former colleagues, consider you their chief suspect?"

"He was not involved," Gillian said shortly.

"How do you know, Frau Delvaux?" Conrad asked, spitting

the words from between clenched teeth. "Is it because he whispered his secrets in your ear every time he enjoyed your body?"

Ross lunged. Hugh grabbed his arm. Aldous pursed his lips as if he were about to spit at Gillian's feet. "Do you claim that this man is innocent of both crimes?" Aldous asked. "Is it merely coincidence that Kavanagh arrived here so soon after the second murder was committed?"

Confusion passed briefly over Gillian's face. Ross had never found the right moment to tell her about the girl who'd been murdered near his apartment.

You idiot. You blasted, arrogant, son of a—

"Your supposed evidence might be more compelling," Gillian said, "if you had not committed a cowardly and unannounced attack on Mr. Keating."

The Earnshaws' flushed faces told Ross they'd relied on their shocking revelations to squelch any mention of that incident. "A lie!" Aldous exclaimed.

"Would you also care to challenge me, Earnshaw?" she asked.

"Not likely," Ross said, "considering what a licking she gave both of them."

"He avoided the Hunt," Kenneth sputtered. "We meant to prove that this human could not Change. Had he done so instead of relying on firearms and a female to protect him, we would not have pressed our advantage."

Gillian's expression was all aristocratic disdain. "Give me the paper," she said, holding her hand out to Earnshaw. He passed it to her, rigid with hatred, and she skimmed the article just as de Gévaudan had done.

"The photograph proves that Charles Keating is Ross Kavanagh, a former policeman, wanted for the slaying of two humans," Aldous said.

Gillian crumpled the newsprint in her fist. "In England," she said, "even a human is innocent until proven guilty."

"That will soon be tested in combat," Count von Ruden said.

"Unless you and your lover are prepared to confess the purpose behind your deliberate deception of all who attended this Convocation in good faith."

"Da!" Vasily shouted. "How long have you known this man? What was your purpose in deceiving us?" He stared at Hugh. "You claimed that Sir Averil employed him to observe the delegates. Would you have us believe that your father would engage a *human* to carry out such a task?"

"I'm not exactly human," Ross responded. "Sir Averil knew my father, and no one ever questioned *his* wolf credentials. When he needed a neutral observer, someone to keep an eye on certain delegates, he called me. He just didn't see any need to inform Mr. Maitland or Mrs. Delvaux that my mother was human."

"And I brought him here at my father's request," Hugh said, belatedly joining in. "My sister never knew him before he arrived."

"Yet she took him to her bed," Conrad snapped.

Ross imagined what the Hun would look like with his nose reduced to bloody pulp. "Mrs. Delvaux never looked twice at me," he said. "And I was here to do a job, not attract attention by putting the make on Sir Averil's daughter."

"If you were employed to prevent just such an incident as Sir Averil's murder," Count von Ruden said, "you failed. Or did the baron object to his daughter's miscegenation, and that is why he is dead?"

De Gévaudan made a sound of derision. "Only a fool would listen to your lunatic ravings, *bübchen,*" he said. "I find Monsieur Maitland's explanations far more convincing."

Whether he did or not, Ross estimated that maybe half of the delegates were prepared to believe the preposterous story he, Hugh, and Gillian had concocted on the fly. But that wasn't good enough.

More bluffing was all Ross had left. "Sir Averil and I both underestimated the enemy," he said. "But I'm going to make sure whoever killed him doesn't benefit from their crime."

Count von Ruden gave a short, harsh laugh. "We shall see how capable you are of achieving that goal," he said. "Conrad, you will meet the human at dawn tomorrow. Sir Hugh and I shall follow."

Conrad grinned. *"Ja, mein Herr."*

"There are no provisions in our laws for challenging humans," Gillian said.

"But he claims to bear werewolf blood, *nicht wahr?* And he accepted Conrad's challenge. Are you so afraid that my son will prove you both liars?"

"I have no fear that Mr....Kavanagh will acquit himself admirably."

"Then he and Sir Hugh will meet us tomorrow."

She met von Ruden's gaze with such sheer force of will that the count's smug expression vanished. "Very well," she said. "It will be done."

"If Kavanagh doesn't run away," Conrad sneered.

"No one's running away," Ross said. "I look forward to pushing that ugly mug of yours in the dirt where it belongs."

"As do I," Hugh said. He must have known he'd lost any ground he'd gained during the Hunt, but he put up a good front. "As for you," he said to the Earnshaws, "slink back to your filthy dens and don't ever presume to cross Snowfell's borders again."

The brothers bristled and looked around the room, clearly hoping to find advocates among their fellow delegates. Even von Ruden and the Russians ignored them. Without a word, they spun around and charged out the door.

"This meeting is concluded," Gillian said. "You will all return to your rooms until dinner is served."

Even the most hostile contingents had apparently exhausted their stores of bile and left quietly, though there were a few burning glances directed at Gillian and Ross. Conrad shoved Ross's shoulder as he walked out of the room, and Count von Ruden gave Gillian another of his unsavory smiles. After lingering near the door to watch the others climb the stairs to their quarters, the French and Marcus Forster returned.

"Is there anything we can do?" de Gévaudan asked.

"Don't you want to know how much of what we said wa true?" Ross countered.

"I trust you were as accurate as you could afford to be," th Frenchman said mildly.

"Yeah." Ross stared at the carpet, aware of how close he wa to snapping. "You didn't have to stick your neck out for us Thanks to you, the Huns didn't have it all their way."

"We are grateful," Gillian said with consummate dignity.

"And I *could* use your help," Hugh said, touching Gillian' arm with his own slightly shaking hand. "Stand by my sister i the worst happens." He nodded to Ross. "Neither one of u intends to lose, but the Germans are out for blood. I doubt they'l play by the—"

"The worst will not happen," Gillian said. "*Both* of yo must leave."

"All that will do is bring a bloody load of trouble down o your head," Hugh said. "This is it, Gilly. My chance to do wha I promised."

"And I came to Snowfell for a reason," Ross said. "Maybe it' changed a little since I first got here, but…" He barked a laugh "You don't really want to go through this all over again, do you?"

"I see that it will do no good," she said with a lack of emotio that roiled Ross's insides. "But you may rest assured that I an quite as prepared as the Germans to break the rules." She turne to de Gévaudan and Forster. "If you are willing to help."

"You may be sure of us," Forster said. "I believe we may als count on Señor Tovar, and possibly Macalister."

Thierry, Dominique and Yves added their agreement. Ros badly wanted to speak to Forster and the others in private, bu he knew any attempt to do so would get them in hot water. Eve remaining in the same room as Gillian was a serious risk. A apology for his failure to inform her about the second murde would be only an empty gesture now.

Just like her promise to come away with him. Hugh had guts and the will to try, but he would never assume leadership of the Convocation now, even if he made it through the challenge in one piece. And as long as there were enemies to threaten Snowfell, its inhabits and its heritage, Gillian would never let go.

Unless someone forced her to.

CHAPTER TWENTY-FOUR

WHO? ROSS MOCKED HIMSELF. *You? After the mess you've mad of her life?*

All because he'd convinced himself that he could actually d some good by staying at Snowfell and finding the killers, tha *he,* carrying all the disadvantages of his human blood, wa capable of protecting her from the criminals and anyone else wh might want to hurt her.

It hadn't been a rational decision. She'd tried to warn him ho bad it could get once he was exposed as a fraud. Now, thanks his lousy judgment, his petty anger and his damned animal lus Jill was in a worse position than ever.

Yet she'd continue to defend him just as she'd defended Hug breaking all the rules she'd lived by.

She wasn't willing to bend anymore, but this time she wa bound to break. Hugh had to realize that. Forster and the de Gé vaudans had to be made to understand that the only solution wa to get Gillian the hell away and keep her away.

"Jill," he said, no longer caring who heard him, "don't d something you'll regret long after the Convocation is over."

"He's right, Gilly," Hugh said.

She stared at Ross, no softening in her eyes. "I suggest yc go to your own room and rest. You will require all your strengt tomorrow." She nodded to Forster and the de Gévaudan "Gentleman, Mademoiselle de Gévaudan, if you will con with me…?"

With a troubled glances at Ross and Hugh, the others followed Gillian from the room.

"We'll never get her to leave," Hugh said, reading his mind. "You know that, don't you?"

"Yeah. But I'm not going to let her destroy herself."

"I'm younger and faster than the count," Hugh said with very shaky conviction. "I could beat him. But you…"

"Worry about yourself. Jill's going to need you, no matter what happens tomorrow."

"Did you… Were you and Gilly together as von Ruden claimed?"

"It was a mistake," Ross said. "I don't know how the Huns found out, but what's done is done."

Hugh met Ross's gaze. "You and Gilly…it can't end like this."

"I've got a few ideas."

"For God's sake, tell me!"

The sibilant tones of the Hungarians' native language outside the door gave Ross an excuse to escape. "I'll be all right, Hugh," he said, as he edged toward the door. "And you're going to win."

He was able to get out of the house without interference and set out for the gardener's cottage. Fifteen minutes' brisk walking brought him to a winding dirt footpath that led to a small house almost completely hidden between overgrown bushes and trees. Ross knew even before he opened the door that the cottage was empty.

He retraced his steps back to the house, where, ignoring the stares of the delegates who crossed his path, he climbed the stairs to Toby's room.

The bed was made, everything was in its place, and it didn't smell as if Toby had been in the room for several hours. Ross leaned heavily against the wall. He'd wanted to talk to Toby one last time…not that there would have been any way to explain.

And wherever Toby had gone, it must be far enough away tha
Ross wouldn't have time to get the particulars from Gillian and
see him before the challenge.

He looked slowly around the room, absorbing what was left o
his son. If he hadn't been memorizing every little detail, he neve
would have seen the piece of paper sticking out from under a stac
of books on a high shelf near the bed. Without really knowing why
he crossed the room, lifted the books and pulled out the paper.

It had obviously been hastily torn out of some kind of journal
a blank page packed with slightly crooked and painfully rendere
handwriting. It was marked with the date: about three weeks ago
before Toby had run away to America. Ross took the paper t
the small desk in the corner of the room and spread it out.

*I can't believe it. At the dig today, I uncovered a bone.
I thought it belonged to an animal, so I kept digging. I
found a skull instead. A human skull. I didn't have time to
dig up much more, but I know there's a whole body there.*

*It isn't old enough to belong to the people who built the
garrison. There are still bits of flesh left, and clothing, so
it must not have been there so very long. It isn't nearly as
horrible as one might expect. Whoever left it there wrapped
it in layers of heavy cloth. The whole thing smelled of petrol
when I first cut it open. It's all a bit dodgy, if you ask me.*

*Could this be foul play? And if it is, who could have
done it? There was a locket, too, and it could be important. It's engraved on one side, with two initials.*

*I know I ought to go to the police, but that will ruin all
the fun. I'm going to find my real father. He's a Detective
Inspector, with all sorts of experience. He must be
champion at finding clues and catching criminals. When
he comes back to England with me, I will show it to him.
He will know what should be done next.*

Ross choked on a laugh. The little devil had arrived in America already planning to drag Ross to England. He'd had faith in his unknown father's investigatory skills long before they'd met.

And faith that I'd love him and Gillian enough to come.

Swallowing the heavy obstruction in his throat, Ross flipped the page to read the writing on the other side.

Bollocks! How stupid can I be? I could have told Father about the grave as soon as he came to Snowfell, but I was so happy to see him that I forgot entirely.

I haven't had any time to gather more evidence. I thought I might have done after I spoke to Father on the fells, but when I heard him and Mother coming to the ruins, I imagined how upset Mother might be to see a dead person, so I covered it up. Now that I am no longer ill, Mrs. Rownthwaite is hovering over me like a nasty old vulture, and everything is at sixes and sevens.

But perhaps it really doesn't matter, with Grandfather dead. Mother will have to look at a dead body, now. I wish I could…

The words stopped there, as if Toby had been interrupted. Ross folded the paper and put it in his pocket. Why had Toby tried to hide the page? If it was part of a regular journal, had he considered that particular entry too inflammatory for anyone else to discover?

Maybe Toby would like to know that his father had found out about his discovery and gone to investigate, even though he wasn't able to participate. Ross decided to take a look at the grave and jot down a few notes for Toby to read afterward. Toby could at least have the exciting experience of leading the police to the body, seeing as he'd apparently uncovered a murder.

Yeah. Quite a thing for him to remember you by.

At least Toby was in a safe place. But he would feel a damned

sight better knowing just where that place was. He would hav
to risk one more meeting with Gillian.

As it happened, Ross didn't find her. Faulder said she'd gon
out to the fells, and he didn't expect her to return before dinne

Ross closed his eyes, momentarily paralyzed by despair. Rur
ning after her would be the worst thing he could do...

"Sir?" Faulder's voice was hollow, and the skin below his eye
was puffy and pale. "May I assist you in some way?"

"Yeah. You can tell me where Mrs. Delvaux sent Toby."

Eventually Faulder did tell him, though he had to be pe:
suaded. Afterward, furious with himself as much as Gilliar
Ross stood alone in the entrance hall and weighed the likelihoo
of getting to Toby before he left the area.

No wonder she hadn't wanted to tell him where she'd se:
their son. If he went to her now and demanded an explanatio:
she would tell him that Warbrick had always been a good frien
in spite of his occasional misjudgments, and that she could tru:
him as long as she kept him away from Ross, on and on, just lik
every time before. And he wouldn't have a single argumer
strong enough to dissuade her.

From her point of view, Ross's suspicions seemed ridicu
lous. He had nothing concrete to back them up. Nothing bu
instinct. Warbrick didn't give a damn about Toby; the conceite
son of a bitch was willing to help Jill out only because he thougl
he might get somewhere with her if he protected her son.

And as close as Jill and Warbrick were, she had almost ce:
tainly told him about the arranged marriage. Being huma:
Warbrick wouldn't have any way to stop it.

*So what is the bastard going to do? Kidnap Toby? What wi
he have to gain by that?*

Probably nothing. But Ross couldn't let it go. Not until he'
seen Toby himself.

Benedikt von Ruden was wandering alone in the form:
garden when Ross left Snowfell. Ross met his gaze, and th

German lifted his hand in what Ross could only interpret as a tentative greeting.

The German's odd behavior distracted him from his worries as he ran toward Highwick. The guy had always been a cipher, never speaking except when he'd offered to put the issue of his relatives' challenges to a vote, for which the count had looked ready to kill him.

They aren't all the same. He had better reason to remember that than anyone. Not all werewolves were like the pack enforcers, Friedrich von Ruden or Vasily. Not all humans were what Sir Averil had believed. There was no one type that accurately represented any group, whether that group was a race, a religion, a nationality or people with the ability to become something other than human.

That was the hope that might still emerge from this deadly mix of hatred, prejudice and remorseless pride. If Jill was relieved of Friedrich and Conrad's malice, she had a real chance of winning over the neutral delegates, driving out the bad ones and turning the Convocation into something that could save werewolves in a way her father had never imagined.

Funny how he was finally beginning to see it her way just when the likelihood of peace was more shaky than ever.

Ross's heart was still tracing a downward course as he arrived at Highwick's rickety iron gates. He continued up the long drive at a fast walk, readying himself for a confrontation that might turn ugly in an instant.

He'd never seen Warbrick's manor before; it was even more of a pile than Snowfell, but run-down and in desperate need of repair. The house was dark; no lights shone through the mullioned windows.

Ross pounded on the front door. No one answered. He was considering kicking it down, solid oak and all, when an elderly man in formal clothes finally answered.

"May I help you, sir?"

The guy was enough like Faulder that Ross figured he w&
the requisite butler. "I've come to see Warbrick," he said.

The butler's expression was polite but unencouraging. "Lo&
Warbrick is not at home, sir."

"Then where is he?"

"I fear I do not know, sir. Would you care to leave your card&

"Sorry, I'm fresh out." He looked pointedly over the old man&
shoulder into the entrance hall. "Look, friend, I don't want &
cause you any trouble, but I know Warbrick's here. It would b&
a lot easier for all of us if you just told him Ross Kavanag&
requests an audience."

The butler seemed to shrink about three sizes. "Yes," he sa&
faintly. "If you will wait here, sir."

The entrance hall was very plain, almost bare of decoratio&
The parquet floor was worn and scuffed. Ross didn't bother &
sit in the single chair, which he suspected hadn't been used in&
long, long time. The hairs at the back of his neck stood up as &
breathed in Warbrick's scent.

And Toby's. The boy *was* here.

Minutes passed. Ross was on the verge of searching the hou&
himself when Warbrick arrived. He wore what Ross recognize&
as English riding clothes: tall boots polished to a mirror shee&
jodhpurs, a tailored jacket and snug-fitting gloves.

"Going out for a ride, Warbrick?" Ross asked.

"Kavanagh." Warbrick gave Ross the familiar up-and-dow&
with the usual results. "I would have thought you'd run back &
America by now."

"Oh? And just why would you think that?"

"Haven't the others uncovered your ruse yet? Haven't the&
noticed that you can't Change?"

"Don't worry your pretty head about me, Warbrick."

The other man removed one glove. "Ah," he said. &
surmise that they have. But you're still possessed of life a&

mb. How much longer do you suppose that Gillian can
rotect you?"

"What did she tell you, Warbrick?"

"Enough to make it clear that you have done nothing but
ause her grief."

On that point the bastard was exactly right, but Ross wasn't
out to let him gloat. "Where's Toby?" he demanded.

Warbrick raised a brow. "Doesn't Mrs. Delvaux confide in
ou anymore, Kavanagh?"

"I wouldn't be here if she didn't. Let me see my son, or I'll
 get him myself."

He waited for Warbrick to refuse. Anticipated it. But the
scount gave a half shrug and called over his shoulder,
Cruthers, fetch Master Toby."

Heavy human footsteps moved away and climbed unseen
airs. Toby was almost as noisy when he ran down them. He
peared in the entrance hall, paused, then walked the rest of the
ay to Ross with rigid dignity. Like Warbrick, he was dressed
r riding.

"Fa— Mr. Keating," he said formally. He flicked a glance at
arbrick, and Ross felt his constraint. "You wished to see me?"

"Keating?" Warbrick repeated. "Is that what you're calling
ourself these days?"

"I want to talk to my son alone," Ross said.

"I think not. Toby and I are leaving Highwick presently. Say
hat you wish to say and go."

Ross dropped into a crouch in front of Toby. "Are you all
ght?" he asked.

"Yes, sir. I'm very glad to see that you are also well."

Ross parsed the boy's reply for signs of strain or fear. If Toby
lt either emotion, he was doing a very adult job of hiding it.

"Did you know your mother was sending you here?" Ross
ked.

"Yes."

"And you agree with her reasons?"

Under other circumstances, Ross would have expected To[by] to launch into another impassioned speech about how he sho[uld] be allowed to stay at Snowfell to help fight the Huns and fi[nd] the murderer. But Toby let his answer stand. He didn't li[ke] Warbrick, Ross knew, which could account for his silence in [the] viscount's presence. Somehow that didn't put Ross at ease.

He had two options: let Warbrick take Toby to whatev[er] "safe" place he and Gillian had arranged between them, or fig[ht] the bastard just so he could steal his son away…to where? N[ot] back to Snowfell. And he couldn't stay with Toby. There we[re] things that had to be done, and the boy couldn't be anywhere ne[ar] when they happened.

Toby wasn't a prisoner, that much was clear. Maybe he finally realized that he could only get in his mother's way wh[en] she needed all her resources to fight her enemies and now trust[ed] his father to do what he couldn't.

I wish to God I had a better way, son. I wish I could ma[ke] you proud.

Ross stood up. "Where are you taking him?" he asked Warbri[ck].

"Gillian thought it best that the location remain a secre[t]." Warbrick slapped his glove against his other palm. "It is qu[ite] comfortable, I assure you."

"Where?"

"To one of my family's properties. That is all you need kno[w.]"

And that was it. Ross still had nothing on Warbrick, and [he] was fresh out of ideas for getting answers—other than resorti[ng] to violence.

"Will you be okay, Toby?" he asked, looking into his so[n's] sober, intelligent eyes.

"Of course." He gnawed his lower lip. "You *will* look af[ter] Mother, won't you?"

"You bet I will."

"Don't leave her alone. No matter what she says."

"You have my word."

Toby nodded. "Goodbye, sir."

"We'll…we'll see each other again soon." Ross almost touched Toby's hair, but his own lie stopped him. "Just remember how much your parents love you."

"We must go," Warbrick said. "Toby, wait for me by the stables."

"Yes, sir." Toby turned smartly on his heel and returned the way he had come.

Ross stared after him. "You take good care of him, Warbrick," he said. "If I ever have reason to believe you've done otherwise—"

"I shall be happy to resolve our differences in a more permanent fashion when this is over," Warbrick said. "If, of course, the guests at Snowfell don't take care of the matter first. Cruthers, show Mr. Kavanagh out."

Ross let the frail old human lead him the short distance to the door. By the time he turned to look back, Warbrick was gone.

The sun was just beginning its slow descent toward the western horizon as he walked back toward Snowfell. Impulse made Ross veer in the direction of the ruins and Toby's mysterious grave. He easily made out the large patch of darker earth that marked where Toby had dug deep into the soil and patted it back into place, something Ross hadn't noticed on his previous visit.

He crouched beside the dirt and brushed at it with his palms. Then he began to dig in earnest.

The body was much deeper than Ross had expected, a good two feet under the surface. Toby had done a remarkable job of excavation, but luckily the soil was loose enough for Ross to remove with his hands. His fingers scraped against heavy, partially disintegrated canvaslike material that had been raggedly sawed open with a small knife. The cloth smelled of gasoline, as strongly as Toby had described. Only the upper third of the wrapping was accessible; the ground past that was hard and unworked.

Ross spread the layers of cut cloth apart to expose what la
inside. His first impression was that the body had been in th
ground for quite some time; it was in a state of dry decay, th
fleshy parts covered with grave wax that had formed during de
composition and preserved some areas of tissue, including
portion of the face around the gaping jaws. There was hardly an
sign of insect damage. Fragments of clothing clung to randor
areas of the body, and a few long strands of light-colored hai
drifted around the skull.

A girl. Or at least a young woman, one who might conceiv
ably have been pretty when she was alive. A swathe of fabri
below the partially exposed cervical vertebrae showed traces o
a pattern, obscured by a dark, wide stain.

Blood. Ross rocked back on his heels. Some combination o
factors had kept the body from becoming completely unrecog
nizable, but he doubted any friends or relatives, if they existec
would find it easy to identify her. She had not died easily. Th
delicate hyoid bone just below the jaw had been shattered wit
great force, and there was a gaping laceration that exposed th
vertebrae beneath the grave wax around the neck.

Bending close again, Ross noted that the shoulders had bee
nearly dislocated, arms forced behind the back at an unnatura
angle, as if the girl had been bound before her death. Ross ha
seen far worse, but it was something he never quite got used to

Toby had suspected "foul play," and Ross was quite certai
he'd been right.

Whoever had killed this girl had not only crushed her neck
but nearly severed her head from her body. Sloppy knife work
the mark of an amateur. The murderer hadn't done this before
But there had been hate behind this crime. Ross could feel hi
skin crawling with the residual emotion.

Struck by an all-too-vivid memory, Ross turned aside as hi
stomach heaved. This was the way the other girl had died.
Bonita Bailey, Broadway showgirl and would-be informant. He

neck had been all but severed, a clean cut with a very sharp blade. And that poor girl found in his neighborhood had died the same way.

He swallowed and bent over the grave again, his heart beating faster. If he dug the body out and rolled it over, maybe he would find that the hands and feet had been tied using a very specific kind of knot. Maybe he would discover that the girl's genital area—if anything was left of it—had been horribly mutilated.

You're crazy, Ross told himself. The odds were a million to one. But the victim appeared to be the right age and had the same light hair.

Sickened by his ghoulish speculation, he closed his eyes. There wasn't a damned thing he could do about this. He didn't have the resources or the time to spare, even if anyone would listen to a man suspected of murder himself.

And yet...

Going back over Toby's journal entry in his mind, he remembered the mention of a locket engraved with initials. That alone might provide a way to identify the victim.

Taking great care, Ross examined the area around the exposed part of the corpse. It soon became obvious that Toby must have taken the locket. He'd probably hidden it somewhere in his room. But Ross couldn't exactly conduct a full-scale search without attracting unwanted attention.

He had to lie low until the challenge. Contacting the police was no better an idea now than it had been after Sir Averil's murder. And even if he didn't get a chance to tell Jill about Toby's discovery, she would find out from Toby sooner or later.

Eventually this poor girl's remains would be identified and restored to her family. If there was any justice left in the world, the murderer would be caught and punished. And that same justice would send Friedrich and Conrad von Ruden the comeuppance they deserved.

Ross set to work rewrapping the corpse and restoring the burial site to its previous condition. No one who wasn't looking for it would know it was there.

He stood up, brushed the dirt from his shoes and trousers, and was just about to start for Snowfell when he smelled a human presence approaching from the stand of trees to the east. He moved quickly away from the grave site and pretended to be examining the remains of the Roman wall.

The man appeared to be one of the locals, thick of build and wearing rough work clothes. He had the kind of face that suggested a back-street enforcer, rather than a farmer or laborer, and his eyes were sharp and watchful. He nodded to Kavanagh as he came near.

"Barie mornin'" he said affably.

"'Morning," Ross said.

"Smart day fur a stroll."

"Yeah." Ross shifted to keep an eye on the man as he joined him in studying the wall.

"Thoo're no' fre abou' 'ere," the fellow remarked. "American ist thoo, eh?"

"That's right." Ross stuck out his hand. "Charles Keating."

The man gripped Ross's hand with his own roughened palm. "Is thoo fre Snowfell? Ah 'eard there wuz a large party stayin' there."

"Yes," Ross said, wondering why this guy was so interested in chatting about Snowfell when the locals had long since been discouraged from having anything to do with the estate and its residents. "I heard there were some old ruins here. Thought I'd stop by and have a look."

"Aye, the arl Roman for'. Bin stories abou' i' since ah wuz growin' up, bu' ah didn't know anyone 'ad dug i' up, like eh."

"It's not a place most people would happen to find by accident."

"Aye." The man pushed his hands into his pockets. "There is

many other ruins in the parish, if thoo'd be interested in seein' them, like. Ah'd be 'appy ter show thoo."

"I think my hostess is expecting me for lunch," Ross said. He backed away. "If you'll tell me where you live, I might take you up on your offer later."

The man withdrew his hands from his pockets. The right one was holding a gun.

"Sorry, guv," the man said, his accent taking on an entirely different cadence. "'Fraid it's na or never."

Ross raised his hands, rapidly calculating how far he would have to jump while cursing himself for an idiot. He had the advantage of speed and strength, but he had to plan his next move with precision.

Maybe this guy *was* the killer and he'd finally returned to the scene of his crime, which pretty much put the kibosh on Ross's wild theory that the Manhattan murders were related to this one. Or possibly the gunman's appearance had no connection to the body at all but had something to with the Convocation and the delegates who would be pleased to see Ross dead even before tomorrow's challenge.

Either way, Ross had to get the man to let down his guard. And to do that, he had to take a chance.

"Did you come back to gloat over your handiwork?" he asked.

For a moment the guy looked genuinely puzzled. "Don't know wot yer talkin' about, guv."

"Why did you kill her?"

"Kill who?" The muzzle of the gun dropped an inch. "Oi never…" His eyes narrowed. "Oh, yeah. Yer a bluebottle, in'cha?"

"Never heard the word," Ross said. He smiled. "Do you really think you can get away with it, even if you shoot me?"

"You got it aw wrong, rasher. I ain't never snuffed nobody."

"Then you'd better not start now. This is a small country, and you're trespassing on Maitland property. If one of their guests turns up dead…"

"Nah wan wants ter kill ya, rasher." The gunman grinned, showing off a prominent gold tooth. "We just wanna give ya a good night's Bo-Peep."

Ross realized his mistake before the man had finished his sentence. The second man's scent washed over him just as the blow sent him spinning into darkness.

CHAPTER TWENTY-FIVE

ETHAN HELD THE REINS lightly in his hands while Cruthers helped Toby mount the pony selected for him from amongst Highwick's scanty stock of riding horses. The beast wasn't young, nor particularly fast, but it was sturdy, and they would be riding for several hours, with few stops along the way.

Mother had already gone on ahead, of course. She couldn't be counted on not to talk. Cruthers had been thoroughly instructed on his own part in the play, and one of the three men Ethan had hired would stay on to make sure the ancient butler didn't try to run. Not that he would ever have the courage.

"Are you ready?" Ethan asked Toby.

The boy only glared at him, the set of his jaw reminding Ethan all too well of his father. Without another word, Ethan reined his mount away from the stableyard and turned the gelding toward the drive leading to Highwick's ramshackle gates. Though it might have seemed strange to a human that he'd chosen to travel by horse instead of motor car, and on established roads instead of cross-country, he knew that the last portion of the journey would be over rough ground more suitable for horses than cars. And during the first leg of their trek, it would be far safer to hide his and Toby's scents and the signs of their progress by mingling with others who used the busier thoroughfares.

Not that Ethan expected pursuit any time in the near future. Gillian believed he was taking Toby to his father's decrepit estate in Lancashire, but he had chosen a much closer and, to her, completely unknown destination. Events at Snowfell would fully occupy those who were most apt to realize that he didn't intend to keep Toby except as a hostage. Kavanagh would soon be out of the way, Hugh was certainly not worth a moment of concern, and Gillian…

When she learned the truth, she would be entirely at his mercy.

Ethan turned his switch on the gelding, though the beast was already moving at a brisk trot. The horse laid back his ears and broke into a canter.

Rage, Ethan reflected, was a pointless emotion now that it had served its purpose. True, the Hunt had left Kavanagh unscathed, doubtless due to Gillian's direct intervention. Her aptitude for leadership was quite remarkable. Sir Averil hadn't foreseen it, and neither had Ethan. It was a quality that would make her inevitable humiliation that much more satisfying. And Kavanagh's fall would have the same savor of poetic justice.

Twisting in the saddle, Ethan looked to be sure that the boy had not lagged behind. The only danger now was the possibility that he might try to escape, or that the men Ethan had employed to deal with Kavanagh had failed to do as he'd instructed. But the petty felons had come highly recommended and were greedy besides, and the little brat was bright enough to understand the consequences of failure. He simply didn't know that those consequences would occur no matter what he did.

They rode steadily for the next few hours, stopping briefly to rest and water the horses, and take their own refreshment. Ethan was careful to stay on the road, warning Toby not to venture onto the fells. They passed over the Scottish border near six o'clock. A few miles south of Gretna Green, Ethan led Toby off the road and into the hills. The westerly path was deeply rutted and used primarily by livestock, whose various hoofprints would disguise any new incursion. They reached the hunting box within the hour.

Ethan knew Mother and her escort had already arrived,

though the motor car that had carried her most of the way would have been driven to a hidden place by the main road, where he could pick it up on his way back to Highwick. Toby nearly fell off his pony when they reined up in front of the lodge, his face drawn with exhaustion and his eyes heavy-lidded in spite of his attempts to remain alert.

Had he been capable of such observations in his present state, Toby might have noted that the unsightly structure was even more badly in need of repair than Highwick. The hunting box had never been much more than a country cottage, catering to the last viscount's craving for the "simple" life, and had been abandoned since he had stopped visiting years ago.

One of the hired men, who went by the name of Algie, emerged, touched his forehead in grudging respect, and took the horse and pony to be cooled, watered and fed. Ethan stretched until his bones popped, took Toby by the arm and entered the box.

The smell of dust and vermin nearly overwhelmed him. Toby stood stock-still and wrinkled his nose. The second man, Ged, was waiting near the door, but he quickly backed away as Ethan dragged Toby through the hall and into the central drawing room. Mother, wearing an ensemble hardly appropriate for the countryside, was ensconced on the hard and very masculine sofa. Her trunks were sitting close by, unopened.

She rose as soon as she saw Ethan. "Why was it necessary for me to come here?" she demanded petulantly, not bothering with the usual greetings. She glared at Toby. "If you merely wanted to take the boy while your…Mrs. Delvaux enjoys her guests, you required no assistance from me."

Of course she was correct. She had no concept of what it was to be a mother, no trace of maternal instinct in her once-beautiful body. And he had told her no more than she needed to know. Any thought of disobedience on her part had been rapidly quashed by her still-fresh memory of the abilities Ethan had so recently displayed for her.

Ethan waved Ged outside and pushed Toby farther into the room. "You know I can't do without you, Mother," he said.

Her pique gave way to self-pity. "Where is the liquor? You promised there would be a good store in this dismal place."

"Oh, there is, Mother. Be patient."

Lady Warbrick flounced back to the sofa and folded her arms, resuming her examination of the boy. Her resentment had begun to give way to something keen and predatory. Even Toby noticed. He retreated into the shadows of a poorly lit corner and seemed to take an undue interest in the rack of antlers displayed on the wall above him.

"Don't you think the poor child ought to be put to bed?" she asked, solicitation thick as honey in her voice.

Ethan felt his face growing hot. He strode to the locked cabinet at one end of the room. Lady Warbrick had already tried to open it; he could smell her flesh on the wood. He produced a key from his pocket and unlocked the door to reveal a number of unopened bottles of Scotch, cognac and other liquors. "Here you are, Mother," he said. "All you could possibly need."

She forgot her interest in Toby and went straight for the cabinet. Ethan grabbed Toby and steered him through a side door into a hall and up a rustic oak staircase. At the landing, he went directly to the first room on the left.

"This is yours," he said, indicating the sparsely furnished chamber. "I shall be next door. Should you attempt to leave the lodge…"

He didn't need to finish. He pushed Toby into the room, and shut and locked the door. Then he went downstairs and out the lodge's rear door to find his employees and make certain that they had completed their most important task.

When he returned to the main drawing room he found Lady Warbrick well on her way to complete intoxication. She barely looked up as he passed through the room.

"Remember that you must stay here, Mother," he said. "You

are not to wander away, nor are you to disturb the boy. Do you understand?"

She lifted her head with an effort and smiled, her painted lips crooked. "Oh, pish," she said. "That spindly thing? You were much larger when you were his age."

"You might remember that he is your grandson."

"And your nephew. But that has not stopped you, has it?"

"Very little can stop me, Mother."

Her plucked brows rose, and she toasted him mockingly with her glass. Ethan left the hunting box and went round to the tiny stable where Algie and Ged had a fresh horse waiting for him. Algie, who was barely capable of staying on a horse at all, heaved himself into the saddle of the second nag, and the two of them retraced the path by which Ethan and Toby had come. At the designated spot, he found the Daimler well hidden with branches amongst the trees. Algie uncovered the motor car and took the reins of Ethan's mount. Ethan slid behind the wheel, waited until Algie had led the horses some distance away and pulled onto the road.

He reached Kendal by evening, with time to spare before he was to rendezvous with Cora. He left the Daimler at a farm whose owner owed him a considerable amount of money, ate the plain fare the obsequious farmer offered, confiscated his only riding horse and rode most of the way to Snowfell. There he released the animal among the fells to either find its way home or be picked up by another local farmer. He walked the remaining distance and bided his time until Cora should arrive.

She appeared minutes late, disheveled and flustered.

"Oh, Lord Warbrick," she said, breathless as she came to a stop beside the old oak that stretched its twisted branches over Cuddy Beck. "It's terrible. Simply terrible."

Ethan was in no mood to indulge her, even in her final minutes of life. "What is it? Quickly, girl."

She nervously explained everything that had occurred since the Hunt, including the fact that the Earnshaws had taken the bait she had left where they could conveniently find it, and exposed Kavanagh as a fraud and murder suspect before all the guests. Ethan wondered if Kavanagh had told Gillian of the second murder, and how she had reacted if he had not.

"Is the challenge still to go forward?" he asked.

"Yes." She wrung her hands. "Oh, what if the count should hurt Hugh?"

Ethan made the appropriate soothing comments, reminding Cora that Hugh was younger and undoubtedly faster than von Ruden. "Mrs. Delvaux has not been molested in any way?" he asked.

"No, my lord."

Good. Matters were developing to his satisfaction. The challenges were not to the death, but Kavanagh might still be killed. "The Germans do not know that they have been identified as suspects?" he asked. "Kavanagh did not mention you?"

She shuddered. "No, your lordship."

"You are quite safe? No one knows you are here?"

"Yes. I mean, no, Lord Warbrick."

"And Hugh will come as we planned?"

"Yes."

"Very good. You have done very well indeed, Cora."

"Thank you, your lordship." She bobbed like a frightened sparrow. "I can tell Hugh tonight? Tell him what we've planned?"

"Oh, yes, my dear. He shall soon know everything."

She was just intelligent enough to realize, as he began his work, that his true plans had nothing to do with her living to see her wedding day.

HUGH SMELLED the perfume first. It was the same stuff he'd caught a whiff of in Cora's room when he'd finally found a chance to talk to her this morning. Poor girl, she'd been virtually frozen with horror over what she'd seen, apologetic for not having gone straight to him when she'd realized Sir Averil was dead, and relieved to learn that she was in no way considered the instigator of the murder.

It was strange that Cora was still wearing clothing that had become saturated with the scents in Sir Averil's room. He was still puzzling it out as he approached the meeting place and realized that another scent had joined the first, acrid and utterly unmistakable.

He ran the rest of the way, a cry building in his chest. Cora was there, where she had promised to be.

And she was dead.

Hugh fell to his knees, the scanty contents of his stomach surging into his throat. He had no doubt that she was beyond help. The deep slash across her neck was like a second mouth, leaving only the spine to connect head to body. Her hands and feet were bound, and the hem of her dress…

Giving way to his sickness, Hugh turned and retched. He was too ill to hear the approaching footsteps until they were almost on top of him.

"My God."

Hugh looked up, his vision blurred with tears. Ethan stood a few yards away, an expression of horror on his face.

Somehow Hugh got to his feet. He wiped his mouth on his sleeve and stepped around Cora's body, as if he might protect her from the final indignity of exposure to curious eyes.

"She's dead," he croaked. "She's dead."

Ethan stared at the body, his skin pale as a cameo in the darkness. "I am…too late," he whispered.

His words made no sense. Hugh shook his head, wondering if the world might suddenly snap back into focus with enough concentration.

"Too late?" he repeated. "What are you…what are you doing here, Warbrick?"

Ethan was long in answering. His face remained gray even after he turned his gaze from the thing that had been Cora Smith.

"Toby told me that Kavanagh was behind it," he said, "but I couldn't believe it."

"Behind what?" All the liquid in Hugh's body seemed to freeze. "What…what are you saying?"

It took some time for Ethan to explain, and with every word, Hugh felt his body turn colder.

"You're mad," Hugh said. "Kavanagh would never do…what you said."

"Even if he believed he was helping Gillian escape a tyrant's control? He wanted her, and the only way to get her was by eliminating Sir Averil."

"No." Hugh staggered backward until his hip struck the trunk of an ash behind him. *But Kavanagh was the one who discovered that Father was dead, wasn't he? No one else saw the body right away. And Cora asked me to meet her tonight because she had something important to tell me. Something she didn't dare tell anyone else…*

"Cora would never have helped him," he said aloud. "She wouldn't kill anyone."

"Kavanagh offered her the desperate hope that you might finally be hers, but only if Sir Averil were out of the way." Ethan sagged, as if he, too, found recent events too horrible to bear. "We must warn Gillian immediately."

Something in the viscount's words punched through the wall of Hugh's misery and shock. "Why," he asked slowly, "should I believe anything you say? You hate Kavanagh. You have from the beginning."

Warbrick didn't deny it. But then he spoke of the second New York murder, of which he'd recently learned, and removed an envelope from inside his jacket.

"I was on my way to Snowfell to give this to Gillian."

Toby's uneven handwriting snaked across the pages, a damning description of a conversation between Cora and Kavanagh that he had overheard the previous night. Hugh read to the end.

"If Toby heard this," he said, his voice cracking, "why didn't
we tell Gilly and me?"

But Hugh already knew. Gillian had kept Toby strictly confined, a prisoner under the inflexible guardianship of Miss
Rownthwaite. What he'd heard—*if* he'd heard it—would have
been a terrible shock. He wouldn't have wanted to believe his
father capable of murder.

"Toby informed me as soon as we reached the old estate,"
Ethan said. "I came as quickly as I could, but…"

Hugh was no longer listening. Ross had presumably killed
Cora to silence her. But what about those other girls? What could
drive anyone to such depravity, especially a man like Kavanagh?

And how could an experienced detective make the blatant
error of leaving a body in plain view on Snowfell land?

He's not sane. Madmen make mistakes. Kavanagh hadn't
been seen at the house since morning. Gillian had been worried,
though Hugh knew she'd hoped that Ross really had run from
the challenge. He himself had been too concerned with his own
problems to think of searching for Kavanagh.

"Kavanagh may, against all logic, attempt to return to Snowfell," Ethan said. "He may intend to abduct Gillian before his
crime is discovered."

And before he had to face Conrad's challenge. With an effort,
Hugh tried to form some sort of plan, no matter how tenuous.
"Learning about the second Manhattan murder didn't weaken
Gilly's trust in Kavanagh," he said. "I'm not sure that even
Toby's journal will convince her."

"Then *we* must act for *her* sake, even if we do so against her
will." He caught Hugh's gaze. "I know you have never held any
great esteem for me, Hugh. We have not been friends. But we
can both agree on the necessity of protecting Gillian and Toby
from a savage killer." He glanced in Snowfell's direction. "You
must find a pretext to get Gillian away from the house within the
next few hours."

As if that hadn't been tried before. "Supposing I do…" Hugh glanced at Cora's body and felt himself tumbling toward a pit of grief and despair. "Supposing I *can* convince her," he said hoarsely, "where should I take her?"

"You will bring Gillian to the crossroads at Mott Fell by no later than half-three this morning. By the time we meet, I will have alerted the authorities."

"You mean bring the police here?"

"They must be told about Kavanagh."

In which case they would inevitably wind up at Snowfell right in the middle of the Convocation. "That's insane," Hugh said. "No one outside Snowfell has been told of Sir Averil's death. We've got him in the ice house, but someone's bound to talk if the authorities come to the house. And the rashers won't stop with questioning Kavanagh, even if they catch him."

"I will not mention Sir Averil. I doubt anyone will wish to call attention to his death."

"They'll want to interrogate anyone who had contact with Cora. Especially Gillian."

"I will keep Gillian away until Kavanagh is in custody."

"And the delegates? Do you think they'll cooperate?" Hugh found it difficult to breathe, and jerked at the studs of his collar with such force that they popped free and went flying away. "Kavanagh made all of us believe the Germans had killed Sir Averil. He may have evidence planted against them, and they won't let anyone damage their honor, especially not humans." He swallowed. "Even if the delegates don't all run off when the police arrive, the Huns aren't just going to forget about the challenges. They have too much to prove."

"Naturally you have reason to be concerned about your own safety. You must come with us."

A blazing current of shame scorched Hugh's body. If he went with Warbrick and Gillian, it would be over. He would be throwing away the last vestiges of his honor and cementing his cowardice in the eyes of his sister, the Convocation, the world. Cora would have despised him. And he would despise himself.

Hugh slid to the ground. Cora was dead. Kavanagh had used her, forced her to help him because he knew she was in a highly vulnerable position. Hugh had put her in the line of fire simply by daring to care for her and letting her love him.

"All right," he said, staring at Cora's ravaged face. "I'll do as you ask. But I won't be coming with you."

He covered his face with his hands and wept.

ETHAN HELD IN his laughter until he was well beyond the range of Hugh's hearing. It had gone even more smoothly than he could have planned. The boy was hooked completely. He had accepted the story with only the most cursory of questions.

He was, of course, entirely incapable of thinking for himself. He had always been that way: impressionable, selfish, weak-willed, readily influenced by any stronger character he encountered, even one he disliked. But he was also easily swayed by an appeal to his long-abandoned duties as a brother, convinced that this time he might become the man Sir Averil had imagined him to be.

The son Ethan might have been.

This is on your head, Father. May you watch the fall of your house from your station in hell.

Ethan climbed into the waiting Daimler, brooding over the one flaw in his plan. It was likely that he would be unable to mete out Hugh's punishment until his other work was completed. The idiot boy undoubtedly planned to confront Kavanagh himself.

A pity Ethan wouldn't be there to witness those final moments before Kavanagh lost what was left of his dreams.

LEAVING CORA was one of the most difficult things Hugh had ever done. Every fiber of his being resisted the idea of letting her lie there in her own blood, her beauty destroyed, nothing left of her vitality and passion. It was obscene.

But if the police were to make a case against Kavanagh, they must have access to every bit of incriminating evidence the former cop might have left behind. The perfume the killer had splashed around filled Hugh's nostrils as he took one last look at Cora.

Rage nipped at his heels as he ran back to Snowfell, the tears drying on his cheeks. He had to find a way of telling Gilly the truth before Kavanagh returned…if, God forbid, he hadn't already done so.

The estate was as silent and shrouded as if it were draped in mourning. Only a few lights still burned, chiefly for the convenience of the servants who maintained a nighttime vigil in case one of the guests should require their services.

Hugh trudged through the unobtrusive back servants' door and made his way to the kitchen, to which Gilly so often retreated when she was troubled. It was deserted; Mrs. Spotterswood wouldn't be up and about until four. He went on to the entrance hall, caught Gillian's scent and continued to the Yellow Drawing Room, largely unused since the Convocation had begun.

Gillian was sitting in one of the wing chairs by the cold hearth, staring into the darkness. She looked up as Hugh entered.

"Where have you been, Hugh?" she asked, her voice thin with worry. "Have you seen Ross? What has happened?"

It was gone eleven, and Hugh knew he had to make his explanation good. "Nothing," he said. "I did look 'round for Ross, but I didn't find him." He positioned himself against the mantelpiece, covering his anger and his fear for Gillian with a concerned and serious air. "I…don't know what to say."

She released her breath in a long, shuddering sigh. "Von Ruden says that he has fled rather than face the challenge."

"Don't listen to anything that blighter says, Gilly."

"I hope he *is* gone. I hope he goes far away, to some place where they can't find him."

The American authorities who wanted to charge him with a second murder? Hugh wondered. The Germans who very likely wanted him dead? The man would soon have more enemies than he could ever hope to evade.

"He must have left for a reason," Hugh said, feeling the worst sort of traitor.

She rose and paced from one end of the room to the other, her plain skirt hissing with every long stride. "I thought he might have gone to find Toby," she said. "I telephoned Highwick, but no one answered."

"Warbrick would have contacted you if he'd…if Ross had taken Toby."

"Could someone have hurt him, Hugh? Could the Germans have tried to…make sure of him before the challenge?"

"They haven't been away from Snowfell, have they? And von Ruden is too arrogant to think that Ross might defeat him."

His words obviously gave Gillian no comfort. She stopped pacing and turned to Hugh again. "We must find him."

"Yes." His tongue moved sluggishly as it shaped the word. "Yes. I'll help you. Gillian, I think—"

"Have you seen Cora?"

CHAPTER TWENTY-SIX

THE QUESTION PLUNGED into the silence like the downward strike of a knife. "You—you haven't seen her?" Hugh stammered.

"I assumed that you were meeting with her tonight," she said, pushing her fingers through her already disheveled hair. "She has been behaving very strangely since…since Father died."

Hugh realized that his own fingernails were cutting deep crescents into his palms. He relaxed his hands. "She has been quite upset," he croaked. "I'm sorry that her work hasn't been up to her usual standard."

"I'm not concerned with her work. But I do worry that recent events have affected her more deeply than I would have supposed." She looked searchingly into Hugh's eyes. "I know that you were fond of her, Hugh, and that she felt the same. Did she think Sir Averil's death would allow you to marry her?"

Oh, God. Hugh tried desperately not to look away. Gillian knew about the affair, which shouldn't have surprised him. But she'd never mentioned it, perhaps believing, as Sir Averil had, that it was only a passing dalliance, like so many before.

"She…" he began. "*We*…had hoped…" He blinked, hoping to stave off the tears a while longer. "I loved her, Gilly."

He realized with horror that he had been speaking of Cora in the past tense. "I should have told you sooner," he said. "She's gone away for a little while. Will you mind very much?"

Her expression told him that he wasn't making sense, but she was too preoccupied to pursue the subject. "I asked Father to employ her at Ethan's suggestion," she said distantly, "but perhaps I should have considered—"

"Warbrick recommended her?"

"Yes." She glanced at the antique ormolu clock on the mantelpiece. "We should leave, before…"

The thoughts roaring inside Hugh's head drowned her out as if he were standing by the Bristol seashore at high tide.

Warbrick recommended Cora. Someone who would owe him her position when decent employment was in short supply, who might inform him of all the goings-on at Snowfell when he could not possibly be there.

Hadn't Ethan also described *himself* when he'd said that Kavanagh would do anything to possess Gillian?

"Hugh! Are you ill?"

Hugh's skin was icy cold. "I'm only concerned about Ross," he said.

"It will be all right," she said, touching his cheek with a warm, gentle hand.

Comforting *him.* But before the sun rose, all Gillian's brave, resourceful strength would finally crumble. She might doubt Warbrick's claims about the man she loved, but if her own brother, who had seen Cora's body, was convinced of Kavanagh's guilt…

Was he convinced?

You'll know when you see him. That was the key. For now, he had to act as though no doubt had ever entered his mind.

"We'd better go," he said. "You should change into something more comfortable."

She shook her head. "Better not risk anyone seeing or smelling me. I shall inform Faulder that we are leaving."

As she went to find Faulder, Hugh sank down in the chair, lowered his head into his hands and listened to the clock on the mantelpiece count out the most terrible night of his life. Gillian's light tread warned him of her approach, and he was up and ready when she came to the drawing room door.

"We should take the Bentley," Hugh said before they had gone more than a few steps outside.

"The Bentley? Why?"

"Because… Because it'll take us around the countryside much faster than if we travel on foot. And we can divide the parish by the roads that run through it."

His argument was weak; as wolves, they could cover ground far more efficiently. But Gillian accepted his suggestion, climbed into the passenger side, and remained quiet while Hugh pulled out of the garage and turned into the drive.

She knows. She knows something is very wrong, but she hasn't dared admit it to herself.

Hugh drove away from Snowfell, his fingers numb on the steering wheel. He took one narrow track and then another, making his way by a roundabout route to the rendezvous point Warbrick had suggested. Gillian's gaze moved ceaselessly over the fells, searching for any trace of Kavanagh. Every so often they would stop, Hugh would set the brake, and Gillian would climb the nearest fell for a sniff and a closer look.

They had nearly reached the intended destination when Gillian stretched out her hand and laid it over Hugh's.

"This isn't working," she said. "Ross hasn't been this way."

"No," he whispered. "I don't think he has."

Once he had begun speaking, he found it impossible to stop. He told her about Cora's death and Ethan's accusation. Gillian sat absolutely still until long after he had finished.

"I'm sorry, Hugh," she said, looking as detached and rational as a professor of dead languages in a room full of dusty books. "Do you believe what Ethan said?"

The tears rolled over Hugh's chin and splashed onto the lapel of his jacket. "I—I don't know what to believe." He clenched his fist on the wheel. "We should go back to the house."

She dropped her hand, and he wheeled the Bentley about and drove recklessly toward Snowfell, twice scraping the gleaming finish on fenceposts and shrubbery.

Faulder ran out to meet them as Hugh pulled up in front of the garage. The butler's white hair was standing nearly on end, and he stumbled as he reached the motor car.

"Madam," he gasped. "Sir…"

Gillian had leaped out the passenger door before Hugh could open his own. He ran after her across the carriage yard and plunged into the kitchen court. He didn't need to see where Gillian had gone to know where to find her.

The kitchen should have been bustling in the hours before dawn, as Mrs. Spotterswood and the scullery maids prepared breakfast for the guests. But this was no ordinary morning. The vast hearth was cold, and the fire in the range had not been lit.

Ross was leaning over the sink, his hair sodden with perspiration, his torn clothing stained with blood. His face was drawn, and Hugh detected the faint discolorations of healing cuts on his cheek and jaw.

Gillian had paused halfway across the room, arms half-raised, as if she had been about to embrace Ross, then stopped herself at the last moment.

"Where have you been?" she asked in a thready whisper. "Are you hurt?"

Ross gazed at her, confusion in his eyes, and stepped away from the sink.

"I came back…as soon as I could," he said. "Is everyone all right?"

"Yes," she said. She moved closer to him. Hugh barely restrained himself from stepping between them. "The blood…"

Ross looked down at his shirt and trousers, studying the scarlet stains as if he had no idea how they had come to be there. "It's not as bad as it looks."

Hugh took Gillian's arm, amazed at his own self-control now

that he was in Ross's presence. "Sit down," he ordered. "Both of you. Tell us what happened, Ross."

Clumsy as a newborn lamb, Ross sank down into the nearest chair. In disconnected sentences, he spoke of how he had been walking near the dig site when he had met a stranger who had pretended to be a friendly local, but had turned out to be something else entirely.

"I must have been out for hours," he said, rubbing the back of his head. "I woke up once in a different place, but they must have been watching me. They hit me again. I was only able to get away an hour ago."

It was as fantastic a story as Hugh had ever heard. Ross had been coldcocked by strangers on Snowfell grounds and kept unconscious during the very span of time when Cora had been murdered?

"Who were these men?" he demanded. "What did they want?"

"They never told me. But I think I know why they attacked me."

He went on to describe the contents of the journal entry he had found in Toby's room and how he had gone to the old ruins to look for the body. "It was there, just like he said."

Hugh felt the blood curdle in his veins. Another girl. Another horrible murder. And two different men who based their claims of foul play on writings in Toby's journal.

"Who was she?" Hugh asked, half-afraid he was about to be ill.

"There wasn't much on the body to identify her."

"And you think the men who accosted you were the murderers?"

"The murderers, or somehow connected with the crime. Maybe they discovered that someone had been disturbing the burial site and came to investigate."

"Then why did they only knock you out? Why didn't they kill you?"

"I don't know." Ross shook his head slowly, as if it were too heavy for his neck to bear. "They would have been smarter to get me out of the way."

But they didn't, did they? Hugh thought. Something didn't add up.

"How was she killed?"

Ross's description was succinct and brutal. *Just like the American girls,* Hugh thought. *The way Cora was...*

He tried to push the image out of his mind. Innocent or not, Ross must have noticed the similarities. Why add such embellishments if they weren't true? Why deliberately remind them about the Manhattan murders if he'd just killed Cora in the very same way?

"Did you see Toby?" Gillian asked suddenly. "Did you speak to Ethan before...before this happened?"

"I had to make sure Toby was all right." A feral light came into his eyes. "Toby knew about the body. He may not be safe with Warbrick. We have to get him back."

Which was exactly what Hugh would have suggested, but coming from Ross, the idea might have a more sinister purpose. If what Ethan had said was correct, Ross had risked a great deal by returning to Snowfell in his present state. But if he could make Gilly believe his story and lure her away before dawn, he could have her *and* escape the challenge.

Yet Warbrick had never mentioned that Kavanagh had come to see him. Who was lying?

Gillian pulled a chair close to Ross's and sat on its edge. "Do you believe these men know about Toby's involvement?" she asked, her steady voice as much of a lie as anything that had been said in the past few hours.

Ross looked from Gillian to Hugh and back again. "I don't know," he said. "Do you know where Warbrick is taking Toby?"

"To an old family estate south of Lancaster."

"That isn't far, is it? Hugh, you'll have to ask the de Gévaudan brothers and Forster if they'll help you track Warbrick down and convince him to turn Toby over to them." His gaze shifted to

Gillian's face. "I didn't want to get the police involved, but they'l
have to look at the body before the killers try to get rid of it."

Hugh remembered Warbrick's precise instructions: *"You wil.
bring Gillian to the crossroads at Mott Fell by no later than half-
three this morning. By the time we meet, I will have alerted the
authorities."*

He didn't have to check his wristwatch to know it was gone
four. What would Warbrick do when he and Gilly didn't show
up at the rendezvous? Would he wait? And what about the
police? They would no doubt go to look at the body first, so there
should be a couple of hours left before they turned up at Snowfell, depending on how much Warbrick had told them.

Ross didn't know that, of course. But would a guilty man want
to call in the authorities? Had Ross truly gone mad, even committed the crime without being aware of it?

Or am I the one going mad?

Gillian must have wondered the same of herself, but for her
it was much worse. Either the friend she had trusted with her
deepest secrets was deliberately attempting to send an innocent
man, her lover, to the gibbet, using Toby to do it, or the man she
loved—no matter how much she denied her feelings—was a
vicious murderer.

But was she thinking of everything? If Ross *had* visited
Warbrick before the viscount had taken Toby away, Ethan could
have sent someone to follow his rival and ensure that he didn'
have an alibi for the time of Cora's death.

And Gillian hadn't seen how bizarrely unemotional Warbrick
had been after his first display of horror, as if the body lying at
his feet had no real importance except as an object he could use
to condemn a man who already walked under a cloud of suspicion. A man he hated.

She will not be compelled to suffer much longer. That was what
Warbrick had said in New York. Hugh had assumed that he meant
to make another futile attempt to get Gilly away from Snowfell

t what if *he'd* done all the evil things he'd blamed on Ross? rcing Cora to help him kill Sir Averil, murdering her…

"Gillian," he said, "I need to speak with you alone. Ross, u—"

"Cora is dead," Gillian said to Ross, speaking over Hugh. "Is at her blood on your clothing?"

Ross's face went so pale that he might have lost every last op of blood in his body. "Dead?"

"Murdered." Gillian leaned forward, her hands clenched in r skirt. "She was killed on the estate. Her throat was slit."

Ross made a choked sound and squeezed his eyes shut. "God. hould have protected her. I should have…" He jerked up his ad. "You think I— Gillian, what are you saying?"

"You have been accused of murder."

Color rushed back into his face. "I don't have to ask who did e accusing. For God's sake, when did this happen?"

"While you were away," Hugh said. "We were…told that you urdered her to hide the secret that you killed Sir Averil."

The horrible sound that came out of Ross's throat might have en a laugh. "Cora did know a secret," he said. "She confessed me that the Huns had blackmailed her into giving Sir Averil e poison." His gaze locked on Gillian's, and there was a deep, tter sorrow in his eyes. "If anyone did this, it was von Ruden. nd if he's made you believe I'm guilty, then I guess he's won."

Gillian didn't flinch or look away, but an almost invisible emor ran through her, leeching the starch from her spine and laxing the rigid muscles in her face and hands. In a single otion Ross jumped out of his chair and began to tear off his irt, breathing harshly as cloth ripped and buttons scattered.

Gillian rose and reached for him, the instinct to comfort him vercoming her bewilderment and suspicion. Ross paused with s fists trailing streamers of dark red fabric.

"They wanted to keep me away," he rasped. "They…did this make it look as if I…"

"Why didn't you tell us what Cora said?" Gillian aske[ ]
hoarsely. "If you had told us—if you had trusted me—we cou[ ]
have helped protect her and stopped the killer."

For a few dizzy moments Hugh hated Ross as much as if *h[e]*
had killed Cora. *He should have told us. Cora would still [be]*
alive….

But Gilly was wrong. They couldn't have stopped the re[ ]
killer, because none of them would have suspected him. And eve[n]
if they had, Gillian would never have believed without evidenc[e]

"It wasn't the Huns. It was Warbrick," Hugh said to Ross. "[He]
told me that Toby had overheard you threatening Cora if she to[ld]
anyone about your part in Sir Averil's murder."

"That never happened. Toby wouldn't…" His lips narrowe[d]
into a grim line. "My God. I had the chance. I could have gotte[n]
him away."

Hugh looked at Gillian. The meaning of what he and Ross ha[d]
said seemed to be reaching her through a thick fog.

Not Ross. She would grasp at that thought like a lifeline. *N[ot]
von Ruden.* That would be far more difficult to let go, becau[se]
the alternative was devastating.

Gillian was being asked to reassemble her repeatedly sha[t-]
tered world into yet another configuration, one in which h[er]
dearest friend was her direst enemy. She was being compelle[d]
to acknowledge that she'd sent her own son into unimaginab[le]
danger because she had trusted a murderer.

"Gillian," Ross said, very low.

She turned and walked blindly across the room. "Ethan? B[ut]
that can't be true." She laughed, a strangled note that obviousl[y]
scared Ross as much as it did Hugh. "He wouldn't harm Toby[,"]
she said. "He would never—"

Ross knew she wasn't yet ready to see reason. "Talk to Forst[er]
and the de Gévaudans," he said to Hugh. "Take anyone else yo[u]
trust to find Warbrick. Do whatever you have to. *Whatever* yo[u]
have to, Hugh."

"I understand."

"I must go to Toby," Gillian said, moving about the kitchen a dazed circles.

"The challenge is less than an hour away," Hugh said to Ross a near-whisper. "What do we do about that?"

"That's why I'm staying. It won't matter much what I do now, ill it?"

Ross wasn't stupid enough to meet von Ruden in an unequal attle. He was going to eliminate the Germans before they caused ny more trouble.

"Warbrick said he was going to inform the authorities about ora's death," Hugh said. "The police could be here at any time."

"Then we'd both better work fast."

"Think, Ross. None of the delegates will try anything with e cops here. And you aren't guilty."

"Didn't *you* think I was, at least for a while?" He glanced at illian, and Hugh heard the words he didn't speak. *Didn't she?*

"Don't you want to make Warbrick pay for what he's done?" ugh asked, desperate and angry.

Gillian turned toward Hugh. "The police…are coming here?" e asked.

"Warbrick will have made sure of it."

She didn't have to be told that all hell was going to break loose nce the police arrived. The Convocation would fracture like awed glass. Their father's life's work would be condemned to issolution.

That was a fate it deserved, Hugh thought. And Gillian ouldn't care, not after what had just been revealed. The only emaining choice she faced was between standing by Ross or oing after Toby.

A mother would always choose her child. But Warbrick *anted* her to come to him, which meant it would be far safer if e didn't.

Hugh went to Gillian and gently took her shoulders in his

hands. "I know you want to go to Toby," he said. "But Warbric
expected me to bring you to him. You'll walk right into his tra
if you come with me." He met Ross's gaze over his shoulde
"You have to take her away from here."

"I can't. It'll look as if I'm running, and that won't do Gillia
any favors. One of the others—"

"No!"

Gillian pushed Hugh away with such force that he crashe
into the kitchen table, the breath exploding from his lungs.

"No!" Her lips lifted in a snarl that was all wolf, humanit
collapsing beneath the weight of her despair. She swung aroun
to face Ross.

"Run!" she taunted. "By all means, run! You have don
nothing but ruin everything you have touched since Toby foun
you. Your actions have destroyed the Convocation. You drov
Ethan to this jealous insanity. You let Cora die. You provoked th
Germans because you wanted to *protect* us." She laughed wildl
"Protect us? Toby would have been better off if he had never bee
conceived!"

Her final declaration echoed into a terrible silence, made
hundred times worse by Ross's reaction. He didn't move at al
and his expression never altered. It was as if he had no argumen
with which to defend himself. As if he believed that everythin
Gillian had said was true.

Hugh couldn't bear it. "You're wrong, Gillian," he said. "He
made mistakes. We all have. But without him—" He smelled th
intruders outside in the corridor and rushed to the door.

"Von Ruden," he whispered.

There was no time to alter Ross's appearance or discuss wh
should be said to explain it. Von Ruden burst through the doc
with his son, barefoot and dressed only in a lawn shirt and ligh
weight flannel trousers.

"Kavanagh," he said, bracing his legs wide as he regarded h
intended prey. "I thought you had fled, and that Mrs. Delvau

had assisted you. I see that I was mistaken." His gaze swept over Ross. "But what have we here? Have you been hunting, Mr. Kavanagh?" He sniffed. "That is not the blood of the red deer or any local game with which I am familiar."

"It's human blood," Conrad said. His eyes lit with hungry interest. "But whose?"

Gillian, whose expression had lost none of its rage, placed herself toe-to-toe with the count, somehow fostering the illusion that she was every bit as tall as he. "Get out," she snarled.

Hugh and Ross moved to shield Gillian at almost the same moment. Hugh managed to force himself ahead of Ross, stopping so close to Conrad that the German's unpleasant breath nearly overwhelmed him.

"There's been a murder," he said.

"A murder?" Von Ruden glanced at Conrad with raised brows. "Who is missing? And what is Mrs. Delvaux attempting to hide?"

"Maybe *you* have something to hide," Hugh said. "The girl who was killed named you as the ones who murdered my father."

CHAPTER TWENTY-SEVEN

THE GERMANS' ASTONISHMENT lasted all of five second
before unfamiliar human scents, drifting into the kitchen from
the corridor, ended any chance of a fight. Gillian's hackles
rose. She stared at each of the men in turn—these men who
had become her enemies—and began to work at the buttons
of her blouse.

Drive them away, the wolf insisted, powerful emotions trans
lated into words her human half could understand. *Drive them
all away.*

But somewhere inside, refusing to be ignored, the woman
who had called herself Mrs. Delvaux clung precariously to the
wolf's leash and would not let go. She spoke of the need for
sanity, for reason, for cunning—human cunning, steady and
subtle. The kind that might yet save them. Save Toby.

And save the one she loved and hated in equal measure.

"The police have arrived," she said, speaking in Mrs. Delvaux'
voice as if she were a ventriloquist's doll. "I suggest that you
return to your rooms, *mein Herren.*"

"Die Polizei!" Conrad exclaimed. "She summoned them here
with lies to interfere with our lawful challenge and save her
American pet!"

"I didn't summon them," Gillian said. "They know nothing
of challenges or what we do here. But they will be looking for
the murderer of an innocent girl, and many British police are
former veterans of the War, with no love for your people."

"Who is this girl you speak of?" Conrad demanded. He glared at Ross. "Look at him! It is *he* who is wanted in America! He is—"

Voices rose from another part of the house: Faulder's, and a deeper and more authoritative baritone. Count von Ruden bristled, nearly trembling with rage. "You shall regret this," he said, then signaled to Conrad and strode for the door that led out to the kitchen garden.

Gillian stared after them, her vision clouding as wolf and woman warred for control of her mind and body. Both wanted the same thing: to find Toby and keep Ross safe. But the wolf was ready to run south here and now, leaving ruin in her wake. The woman…

The woman looked at Ross and remembered what she had promised him in another life, in a dream of hope that no longer existed. She gazed into his eyes…so empty now, devoid of emotion, returning her wordless glance without anger or fear or regret.

"Ross, you've got to go," Hugh said. "The Huns have been neutralized. They're out of the game." He met Gillian's gaze. "For the last time, I'm begging you to trust me. I'll find Toby and set him free."

She realized that she might endanger Toby all the more if she tried to free him herself. She saw how very blind she had been, refusing to acknowledge long ago that Ethan's affection had become dangerously unbalanced. She could no longer cling to the belief that Ethan, the Ethan she had loved in her own passionately childish way, was still the sympathetic, loyal friend he had been in the days of their youthful intimacies.

Yet there must be a chance, a thin thread of hope, that he could still be reached.

She half turned toward Ross. "My brother is right," she said. "I will stay here and distract the police as long as I can. Run west, into the mountains. They won't find it easy to follow you there." She embraced Hugh tightly. "Take great care, Hugh."

"I will." He smiled—not to cover his fear or get in anyone's

good graces, but to comfort her. "Have faith, Gilly," he whis
pered. Then he let her go and offered his hand to Ross.

"Good luck," he said, gripping Ross's hand. "Toby's goin
to need both his parents when this is over."

Ross kept his hands at his sides. "Save him," he said.

Hugh pivoted and strode for the door to the garden. Ross wa
already halfway to the door to the main part of the house by th
time Hugh was gone.

"Ross!" Gillian cried, running to catch up.

The human voices, addressing questions to unseen servants
waited on the other side of the green baize door. Ross stopped, hi
back a more imposing barrier than anything made of wood or stone

"You were right," he said. "Everything you said was right."

"No. I was—"

"I'm done for, Jill," he said. He lifted his hands, staring at hi
palms. "Even if the cops realize it was Warbrick, these stains wi
never wash clean. I couldn't protect any of you. But I can sav
you more trouble now. Tell them you didn't really know me. Te
them I deceived you." He laid his palm on the door. "Goodbye
Gillian."

For a full minute Gillian's limbs refused to answer her wil
There was a commotion in the entrance hall, exclamations, the
Ross's quiet voice as he submitted to the authorities.

Gillian leaned against the door, her eyes dry and burning. Sh
felt the wolf fighting to take control again, longing to charge int
the hall and attack the ones who were stealing Ross from her.

She opened the door.

Ross was gone. Two humans stood by the foot of the stair
case: a constable and a man she presumed to be his superio
Gillian could smell the heightened tension in the air, not onl
from the police, but from the servants, who had retreated int
their own safe corners, and the werewolf guests. She assume
that most of them had overheard enough to realize that th
visitors were members of the local constabulary.

By the end of the day, if circumstances permitted, many of the delegates would be gone. And of those that remained…

"Mrs. Delvaux?"

She focused on the man standing before her, the higher ranking of the two policemen. He was of average height and appearance, still young in age, but he wore his uniform as if he had grown into it over years of service and knew precisely what the world expected of him.

What he asked now—and how she answered—would determine how much freedom she would have in the coming hours. Freedom Ross had bought for her with his sacrifice, a gift she couldn't afford to waste.

"Mrs. Delvaux?" the man repeated.

"Yes," she whispered.

He touched the brim of his hat. "I am Detective Chief Inspector Abbott. I am sorry for the necessity of this intrusion." He cleared his throat. "I know this is a very difficult time for your family. I had hoped to speak with you before any action was taken, but my men were unable to locate Mr. Maitland."

"He is away."

"Yes. Do you know why we are here?"

Gillian allowed something of her turbulent emotions to show on her face. "You have arrested one of my guests."

"Taken him into custody, ma'am." Abbott frowned in concern. "This must come as quite a shock. Perhaps you ought to sit down, Mrs. Delvaux, and allow me to explain."

"I am…quite all right, Chief Inspector."

His frown deepened, but he took her at her word. Even in these modern times, respect for the peerage had not entirely vanished. And perhaps he was beginning to sense, as most humans eventually did, that she was not an average woman.

In clipped but simple sentences, he told her how the Kendal station had been contacted early that morning by a local landowner, who had provided information about a serious crime committed at Snowfell. Abbott hesitated, still obviously concerned for her sensibilities, and asked if she had been aware that one of her household staff was missing.

Recognizing that she must conform to Abbott's expectations, Gillian pretended to swoon when he informed her of Cora's death. He apologized, took her arm and found his way to the Yellow Drawing Room.

"I must insist that you sit down, ma'am," he said, guiding her to the armchair near the hearth and taking a chair opposite.

"I do apologize for not ringing in advance," he said, "But such a serious matter should not be discussed on the telephone, and we felt it prudent to take the suspect into custody as quickly as possible."

"You…suspect Mr. Keating?"

"We understand his name to be Ross Kavanagh, a man wanted for questioning regarding a murder in the United States."

He went on to ask her about Sir Averil and the circumstances of his death, of which Ethan had evidently informed him. "There is a strong possibility that Kavanagh had a part in it," he said. He asked her about the body, and suggested the necessity for an autopsy. Then, with another apology, he began the interrogation.

In the end he was satisfied that she had not realized the true nature of her guest—whom Sir Averil had invited to Snowfell— or had ever suspected him capable of murder. She knew of no motive Kavanagh might have had to kill either her father or Cora. Yes, she had seen Kavanagh's bloody clothing, but she had thought it was his blood and had believed him when he told her he had been assaulted by parties unknown.

She didn't ask what evidence the police had, or why they had been so quick to trust the unnamed tipster. Abbott seemed to accept her lack of curiosity as another symptom of shock.

"May we call someone to stay with you?" he asked. "I shall leave a constable to assist you, but if you've any kin you'd like us to inform…"

Gillian pressed her palm to her forehead. "Thank you, Chief Inspector, but I have no other close relatives in the county. I know our guests will be of…immeasurable help in this time of…"

Abbott rose. "I will not disturb you further, Mrs. Delvaux. I would ask that none of your guests leave Snowfell for the time being. I will return presently to continue establishing the facts of the case, and my man will begin speaking to your guests later this afternoon."

Gillian nodded, staring into the empty grate. Inspector Abbott touched his hat brim. "Please don't give a thought to Kavanagh, Mrs. Delvaux," he said. "He has apparently deceived many people, but he shan't get away with it again." He paused. "If you recall any information of importance…" He produced a card and set it on the mantelpiece. "Should you require anything at all, simply speak to Constable Blackburn, and he will see that I am informed."

He left the room. Gillian rose, straightened her skirt and followed him into the corridor.

The constable Chief Inspector Abbott had left behind still stood guard at the foot of the staircase. Gillian made short work of getting rid of him by requesting, in a desperate and trembling voice, that he visit the parish church in Kendal and ask that the curate call on her at his convenience. "He has a telephone, but it often seems to be out of order," she whispered apologetically. "If you might… If it isn't too much trouble…"

Constable Blackburn undoubtedly knew that he ought to telephone his superiors before leaving the premises, but either pity or subconscious unease inspired him to disregard his common sense.

"I'll do what I can, ma'am," he assured her. "Please don't venture from the house."

"No. I think I shall go up to my room."

The constable made the appropriate noises and hurried outside. Gillian waited until she could no longer hear him and went directly to the Great Hall. Behind the door, Count von Ruden was speaking to the others who had gathered there in a whisper that to werewolf ears, carried as effectively as a shout.

"Their stupidity in trusting the American has brought these humans to disrupt our crucial work here," he was saying. "It is time to select a new leader, one who will…"

Gillian lost the thread of his speech. The wolf had begun to gnaw at her insides, eating away at her heart.

Toby is in danger, it moaned. *Ross…*

But the familiar voice that answered silenced the wolf with a shattering roar of contempt.

Toby? it mocked. *Kavanagh? How do they matter now?*

Gillian pressed her hands over her ears, but she knew the voice too well. A few days of its absence had not cured her.

Do you see what you have done? Do you see what has become of all my work?

She shook her head and whispered, "I have done all I could…"

You have failed. The Convocation as I planned it, as I alone could create it, is dying. You have failed not only me, but the future of our kind. We will become as extinct as the mammoth or the dire wolf, and our extinction will lie upon your head until the day of your own welcome death.

"The Germans," she said, defying him openly as she had never been able to do while he was alive. "They are like *you.* Let *them* carry out your plan."

The Germans? They would have been useful tools, but we must maintain control. We alone possess the intelligence, the vision, the commitment and loyalty to our own great purpose, and not to any human ideology.…

Gillian heard the rise of Count von Ruden's voice in the Great Hall, followed by Vasily's, furiously arguing.

You have failed, the inner voice raged on. *But there is yet a chance to recover your honor and your name. Stand before them now. Forget every distraction, every weakness. You must live as I have lived. You must become what Hugh could never be. Redeem yourself, daughter. You are my heir.*

Redeem yourself, and save us....

Gillian took a step toward the door, put her hands on its heavy wood surface and imagined Sir Averil standing at her shoulder, smiling as he had so seldom done. Proud of her. Accepting her. Loving her at last.

She turned and raced up to the first floor, taking the stairs two at a time. She ran to one of the bedroom doors and opened it without waiting to knock.

Dominique was standing over a small trunk lying open on her bed, holding a gauzy blouse in her hands as she gazed out the window at the sun rising over the wood. Her bright russet hair was loose, her usually impeccable clothing in disarray. She spun round when Gillian strode in.

"Mrs. Delvaux!" she cried. "Are you well?"

"Yes." Gillian wasted no time getting to the point. "How much do you know?"

"I know that my brother left Snowfell with yours, to find your son. And that Mr. Keating has been taken by the police."

She probably knew much more, but there was no time for discussion. "Where is Yves?"

"He has gone downstairs to observe those who have assembled in the Great Hall, but these police—"

"They are gone for the time being," Gillian said. "Ross has been accused of murder and arrested. I am going to help him. The police will be returning presently to question every delegate who remains at Snowfell."

"Oui," the Frenchwoman said, grim understanding on her normally sunny face. "Some I think have already left."

"Only those willing to risk questioning and exposure will remain. I believe the Germans are insane enough to try to seize control of the Convocation and establish dominance before the others flee." She paused for breath. "If they can lay the ground-work, they will be able to resurrect the Convocation and build it according to the principles of their new political party."

"There will be trouble from these Nazis," Dominique muttered.

But any future beyond the next few moments had no meaning for Gillian. "I am leaving. Advise anyone you trust to leave as well. I would wish to warn Señor Tovar and Mr. Macalister and his wife, at the very least."

Dominique bit her full lower lip and nodded. *"Je comprends."* She took Gillian's hands. "Will you not be held responsible for this by the human authorities?"

"Let them think what they wish. I shall deal with them when I return…if I do."

"Ah. Is there nothing more we may do to help?"

"Marcus is assisting Hugh and my brother. Toby and Ross are my sole concern."

"Then I wish you all the luck."

Gillian squeezed her hands. "Take great care. We shall meet again."

"Au revoir." The Frenchwoman gave Gillian her remarkable smile, turned to the bed and resumed packing her trunk.

Gillian left, shut the door and walked briskly to her own room. After collecting all the money she could find in her pocketbook and the hidden cache behind the armoire, she ran downstairs. She suspected that some of the servants had already left Snowfell. She found the rest—two of the parlor maids; Robert, the footman, a scullery maid; Mrs. Spotterswood; Mrs. Mossop; and Faulder—in the servants' hall, huddled together like sheep awaiting the wolf.

"Listen to me," she said. She briefly explained what had happened in the past several hours, though she knew the servants had their own ways of obtaining vital information.

"The guests can no longer be trusted," she said. "You must go at once to your families or to local inns. Should the police seek you out for questioning, you must not appear to be avoiding them." She laid a sheaf of banknotes on the table. "Take what you need. My brother and I shall see that you are all paid in full when this is over, and that you find acceptable employment, or are settled with a comfortable retirement."

Mrs. Spotterswood was deeply distressed, her eyes wide. "You are discharging us?"

"Not because I wish it. It may be only a temporary measure, but it is safer to assume…" Gillian's eyes began to fill with tears. "You have all served with great loyalty and skill. I shall not forget you."

Faulder stepped forward. "Master Toby? He will be all right?"

"Yes," she said fiercely. "He will be all right. There is one last thing you can do for me, Faulder."

He bowed deeply. "I will always at your service, madam."

She drew him aside and gave her instructions, then firmly shook his hand. She did the same with the lone footman, and kissed the startled maids and Mrs. Mossop on their cheeks. For Spotterswood she reserved a close hug.

"You I shall miss most of all," she said.

"You are not returning to Snowfell," Mrs. Spotterswood said solemnly, her own tears falling thick over her wrinkled cheeks.

"Perhaps someday. And if I do, I shall be sure to find you."

Mrs. Spotterswood sniffled and raised her apron to dab at her eyes. The others, all in good order, distributed the cash amongst themselves. They were on the verge of returning to their various quarters when the footman Peter burst into the room, dragging a terrified Miss Rownthwaite behind him.

"I didn't know!" she was crying. "The viscount only said he wanted to protect the boy!"

"We found her trying to sneak out like a thief, ma'am," Peter said. "She had a right mountain of banknotes in her bag."

A few moments was all it took to pry the story from the governess. She'd been paid by Ethan to help spy on the Maitlands, and to watch Toby and prevent him from communicating with his parents after he'd returned from his late-night foray. And she knew that the viscount wasn't taking the boy south into Lancashire, but north, over the Scottish border.

That meant, Gillian realized in horror, that Hugh and his allies were going in the wrong direction.

After asking Robert and Peter to hold Rownthwaite for the police, Gillian ran upstairs to her room and removed her skirt, replacing it with full trousers and walking boots, and shrugged into a light wool jumper. She selected a change of clothing and a few essentials, then visited Toby's and Ross's room to do the same. She packed everything tightly in a duffel fitted with a special handle designed to be carried in a wolf's jaws, one she hadn't used since her first few explorations she'd ventured after her initial Change. She made certain her hair was firmly secured in place close to her head.

Then there was nothing to do but follow where her heart led her.

The ugly clamor of fighting in the Great Hall had begun as she walked out the front door. Constable Blackburn had not come back, but when he did, he would be safe. The delegates might destroy each other, but they wouldn't dare touch a human constable.

Gillian ran as far as the wood, stripped off her clothing, pushed it into the duffel and Changed. Power and a new sense of purpose galvanized her body. She ran cross-country, the duffel dangling from her jaws, the warmth of the morning sun bathing her coat as the ground rolled away beneath her feet. The house vanished from sight, taking with it all the years of denial and misery and fear.

The scant three miles to the outskirts of Kendal passed by in minutes. She descended into the rolling hills bordering the Kent Valley, following the course of tree-lined becks and skirting the green patchwork of farmers' fields, leaping dry stone walls and carefully tended hedges. Other than a few watchful farm dogs, no one noticed her presence.

When she crossed the last field and the town's outermost dwellings rose up before her, she darted behind a hawthorn hedge and Changed again. She removed a skirt and blouse, smoothing them as best she could, and pulled on stockings and low-heeled pumps.

Kendal was not so large a town that she could not easily find her way to the borough police station, a modest building of Cumbrian red sandstone. She paused, gazing at the station's deceptively peaceful facade, and moved round to the back.

The rear door, however, was locked. She scanned the narrow windows, most barred, and considered simply breaking in. Her werewolf strength was sufficient to the task. But if there were any police in this part of the building, they would be alerted immediately.

She returned to the front door and walked in, the duffel over her shoulder. The constable at the desk looked up from his paperwork and greeted her pleasantly. She saw at once that he didn't recognize her; he was young, and probably only recently employed by the Borough Constabulary.

The right words came to her as if my magic: a false name, a claim of distant kinship to the prisoner, a request her obvious breeding and worried manner—and a touch of subtle werewolf intimidation—made it impossible for the inexperienced policeman to refuse. He confided that he was temporarily the lone constable in the station due to the severity and unusual nature of a local crime, and could not abandon the desk to remain with her, though it was very much against the rules to allow her into the lockup. He warned her to stay well away from the bars and ring the buzzer should she require any assistance whatsoever.

He led her into the rear of the building, unlocked one door and then another, and continued into a narrow corridor lined with barred cells. The sour smells of the human inebriates and other petty offenders did nothing to conceal the scent of the one Gillian sought. When she and the constable reached Ross's cell, he was looking out at them, standing clear of the bars. He wore gaol-issue shirt and trousers, his own clothing confiscated for evidence.

The constable pointed his truncheon at Ross and sneered with disgust. "You have a visitor, Kavanagh. Cause any trouble and you shall face the consequences." After one long, worried look at Gillian, he backed away. She let go her pent-up breath as the door closed at last.

"Ross," she said, her voice cracking.

He continued to stare through the bars. "You shouldn't have come," he said.

Gillian glanced from cell to cell. At least two of the prisoners were sleeping off their drink. But two others were obviously listening, seeking any distraction to relieve their boredom.

She moved closer. Ross had been roughly handled, though his bruises were fading. His eyes were empty. He didn't intend to fight the charges against him.

And why should he? Who had stood by him without question, either here or in America? No one. Had *she* tried to stop the police from arresting him? Hadn't she denied knowing his true identity? Hadn't she hesitated at the door to the Great Hall, listening to the voice in her head, a part of her still treacherously longing for her dead father's approbation?

You have done nothing here but ruin everything you have touched since Toby found you. Ross could not have forgotten those words, nor what followed: *Toby would have been better off if he had never been conceived!*

And he had accepted her condemnation as he would accept a punishment he had never earned.

Gillian bowed her head until she could control the tears. They would solve nothing. The road had become clear, her mind and heart completely unobstructed for the first time since she had learned to Change and accepted her "place" in her father's world.

"You were wrong," she said to Ross in a voice that was hardly more than a sigh. "Hugh was wrong. Only *we* can save Toby, Ross. You and I."

He met her gaze. She imagined she saw a response in his eyes, but it was swiftly gone.

"You know what will happen," he said, matching her muted tone. "If they catch you helping me, you'll be subjected to interrogation, confinement and humiliation."

"I don't fear humiliation. If we prove your innocence..."

He shook his head, denying her hope, denying even the possibility. "If your name means anything to you—"

"It doesn't."

"But the Convocation—"

"The Convocation be damned."

He retreated to sit on the barren cot pushed against the rear wall. "Get out of here before the constable comes back."

Instead of obeying him, she reached out and touched the bars. They were strong, certainly strong enough to foil any human without the proper tools to bend or weaken them.

She turned and walked along the corridor, pausing at the first cell with a conscious inmate. "Listen to me," she said softly. "You are going to forget everything you see and hear during the next few minutes."

The prisoner, who had the lean and hungry look of a sneak thief, grinned around blackened teeth. "Now why should I do that, missus?" he asked.

Gillian leaned into the bars and bared her teeth. "Because, if you do not, I shall hunt you down and kill you."

The man's face underwent a rapid transformation from amazement through mockery and settled at last on startled belief. "What the bloody hell are you?" he whispered.

She didn't answer but continued to the next occupied cell. When she was done, each prisoner had shrunk as far back into his cage as he could go, and nothing but the harsh sound of breathing indicated that anyone but Ross and Gillian shared the cell block.

Gillian returned to Ross, wrapped her fingers around the bars and stared at him until he met her gaze. "Help me," she said.

And he did.

CHAPTER TWENTY-EIGHT

THEY WERE fighting again.

Toby listened at the door, his ear pressed to the wood, though he could scarcely have avoided the noise even if he'd buried his head under his pillow. Lady Warbrick was doing most of the shouting, but it was the softness of Ethan's voice that frightened Toby most.

He'd used that same voice when he'd made Toby write that nasty bit about Father, saying that otherwise he would make sure that Mother suffered terribly when she came looking for him. That was when Toby realized that everything Ethan had ever said to him or Mother was a lie. And Mother had no idea at all.

It had been so very hard to make Father believe that nothing was wrong.

Toby clutched at his stomach, trying to ignore the queasy sensation that had begun a few hours ago, making him feel as if he wanted to crawl right out of his skin. His teeth ached, and his arms and legs felt as if they were attached to somebody else. He leaned more heavily against the door. The voices outside got louder.

"I told you to stay away from him," Ethan was saying.

"I brought him food and water!" Lady Warbrick cried. "You didn't tell your thugs to make sure he was fed."

"And what else did you do, Mother? What else?"

Toby rubbed at the painful spot right above his nose. He didn't know exactly what Ethan thought Lady Warbrick had done, but she had only been kind to him. She had brought him sweets and other things to eat and drink, and she had asked him what he liked to read and if he was good at drawing or sport. Sometimes she didn't talk very clearly, and she always smelled of alcohol. But once when she'd come to his room, she'd sat beside the bed and started talking…not about Ethan, but about herself.

Toby reached inside his trouser pockets, touching the warm piece of metal he'd carried since he'd found it in the grave. PP, the engraving said. He'd thought it might be the name of the poor lady who had died, but now he knew to whom the locket had really belonged.

Phoebe Pickering. That had been Lady Warbrick's name when she was a little girl, before she got married to Viscount Warbrick. She had told Toby about the pony she had ridden when she was his age, and how she sometimes picked wildflowers in the meadow near her house. And she had become very sad when she'd talked about her father, who had sounded even nastier than Sir Averil.

After their last talk, when Toby felt the most like weeping, he had shown her the locket. She had held it in her hand, and tears had rolled over her cheeks, making little rivers through the white powder. She touched a secret catch on the side, and it opened up to reveal a tiny picture of a girl with pretty golden hair, and a boy who looked very much like her.

"Ethan said he lost it," she'd murmured. "I never did believe him." Then she had closed it again, given it back to Toby and wrapped his fingers around it.

"Remember me," she said. "Remember that I wasn't always wicked."

He had promised. But he knew that Ethan hated her, and he wondered if she thought he would hurt her. Lady Warbrick's voice rose higher and higher. He closed his eyes and listened again.

"What you are doing is evil!" she shouted. "As evil as anything I have ever done. You will not harm the boy."

After that, the cottage became very quiet. Toby's heart beat fast, because he knew something was happening. Something very bad. A muffled sort of cry followed, quickly ended.

He took one step backward, and then another, until he was standing straight against the wall. He looked again at the window. It had been boarded up, and his efforts to work the nails loose had failed each time he'd tried. The lock on the door had proved equally unbreakable. So he waited, bucking up his courage, until the doorknob rattled.

The ugly man called Algie poked his head in. "Come on," he said. "We're garn."

"Where?" Toby asked in a small voice.

"Away from 'ere." Algie walked into the room and made a grab for Toby, who bent low, ducked under the outstretched arm and dashed for the open door.

He wasn't sure afterward why he ran toward the main drawing room instead of the door that led to freedom. He knew from the smell what he would find.

Lady Warbrick lay on the floor, her skirt pushed up around her knees and her white blouse red as current berries. There was a second, gaping mouth below her chin, and her eyes were staring up at the ceiling, as if she were looking straight at Heaven.

Toby choked and stumbled away, right into Algie.

"Ya li'l bugger," the thug swore. He dragged Toby toward the back door, muttering all the while about the "barmy guv'nor" and how he'd "made a dog's breakfast o' the whole bleedin' fiddle."

Toby was hardly listening. He knew that Ethan had killed Lady Warbrick. He thought that Ethan had also killed the girl in the grave. He would probably kill anyone else who made him angry enough.

I can't let Mother come here, Toby thought. He stumbled along with Algie, dragging his feet, trying to think. The scent of burning stung his nose. Algie stopped and looked behind him.

The hunting box was on fire, the flames already eating at the wood and casting up great plumes of smoke.

"Get movin'," Algie grunted, nearly jerking Toby off his feet. But the peculiar feeling in Toby's stomach was getting stronger, and he realized that it wasn't really illness at all.

I don't want to. I want to be like Father.

But he had no choice about it now.

He let himself fall back, slowing Algie just enough as he reached into his pocket, pulled out the locket and dropped it to the ground. He scuffled his feet, covering the locket with a layer of old leaves and dirt. When Algie jerked him again, he followed passively, unbuttoning his jacket and shirt as he walked.

It took a great deal of concentration. Toby wasn't sure he could do it. The dodgy feeling made it difficult to focus, but a deeper knowledge was already at work in his body. His belly cramped, and he lost his footing.

Algie swore. "You li'l—"

"I have…I'm going to be…" Toby doubled over and retched, splashing Algie's boots. Algie exclaimed in disgust and hurled Toby away.

Immediately Toby undid the buttons of his trousers and staggered toward a low clump of shrubbery. He had never undressed so fast in his life. He heard the heavy tread of Algie's footsteps and knew he had only one chance to make this work.

"Where're ya, ya blighter?" Algie growled. "Ya come aahhh o' there, or I'll—"

He never finished his threat. Toby leaped out, clearing the shrubbery in one easy jump, and landed forepaws first on Algie's chest. The impact drove the breath from the man's lungs, and he squeaked in terror. Toby permitted himself the indulgence of snarling in the man's face, then bounced aside and began to run.

The glory of the Change, the joyful freedom of it, beat in his blood like a magic potion. He was strong, far stronger than any human; he was fast, so fast that neither Ethan nor his henchmen could ever catch him.

Find them, his wolf's brain insisted. He must find Mother and

Father, and tell them everything he'd learned, so they could call the police and stop Warbrick. But he found himself turning round as he reached the road that would lead him home. He had to make Ethan understand that he would never get away with what he'd done. He would show the viscount what Maitland blood could do.

He caught Ethan's scent only a half mile from the hunting box, its unique tang hovering beneath the stronger smell of scorched wood like a cold current under tropical waters. Toby leaped over a beck, wound his way through an isolated grove of oaks and was suddenly engulfed in the odor of a killer.

But Ethan wasn't there. In his place was a wolf, twice as big as Toby and bearing a gleaming golden pelt just a shade darker than Mother's.

Toby skidded to a stop, his nails clawing at the soft earth.

The wolf Changed before his eyes, shedding fur and rising on two hairless legs. Ethan smiled.

"Hallo, Toby," he said.

Toby tried to escape. He flexed his spine, attempting to run and twist at the same time. His paws tangled, and he fell with a *whoof* of pain.

"You have much to learn, boy," Ethan said, coming to stand over him. "But I doubt you will ever get the chance."

ROSS KNEW they couldn't afford to wait for darkness. He heard the constable returning just as he and Gillian left through the station's back door.

There was no telling if Gillian's attempts at intimidation would work on the other prisoners, but they would have been smart to take her threats seriously. Gillian had become a whirl-wind, carrying Ross with her from once place of concealment to the next as they made for the car Faulder had left at the edge of town. She was all ferocious purpose, just as she'd been when she had confronted him in Snowfell's kitchen.

He hadn't blamed her for what she'd said, not then and not

now. He and Hugh had been idiots for thinking she wouldn't try to rescue Toby herself; she'd turned her back on her father's world and would never regret it.

But she had come for *him,* and he still didn't know why. She couldn't consider him an asset in rescuing Toby. And he had no intention of letting her sacrifice her future, whatever she chose it to be, because she'd helped him escape.

He asked no questions until they reached the Bentley and Gillian took the wheel.

"How long will it take to get to this estate?" he asked, bracing himself in his seat as she sped away from the dry gully where the car had been hidden. "It won't be long before someone notices I'm gone."

Gillian bent over the wheel, her hair flying loose. "Ethan didn't take Toby to Lancashire," she said. She filled him in on what had happened since he'd been taken into custody. She said nothing more about the Convocation or the delegates, only indicating that she had paid off the servants and suggested they leave Snowfell.

"We shall go directly to Highwick," she said. "If Warbrick has left any trail at all, we shall find it there."

"Warbrick was laying a trap," Ross said as Gillian raced over a narrow bridge. "Maybe Rownthwaite was supposed to tell you where he went in case you didn't go with Hugh to meet him."

"Ethan shall get his wish," she said, leaning hard on the gas pedal.

She drove like a madwoman, bumping recklessly over farmers' fields and across creeks until she reached a country road. Within twenty minutes they were pulling into Highwick's gravel drive.

Ross was first out. He expected the place to be deserted, but it wasn't. He found Cruthers in what must have once been a gardener's shed, sitting against the damp wall with his knees drawn up to his chest. He flinched when he saw Ross, and his mournful face grew new lines of fear and grief.

"Where are they?" Ross demanded. "Where did he take Toby?" He grabbed the stained front of the man's shirt and lifted him to his feet. "Answer me!"

Cruthers' red eyes flickered to Gillian, who had come up behind Ross. "To the hunting box," he whispered.

"Where is it?"

The butler's full weight sagged in Ross's grip. "She knew," he said. "She knew she wouldn't come back alive."

"Who?" Gillian asked.

"Should have told someone…"

"Where are they?"

"You mustn't…oh, he must be punished, but not…" He began to weep. "He has suffered, too."

Ross eased the servant to the ground and exchanged a puzzled glance with Gillian, who took his place. "What are you afraid of?" she asked Cruthers with a patience that belied her urgency. "Why are you here?"

The old man covered his eyes. "I was…I was to remain at Highwick and tell you where the viscount had gone if you should determine that Mr. Kavanagh…" He trembled violently. "It is a trap, ma'am."

"We know that," Ross snapped.

"He left a man behind to make certain I obeyed. But Mr. Maitland and two others arrived, and he shot—"

"Who?" Gillian demanded. "Who was shot?"

"The Frenchman. He was still alive when I…last saw him."

"Did you speak to them?"

The butler shook his head.

"Hugh and the others figured it out somehow," Ross said grimly. "They knew that Warbrick was headed north."

"I…couldn't…the child…" Cruthers swallowed convulsively and raised his head, his bleary gaze focusing on Gillian. "The boy is ill. I tried to stop it, but—"

"Toby is ill?" Gillian cried.

"Master Ethan." Cruthers coughed. "Your mother...she wa ill...ill in her mind."

"My mother?" She crouched beside him, her breathing harsh "What are you saying?"

For a moment the old servant was almost lucid. "Lady Warbrick." He reached for Gillian's hands. "She—she neve treated Ethan as a son. She was lonely. She made him do—" Hi eyes were hollow pits, brimming with horror. "I kept the secret I kept all the secrets. No longer. Sir Averil was his father. The viscount..." He clutched her fingers until his own turned blue "Ethan is your brother."

Gillian wrenched her hands away. Her lips moved but made no sound.

"You're crazy, old man," Ross said, ignoring the taste o bile in his mouth. "You're going to shut up and lead us to them right now."

Maybe the geezer would have been willing, but it was soo apparent that he lacked the physical strength to lead them anywhere He head lolled against the wall, and his muscles went slack.

"I will tell you," he said.

As if he had been relieved of an unbearable burden, Cruther spoke in tumbling sentences that made little sense to Ross, bu obviously meant something to Gillian.

"Do you recognize the area?" Ross asked her.

"Yes." She rose. "We shall require your services as a witness Cruthers. Where is the man who shot de Gévaudan?"

"He—he ran away."

"Have you money?" The old man's chin moved fractionally on his chest. "When you are able, find an inn and stay there unti we come for you."

Cruthers closed his eyes without acknowledging her com mand. He might run away, but there wasn't much they could d to prevent it except tie him up. Complicit or not, the butler didn' deserve to be treated like a criminal.

Gillian had reached the same decision. She strode out of the shed. Ross followed, staring at her rigid back.

Ethan is Gillian's brother.

Had the old coot been lying? Hell, he hadn't been in any state to invent a story like that on the fly. But what did it mean? What had he intended by telling her now?

If such speculation troubled Gillian, she refused to let it affect her. She had left the engine running and barely waited for Ross to climb into the passenger's side. She spoke only to tell him that the hunting box was over the Scottish border, in an area as yet largely unserved by the network of paved roads gradually being built across Britain. The distance was a little over ninety miles, and the last part of the journey would have to be taken on foot.

They crossed the border three hours later. A steady drizzle had begun to fall, stuttering across the roof of the car. Gillian pulled up at a crossroads and turned west onto a rutted dirt track. The landscape wasn't much different from what they'd passed through all along: rolling hills populated by sheep, dry stone walls, and isolated farms tucked into narrow valleys or perched on the slopes of low fells. Ross could feel how close they were to their destination even before he began to smell the smoke.

Gillian pressed her foot on the accelerator, her profile grim above the wheel. Ross reached inside the jacket she had provided, searching for his revolver.

Of course it wasn't there. He was going into this fight knowing that Gillian was, by her very nature, far better equipped than he was. But he had to know exactly what they would be facing.

"Can Warbrick Change?" he asked. "If he's your brother, he could be like you."

Gillian's knuckles went white. "I never saw him do it," she said. "I never saw anything to suggest..."

And why would she? Cruthers had spoken of secrets. If Warbrick had known of their true relationship, he hadn't seen any percentage in telling her. Sister or not, he wanted her. The

English countryside wasn't exactly crawling with werewolves, and questions of his parentage would inevitably arise if he revealed such an ability.

But maybe he *didn't* know. Gillian had told Ross how much Sir Averil despised Ethan, just as he despised all humans. Had the old tyrant actually betrayed his own principles with Lady Warbrick? That would explain why he'd always treated Gillian with such scorn. But how had brother and sister come to be living in two separate households, each growing up in ignorance, each knowing only one parent?

Whatever the answers, only one of them mattered now. If Ethan could Change, he would be stronger than Ross and at least Gillian's equal. Also, he might have others with him, like the thugs who'd waylaid Ross by the grave and the one who'd shot de Gévaudan.

And he had Toby.

The stench of burning grew stronger, and Ross saw a haze of lingering smoke beyond the hills ahead. Gillian rounded the next corner so fast that the car tilted on its wheels. The road came to an abrupt end. She shut off the engine, opened the door, and ran to the broken gate that stood between the road and a narrow track that curved around the next hillside.

Ross removed his jacket, threw it in the back of the Bentley, and joined her at the gate. He examined the path, searching for clues he didn't expect to find. Some previous downpour had erased any footprints, human or otherwise, but this had to be the right place.

Gillian pulled off her sweater and flung it over the gate, kicked off her boots and began working at the buttons of her rain-soaked blouse. Ross swung the gate open on its rusted hinge and ran ahead. She caught up with him in less than a minute, golden and beautiful and deadly. One glance at his face through slanted, green-gold eyes, and she was skimming over the muddy ground at a pace his human legs couldn't match. He lowered his head and imagined his body as a machine, immune to discomfort and driven by a single purpose.

The lodge was in ruins. The walls had collapsed, the jagged black teeth of the building's foundations enclosing the smoldering remnants of its interior. The trees nearest the building were partially scorched, their branches pointing accusing fingers at the source of their destruction.

Gillian had stopped, her tail held stiffly behind her, her head swinging from side to side as she sifted the air. Ross bent to catch his breath. His nostrils stung and clogged with the acrid odors. It would be almost impossible to separate the smell of burned flesh from the rest. He closed his eyes.

Let him be safe. Dear God, let him be safe.

A cool, moist nose nudged his hand. He raised his head. Gillian was moving east, away from the lodge. The drizzle gave way to a more aggressive rain, but not before Ross caught a glimpse of what Gillian had found.

Footprints: large and small, human and wolf.

Gillian broke into a lope, her muzzle close to the earth. Ross ran parallel to her, careful not to obscure the tracks. He splashed through a creek, caught his shoe on a submerged branch, and paused just long enough to remove both shoes and socks. His bare feet squelched in the mud, but his toes found purchase, and he hurled himself up the hill that stood between him and Gillian.

Suddenly his nose cleared. He forced his body into a final push, crested the hill and lurched down the slope. He dug his fingers into the rough grass to slow his descent, stunned by the tableau at the bottom of the hill.

Ethan and Toby were standing in the shelter of an ancient, twisted oak, naked and drenched. Gillian had Changed, her golden hair streaming water, droplets gleaming on her shoulders and hips. Her gaze was fixed on the hunting knife Ethan held against Toby's throat.

"I knew you'd come," Ethan said in a mild voice that should

have belonged to another man. "Though I had hoped it would be under different circumstances."

"Let him go, Ethan," Gillian said softly. "I know you don't want to hurt him."

The viscount cocked his head, his gaze sweeping over Gillian in a way that made Ross more than willing to kill. "You were supposed to give up long ago," he said. "You should have realized that I was the only one you could rely on."

"I *do* rely on you," Gillian said. "I have al—"

"When Hugh didn't bring you to the rendezvous, I knew something had gone wrong. I would not have thought it possible to overestimate our dear little brother's gullibility." He glanced in the direction of the lodge. "That part wasn't planned, you know. Mother made a such a bother of herself. I thought I'd have more time to prepare, to make everything ready for you."

"I'm here now," Gillian said. "Why don't you release him?"

"You do resemble her," Ethan said dreamily. "I never realized how much."

Ross inched his way down the hill, watching Ethan's face. He'd expected to see triumph, satisfaction, lust. But there was more there he couldn't define: confusion, despair, grief. And maybe just enough distraction to give Ross a very small chance to take him down.

"Who?" Gillian asked, sliding one foot closer to Ethan. "Who do I resemble?"

He sighed. "I grow weary of this game, Gillian. When did you learn the truth?"

"How can you think that I…? If I had ever guessed…"

"They had a bargain, the two of them. He chose you, and she chose me. It would have been better if she'd smothered us both in our cradle." His hand slackened on the knife. "We could have had everything, Gillian, you and I. If it hadn't been for *him*. Dear old Father."

He looked directly at Ross, ending any hope of an unex-

ected attack. "Stay where you are!" he said. He took a firmer
rip on the knife, and Toby winced. His thin body shivered, but
is jaw was clenched in defiance.

"I tried, Mother," he said, his voice much deeper than it had
ver been before. "I tried."

"Let him go!" Ross shouted.

But Ethan had already dismissed him as of no importance. He
miled gently at Gillian.

"It's too late," he said. "Much too late."

Gillian leaned toward him, the muscles at the slope of her
ack and buttocks tense with the emotions she didn't dare reveal.
No," she said. "It's not too late. I always sensed there must be
reason why we were so close, why I trusted you from the mo-
ent we met. It's why I know you would never harm your own
ephew."

"My nephew. My flesh and blood." He moved his free hand
wkwardly to stroke Toby's hair. "He could have been part of it,
o. But you chose a human over him. Over me."

A hard education had given Gillian the skill to make herself
ppear as meek and submissive as a frightened child. "Kavan-
h...I was wrong about him, Ethan. He could never be like
...like you and me." She hesitated, and Ross knew she was
thering any and all arguments she hoped might sway Warbrick.
le used us to escape the authorities in New York. He ran away
om a legitimate challenge because he was afraid. He returned
Snowfell covered in blood, and Cora..."

"He's lying!" Toby shouted. "Ethan killed her!"

Ross yelled in horror, "I did it, Toby! It was me!"

Warbrick shook his head. "Your lies accomplish nothing," he
id. "Do you expect me to think that you still suspect him,
en his presence here is living proof that you believe in his
nocence?"

"I didn't know he was following me," Gillian said. "The last
aw of him, the police had taken him into custody for murder."

"How clever of him to escape gaol so quickly," Ethan said. "And to evade your notice, human that he is."

Ross felt very close to being sick. *If I'd stayed out of sight and smell, if I'd let him believe she didn't know I was here....*

But even Gillian hadn't considered that possibility. She hadn't been thinking clearly. *He* should have been thinking for both of them.

Once again he'd failed her.

Almost casually, Ethan pressed the knife into Toby's throat. A minuscule drop of red beaded on the boy's fair skin. Gillian made an agonized sound, and Ross almost lost the rigid discipline that held him where he stood.

"I am curious, dear Gillian," Warbrick said. "When did you realize that I had killed Cora?"

"What reason would I have to think such a thing? What possible purpose could you have?"

"You would not be here if you hadn't thought Toby was in some danger from me, would you?"

The muscles in Gillian's shoulders twitched. "I am here to make peace with you, Ethan. Toby and I will go with you whenever you wish."

"Even though I killed our father?"

She understood how pointless it had become to deny Warbrick's guilt. "Did you think I would mourn for him?" she asked. "Did think I would not be grateful to be set free at last?"

"From our loving pater, to whom you were so unquestioningly loyal?"

"He was an evil man, and I was a fool to obey him."

"Were you?" Ethan dropped his hand from Toby's hair. "You had everything, you and your brother. I had nothing but..." He sucked air through his teeth. "Oh, the great hypocritical Maitlands. Believing in their own superiority, their purity. But you weren't pure. Sir Averil knew it. He lied to his own people." Warbrick bent his face close to Toby's. "This little mongrel night never have been able to Change at all, just like his father. What would you have done then?"

"It wouldn't have made any difference!" Toby exclaimed.

Ethan jerked his chin toward Ross. "Do you imagine *he* ever cared for you, child? Do you think he wouldn't cast you aside if he could have your mother in exchange?"

Tears mingled with the rain on Toby's cheek. "You're nothing but a bloody liar!"

Ross skidded the rest of the way down the slope, desperately afraid that Warbrick would simply lose patience with his hostage. But the viscount seemed almost bored.

"I told you not to move," he said.

"You don't want the boy," Ross said. "You want revenge." He held his hands open in front of him. "Gillian doesn't want anything to do with me. She isn't about to expose you. You've set it up so that everyone is going to believe that I killed Cora and Sir Averil, and it will be only a short step for them to add the murders of those girls in New York. The only thing you need is a confession."

Ethan looked not at him, but at Gillian. "Would you let him confess?" he asked. "Would you hold your silence, knowing what I've done?"

"Yes."

"No, Mother!" Toby yelled. "He'll kill you, too, just like he killed Lady Warbrick!"

Gillian lunged. Ethan stumbled backward, thumped into the oak's scarred trunk and nearly lost his grip on Toby. But the hideous strength of insanity gave him an almost supernatural speed. He swung Toby around, slammed him into the trunk and positioned the knife so that the point rested against the soft flesh just beneath the angle of Toby's jaw. Gillian retreated, trembling.

"Foolish, my dear," Warbrick said, "Very foolish." He turned to Ross. "No confessions, Kavanagh," he said. "They'll have you

anyway. They're out for blood." He laughed at a high, hysteri
cal pitch. "No doubt you thought you had a secure place among
them, those humans you served with such devotion. But the
betrayed you. We have that in common. Those who should have
trusted us, loved us…" He stopped himself. "The police neve
would have learned anything useful about that showgirl—Bonit
wasn't that her name?—if you hadn't walked into the apartmer
after I left and provided them with a ready suspect. I held no i
will for you then, of course. You were merely a convenient pats
But the second girl…think how much suffering might have bee
avoided had they caught you."

"You still would have killed my grandfather," Toby said, pa
thinning his voice.

Ross glanced at Toby, trying to make the boy understand th
his outbursts weren't helping the situation. He had to kee
Warbrick talking.

"Why *did* you kill Bonita?" Ross asked. "A lovers' quarrel"

"Ah." Warbrick tilted his head back and closed his eyes. "
would not expect you to understand." He shuddered, and Ro
saw with disgust that the viscount's cock had grown hard. "Ha
you killed, Kavanagh?"

The memories were not pleasant, but Ross had learned to fa
them. "Yes," he said. "In the line of duty."

"And you did not enjoy it?"

"That wasn't part of the job."

Ethan dropped his head, but his eyes were still shut in an e
pression close to ecstasy. "A pity."

"The first one was an accident, wasn't it?"

The depraved smile left Warbrick's face. "It was no accider
I—"

"I don't mean Bonita. I mean the girl in the grave by t
Roman wall."

Toby gave a half-stifled gasp. Warbrick started.

"You didn't realize that Toby had taken an interest in t

uins where you buried her. He found what you tried to hide. I'd
ust finished covering the corpse back up when your goons came
or me, but they never noticed."

Warbrick looked genuinely shaken. "A naive country girl.
No one ever missed her."

"I had an idea that she'd died the same way as the women in
New York, but I didn't have any proof. Now it all makes sense.
You were only getting started, weren't you?"

"She made a grave error in judgment."

"By turning down your gracious offer to make love to her?
Like Bonita Bailey? Did Cora turn you down, too?"

"Cora? She was a convenient tool, no more."

"And she wasn't like the others. Her hair was dark, not gold.
She didn't look like your mother or Gillian. She wasn't right, was
she?"

Wabrick's gaze grew unfocused again. "Mother used to be
so beautiful," he murmured. "But she wasn't nice to me. Not nice
at all."

"What did she do to you, Ethan? She hurt you very badly,
didn't she?"

Tears leaked from the corners of Warbrick's eyes. "I don't
want to, Mummy. I want to sleep in *my* room. Can't I—"

Whatever he might have said was lost in the deafening boom
of thunder. Warbrick shook himself out of his dream world, scattering water from his hair.

"No more talk," he said. "One more word, Kavanagh, and the
boy is dead." He looked into Gillian's eyes, and Ross could only
imagine what horrors she saw in them. "Your pride has betrayed
you, Gillian. I am your brother. Your punishment is mine to de-
liver."

Gillian's voice was raw, the croak of a woman who had almost
forgotten how to use a human tongue. "Give me another chance,
Ethan. I can make you happy. We can live as we were meant to
live."

"Not now," Warbrick said. "Not ever." He gestured toward t[
ground between them. "You have learned to embrace the bea[
Now you must begin to behave like one. Down. Down on yo[
knees."

She dropped into the mud. Ross's pulse boomed beneath t[
skin of his temples. He wasn't quick or strong enough to sa[
her, to save Toby.

Warbrick's purpose wasn't just to humiliate Gillian. F[
wanted Ross to watch while Gillian bowed at his feet for the sa[
of her son. *Their* son.

Ross turned his back on all of them and started up the hill

CHAPTER TWENTY-NINE

KAVANAGH!"

Gone was the unnatural calm with which Ethan had ordered Gillian to her knees. She heard Ross moving away, and a dozen thoughts tumbled over themselves in her mind.

He wasn't abandoning them. That was as far beyond Ross's nature as mercy was beyond Ethan's. Ross knew she would do anything in the world to save Toby, anything that Ethan demanded of her.

But Ross would never accept her surrender. He was drawing Ethan's rage to himself, permitting Warbrick to assume—as, in his madness, he surely would—that Ross had chosen his own survival over hers and Toby's. For the span of a few seconds, Ethan would be distracted.

Before her human self fully grasped the implications, the wolf was moving. She sprang up, her feet slipping in the mud, and lunged at Ethan.

He was too fast. She pushed him off balance, but his hand was still on the knife, and he kept his grip on Toby's arm. Toby struggled valiantly, but his efforts were doomed from the start.

Gillian howled. She twisted on her feet, ready to throw herself at the knife before Ethan could use it against Toby.

That was when the other wolf leaped from behind the oak and sank its teeth into Ethan's leg.

But Ethan was beyond pain. As the wolf turned and Gillian began a fresh attack, Ethan reversed the knife and struck Toby's

temple with the handle. Toby fell and lay still. Gillian took Eth
down with her. She Changed and opened her jaws, ready to te
out Ethan's throat.

The memories that came to her then were no more than flic
ering images, mere glimpses of lost childhood friendship. B
the instant of hesitation was enough. Ethan Changed beneath h
his writhing body impossible to grip. Then he was somehow
top of her.

She clawed frantically at Ethan's chest, scraping at pa
heavy fur. She thought she saw Hugh, nakedly human, draggi
Toby's limp body away. She tore at any part of Ethan she cou
reach, mad with hatred, but he outweighed her by at least eig
stone. His jaws worked into her ruff, seeking flesh, stopping h
breath.

And then, without sense or warning, he Changed and let h
go. She clambered to her feet, dazed and shaking, but Ethan h
vanished. At the foot of the hill behind her, Ross, wielding a thi
branch like a club, was fighting a wolf with fur dark as a moo
less night.

The wolf was Count von Ruden. And there were other wolv
with him, some paired off for battle, the rest watching from
sidelines like a jury of peers waiting to render a verdict.

Gillian had no time to wonder how they had found her a
Ross, or what they intended. She made the only choice she cou
the one Ross would have wanted her to make. She ran in the
rection she'd seen Hugh take Toby.

Hugh was crouching over his nephew, his hand on Toby
forehead. He looked up as Gillian appeared.

"He's all right," Hugh said. "He's already waking up."

She saw that Toby was breathing steadily and crouched
touch his cheek. "Thank God you found us."

"Forster and Yves are here, as well, and Thierry is on his wa
He pressed her shoulder. "Warbrick's gone, run away like
coward he is. Help Ross."

Without hesitation she raced back to the foot of the hill. Ross was holding his own, though his legs were bloodied with the numerous lacerations of teeth and claws. He wielded the branch with expertise, but von Ruden eluded his swings.

Gillian charged. Ross turned his head just long enough to meet her gaze, and the wolf within her understood.

He must do this alone. He would never regain any self-respect if he accepted her aid now. Either he would win—or he would die. It was as simple and as terrible as that.

And though she understood, her heart wailed in agony as Ross fell, the branch knocked from his hand, and was buried beneath von Ruden's heavy body.

Time ground to a halt. Von Ruden lowered his head, poised to kill. Ross seemed to surrender, welcoming his fate. And then he bucked, and his bunched fist slammed into von Ruden's muzzle. In a remarkable, entirely inhuman motion he threw von Ruden off, bent at the waist and flipped backward, landing on his feet. Von Ruden staggered, blood dripping from his mouth. Ross snatched up the fallen branch again.

The air exploded with sound—not thunder, but the unmistakable report of a gun. The bullet struck Ross in the shoulder. He stumbled. Gillian heard the source of the shot and dashed for the oak.

Ethan held the gun in his right hand, taking aim for a second shot. He never completed the movement. A furious blur of motion in the form of a half-grown wolf clamped sharp white teeth around his injured leg and pulled.

Toby couldn't maintain his grip for long, but his effort at distraction worked. As he dodged Ethan's striking foot, Gillian rushed the viscount. Ethan brought his weapon to bear for the third time, but the muzzle wavered wildly between her and something—someone—behind her.

Everything happened at once. Hugh the wolf dragged Toby out of the line of fire by the scruff of his bristling neck. Ethan swung his gun at Gillian as she rushed headlong to attack. And Ross, bleeding profusely from the wounds in his shoulder and legs, surged past her and tackled Ethan with a roar of rage.

The gun flew away. A naked, dark-haired man—Marcus Forster—snatched it up, Tovar close behind him. Ross used his fists on Ethan with great effectiveness. He only stopped when Gillian pulled him off, avoiding his wound. His breathing was harsh with pain, and his punishment of Ethan had worsened his bleeding, but he stood upright and met her gaze.

"The bullet…" she said, panting.

"It passed through. I'll heal."

She knew he was right, but the knowledge brought no comfort. In that small, deceptive bubble of calm, she took in the state of the world around them. Hugh was with Toby, who had Changed again. Forster and Tovar stood guard over a prostrate Ethan. Several of the delegates were fighting; she recognized Conrad struggling with Vasily, while Dominique, who had not followed her advice to leave the Convocation, lithely dodged Károly's erratic attacks. Hasty alliances had been formed, only to shatter again, their original purpose lost in animal violence.

How she hated them. How she hated herself.

Ross extended his bruised hand toward Gillian, then lowered it again. He would not touch her, but she longed for his touch. She wanted his arms around her, comforting, accepting. She wished she could thank him for his courage, his faith in her, his refusal to give in to despair.

Instead, she went to Toby and engulfed him in her embrace. His thin arms—not so thin now as she remembered—wrapped around her waist.

"You were so brave, Mother," he said in that unfamiliar, husky voice.

"So were you."

Toby looked over her shoulder anxiously. "Has Ethan been captured?"

"Yes, thanks to you."

His Adam's apple bobbed. "He really did kill Lady Warbrick. And he killed the lady in the ruins."

"Yes."

"I have to tell Father I didn't want to write those horrid things about him and Grandfather and Cora."

"He already knows that Warbrick forced you to do it," she said, "but you can tell him later. There are more important things I must attend to now."

She walked past Ross and faced the delegates. The mêlée had consumed all but a few in a frenzy of savagery. Dominique had broken free of Károly, limping as Yves chivvied her away from the tumult, but her opponent lost no time in attacking Sigurd. The other Norwegian was locked jaw-to-jaw with another of the Hungarians. Count von Ruden had disappeared, leaving Conrad to face Vasily and his comrades alone.

Gillian retraced her steps to stand before Marcus. She extended her hand for the gun he had been holding gingerly between two fingers, strode clear of the ancient oak and pointed the gun at the heavy gray sky.

The weapon's report brought an instant response. The frenzy came to a stop, the antagonists leaping apart almost as violently as they had come together. Most immediately Changed, healing whatever wounds they had taken in their battles. They glared at each other and at Gillian, and she knew there would be no escaping the madness if she did not take absolute charge of the situation.

Yet she hesitated, accepting in her soul what had only been theory until this moment. She had deliberately left the delegates to gather the scraps of the idea Sir Averil had bequeathed to them and reassemble those pieces however they chose, but they had failed to find a leader or make any peace amongst themselves. Whatever instinct or compulsion had brought them to this place in the borders of Scotland, Sir Averil's dream had been torn apart by the very men he had considered most worthy and capable of carrying out his scheme.

And yet now they, the finest and purest specimens of their kind, were waiting for *her* to speak. In the eyes of a few—one of the Russians, Señor Tovar, the youngest Hungarian, whose name she had never been able to pronounce, Dominique and her cousin; and, not too much to her surprise, Benedikt von Ruden—she saw the tiniest chance of salvation.

Salvation not of her father's ambitions, but of something much finer. Once she had asked Ross if he would want someone like von Ruden to set the course for the future of the werewolf kind. Gillian doubted that was possible now. But who *would* set that course? Could the right leader offer a new way, a new philosophy, that would include those like Ross, like Toby…like her? And like Ethan, who might never have been lost to madness if he had only found somewhere to belong?

Any new leader would have to be strong, confident, utterly sure of his abilities and purpose.

Someone who could bring together *loups-garous* of a dozen or more different nations and convince them that there was a greater truth than purity or mere survival.

She spun on her toes, returned to the Oak and gave the gun to Marcus, who took it with a sympathetic nod. She marched back to the gathering and found herself meeting Benedikt's gaze. The young man had turned against the vicious, ruinous path of his kin, but he needed guidance. And he was looking straight at her.

No, she thought. *Not me.*

Dominique broke from the crowd as if she meant to speak, but she waited for Gillian, her posture that of some ancient Celtic warrior ready to go into battle at her chieftain's command.

No! I've chosen my path.

And what was that? To defend Ross against his accusers and make certain that his name was cleared, in both England and

America. To support Hugh as he assumed his new position as Sir Hugh Maitland of Snowfell. To create a new life and new meaning for herself and Toby.

And when Ross is free?

She felt his presence at her back, smelled the blood and perspiration and beloved masculine scent that was uniquely his. He, too, was waiting, and she was afraid to turn and see his face.

Again and again he had offered to take her and Toby to a place where they would be safe. The last time she had agreed. But so much had changed since their lovemaking in the cave by the beck. He had suffered the shock of being attacked and labeled a murderer all over again, not only by the police, but also by Hugh's suspicion and her own brief but damning hesitation in believing his claims of innocence.

She had doubted, but that was not the worst of it. She had blamed him for everything that had gone wrong since his arrival in England and even before, afraid to acknowledge her own part in the suffering Sir Averil had created.

Ross hadn't even denied her accusations. With his silent acquiescence he had helped her resurrect the barrier she had begun to build on the day she'd left him in London, raising it stone by stone over all the years of blind obedience to Sir Averil, cementing each block in place with her need for her father's love. And she had never truly let it fall.

"Madame Delvaux."

Gillian heard Dominique's clear voice and roused herself to face the present again. Thierry de Gévaudan had arrived, dragging behind him a pair of dazed and bedraggled humans. He tossed them to the ground at Gillian's feet.

"Two of Warbrick's henchmen," he said, panting, but wearing a very satisfied smile. "I regret the delay, but this one—" he aimed a light kick at the bigger of the two men "—was at Highwick when we arrived and shot at us. I was a little indisposed for a short time before I was able to hunt him down and locate his comrades. The third is unlikely to leave the place where I found him." He kicked at the second man for good measure. "They confessed everything, including their part in attacking Ross and witnessing Warbrick's murder of his mother." He looked keenly into Gillian's eyes. "Warbrick meant to kill you and Toby, as well. Shall we hold them for the police, or have you another form of justice in mind?"

She closed her eyes. Even de Gévaudan, so courteous and civilized, was prepared to kill these men for their part in Warbrick's crimes. That was how closely all of them, even those who bore no grudge against humans, walked to the edge of savagery.

But someone else walked behind her, a man who would not abandon her even when she had left him with no legacy but grief.

When she opened her eyes the fear was gone. She raised her hands high.

"The time for violence is over," she said, staring first at Conrad and then at Vasily. "You may behave as you choose in your own countries, but this is my land. This is England. Here you will be civilized. And if you remain, if you choose to return to Snowfell, there will be new conditions and new laws. We will adapt to this world we live in, and we shall do it peacefully and without hatred or prejudice." She turned and held out her hand to Ross. "No one shall be judged by the purity of their blood. Not ever again."

ROSS LISTENED, as mesmerized as the others by the power in Gillian's bearing and simple words. She had stood up to them before, after Sir Averil's death, kept them negotiating instead of fighting, gathered them in with her unexpected and unwilling ability to lead. He had thought her changed then, but this…

This was different. *This* was the Gillian who always should have been, a woman complete, a natural leader, a voice of reason to counter Sir Averil's appeal to the darkest instincts of the werewolf kind.

Even as he took her hand, Ross felt the brief glow of victory slip out of his grasp. After Toby and Gillian had taken Warbrick down, he'd hardly noticed the pain in his shoulder where the bullet had passed through; all he'd been able to think was that the ones he loved were safe.

He'd looked down at Ethan, who hadn't moved from where he'd fallen. The man's stare was blank, almost senseless. Blood was drying around his mouth and nose. Yet the thrashing Ross had given the bastard hadn't satisfied him; he wanted to see Warbrick hang. That alone was reason enough to keep fighting to prove his own innocence. And when he'd seen the pride in Toby's face, knowing how brave the boy had been—seen, too, Hugh's calm and steadfast bearing—he'd begun to believe that everything might come out all right in the end.

Yet now, with Gillian's hand in his, he was aware of a growing detachment within himself, the deliberate shift within his heart as it prepared to let go.

She was speaking to the delegates in clear, firm sentences, explaining what had happened since Sir Averil's death and Hugh's discovery of Cora's body. She left out any reference to the initial suspicion that the Germans had caused her father's death. She gave a brief description of her acquaintance with Warbrick, relating how he had attempted to frame Ross for the murders while intending to lure Gillian into his trap by using Toby as bait. He had murdered his own mother, and it was very probable that he had killed two other women in America, as well as an unknown victim buried near Snowfell.

"But why?" the youngest Hungarian asked. "Why did this human murder these women? Why did he wish to harm you and your son?"

"Isn't it obvious?" Vasily said loudly. "He was infatuated with Maitland's daughter, and she encouraged him—until Kavanagh appeared to take his place in her favor."

"Warbrick and I were friends, yes," Gillian admitted without a trace of apology "But I never truly knew him. He is half-werewolf. Like me."

"How can this be?" Señor Tovar asked.

"Warbrick is Sir Averil's son," she said. "And my twin brother."

Speaking over the astonished burst of exclamations and protests, she told them how Warbrick had been raised by their human mother, while she had gone to live with Sir Averil. "My father refused to acknowledge him," she said. "Both of us were ignorant of our true relationship until recently. I myself knew nothing of it until today."

"Sir Averil mated with a human?" Vasily asked, pushing forward. "No wonder you desire an end to what you call prejudice! *You* are not pure! You—"

Ross let go of Gillian's hand. "Shut up."

Amazingly enough, everyone did. "It seems to me," Ross said, "that Sir Averil was wrong about everything. Toby can change, human blood or not. And if he could be such a hypocrite, Mrs. Delvaux is right. There's no percentage in doing a single damned thing he said."

"My father deceived us all," Gillian said calmly.

Arguments broke out among the delegates as they reacted to her confession. Finally the Spaniard stood forward.

"Was the Russian correct?" he asked. "Did Warbrick attempt to implicate Kavanagh out of jealousy?"

"Yes." She raised her chin. "He knew that Mr. Kavanagh is the father of my son."

Ross accepted that any denial on his part would be useless. Gillian had made a courageous decision, standing by the principles she'd so staunchly announced.

She'd played the right hand. The racket gradually subsided. No one had taken so much as a step in Gillian's direction. No one asked her why Sir Averil had chosen her over Warbrick, how she had met the American, or why he had really been at Snowfell.

Conrad, who hadn't said a word since Gillian had fired the

gun, was the first to speak again. "You never intended to hold to our bargain," he said, his anger muted by his isolation. "For that I am grateful."

"You're wrong, Herr von Ruden. I was fully committed to our agreement until I came to my senses."

Conrad went red in the face. "Your kind cannot win," he said. "Ours will be the victory. Look to the East, Frau Delvaux. You will see us again."

He marched up to Benedikt, spat at his feet and Changed. He raced up the hill in a flurry of fur and outrage, his threats carried away by the rain-freshened wind. After a moment's pause, Vasily addressed his compatriots in his own language, and the three of them began to follow Conrad. Only one looked back, genuine regret on his face.

It was if the air itself had lightened with their absence. Those delegates who remained, including the Hungarians, gathered closer to Gillian. Hugh and Toby, who had listened quietly in the background, came to join her, as well. Ross felt their anticipation like the sudden warmth of the sun breaking through the clouds overhead.

No one noticed him as he retreated to stand watch with Marcus Forster.

"What now?" Dominique asked. "What of Warbrick and these *minables*?"

Gillian looked down at the viscount's hatchet men, who'd had the sense to lie absolutely still. "I believe these men will find it advisable to repeat their confessions to the authorities. Warbrick has also made a confession before witnesses. They must all be surrendered to the police."

"Humans?" János asked.

"We are not above the law. I assisted Mr. Kavanagh in escaping gaol, and I shall deal with the consequences of my decision. I am fully confident that his innocence will be proven beyond all doubt."

"And if Warbrick should reveal his true nature?"

"Then he will be no more than a legend, a myth, a freak. Common men seldom seek rational explanations for what they don't understand."

János nodded brusquely. But Ross knew Gillian wasn't finished.

"In light of what will soon occur," she said, "I suggest that you all leave this place at once. The smoke and gunshots will have attracted attention, and you will be subject to questioning by the police should you stay."

"We do not fear such questioning," Tovar said, "and we will not leave you to face the authorities alone."

"*Gracias, señor,*" she said, momentarily losing her voice. She recovered quickly. "Once matters are settled, you are all welcome to return to Snowfell as long as you are prepared to pursue a new and civilized doctrine for our people. You will be free to choose your own leader without interference."

"And if we choose you?" de Gévaudan asked.

The others murmured agreement. Gillian didn't answer, but Ross could see that she was deeply moved by their faith.

And how could she refuse? How could she deny the birthright that shone from her like a beacon of sanity and compassion? How could she not lead her fellow werewolves to this new world of hope she had proposed as an alternative to a legacy of hate?

"I would second this proposal," the young Hungarian said. "We see, from your own example, that human blood does not confer weakness, but strength."

Ross hardly heard the rest of the conversation. He retreated into that remote, increasingly familiar place where emotions had no power to lift him into the sky or tear the ground out from beneath his feet. He was so far away that he responded too late when Forster's shout finally penetrated his consciousness and he spun to face the commotion.

Marcus was just rising to his feet, his normally mild expression contorted with anger. Hugh was crouching several yards away, and in between them stood Warbrick, with the gun in his hand.

He smiled at Ross. "Well, Kavanagh," he said. "You haven't won after all."

"Maybe not," Ross said, moving as close to the viscount as he dared, "but you're finished either way, Warbrick."

"And you'll finish with me. I shall not miss a second time." He aimed the gun. Ross heard a disturbance behind him: Gillian and de Gévaudan and a number of the others, all ready to bring Warbrick down.

"I see that you have gained allies," Warbrick said mockingly. "I trust you realize that it was Gillian who won them for you."

"I realize it," Ross said. He moved closer still, so near that only Warbrick could hear his next words. "Go ahead," he said. "You'd be doing me a favor."

He should have known it wouldn't be so simple. Toby appeared out of nowhere, as he was so good at doing. He glared at Warbrick with fearless defiance.

"I have the locket," he announced. "The one your mother gave you. You left it in that poor lady's grave." He frowned. "Why did you kill that lady? Why did you hate your mother so much?"

Warbrick could easily have shot Toby before Ross or Gillian or anyone could stop him. But he moaned deep in his chest, and tears glazed his eyes.

"Mother," he whispered. "I'm sorry."

He thrust the muzzle of the gun into his mouth and pulled the trigger.

CHAPTER THIRTY

THE CHAOS Ethan had left in the wake of his death required every ounce of Gillian's attention. Emotions she might have permitted herself to feel at another time became burdens to be quickly shed; she knew she'd never understand why her father had taken a human lover and chosen her over Ethan, or why he had been willing to raise a half-human child and pass her off as pureblood. Nor could she fully confront her guilt for failing to recognize Ethan's obsession and finding a way to stop his descent into murder.

Nevertheless, easing Toby's guilt over triggering Ethan's ugly suicide was of far greater concern, as was organizing a hunt for Warbrick's missing henchman, who had turned out not to be dead after all, and considering how best to approach the police.

The mood at Snowfell was both grim and expectant; none of the delegates who had supported her chose to leave, even in the face of the interrogations to which Chief Inspector Abbott subjected them. And though Gillian had prepared herself for obstacles in presenting the convoluted evidence for Ethan's guilt and Ross's innocence, her testimony, along with Toby's, Cruthers' and that of Warbrick's men—and Ethan's witnessed confession, most of all—quickly laid the groundwork for Ross's provisional release. The authorities would communicate with their American counterparts, but Hugh promised to use his inheritance to hire the best barristers and solicitors for his defense.

As for Gillian's own part in breaking the law, the police

proved unwilling to press charges. In fact, they were most co-operative, especially when she looked them in the eye and smiled ever so gently, revealing the slightest glint of her teeth.

Only when the preliminaries were completed, Snowfell had settled, and both Sir Averil and Cora had been given quiet burials, did she begin to feel anything again.

It was strange, she reflected, how little the years of suppressing her emotions had lessened their intensity. Her overwhelming relief, her pride in her son and in her brother and Ross, her unexpected grief over Ethan's descent into madness and horrible death…all existed in her heart simultaneously with an incredible sense of freedom and a new acceptance of her own new-found strength. She had gained a mother and then lost her without ever having really known the woman, though Lady Warbrick had been deeply ill herself. And she had begun to consider the real possibility of making peace with her memories of Sir Averil and what she had done for the sake of a man who could not love her.

Hugh had changed immeasurably, though Gillian couldn't put a finger on the specific event that had instigated his transformation. He was dignified and responsible, taking up his position as the heir of Snowfell as if were the most natural thing in the world. His spendthrift ways were finished. He quickly reemployed the staff Gillian had dismissed, and Snowfell was truly whole again for the first time since Sir Averil had inherited the baronetcy.

Then there was Ross.

Gillian saw little of him in the days following his release from a second stay in gaol. Their reunion had been as formal and strained as their first meeting in New York. He had dodged her so deliberately since that she couldn't mistake his desire to avoid her company. And though she had thought of asking him to join the new Convocation as a full and valued member, hoping he might openly and freely contribute to the dialogue, she soon realized that he wanted nothing to do with it. He kept to himself, often wandering the fells, a lone figure silhouetted against the sky. She was too much a coward to break his solitude, and she couldn't blame him for choosing it.

So she watched…wanting him, needing him, afraid to find she was just as weak now as she had been for so much of her life. Once she caught him arguing with Hugh at the edge of the wood; their voices carried across the park, but she didn't allow herself to listen. And she made no attempt to interfere when Toby tagged along after his father, knowing that he had found the one man he could love and emulate without hesitation.

But Toby, for all his recent experiences and his ability to Change, wasn't quite as grown-up as he wanted to believe. He must have known that Ross was moving farther and farther away from them both. Gillian's apologies for her lack of faith in him weren't enough to hold him, nor was her sincere admiration for his courage and loyalty. Not even the wanting they both tried so fiercely to deny could hold him.

Would her love have been enough, if she'd told him? Or had his pride and trust been too badly damaged by the things she had said and done? Had he become so disgusted with the sham life she had clung to, the egregious mistakes she had made, that he couldn't bear to be in her presence?

Even if he loved her, could that possibly overcome the pain and shattered illusions of the past few weeks?

Unable to answer her own questions, she flung herself into the recreated Convocation. Though the others were glad to follow her lead, she began to see that the privilege she had won meant nothing to her. With little encouragement on her part, Hugh slipped into her place as easily as he might don his favorite tuxedo.

Afterward, she spent as much time with Toby as she could, recognizing that this period of special closeness to her son was coming to an end with his growing independence. One morning she rose from her bed, preparing herself to face another day, and discovered that Ross was gone. He'd left the dress suits she and Hugh had bought for him, but his ordinary clothes no longer hung in the armoire, and his small suitcase was missing.

So was Toby.

Gillian dressed haphazardly, ran down the stairs past a startled Faulder and flung open the front door. She couldn't smell either Toby or Ross. She dashed across the lawn as far as the wood, desperately sweeping the air. Nothing.

They've gone out to the fells, perhaps on a longer walk than usual. But she knew it wasn't true. She *knew*. Ross had finally left Snowfell, and he'd taken Toby with him.

She rushed to the garage. All three of the motor cars were still there, but it was only a three-mile walk to Kendal and the railway station. Her first impulse was to Change, but she saw the impracticality of that at once. She leaped into the seat of the Bentley and sped toward Kendal.

The small, unstaffed brick railway station seemed deserted at first. Gillian parked the motor askew at the kerb and jumped out, rounding the corner of the building to the platform.

Two people stood beside the tracks. The smaller one stood proudly erect, facing the bigger, who knelt before him. They were engaged in conversation, heated on the boy's part, calm on the man's. Ross laid his hand on Toby's shoulder, and Toby shook his head.

Gillian didn't have to hear the conversation to know what was being said. Ross hadn't stolen Toby away. Toby had followed him. He had chosen his father over his mother.

And who could blame him? He was a remarkably resilient child, but she could have made his life a misery had she gone through with Sir Averil's plans. She had denied that his father even existed. Mistake after mistake after mistake.

Yet Ross was trying to make Toby go home. He was already breaking his parole by leaving the area, though Gillian had no

doubt that he planned to give himself up to the American police
She knew that at least she could prevent the English authoritie
from chasing after him.

But if he succeeded in sending Toby back, their son woul
obey only with the greatest resentment. If he didn't want to sta
at Snowfell, he would simply run away again.

The is no reason for us to stay. We might go anywhere.

Homeless, rootless, always lacking the one thing that woul
make them whole.

She took one step back, and then another. They still hadn'
seen or smelled her. Perhaps she could escape before they eve
knew she had been there.

But then Ross looked up. Their eyes met across the distance
and Ross sprang to his feet. Toby turned, and there was such
look of joy on his face that Gillian could barely stand up hersel

"Mother!" he cried. "Why did it take you so long?"

Ross continued to stare at her, expressionless, his brown eye
as flat as tarnished pennies. He took Toby's hand and led hin
up the platform to Gillian.

"I'm sorry for the trouble," he said. "I didn't know he'd fol
lowed me."

Toby opened his mouth. "I—"

But neither his father or mother was listening. Gillian couldn'
avert her eyes from Ross's face, though the pain was so intens
that she thought her heart would stop beating.

"You're going back to America," she said.

He shrugged. "Got to face it sooner or later. And there's
good chance now that I can clear my name."

"You will. Hugh and I..." She swallowed. "Hugh and I wil
make certain of that."

"I'm grateful. It's not like you owe me anything."

"We owe you more than we can possibly repay."

His gaze slid away. "You don't have to worry about the cop
blaming you for my leaving. I worked it out with them. The Liv

erpool police will make sure I get on the boat, and there'll be cops to meet me in New York."

So it had all been planned. He had never really considered staying in a place where he had been treated so badly. Without a good reason, a reason that touched his heart…

"Mother!" Toby cried. "Father! You can't—"

Ross squeezed his shoulder. "Time to go with your mother, son. I said I'd keep in touch, and I will. We'll write to each other, and—"

He stopped at the sound of a shrill whistle. The noise made all further conversation impossible as the train puffed and chugged its way up to the platform. A middle-aged woman and a nervous man in a suit detrained with the help of a uniformed porter, who looked inquiringly at Ross, Toby and Gillian.

Ross pulled Toby round and embraced him, lifting him off his feet.

"Be good," he said into Toby's hair. "Listen to your mother."

He let Toby down, pretending he didn't see their son fighting his unmanly tears. "Goodbye, Gillian," he said, offering his hand. She took it, too numb to feel her own fingers or his touch.

The porter called out. With another blast of its whistle, the train began to lurch forward.

Ross released Gillian's hand and picked up his suitcase. He walked briskly toward the moving train. Toby stood stock-still. Gillian didn't dare touch him. They watched Ross hop up and swing through one of the compartment doors. He held the door open and looked back as the train picked up speed. His lips moved. Gillian read the words without hearing so much as a whisper.

She grabbed Toby's hand and began to run. They caught up as the last coach was passing the end of the platform. Gillian swung Toby up ahead of her, pulling the door open just in time.

Toby plunged past the startled passengers and ran as fast as the narrow corridor allowed, Gillian right behind him. They passed through two more coaches and a saloon, where a few passengers were eating breakfast and Gillian lost a shoe. Halfway into the third coach, Toby careened to a stop and stared at the compartment door in front of them. Ross was not alone inside, but his scent, his presence, was all that mattered.

Toby stood back. Gillian opened the door.

Two men, one reading a newspaper and the other half-asleep, started up from their seats. Ross, alone on the bench opposite, was staring out the window, but she could tell from the tension in his muscles that he knew she and Toby were there.

Gillian smiled at the two bewildered passengers. "Will you gentlemen kindly excuse us?"

The man with the paper glanced at Ross and hastily edged past Gillian and out of the compartment. The other man stared at Gillian belligerently.

"Is this your compartment, ma'am?" he asked

Ross turned to look at the man, who suddenly abandoned his truculent attitude and followed his fellow passenger. Gillian smiled at Toby, stepped inside and closed the door, then sat in the seat opposite Ross.

"You shouldn't have said it, you know."

He released a sharp breath. "Said what?"

"I love you."

He finally looked at her. "You're right," he said. "I shouldn't have said it."

She refused to let herself falter. "Are you saying it isn't true?"

His expression went from a perfect blank to hope and anguish in an instant. "It's true," he whispered. "It always has been."

"Did you think it was any different for me?"

If a man like Ross could gape, he came very close. He shut his mouth with a snap. "Even when you left me in London?"

"Then, and every day since."

His hand, resting on his knee, began to shake. "I was never worthy of you, Jill. We both knew it then. It's still true."

"You have it the wrong way round. I was never worthy of you."

They gazed at each other for a long time. Gillian expected Toby to burst into the compartment, but he left them alone. A knot began to form in her throat.

Then Ross laughed, his eyes crinkling at the corners and shining with real humor. Gillian felt the corners of her own mouth begin to tilt upward. All at once she saw the sheer absurdity of the situation, and laughter bubbled up in her chest.

When they were finished, gasping and shaking, Gillian knelt on the carpet between the seats and rested her hands on Ross's knees.

"Do you suppose," she said, "that two such unworthy souls might find happiness together?"

He took her hands and lifted her as he rose. "Jill," he whispered, "it won't be easy. I can't stay in England. And if you and Toby come with me…"

"We'll stand beside you." She put her arms around him. "We will love you."

He pulled her close and pressed his face into the hollow of her shoulder. "Toby—"

"Will, with any luck, grow up to be a man just like his father."

Ross lifted his head. He searched her eyes and then met her lips with his. They were thoroughly lost in the kiss when Toby finally opened the door, his hands planted on his hips.

"Well," he said imperiously, "it's about time."

And they all laughed together.

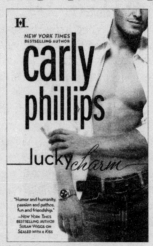

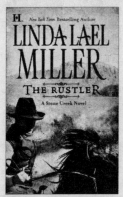

SUSAN KRINARD

77258	DARK OF THE MOON	___ $6.99 U.S.	___ $8.50 CAN.
77139	LORD OF THE BEASTS	___ $5.99 U.S.	___ $6.99 CAN.

(limited quantities available)

TOTAL AMOUNT	$ _____
POSTAGE & HANDLING	$ _____
($1.00 FOR 1 BOOK, 50¢ for each additional)	
APPLICABLE TAXES*	$ _____
TOTAL PAYABLE	$ _____

(check or money order—please do not send cash)

To order, complete this form and send it, along with a check or money order for the total above, payable to HQN Books, to: **In the U.S.:** 3010 Walden Avenue, P.O. Box 9077, Buffalo, NY 14269-9077; **In Canada:** P.O. Box 636, Fort Erie, Ontario, L2A 5X3.

Name: _____
Address: _____ City: _____
State/Prov.: _____ Zip/Postal Code: _____
Account Number (if applicable): _____

075 CSAS

*New York residents remit applicable sales taxes.
*Canadian residents remit applicable GST and provincial taxes.

HQN™

We *are* romance™

www.HQNBooks.com

PHSKI008BL